Human Mules: The Kayayo Girls

Carol Larratt

Published by New Generation Publishing in 2013

Copyright © Carol Larratt 2013

First Edition

The author asserts the moral right under the Copyright, Designs and Patents Act 1988 to be identified as the author of this work.

All Rights reserved. No part of this publication may be reproduced, stored in a retrieval system or transmitted, in any form or by any means without the prior consent of the author, nor be otherwise circulated in any form of binding or cover other than that which it is published and without a similar condition being imposed on the subsequent purchaser.

www.newgeneration-publishing.com

 New Generation **Publishing**

For the brother I never knew. To Terry.

Acknowledgements

Thanks to Jane Cameron in New Zealand for help with artistic direction. Thanks to Idrissu Sumani, Kubara Ahmed, Hazirah Adnan, Kwaku Opoku, Joan Asamoah, Morris Abugah, Miriam Boateng, Al-Hassan Wapana, Usman Napare, Kubara Mahama, Miriam Nakpambo, Mohammed Ziblim , Mary Kombat, Yennu Duut, John Manful, Comfort Gyamfi, Akosia Sawyer, for all your help and patience, and for never giving up,

Thanks to Yea Won Choe for inspiring anecdotes
…and to all the kayayo girls of Accra without which this book would not have been possible.

All personal and place names in this book have been changed to protect identities.

The description of Ghana within this book depict only a very minute area of the city of Accra and in no way is it representative of the country as a whole.

Chapter One

Kayayo Girl

Leila walks tentatively through the sweltering market, teeming with humanity. Little Aysha, born exactly nine months after the start of Leila's first period, bounces on her back as she pushes her way through the crowds. It's her first day in Accra. For the past year she had been planning to come. To leave her impoverished village in the dried up north of the country. She had been afraid. Had heard many rumours of terrible things that happened to those who ended up on the streets of this big city. Several times in the village she had packed her small ragged bag, only to change her mind at the last minute. Were the dangers, the threats and maltreatment that awaited her there worth the rewards of prosperity and the prestige that would await her on her return to the village? Wouldn't it be better to just stay in her cocoon of security and poverty, knowing at least herself, her daughter and family would never have to experience loss and danger?

Unfamiliar faces sneer at her from left and right as she attempts to weave her way through the narrow alleyways, piled high on either side with goods and strange foodstuffs she had never seen before. Huge, fat, ebony skinned women (she had never seen people so fat before) push past, knocking her sideways. Baby Aysha screams from behind her.

Leila's mind retreats back to the familiarity of her village. The parched, ochre landscape dotted with baobab trees. Rabia, with whom she had walked, both of them balancing baskets of bright yellow maize on their heads, for almost her entire life, is walking by her side, laughing at her stories. She remembers the day

Rabia returned to the village after her hasty and nervous departure the year before.

It was early morning. The large pink sun was just beginning to appear on the horizon beyond the brown hills. She was returning from the well with a group of other young women and heard the sound of a motor being followed closely by a cloud of dust. Minutes later Rabia stepped out of the bus, a mountain of luggage by her side. The city was brushed over her like a coat of paint. Her gait exuded haste and confidence, mocking the quiet resignation of the villagers. An air of mystery now surrounded her as the village girls looked on with incredulity at the goods she handed out.

'I wanted to bring more, but just couldn't get it on the bus,' Rabia announced, triumphantly glancing at Leila.

They had planned to leave together a year earlier. To work as 'kayayo', the human mules of Ghana's big cities, carrying massive loads of goods upon their heads, within the labyrinthine markets where cars cannot reach. Again Leila had pulled out at the last minute. Should she trade in what she had for the uncertainty of life in the city?

'Mother, here's the set of drinking glasses you asked for, you can see they are decorated with gold and silver. Rahima, here is your sewing machine, I wanted to buy you an electric one but there's no power in this village, so what's the point?'

Leila smiled, now intimidated by her old friend.

That evening, in the compound, Rabia's stories of city life washed over the village, draining the life and colour from every hut, intensifying its dullness with each and every new embellishment.

'All the houses have glass windows, and they all light up at night, the streets are full of lights and cars. You know there are so many cars they even have special lights in the road to tell you when to cross, it's that bad!'

Leila and the other villagers looked puzzled, remembering earlier stories of abduction, rape and hardship.

'It's not like that at all,' insisted Rabia, 'I live in a house with electricity and water, people are friendly and kind, I can buy so many things.'

'Look at this electric watch,' She lifted her wrist in a nonchalant manner as if to emphasise the ease with which she had purchased it.

That night Leila returned to her hut. The happiness and contentment she had felt only yesterday had been usurped by an awareness of the limitations and dullness of her life. Her parents entered the hut and sat down. She eavesdropped in the darkness.

'Look at how Rabia has excelled, and the way she is helping all her family. Her father now has a bike and her sister a sewing machine. Why is it our own daughter has let us down so badly?' said Leila's mother, bitter and full of animosity.

'The difference between the two of them was marked even from childhood,' added her father, 'Rabia was always so keen to help and run to the town, all our daughter ever wanted to do was to hang around in the village and gossip, and now since Aysha's birth, we have even another mouth to feed. This should be the responsibility of the child's father, but since he left for work in Libya, he never thinks about us and his daughter.'

'That's how they are,' interrupted Jamila, Leila's mother, in a downtrodden tone. 'You know once these young boys leave they forget about us and our poverty.'

'Who knows if he is even still alive, you hear stories of them being attacked and killed in the desert' added Leila's father, full of dread.

Jamila held her head in her hands.

'If only God had blessed us with a daughter like Rabia, we wouldn't have to suffer so much now, how can I face Rabia's mother at the well tomorrow, boasting about all the new things she has?'

Tears streamed down Leila's dusty face, forming bold vertical lines. Her heart ached. How could she let her parents suffer when so many other girls had gone to work as kayayo and brought back so much to help their families?

Crossing the busy road in Accra, Leila recalled that day as the turning point. It was the day she managed to overcome her fears of what might happen to her. Bringing back wealth to help her family. Sending her younger brother, now almost six years, to school. These were now the most important things in her life. This was her motivation as she carried almost twice her body weight in heavy loads across the city, from warehouse to market, earning sometimes only barely enough to feed herself and her baby. She had no home to live in. Neither did Rabia. Soon after she had arrived in Accra with her childhood friend she realized most of Rabia's stories had been fabricated. They slept in the street, under doorways and market stalls. They woke up at dawn when the traders opened their stores and kicked them out.

The sun scorched her shoulders. Little Aysha cried. Her back almost broke from the weight of the charcoal she carried on her head. Insults hurled down on her from passers-by and a wiry young man pushed her sharply as he barged past. She fell.

'You stupid girl, look what you've done to my goods, now pick it all up.' She was kicked into the gutter.

'How old are you?' another woman shouted, 'Shouldn't you be at school?'

Leila had no idea how old she was, the years since her birth had never been counted.

As she continued to pick up the charcoal amidst little Aysha's wailing and the cacophony of slurs being thrown at her, Leila thought about the dinner set she had proudly bought for her mother. She imagined how they would eat from it in the compound in front of Rabia's parents. As she dropped the last piece of charcoal into her metal bowl, she imagined her father, pouring a tin of 'Ideal' milk into his gold embossed cup and saucer. A warmth enveloped her emaciated frame as she thought of this. It was such thoughts that made the hell she must endure here in the city worthwhile.

That night, pain pulsed through her body. Bruises formed on her skin. She lay in the street, surrounded by the other load carriers, or 'head porters', girls just like her, who had all come from the dry villages of the north. She felt secure, surrounded by those she had come to view as her sisters, their legs and arms entwined, each resting on the other. She felt the spidery pit pat pit pat footsteps of the city's rats running over her body as she lay there. She listened to little Aysha's heartbeat, felt her faint warm breath on her face. She again remembered the dinner set, white with gold and silver edging similar to the glasses Rabia had brought for her mother. She imagined her parents' faces as she gave it to them. She fell asleep. She was achieving her dream.

Some hours later she awoke. The girls were shouting and screaming. She had no idea what was going on.

'Kadima, I saw him over there, he bent down and picked up some things and walked away, over there, look!'

'It's one of those thieves that come and take our things when we are sleeping', Rahima screamed.

Leila bent down to pick up little Aysha.

She had gone.

'My baby, my baby, Aysha, she's gone!' Leila yelled.

'He took the baby, the man took the baby,' another girl blasted.

They all ran in the direction the man had taken. As they turned into the main road a large black car was driving away.

Two days later a short story appeared in a local newspaper relating the abduction of a child.

After many months of fruitless searching for baby Aysha, Leila returned home to the village.

She took her family a dinner set, a sewing machine and a radio.

Chapter Two

Under the Mango Tree

The kayayo, who characteristically can be seen thronging the streets with their metal bowl or 'tahili', their sole means of livelihood and income balancing on their head, largely live around transport hubs and markets in the poorer shantytown areas of Accra and Kumasi. The majority are school-aged girls between the ages of twelve and seventeen, but increasingly many are appearing on the streets at even younger ages. It has been estimated that their numbers run into the tens of thousands, yet little is known about them and very few studies have been done into their way of living and why they continue to arrive in Accra in increasing numbers each year.

After living in Accra for over a decade, where I came originally to work as a teacher with my two children, it became increasingly apparent to me that these young girls lived within a society but were not part of it. It was as if they created their own society, their own secret world within another. They were so much part of the urban landscape that they generally existed unnoticed by those around them, like an unsightly birthmark that reluctantly you are forced to accept and eventually no longer see. Their daily lives were played out at ground level, on pavements, under trees and hidden in closed up shop fronts. Thus they rarely came within the eye span of the average Accra citizen, so were conveniently easy to ignore and consequently this helped camouflage their painful existence from the majority of people.

As the years went by, I became more intrigued and fascinated by these young girls whom I would sometimes run into feeding their babies under trucks, sleeping in car parks or bathing behind walls and bushes in the early hours or at dusk in the hope of evading prying eyes. They looked noticeably different from those around them, in both dress and appearance, as if they came from a region or country very different from where they now found themselves. I also came to learn as the years went by, that they were most often despised by those people around them, those with whom they were forced to live. I kept wondering, where did these often stunningly beautiful young girls come from? Why whenever I asked about them no one had any real answers? Why did so many of them carry tiny babies but there was never a man to be seen within their groups? Their world appeared to consist only of women, female children and babies. One day answers started to come to me under the shade of a giant mango tree.

The magnificent tree grew in the gardens of an old, desolate house dating back to colonial times. Its heavily laden branches extended way beyond the perimeter walls, providing welcoming shade onto the pavement outside. It was under this shady oasis, within a city bleached from an incessant and merciless sun, that I first noticed a large group of around thirty kayayo girls.

I continued to see them. Day-in, day-out. Every morning as the weeks and months went by, while driving my daughter to and from school, I would glimpse their daily rituals, played out under the boughs and branches of the tree. By nightfall they had disappeared. I had no idea where they had gone. One morning, I decided I had to go and talk to them. I would go with my neighbour, Vida, who could speak the local language. That morning a feeling of excitement and anticipation started to move me.

As we approached the girls looked around a little

perturbed, some rising nervously from the upturned metal bowls on which they were sitting. The kayayo are unused to anyone taking any interest in them, other than to hurl insults, assault or to evict them from their resting places. Thus the sight of these two strangers, holding friendly mechanical fixed smiles, coming over to join them created some initial hesitation on their part. They were also very suspicious of officialdom, constantly worried that they could be rounded up and sent away from Accra. The recent census in Accra, aptly named, 'YOU COUNT SO BE COUNTED', reported many problems in trying to enumerate the kayayo, as they would often run away on seeing the census officials approach.

Little did I know that this initial hesitation would be so short lived! Vida told them that I was interested in writing a book about their lives. For some reason, this seemed to come across as particularly funny and some burst out into uncontrollable laughter. I showed them a book written by another author describing the lives of African women that had many photographs and the laughter increased to the extent that some were hanging on to the wall of the Blue House from which the mango tree grew, in an attempt not to fall over. One girl took the book to look at the pictures, and then others tried to grab it from her. This resulted in a line of girls, running round in circles trying to chase the girl with the book in an attempt to get hold of it, the girl with the book fell over, and those behind tripped and fell on top of her in a heap. The resulting scene was of a pile of girls on the pavement laughing to such an extent that they couldn't get up, others were holding onto the wall bent double, and Vida and I looking at each other, as if to say, 'where do we go from here?'

Amidst all this hilarity one girl stood out. She was tall, stately and gazed at me smiling mysteriously. She had a serene air and approached me reticently. She was carrying a beautiful baby girl on her back, called Madihah. Surprisingly she spoke a little English. She told us she had a mobile phone and wrote down her number on a scrap of paper she found on the pavement and told us to ring her if we needed anything. She smiled again and walked off with baby Madihah bobbing on her back. They then both disappeared around the corner of the Blue House.

It was not long before I lost Rebecca's scrap of paper. I had to wait again for over two weeks before I once again could get to the tree and I wasn't sure if I would ever find her again. I was overjoyed when pulling up at the Blue House almost three weeks later. I saw both her and baby Madihah sitting amongst the group. Then something strange occurred that I have never experienced before, even after living in Ghana for well over a decade. I later came to realize, that this 'strangeness' only reflected the fear and danger that permeated the girls' lives on a daily basis.

I told them that I had found a nice café where a few of us could sit and have a drink and chat and then told Rebecca and a few others to hop in the car. They all point blank refused. They would not budge from their decision. Accra, until very recently, has always been hailed as one of the safest cities in Africa and was relatively crime free. Most people didn't think twice about hopping into a stranger's car for a lift and I had often been flagged down by mothers asking me if I could take their children to school even though they hadn't a clue who I was. Such was people's kindness that if you stopped to ask a person directions, he or she would usually accompany you in the car, going miles out of their way to get you to your exact destination and then walk back. So the fact that even a whole group of friends would not enter a woman's car did seem very odd in a country where this was the norm, even for those travelling alone. After trying to persuade them for some time I gave up and went home. I would have to find somewhere closer and within walking distance.

However, it was not easy to find a comfortable and relaxing place to sit. The area where this particular group, and later I discovered many thousands of other kayayo resided in was called Kejetia. It was a poor downtown area, which was close to Nima, the largest and most notorious shantytown in the capital. Consequently, there were not many comfortable restaurants or cafés around. However, eventually I did find a 'drinking spot,' a local dive just several hundred metres from where the girls sat under the tree. A few days later I went back, this time without Vida as I thought that now Rebecca would be able to translate for me. I parked the car down the street and approached the group on foot. Some sprang up offering me a seat on their upturned metal bowls, which shimmered in the afternoon sun. Other girls were already sleeping in their bowls, and had engineered many different ways of doing this and still remaining comfortable. The most usual was to sit inside the bowl, which was some distance from the blue wall, then lean out at an angle so their head rested on it. Yet more sat in the bowls resting their heads on the laps of other girls who would also do likewise, thus forming a line or circle of bowls, babies and sleeping bodies. Others would just curl up on the cracked and dusty pavement, lying on the strips of brightly coloured cloth they used to tie their babies while walking. Passers-by as always stepped over this small intimate world around them as if it did not exist.

I asked who wanted to come. Rebecca and two other girls joined me. I pointed out 'The Spot', which we could just see in the distance from where we stood under the tree. We then proceeded to march there in single file, the pavement being too narrow for any other way, and entered the shack-like building. We made ourselves as comfortable as possible on the rickety plastic tables and chairs. The Spot was a flimsy structure consisting of bits of plywood and covered over with a corrugated iron roof. On the wall were several torn posters. One was of a Japanese woman wearing a fixed pearly white smile, urging us to use 'Methane Mouthwash for a Fresher Smile'. I glanced back at the girls. What should I ask them? Where should I start? I had no idea. I started, as did most of us, with names, locations and numbers.

The two girls with Rebecca were called Mahab and Nurah. Nurah had a child that looked a few months older than Rebecca's daughter Madihah. Nurah's daughter was called Romatsu. Mahab had a son about nine months called Adnan. Nurah was very shy and gentle. She often glanced over at me, smiling nervously as if she wasn't sure what to do. Her deep-set eyes twinkled in the sun. She wore a long blue flowery patterned skirt and a grubby white T-shirt. Rebecca was tall and athletic, and possessed a quiet dignity which radiated from within and which appeared strong enough to repel all attempts to crush it. She wore a navy and white striped T-shirt with an orange flower patterned skirt, which came well below her knees. Mahab seemed the oldest of the three girls, perhaps eighteen. She was an extrovert, strong willed and tough. She also wore a T-shirt and a long flowery patterned skirt, which I later came to realize was like a uniform for the kayayo. All the girls wore brightly coloured scarves worn tightly around their heads leaving the remaining pieces of cloth to dangle down their backs. Rebecca told me she was fifteen and Nura said she was sixteen. However this changed from week to week and eventually I realized that both they, and in fact all of the kayayo, had no idea of their ages, which they later admitted to.

I ordered some soft drinks—Coke, Fanta and Sprite. The girls sipped them very slowly, occasionally offering small sips to their babies. I think for many kayayo girls soft drinks would be seen as a luxury they could ill afford. They were determined to make the drinks last as long as possible.

Where did they come from, why were they here?

Rebecca said softly that she came from the village of Bandugu in the Upper East region of Ghana that was near the border with Burkina Faso. Nurah and Mahab also said they came from the same area. The girls said they were from the Mamprusi tribe, and their language was Mamprusi. I asked Nurah if they spoke Twi, the main language of the south of Ghana, but she said that most of the girls from their tribe could not speak Twi very well and some not at all.

Ghana geographically is divided into ten regions. There are three northern regions of the Upper East, Upper West and Northern Region. These three regions, from which almost all of the kayayo originate, are the poorest in Ghana. They also differ remarkably from the rest of the country, both culturally and topographically, being situated within the sahelian belt of Africa. The landscape is dry scrubland, very different from the verdant green of the rest of Ghana. Although Ghana has over seventy languages the main national language in the south is Twi, the language of the Akans. The Akans are a loose grouping of related tribes in southern and central Ghana including the Ashanti. There is also the Ga tribe who inhabit the region in and around Accra. The girls' language is different from the Akans. Many people from the north who have never lived in the south, like the kayayo, are unable to speak Twi. If they have not been to school they also will usually be unable to speak English (the other main language used in

Ghana). It is this predicament that puts the kayayo at a distinct disadvantage in Accra and indeed Ghana as a whole, as almost all of them are illiterate and unable to speak either of the two languages necessary to function effectively in the country or its capital.

Baby Madihah, Rebecca's daughter, had been eyeing me hesitantly for the past few minutes. I went to pick her up and she screamed ferociously

Rebecca laughed.

'She's afraid of you.'

Romatsu, Nurah's baby, seemed unperturbed, and bounced up and down on her mother's lap smiling at me despite the terrible open sores which covered her entire face. I asked Nurah via Rebecca how long her baby's face had been like this?

'For some months, but I don't have money to go to the doctor.' She shrugged her shoulders helplessly.

'The sores are spreading to her neck and shoulders and she cries a lot, but I don't know what to do.'

Nurah bowed her head. She didn't want to meet my gaze.

Generally the kayayo separated themselves from all those around them. It was by doing this that they maintained both their dignity and self-esteem. To be constantly in contact with a whole society which not only despised you but who regularly maltreated you on a daily basis eventually ate away at your own self-image, your worth as a person. Sadly I became acutely aware while sitting huddled together with these girls in the fading sunlight of that Wednesday afternoon that the persistent abuse these girls had to endure on a daily basis had managed to penetrate their very awareness of themselves. I could see they were desperately struggling to maintain a kind of dignity in front of a person whom they presumed viewed them as did all others, that is as little more than vermin. Even Rebecca, who exuded an inner strength despite her gentle manner, was finding it difficult to maintain her carefully protected pride.

Yet this was the world in which they lived, the kayayo world. Everyone saw them as the lowest rung of the ladder. Many people saw them as little more than common criminals, taxis would refuse to take them in their cabs, residents of Accra thought they could bully, abuse and push them around at will with no comeback. I asked them how they were treated by the Twi speaking people of Ghana, the southerners. Nurah answered for them with strong emotion despite her gentle shyness.

'Some of them here they treat us as if we are not human beings, they sack us from our resting places, wherever we try to rest or sleep they sack us, they treat us like animals because we don't speak Twi.'

The term 'sack' is used in Ghana whenever you want to get rid of someone, if you want to get someone out of a place or move someone on. The kayayo girls, due to the nature of their work, often began working before dawn at 5am, where they trudged the city the entire day, carrying heavy loads on their heads. After some hours they must sit and rest, drink water and feed their babies, whom they must carry on their backs in addition to the loads. Yet even the right to sit and rest was often denied them as they searched the city for any empty spaces where they could sit down. In an overcrowded city such as Accra, virtually all available space is 'bagged'. It was therefore not uncommon for the girls after sitting down or while in the middle of a much-needed doze or meal, to be pushed, shoved or kicked and told to move on. Accra residents had often told me they didn't want them hanging around 'their area' as they were 'dirty and messed up the place'. The girls would then have to get up together with their heavy loads and infants, and start to walk again without having even eaten or rested.

Mahab's deep husky voice interjected, full of rage.

'When we go to work they don't greet us, they don't greet.'

She opened her palms in a gesture of seeming indignation.

Greeting was of utmost importance in Ghanaian culture. Not to greet someone you pass by or meet was considered the apex of rudeness. It is simply not done. The fact that a large proportion of the city's population failed to greet the kayayo in the customary way must mean they saw them as less than human. It would also be another hurtful daily reminder for the girls of their seeming worthlessness in the eyes of their neighbours.

In the light of all this I wondered if they liked living in Accra, or did they prefer life in the village?

'We like everything in the village,' said Mahab, desperately trying to restrain Adnan from grabbing her precious bottle of coke.

Mahab was a tall, strong young woman with an equally strong voice. I could imagine that she wouldn't allow anyone to cross her, or if you did it was at your peril.

'We were born there, we grow there, we come to Accra because there is no work in the village, sometimes we can't even eat, we don't like Accra and come here for only the money.'

A very sullen faced middle-aged woman came along to wipe up the mess Adnan had made over the table with the Coke. I wondered why she looked so sad. Inadvertently, I glanced up and saw 'Cheiko', that's what I will call her, yet again smiling down at us with her pearly white teeth. I was imagining her life in Japan and how it could have any connection with what was going on in this tiny shack, yet she continued to smile.

Was she mocking us? Most of these girls here couldn't even afford to buy toothpaste let alone mouthwash. Rebecca, who had been sitting observing the others, got ready to speak, and she glanced at everyone to make sure we were listening, smiled gently and murmured,

'Our parents and brothers and sisters are in the village, we don't want to be in Accra but we have no choice.'

By now the three infants, Madihah, Romatsu and Adnan, were crawling on the broken tiled floor of the drinking spot. In many of the poorer areas of Accra, using 'broken tiles' the cast offs and remnants left over from tiling the more wealthy homes is the customary way to decorate your house, shop or café. The effect is quite dazzling and can at times, depending on what type of tiles and colours are used, look even better than the 'real thing'. The three babies seemed to be enjoying themselves on the cool and smooth floor, which was very different from the dirt floors of the roads and pavements they were accustomed to. Baby Romatsu's open sores were becoming more wet from her constant dribbling.

'The Spot' was becoming very noisy. In the background a tinny radio was blaring and crackling and it was becoming difficult to hear what was being said. We asked the café worker to turn it down, and she looked at us blankly, showing no emotion, but a short while later the music was at manageable levels.

I was beginning to realize that Rebecca's English was quite rudimentary. She didn't always understand everything I said. If I really wanted to understand these girls and their lives in Accra, their emotions and beliefs it was imperative that I found someone to translate who could speak both fluent English and Mamprusi. I glanced over at Nurah and she smiled, her eyes transformed into crescent moons twinkling in the fading sunlight.

Vaguely visible through the swishing bamboo strands that were hanging on the doorway I could see a tatty blue and white sign over the entrance to a compound family house opposite, on the other side of the narrow road: 'Black Volta House'. That could be my answer. The girls came from near the Black Volta so I was sure I could find someone in there who could translate for me. Gradually the noise emanating from Black Volta House was in stiff competition with the crackling high-pitched whine of 'The Spot's' radio. Obviously a family row was in full swing. I went over, leaving the girls to talk among themselves, and asked a tall wiry man at the doorway if there was anyone in the house who wanted a small job translating for me from Mamprusi to English.

'Nobody here speaks Mamprusi as we here in this house are all from the FraFra tribe, we don't speak Mamprusi.'

The Frafra tribe were well known for having extreme tribal markings that often covered their entire face. Just then a man who had been sitting outside the spot playing dominoes came up to us and said he could help me so I presumed he could speak Mamprusi. He followed me back into the now darkening shack and sat down. The four soft drink bottles were looking lost and empty on the table. I asked him in English to ask the girls a question for me in Mamprusi and he asked them in Twi. I told him that I didn't want a Twi speaker as the girls could not really understand the language well, and he then proceeded to ask them in English. I then said there was no point me paying him to ask them questions in English as I could do this myself. At this point the sullen middle-aged café worker, Gifty, suddenly came to life and interjected also telling the man that the girls did not understand Twi. A heated argument then ensued between the café worker and the man. Rebecca started to look annoyed and said that she could understand English. The man then said he knew a lady across the road who could speak Mamprusi so he would go and get her. Everyone was getting confused with this 'language banter'. We continued to sit and wait patiently in the now gathering darkness.

A short while later a plump, middle-aged woman swished through the bamboo curtain wearing an apron and holding a wooden spoon. She look flustered and in a hurry and said she could speak Mamprusi but didn't have time as she 'was cooking beans' and she had left her market stall unattended. The girls were starting to look tired, I was feeling hot and sweaty in the intense humidity and I decided that we should end for the day. It was now dark outside and the flickering yellow light from the naked flames of the kerosene lamps cast a warm glow. I gave the girls some money, and some old clothes. I was aware that the time I spent with then was taking away precious hours of earning potential so they had to be compensated for that. We agreed that we would meet again soon. I watched them slowly disappear in the distance, laughing and squealing with delight as they were holding up and exchanging the clothes and shoes I had given them.

There was so much more I needed to learn about their lives. I had not yet found out about their living and sleeping arrangements, about the fathers of their babies, and how much they earned. I really needed to find a good translator. That night, images of Nurah's baby's face would not go away, Romatsu's constant dribbling was making the sores damp and spongy. I knew of a good cream, a mainstay for all skin infections, so made a note to buy some the next day.

As I drove slowly towards the Blue House, early morning shadows tiptoed over the oasis of domesticity under the tree. As always, many girls were asleep in various stages of contortion, some were bathing their babies in their metal bowls, others washing clothes. Some of the younger girls were playing 'Ampe', a game whereby the girls clap each other's hands and jump in unison. It could have been a scene of family life the world over, found in living rooms, gardens, kitchens and bedrooms. Yet in the kayayo world, 'home' was the street. As I pulled up I saw Rebecca. She came to the car walking slowly and smiling, holding baby Madihah tightly. As she got close, Madihah, on seeing me, screamed. As usual we both laughed. I asked if Nurah was around as I had some cream for Romatsu's face. She went to call her and within a minute shy, gentle Nurah arrived carrying her daughter. I showed her the cream and rubbed some into Romatsu's face. I stopped a man passing by and asked him to tell Nurah that she must rub the cream into the infant's face three times a day. He translated and thanked me for helping Nurah and went on his way. It was ten days or so later, as I was driving slowly past the tree, that Nurah spotted me. She flagged me down and held up baby Romatsu to the car window for me to see. Her face was clear and healthy. Nurah as usual just smiled her gentle smile. The cream had worked!

The word 'kayayo' has its roots in two linguistically different languages. The word 'Kaya' comes from the Hausa language, a common language of trade throughout West Africa and means 'wares or goods.' The word 'Yoo' is derived from the language of the Ga tribe of the greater Accra area and means 'woman'. The word then has a literal meaning of 'woman and wares or goods.' However, although the kayayos' lives are intimately entwined within the commercial world of goods and wares for sale they rarely if ever engage in any commercial activity. Their role is to rather facilitate this often lucrative trade by acting as a means of transport. Predominantly women traders use the kayayo to transport their goods from points of arrival to commercial centres and markets. The design and density of these crowded markets, often consisting of a multitude of extremely narrow alleys, makes pedestrian load carrying much more favourable as compared to motorised transport or even hand pulled carts. These carts can also quickly clog up and obstruct the passageways. Also, the dominance of the petty trading environment in many African countries creates a need for transportation of very small loads, which can easily be performed by 'human transport' carriers or the kayayo.

Indeed the kayayo have been identified as an integral part of the transport system of Ghana's informal economy where transportation of goods in labyrinthine and inaccessible markets cannot be carried out by motorized transport. They play an integral role in the commercial life of the two major cities of Accra and Kumasi. In fact the kayayo do the work that in many developing countries is done by animals or beasts of burden like donkeys and bullocks. They are in fact Human Mules.

There are many reasons given as to why the kayayo started to arrive in Accra. There is however a general consensus that approximately twenty years ago, they were not present in the city. During an interview with a government official, I asked her why she thought the girls had started to travel south. As the bureaucrat sat in her attractive office, near to the Chinese built National Theatre in downtown Accra, she looked perturbed. She didn't know how the 'problem of the kayayo' could be solved. She told me,

'A lot of the kayayo started coming down when the rice industry in the north collapsed.'

She shuffled in her chair, leaning forward, looking directly at me.

'Before this the industry was very vibrant and the girls usually got jobs on the rice farms...harvesting, planting, things like that...it started to become difficult for rice farmers to grow rice when the World Bank forced Ghana to remove their subsidies on agricultural produce...our government as a result could no longer subsidize fertilizer, tractors and other farm inputs.'

Ghana's rice industry has collapsed over the past three decades and the timing would coincide with the first appearance of the kayayo girls on Accra's streets, twenty or so years ago. The slashing of subsidies enforced by the World Bank and IMF would also have taken several years to filter through as harvests progressively worsened. It is common knowledge also that the high agricultural subsidies western farmers continually receive also destroys the livelihoods of African farmers. In 2003 the US government paid $1.3 billion in rice subsidies to its farmers, effectively footing the bill for almost three quarters of the crops' production cost. Cheap rice of much higher quality then flooded developing nations like Ghana. Ghana is now one of biggest importers of rice in Sub-Saharan Africa.

Many local shopkeepers told me that they couldn't sell the Ghanaian rice, despite it being cheaper as the quality was so bad. Due to lack of subsidies the farmers in the north cannot purchase the appropriate technology needed for milling the rice. The result has been a massive increase of rural migration to the cities.

I realized such slashing of farm subsidies would have affected the families of the kayayo disproportionately. Most were from very poor socio-economic backgrounds. One survey revealed that almost seventy five per cent of the kayayo stated that their parents were either farmers or unskilled labourers. A sizeable proportion, ten per cent, said either one or both parents were dead. Although most kayayo were young, the majority (almost eighty per cent in the same survey) being between the ages of twelve and seventeen, their fathers can often be quite old, having married much younger wives. Unsurprisingly, the kayayo generally came from large families. Almost half came from families of between four to six children, around twenty five per cent came from families of between seven and nine children and fifteen per cent came from families of approximately ten or more.

The civil servant and I sat in silence for several minutes listening to the roar of the traffic outside. I was looking at the pile of papers on her desk, as the sun was trying to peep through the venetian blinds, penetrating this cool, shady office with its narrow rays.

Then she continued. She sounded a little indignant.

'I understand they still subsidize their agricultural produce in Europe.'

I asked if the government had any plans that could help the kayayo in Accra. She told me that it was imperative that something was done soon as increasingly the girls were having babies in the city and these children too would be growing up on the street knowing no other life.

She then said that one government ministry had carried out a scheme in conjunction with UNICEF, which offered skills training to many of the girls. After the training in sewing and hair design the girls were given sewing machines and hairdressing equipment. The aim of the project was that the girls would start to set up in business and then the desire to come to Accra would lessen. However, when the parents of the other girls in the northern villages saw the machines they sent even MORE girls down than ever in the hope that they too would get these benefits. So the scheme had the opposite effect!

The civil servant went on to tell me that one Government Ministry was trying to count the number of kayayo in the city, and the recent census had also tried to enumerate them. During the census I spoke to one of the enumerators who explained how they managed to achieve this seemingly impossible task.

'We would visit the areas where the girls slept and interview each girl. After logging their details, the girls were then given a receipt, which they were told to keep and show any further enumerators. This way the girls would not be counted twice.'

With the benefit of hindsight and after being with the kayayo for over a year, I realized it would be relatively easy to be able to find out exactly how many girls there were in each area even after two or three visits.

The official then said that if conditions were better in the three northern regions of Ghana (Upper East, Upper West and Northern Region), they would not have to leave their homelands. It was for this reason that the government had started to instigate measures that would hopefully speed up development in the northern part of the country. For this reason the Savannah Accelerated Development Agency Act (SADA) was passed. It was hoped this would put measures into place that would enhance economic development in the region.

SADA's main remit was to 'coordinate a comprehensive development agenda for the northern ecological zone of Ghana...to promote sustainable development using a forested and green north to catalyse climate change reversal and improve the lives of the most vulnerable citizens in the area.' Indeed the northern region has been badly affected by climate change and in 2007 a severe drought followed by a deluge of rain produced serious flooding which killed hundreds and displaced more than half a million. It was interesting that the SADA Act itself had recognized the problem of the kayayo, stating that as a result of the environmental degradation and consequent floods even more kayayo than before were now migrating to Accra. It stated,

'Thousands of young girls, women and children (have now) joined a teaming underclass of street porters (kayayo) in the urban commercial centres of southern Ghana.'

The Government also recognised that if nothing was done to counter the impact of climate change in Northern Ghana the consequences would be more dire.

Two weeks had passed and I found myself once again sitting in the sweltering dingy drinking spot with some of the girls from 'Under the tree next to the Blue House'. I listened to myself once again asking a sullen faced Gifty if she could turn down the high pitched crackling from her tinny radio. As was the norm a minute or two passed and the noise subsided. This time I had Rebecca and Nurah with me, as tall, husky voiced Mahab was working, carrying plantains from a truck which had just arrived from the Ashanti region, to various shops and stalls around Kejetia. Today, two other very young girls had joined us. Latifa, who looked no older than twelve years, was mischievous, lithe and lean like a gazelle and moved quickly. Her large liquid black kohl lined eyes darted about from left to right as if she was constantly on the lookout. She was wearing a bright green Chelsea FC T-shirt and matching lime green headscarf. The other girl, Aysha, was also very young. Her hands and arms intricately decorated with henna tattoos. Unusually for a kayayo girl she was a little plump. Both Aysha and Latifa had no idea of their ages. From the corner of my eye I could see that Baby Madihah was as usual watching me guardedly from the safety of her mother's embrace, Nurah and the now clear skinned baby Romatsu sat quietly in the corner. The drinks arrived, this time they each ordered different drinks—Fanta, Sprite, Coke and Muscatella. I asked Nurah and Rebecca about the fathers of their daughters. Rebecca answered first.

'My husband, Nurah's husband and all the other girls' husbands, they are in the villages up in the north. We come here alone. Our husbands they don't want us to come. They are against it. We come here against our husbands' wishes.'

If that was the case, what happened when they returned, were their husbands not angry?

'When we get back the anger has gone as we bring them back plenty money and this helps our husbands and our families.'

I asked them how much they generally took back and what it was used for. Nurah smiled, removing Romatsu from her lap and putting her onto the broken tiled floor. She looked first at Rebecca coyly as if to say 'is it ok for me to speak now?' and then at me, then she spoke.

'I have three brothers and three sisters. I am the middle one. I use my money to help my brother continue his education.'

Rebecca also said she handed over the money she earned to her parents. They then shared the money between the brothers to help them go to school. I asked if they themselves wanted to go to school seeing that they were in Accra literally breaking their backs so that their brothers could go to school. They both laughed out loud.

'We have already born (given birth) so there is no need now for us to go to school.'

Nurah said she had attended primary school for a couple of years and I guessed Rebecca had attended school for longer as she spoke English. However, I learnt later that many of the girls had not attended school at all but were often too embarrassed to say so and would therefore often make out they had at least attended primary school for a few years. One reason families are loath to spend money on educating their daughters was that within the Mamprusi tribal tradition, girls traditionally left the home of their birth and went to live with their husband's family. The girls' families were thus not keen on investing precious funds for their daughters to 'go off and build someone else's family', as the civil servant I had met in Accra had put it. They saw it as 'a waste' to educate a daughter who would only go and benefit someone else's family.

I asked them about their families in the village. Both Rebecca and Latifa said their fathers had two wives. Rebecca said she had three brothers and seven sisters. Four of these children were from the first wife and six from the second wife. Latifa said she had two brothers and three sisters from her own mother but did not mention the children of the second wife. Aysha said her father only had one wife, which is unusual. Polygamy is the norm.

The drinks were now circulating the table. Each girl took a mouthful of each drink and then slid it along to the one sitting next to her and so on. Each girl would then get to taste each drink. Latifa and Aysha did not take much interest in the conversation and were finding it difficult to keep still. However Aysha, with her intricately tattooed arms and hands, appeared to want to talk and join in but seemed to be constantly swayed from her desire by her younger friend. They were constantly getting up from their seats, walking around the tiny shack, raising their arms languorously and then sitting down again.

We sat in silence for several minutes. I spent some

time scrutinizing the Spot's fencing which consisted of bits of mismatched pieces of scrap wood nailed together. Frayed dirty pieces of basket matting were nailed and stuck over the gaps in the wood. The rusted corrugated iron roof soaked up the oppressive heat, turning the place into an inferno. Nurah was looking silently but admonishingly at Latifa. After some time our eyes met.

'They are not serious, mummy, they do not behave well.'

She was referring to little Latifa and Aysha who were playing with the drinks, giggling and getting on and off their seats. They seemed to take no interest in the questions and soon got up and left, swishing through the tattered bamboo tassel at the doorway. I asked Rebecca and Nurah where they slept at night. They said they had to sleep out in the open, on the pavement near the Tonga Market Polyclinic. Were they disturbed? Nurah glanced at Rebecca with a knowing look and Rebecca voiced their grievances.

'When we are sleeping in the night, people they sneak up, they try to steal our money when we are sleeping. They try to take it from our pockets. It is only men who do this...sometimes they come and try to have sex with us. It is usually one man who will do this, the men don't come and try and do this to us in groups.'

Many people all over Accra have given testament to this. This was one of the first rumours about the kayayo girls I had heard when arriving in the city, that the girls are often raped. Many people disgustingly talk about them, saying contemptuously,

'Those girls, people can just go and lie on them.'

I have heard this statement many times and it seems to be a standing joke amongst many of the less salubrious men in Accra. Once again the general consensus is the girls are nothing, they can be bullied, insulted and even raped at will and there is nothing they can do. They lie asleep in the open so why shouldn't men just go and take what they want? They are at the lowest rung of a ladder in the pecking order of an already poor and harassed segment of society. Furthermore, the kayayo are migrants in Accra, they have no brothers, fathers or groups of extended family members who could stand up for them. In a society such as Ghana family and connections count for a lot, without them you are particularly vulnerable. People then know they are able to do what they like to you with no comeback.

Rebecca's heart-breaking story continued.

'Where we sleep on the floor at night there is no roof, so if it rains we have to get up and huddle under some nearby eaves, but still we get wet as the wind beats the rain on us. Some nights we have to stand with our babies all night, we cannot lie down as it's too wet, we have to get out of our sleeping place by five or six in the morning as the man needs to open his shop.'

Rebecca then muttered that herself, Nurah and Mahab, and indeed many other girls, slept on a small patch of cement floor in front of a shop. She said there were so many girls around sleeping 'she couldn't count them.'

I later learned that almost all the kayayo girls at Tonga market slept in front of shops and kiosks. Often there would be a small patch of cement, often just a few feet in diameter, where they could huddle together and sleep. Although sleeping on a bare cement floor may seem harsh, for them it was preferable to sleeping on the open dirt tracks immediately in front of the shops. Although many of the shop fronts possessed small awnings these would not be sufficient to protect the girls and their babies from the rain, which was often accompanied by lashing winds. Most of the shopkeepers did not want the kayayo girls and their children sleeping in front of their shops but could do little about it.

Although the radio had been turned down, and Gifty, who looked exhausted, was now sleeping on two chairs put together, the noise from Black Volta House across the road had been gradually increasing. A woman had run out into the middle of the street and was screaming at a man from a safe distance, whom I assumed to be her husband. Other people started to intervene, all shouting at the same time.

Inside our little darkened cocoon, just yards from this affray, I sat stunned by the tales of misery that I was hearing. All five bottles of soft drinks now stood empty in a circle on the dirty plastic table. A fly was trying desperately to extricate itself from a pool of Fanta. Babies Madihah and Romatsu had fallen into a deep sleep with their mothers' nipples still in their mouths. Only Cheiko up on the wall seemed to show any cheer, her smile fixed, snowy white.

From within the darkened shack I spotted some kayayo walking past the swishing bamboo curtain at the entrance, their metal bowls loaded up with clothes.

'They are on their way to the bathhouse,' Nurah said gently

'Can you not bath at home?'

'Where we sleep we cannot bathe, we cannot cook we cannot even go to the toilet. If we want to bathe we have to pay 30psws (15 pence Sterling) for a bucket of water, mummy it cost us (it's expensive), with that one bucket of water we have to wash ourselves, our baby and our clothes. We have to get up at 5am when it's still dark to go and bath. When we go to the toilet we have to pay again and for the paper too we have to pay.'

I asked them where they hung their clothes to dry.

They told me they could only hang their clothes out to dry in the night when the shopkeepers had locked up and gone home. They would tie bits of string across the shop front and hang them there, meaning that the wet clothes would drip on them at night, often the clothes were not dry by morning as there had obviously been no sun, so themselves and their babies had to wear them damp the next day. They also told me that sometimes people stole their clothes when they were drying on the line. They went on to tell me they can never cook food as they have no cooking utensils and there was nowhere to cook. They were forced to buy food every day from street vendors. I wanted to get an idea of their average day. Nurah and Rebecca glanced at each other. Nurah's eyes turned once again into crescent moons as she smiled gently at me. She prepared to speak.

'We get up and go the bathhouse and wash we go and buy porridge for 50psws (25 pence Sterling). We go and sit under the tree and chop the porridge and share with our babies. Then we start to walk and look for work, sometimes we walk and walk and no one will ask us to carry anything. At about 1pm we stop and buy rice for 50psws if we are near the tree we chop there, we feed our babies, but sometimes we are walking far away so we just find somewhere to sit and eat. But sometimes the people around sack us and we have to eat as we walk. We cannot even find somewhere to sit.'

I asked if they ever ate meat or fish or milk or even vegetables.

'We don't have money so we can't buy that, sometimes if we don't get work we have to go to sleep without food.'

Most kayayo exist on this diet of carbohydrates. Very few ever eat nutritious food, the babies largely live on a diet of breast milk, although the girls do share their meagre rations of rice and porridge with their babies. They also eat kenke made out of fermented corn dough, TZ made from millet flour, sometimes they also buy fried or boiled yam. Mostly these foodstuffs are prepared by street vendors in extremely unhygienic conditions. The food is then poured into polythene bags and tied up with a knot at the top. Those buying the food can then take it to wherever they choose to eat. In the case of the millet porridge or 'koko' as it is called, a small hole can be bitten into the 'rubber bag' and the porridge sucked out. The polythene bags are the poor man's way of transporting food, an alternative to take away boxes. Water also is put into polythene bags or sachets and sealed. As with the porridge a small hole is bitten into the top corner and the water sucked out. Only more wealthy people in Accra buy water in bottles. Many of the companies springing up in what has become known locally as the 'sachet water' business, are of dubious character and often the water is contaminated. The government has closed down some of these companies. There have been sporadic cholera outbreaks in the city due to the selling of contaminated sachet water.

Living in such unhygienic conditions I wondered if the girls or their babies ever became ill, what did they do if their children got sick? Again Nurah and Rebecca gazed at each other smiling, Nurah gently raising her head to her friend to signal it was her turn to talk.

'We go to the doctor. There is one in the market near where we sleep. I go there with Madihah yesterday, Madihah she was sick.'

'What was wrong with her?'

'I don't know, she was sick and she was hot, the doctor gave me medicine for Madihah but I didn't have money to pay, I told the doctor I would come the next day to bring the money.'

'Did you take it?'

'No, I don't have money to take to the doctor, so I don't go there.'

Nurah and Rebecca were looking tired. Latifa and Aysha had long gone. Gifty was still sleeping on the put together chairs. Her two beautifully dressed children had just returned from school. I gave her son the money for the drinks and he promised he'd give it to his mum when she woke up. As we swished through the bamboo curtain we watched the ructions, now in full swing, that were going on at Black Volta House. Most of the neighbours were now in various stages of diplomacy along the street trying to sort out the domestic breakdown. Romatsu was now sleeping on Nurah's back and Baby Madihah could now look at me without screaming as long as I was at a safe distance. I walked with the girls back to the tree where they met up with the rest of their group and I gave Rebecca the money to pay the doctor. I strolled home, thinking that I would have to go to visit the doctor at Tonga Market to find out more about the health problems the girls faced and how they coped.

The next morning I passed the tree and the girls, who were all sitting on their tahilis sucking their koko, called out to me. I asked one of them to direct me to the Polyclinc and Nurah, walking gently and tentatively, with Romatsu as always wide eyed and bouncing on her back, accompanied me through the narrow alleys. I had arrived early without eating breakfast or drinking anything so was beginning to feel hungry. The Polyclinic was right bang in the centre of the market. While walking through the market I could not help feeling shocked at how the prices for food were spiralling fast. Some market ladies had been arranging onions on their tables. The onions were tiny, like the pickled onions you get in a jar. They were arranged in groups of four or five which would be the equivalent of one large onion. This was on sale for $1(US). I started to wonder how the poor of Accra could eat at all. How long could this go on before the place erupted, with riots breaking out?

I entered the clinic. It was a dingy place. There were many old posters on the wall that had been torn and repaired numerous times leaving a tapestry of yellowing sellotape covering them. One poster was advertising the 'Measles Campaign', another 'Ways to Avoid Malaria During Pregnancy.' Another poster outlined the list of treatments that were exempt from the recently introduced National Heath Insurance Scheme (NHIS), which provided free treatment and medication for a small annual registration fee of Gh25 (around £12 Sterling). One of these was 'Cosmetic Surgery'. People waited silently and patiently on wooden benches. A tall slim girl sauntered majestically through the waiting area carrying a large silver tray of hard-boiled eggs on her head. Hungry patients eagerly bought them.

Eventually a nurse in a snazzy uniform of a tight fitting beige dress, fastened at the front with giant emerald green buttons came out and told me that the doctor had not yet arrived, but I 'should wait for him in the corridor.' The nurses told me that they were outreach workers who did preventative work in the community such as vaccinations against pertussis, whooping cough, diphtheria, hepatitis, polio and measles. They told me that these vaccinations were now free under the new National Health Insurance Scheme introduced by the government. I asked the nurses how they got their messages across to the kayayo many of whom didn't speak Twi. They told me that,

'There is usually one of them among them who

speaks Twi quite well, one who has been coming to Accra for a long time and they translate to the others.'

The fact that I had not eaten or drunk was beginning to take its toll in the heat. I was starting to feel increasingly dizzy. The nurse with the giant emerald green buttons became concerned and went out to buy me water. After drinking the water I continued waiting for what seemed to be an eternity and I was beginning to feel quite ill so decided to leave and return the next day.

The following day I arrived much later, at 11am, realizing that Dr Asamoah was definitely not an early bird. I also made sure I ate 'plenty' as the Ghanaians would say. As I entered a nurse told me the doctor was expecting me and I was led into the consulting room even though a patient was still being treated in there! I waited while he wrote out the patient's prescription.

Dr Asamoah was a quietly spoken, gentle man who obviously worked very hard in this overcrowded and underfunded clinic. His hair was greying and a giant pair of black-rimmed glasses, concealing large bulbous eyes, framed his large square head. He was courteous and polite. I asked him what were some of the main problems the girls faced living out in the open. He said of the most common problems the biggest was malaria. This applied both to the babies and the kayayo themselves. He said this was directly due to living and sleeping out in the open. He also added that many of the kayayo living in and around the market were between the ages of ten and twelve years. I was not surprised as I was beginning, as I penetrated the interior of the market more, to see very, very young kayayo girls, who were in fact just children.

'The girls sleep next to the open gutters, which are full of stagnant water and a breeding ground for mosquitoes.'

'Can the girls not sleep under nets?'

'We have a programme where we give out free mosquito nets but the kayayo could not take full advantage of them due to not having a good place to hang them and also not having a permanent place.'

He said the second most common problem was gastro-intestinal problems due to unhygienic conditions. Typhoid was also a problem and also respiratory problems due to constant dust and exhaust fumes. Generally the kayayo have to walk through the massive traffic jams that run through the entire city as they take their loads from one location to another. Indeed, if one takes into account the density of the city's traffic gridlock it is probably quicker to use the kayayo than motorized transport.

Dr Asamoah went on to use an expression that I have heard the kayayo girls use many times themselves. He said seriously,

'They get beaten by the rain. Where they sleep there is no cover from the rain and they have to get up from their sleeping places. Sometimes they have to stand the whole night. They get soaked and often have to sleep like that in the cold. The babies get pneumonia because of getting wet and cold and having low immune systems. At times the girls lose their babies, but this is mostly dealt with at the Bilal Polyclinic which is larger and better equipped.'

I mentioned how I had noticed that the girls tended to eat food without many nutrients. He said the girls ate what they term as 'dry food': rice, kenke, TZ and banku, which was basically stodge. However he said the girls did not appear to be malnourished. He said rather it was the babies who were malnourished, with many of them suffering from anaemia.

'They don't have time to look after the babies and don't feed them properly. They use their dirty hands to hold the breast and put it in the babies' mouths. Many of the babies have worm infestations and skin diseases.'

Dr Asamoah went on to talk about what he called the 'occupational hazards' of working as a kayayo.

'They get a lot of injuries. They carry loads that are too heavy for them and they fall down with the loads falling on them and their babies. They also get a lot of lacerations which need to be stitched.'

'Why the lacerations?'

The doctor told me he thought this was due to walking past so many things in the market at close proximity, they brush against things and get cut.

I wanted to know more about the alleged sexual exploitation the girls had to endure and the incidents of rape. Had he heard about this? Sadly, he said rape often occurred.

'When the girls are lying down at night men just come and lie on them, but as the kayayo are often in groups they are sometimes able to fight the men off. So often it can be attempted rape.'

I asked if they ever had to treat girls who have been victims of these crimes.

'Because I am not a gynaecologist, I usually send severe cases of injury to the Bilal Polyclinic, a bigger hospital in the area.'

He added that many of the kayayo girls 'get pregnant when they are down here.'

I thanked Dr Asamoah for the time he had taken to talk to me. I left admiring the man. Government doctors do not get paid well in Ghana yet he worked tirelessly in this downtrodden area, fighting an uphill battle with few resources. After living in Africa for almost fifteen years I had become accustomed to poverty and the heartache it brings. Yet anytime I thought of these poor little girls tears would well in my eyes, as did that day I left Dr Asamoah's consulting room. The plight of these girls brought pity from even those you felt should be pitied most. Their status was so low, their plight so wretched that even the poorest in Accra thought they were fortunate in comparison to them.

It was now mid October. Thirty-three miners had today been trapped seven hundred metres underground in the San Jose mine, Copiaco, Chile. It seemed so far away from here in West Africa but the constant news coverage made it seem it had occurred just around the corner. I decided today I would drive to downtown Accra to find out about the thousands of other kayayo who purportedly lived down there. As I was driving across an overhead bridge a giant larger than life sized poster of Bishop Duncan Williams, a Ghanaian 'Super Pastor' towered over me. He was imploring people to attend his '24 Hour Prayer Spectacular' at his church 'Action Chapel' in Spintex Road. So large was the church that it was one of the first landmarks one saw on descending into Ghana's Kotoka International Airport. The giant pair of marble hands held together in prayer confronted all who entered. So busy was I looking up at him that I did not notice the line of police ahead.

Anyone who lives in Accra will have their 'police stories' that are pulled out at parties and lunch dates. One could be forgiven for thinking that the main reason the police exist in Accra and indeed Ghana is not to fight crime, but rather to extort money from every passing motorist, using an array of unbelievable invented 'infringements' of traffic regulations. After being stopped for having an 'expired license' (when the date clearly shows it isn't), or 'going through a red light' (when it was obviously green) you will then be told that you can be either be 'taken to court' or what has become euphemistically known as, pay a 'spot fine', meaning a bribe which will go straight into their pockets. Most people opt for the latter, pay up and drive on.

So it was under the gaze of Bishop Duncan Williams that I was stopped yet again by the Ghana police for a 'traffic violation'. The pair told me I had just gone through a red light. I replied that I wasn't colourblind, that it had been green.

'Then we will have to take you to the police station and you will appear in court.'

'Take me.'

'Ok.'

One quickly jumped into the back of my car. I had forgotten to lock it. I was really stuck then. An argument ensued with accusations and counter accusations. Just then, in the distance, I saw Mahab and Aysha walking across the bridge laden down with heavy loads of yams. They soon recognized the car and came over. They looked angry and said something to the police in Twi. I was telling the other policeman to get out of my car. I had not 'gone through a red light'. Other pedestrians stopped and it started to resemble an affray with everyone talking and shouting at once. One man started shouting at Mahab and she started to shout back and he pushed her. He tahili fell off her head and the yams tumbled and scattered across the pavement and into the road in front of oncoming cars. Those around and passers-by rushed to pick them up, putting them back into the metal bowl. Mahab did not join in, rather she retaliated, pushing back her attacker. She started screaming at him. I saw Aysha trying to talk to the other policemen. Whatever she was saying would have been rudimentary as her Twi was not good. Nevertheless Aysha seemed articulate and very intelligent. She spoke with fervour and grace. She appeared like an orator. Mahab was still shouting at the man. The police were insisting on their 'fine.' I couldn't stand it any longer. I gave them both five cedis each and drove off, checking on them through my rear view mirror. They laughed and quickly put the money in their pockets. Mahab, Aysha and their loads were in the back, and we drove the short distance to the Spot.

When we entered a man was sitting at the table talking to Gifty, who wore on her face an expression of misery. He had a profusion of fake gold chains, which he was trying to separate ready for sale. Another lady was sitting with them. Mahab, Aysha, and myself sat down at the table and I ordered some drinks. The Japanese girl on the wall had not changed her expression. She seemed trapped in another world. I told the others at the Spot about my ordeal,

'That's how they are,' said the man, desperately trying to wriggle out one chain 'they just try to take your money, they are greedy.'

Aysha went out to buy food and returned with four black polythene bags, two containing a gooey, glutinous, green okra stew and the other, banku. They dipped the banku into the stew and woofed it down. They had not eaten breakfast since starting work before dawn at 5am. It was now almost 11am. Aysha was still adorned with the intricate designs on her hands and arms and she wore a tight fitting pink T-shirt emblazoned with 'Obama Girl'. Little Adnan, Mahab's son, was sitting on the broken tiled floor sucking on a piece of what looked like white rubberized cow's innards. This was popular among the poor who could not afford meat. He chewed and smacked his lips.

Mahab was still angry about the man who had pushed her. She was wearing a green and white striped T-shirt and green skirt.

'This keeps happening,' she told me in her deep husky voice.

'Whenever we are walking around the city with our loads, the other people they insult us and call us names.

As we walk people push us out of the way, as there are many people in the street our bowls fall on the floor with all the goods.'

In one of the few surveys done into the lives of the kayayo on the streets of Accra, harassment, which came second only to lack of accommodation, scored high amongst their grievances. Other complaints included 'customer exploitation and abuse', 'health and finding food', 'exhaustion', 'stealing' and 'no place to rest'. Mahab had now taken the chewy stomach innards from her son and was now chewing on it. Little Adnan screamed for it back. He was dressed beautifully in lemon shorts and a lemon polo striped T-shirt.

It would always baffle me how wonderfully turned out all Ghanaians looked. They always appeared to be wearing the height of fashion, yet imported clothes here cost the earth. It was later I found out the secret. The sprawling second hand or 'home use' clothing markets in downtown Accra where you can pick up a Tommy Hilfiger, Vivian Westwood, Zara, Mango, Next or other designer clothes for literally pennies. Today little Adnan was wearing 'Baby Gap,' not that Mahab nor anyone else around had any idea of the prices people in the west paid to adorn their offspring in such labels.

Mahab continued angrily.

'Sometimes they start to beat us for destroying their goods.'

The loads could be worth up to a few months' salary for the vendor and they would be furious. The perpetrator of the crime, the one who pushed the kayayo usually joined in with the others in the general abuse. No one would listen to the kayayo.

'Then they take us to the police station and we have to pay.'

'How can you pay?'

'Sometimes we have to pay, sometimes also they let

us go.'

I could see from the hatred and anger that flashed across both Aysha's and Mahab's faces that this continued harassment was more than they could bear. Also these kinds of incidents seriously forestalled the kayayo's main aim for coming to Accra in the first place which was to save. The reason the kayayo suffered living out in the open, not eating decent food, was so that at the end of it they would be able to take home much needed goods and money to their families in the impoverished north of the country. In a recent survey almost eighty per cent of kayayo girls interviewed cited that the main reason they had left their homes in the north of the country was to come to look for money, the second biggest reason was to escape abuse and neglect within the home. One of the major reasons given for this neglect and abuse was because their fathers had 'taken another wife'. Many in the survey said their fathers in particular had 'neglected them completely'. They therefore felt they had no alternative but to come to Accra to support their families and act as breadwinners. For many of the kayayo the appalling conditions under which they were forced to live appeared tolerable to them as they saw it as only a 'temporary means to an end'.

Yet so many events occurred which prevented them from achieving this end, from the continued theft of their goods and bouts of sickness and injuries, to constantly having to pay 'compensation' for incidents, that they started to resemble a hamster on a wheel, forever striving but reaching nowhere. I often got the impression they took one step forward and two steps back. I had never met a group of people who suffered so many setbacks in their process towards financial betterment. It was a credit to these girls that despite all these hardships they were still able to save and take money home.

I glanced down at the floor. Adnan had taken advantage of his mum's animated talk to snatch back the white cow innards. The man with the chains had now managed to extricate about ten chains and had laid them vertically across the table. Gifty, stern faced, was gathering our now empty bottles. I didn't want to glance up at the wall and see Cheiko smiling at us.

I looked across the table and saw Aysha and Mahab smiling at me, as if they had a guilty secret to hide.

'Why are you smiling?' I asked

They each produced a 10 cedi note and laid it on the table.

'Look what we earned this morning. The man we worked for he gave us this...look.'

They kept holding the notes and fingering them. They told me they were not going to spend it but save it.

'Still it is not even midday, we can still earn more and save this.'

Aysha put her elbows on the table and held out her beautifully decorated palms, tattooed with henna. She went to speak.

'I want to buy a sewing machine and learn how to sew...then once I learn I will teach my sister to sew and I will come and work again as kayayo and buy another machine.'

It was a good idea. Aysha was so articulate and intelligent, she had good ideas, and wanted to go further in life.

I left my car outside the Spot and walked down with them to the tree. Nurah and Rebecca were sitting on their bowls feeding their babies. Shadows from the tree above imprinted and danced over their faces. They smiled gently as we approached. Mahab quickly told them 'my police story'. Both Nurah and Rebecca looked sad and told me they were sorry. They (the police) had made me waste my money. We said goodbye and I left this bustling world of female domesticity.

Chapter Three

The Policeman and the Banker

I wanted to find out more about why the kayayo girls were constantly dragged to the police station and decided the next day to visit a local police station in Accra. The next day I arrived early at the station. There was nowhere to park outside and I was terrified of 'being done' for yet another 'traffic violation' so drove into the police station car park. I parked and on getting out was approached by an irate policeman who told me that it was not allowed to leave cars in the car park.

'But I am coming inside the station to talk to the police,' I rebuked.

'It doesn't matter - if you leave your car here it will be taken away.'

I continued to sit in my car wondering what to do. Another policeman was standing nearby and started chatting to me through my open window. He was very friendly and helpful and told me his name was Gyedu. He told me he was very keen to help me with the book and that being in central Accra he had a lot of 'dealings' with the kayayo. He explained that one of the main things that caused problems and resulted in the girls being dragged to the police station was 'overload'. He said the tendency was for them to take more than they could carry as they wanted to 'get more money', so if people only very gently brushed against them, they and their loads toppled over. He went on to say that 'due to tiredness' the kayayo, unlike most others carrying heavy loads in Accra, didn't always shout for people to move to the side when they were coming.

The usual cry one hears in Accra when people are

approaching with dangerously heavy or cumbersome loads is 'agoh, agoh'. This basically means, 'get out of the bloody way or you'll be knocked over'. The issue of tiredness I have heard over and over again when talking to people in Accra about the kayayo. It has been cited as the principal reason for many of their problems, such as the ease with which people can steal from them, to the constant fights that break out between them. It must be hard to gauge just how intense their tiredness is after trudging the entire day in intense heat with loads almost as much as their own weight and the added stress of a crying and hungry baby on your back. I also felt that their hesitation in calling for people to move out of the way was not only due to tiredness. The kayayo may also feel shy about drawing attention to themselves for fear of being further insulted by those who they ask to move.

Officer Gyedu went went on to elaborate. He gave other reasons why the kayayo's excessive loads can lead to them ending up in police custody.

'They can't turn their heads to look for oncoming traffic, as the load is so excessive, if they try to turn it would topple over. So when they see a car coming the instinct is to drop the goods and run to get out of the way, this will sometimes fall on people's cars, sometimes smashing their windscreens.'

Suddenly an officious looking man marched sternly out of the station entrance and waved his arm furiously for Gyedu to come over. I learnt it was his boss, the Chief Superintendent. He wanted to know why he was talking to this stranger in the car park. Gyedu explained to him that I wasn't able to get out of the car to sit anywhere more comfortable, as if I did my car was likely to be towed away, even though it was in the Police Station's car park, so that I had decided to do the interview whilst sitting in my car. The commander then came over to speak to me and I put on my sweetest smile and told him how grateful I was that Officer Gyedu was being so helpful in giving me information about the kayayo girls for my forthcoming book. He changed and told me that the Ghana police always liked to help strangers and foreigners and that he knew I was trying to help the girls so they must 'also help you.'

Officer Gyedu then continued.

'When the kayayo drop goods on the people's cars the car owners drag them, that's if they can catch them, up to the police station.'

He quickly dusted off some petals that were falling on his uniform from the overhanging tree.

'If you carry loads you should take care so you won't spoil other people's property, if they damage your car the drivers must catch them, push them in the car and bring them to the station. If there are two or more people in the car they can usually catch them. Other people in the street will also usually help.'

I was picturing the driver, his passenger then the local street vendors around all gathering together to chase the poor kayayo girl and push her in the car.

'Another problem which brings them to the police station is that they hit people in the eye with their loads.'

He said that in addition to carrying things with the metal bowl or tahili, they sometimes used planks of wood depending on the nature of the load. He continued to brush the petals off his impeccably clean and smart uniform. He seemed annoyed and then said,

'If someone asks you to carry four buckets of paint and you can only carry three, why take four? Give one to your sister (friend) to carry. Call your sister to help. But they take loads more than they can carry cos they want the extra money.'

He went on to say that when the accidents occurred

they sometimes seriously injured other people as they 'pushed or dropped the loads on someone's head.'

'How do the kayayo girls manage to pay all this compensation to drivers and vendors of goods, they have nothing?'

Officer Gyedu told me they had associations, so that when these incidents occurred the association's leader would come to talk to the car owner and agree a price.

'What if the girl doesn't have an association to help her, is she taken to court?'

'If the girl can't pay the police will plea on the girl's behalf and the girl will also beg. Because we are human beings they ask the driver to do them a favour and 'consider the girl'. Usually they accept as the kayayo could be their sister, and they know they can't pay anyway.'

I looked up at the overhanging tree laden with hundreds of tiny pink flowers. The air was hot and dusty and I could smell the heavy sweet smell of plantains being fried. A small girl approached us and asked if we wanted to buy iced sachet water. She took some from the bowl on her head and handed it to us and she went on her way.

I told Gyedu how many people had told me the girls were sometimes sexually assaulted and raped. Did he have any knowledge of this? He told me that the men who raped the girls were mostly their own tribe's people. In a way I was both surprised and not surprised on hearing this. Surprised as the girls looked to their 'own people' to protect them in this swollen metropolis, yet not surprised as I knew the girls tended not to mix with other tribes, especially those from the south, so usually any men they did come into contact with would for the most part be those from their own tribe.

Gyedu cited tribal marriage as one of the factors which caused a lot of problems for the girls.

'Any man can tell a girl's father that he would like to take his daughter as his wife, the father then can agree and give his daughter for marriage even if the girl doesn't want it. Often the men are much older than the girls.'

Gyedu said that it was at this stage that the girl may try to run away and often ended up on the streets of Accra. It was then most often the father, the prospective husband or other male members of the girl's family that would come to Accra searching for her. He told me they often tried to kidnap the girl and then take her back to the north.

'How could they ever manage to find her in such a huge metropolis as Accra?'

'It's easy to find them,' he assured me. 'They know where to find them.'

He then went on to tell me about a very similar case which he had had to deal with not so long ago.

'I was patrolling the streets of downtown Accra one evening. A lady had run away from Tamale to come to Accra, and the men from the village traced her and found her. They grabbed the lady and tied her hands and legs with rope and put her into the back of a vehicle. The police heard the screams and ran to the scene and arrested them. The village men then told me very indignantly as if they were doing nothing wrong,

'We are only taking her back to Tamale'.

'And?'

'But later they were charged and sentenced.'

It was getting late and Gyedu told me he could talk no longer but he said he wanted to help me with the book and gave me his number. More small pink petals had fallen on his hat and he brushed them off.

It was much later after finding out a lot more about the kayayo and how they lived that I got to understand what Gyedu meant when he said, 'it's easy to find them, they know where to find them'. It was possible for someone to come to a bustling city such as Accra or a huge mega-city like Lagos and manage to find an individual within a day or sometimes even hours without having any knowledge whatsoever of their whereabouts. For example, certain tribes from certain areas of the country will tend to live in allotted neighbourhoods. You can arrive in a city and ask where the Dagomba people or the Hausa people live. You would have then considerably narrowed down your search. Once there you start to ask if and where the people for this sub-area or village area live, it will not be long before you have located someone from your village, or if it's a small town the area of the town from which you came from. Within a short time you have found someone who knows the person you are looking for. That was why many of the kayayo told me that the girls who had run away could not live with them as it would be too easy for the people from their village to trace them. Indeed, reports have also said that living in the street does not mean in local terms that the kayayo are without an address from which they cannot be found, as friends and relatives can locate them according to their nighttime residences.

It was these girls, the girls that had run away, who were particularly vulnerable as they did not have the safety network of being within the larger kayayo group which served as mutual protection. They would either have to sleep alone in the street or accept 'invitations' from men in the area to share their trotro or taxi. The men would tell them they wanted to 'help them' so they were not sleeping in the open. Other times they were offered floor space in wooden kiosks, which served as shops or fast food joints during the day. It was at these times the girls were helpless and were often either sexually exploited or raped.

A case study looking at the sexual exploitation of children not only just among the kayayo, but on the streets of Accra generally, found that in cases where a boy 'supports' a girl financially or materially, or provides accommodation or 'protection' sex was expected. The study went on to point out that for these young girls sex is understood 'more as a service that females provide for males than as an act of mutual pleasure' and that the idea of rape or exploitation does not seem to be 'appreciated or understood by most of the girls'. Also it was noted that both their concerns about protection and actual incidence of condom use were low and inconsistent and this was 'related to the exploitative nature of the sexual relations, as girls do not feel entitled to negotiate for such protection.' The report concluded, not surprisingly that the sexual exploitation was particularly prevalent among the kayayo who have no accommodation or relatives within Accra. I also came to realize that this vulnerability made them easy prey for men who claimed to be 'protecting' them.

I was beginning to realize more and more the dangers the girls faced. But slowly I also realized how they had learnt to create and structure their own unique society which helped them overcome, survive and even prosper amongst this hell in which they were forced to live. I learnt they had special associations to cushion them against unexpected financial hardships as we have insurance schemes. They formed schemes for incidences of sickness and injury as we have health insurance. They formed their own schemes to enhance and help themselves and each other to save, as we have our saving schemes. They formed and moved in tight knit groups to safeguard themselves from attack by strangers and did not mix with any other people except those within their own tightly knit unit. I was fascinated to find out about these special and truly courageous girls.

As the weeks went by the cooler weather that characterized Ghana during the months from May to September, began to fade and the heat from the sun grew stronger with each passing day. I would pass the girls sitting under the mango tree. I watched their babies grow, got to know intimately their heartaches and joys and their laughter. Often I would stop for a few minutes as I passed. Gazelle-like Latifa would often come over with some of her younger peers, act mischievously in front of my car and pull war like faces. They would raise their fists as if in mock battle then bend forward and laugh. Of the girls I had got to know to date, Latifa was the youngest and also the cockiest. Nurah was the most gentle. Rebecca also had a gentle manner but this went along with an inner resolve and strength. She could speak English, she had been to school longer than the others. Young Aysha was the intelligent entrepreneur, who dreamed or starting her own business. Mahab, with her deep husky voice, was tough and straight talking but courteous and polite to myself, an older person, as their tradition dictated. All of them I thought, maybe with the exception of Nurah, had the toughness necessary to survive on these streets. Nurah was reserved, shy and patient, and she blended with her group. From them she got her strength and protection.

I still had not managed to find an interpreter and it was seriously curtailing my work. Often the girls seemed not to really understand what was being said to them in Twi. I had been up and down the street near the Spot several times asking everyone I passed if they knew someone who wanted a small job translating for me from Mamprusi to English. I had been told there was a watchman at the Methodist Church, who could speak both Mamprusi and fluent English. I had been there a few times but had never been able to find him. I often had to rely on impromptu situations, asking people nearby to help me.

I had not been to the Spot for about two weeks so one morning I arranged with the girls that we would go that afternoon. It was around 4.30pm, and it was just after picking up my daughter from school when I arrived at the tree. I could never be sure who would be there. They could make an arrangement to meet me at a certain time but if someone called them to carry or they were trudging miles away in a different part of Accra, it would not be possible. As I approached, tiny Latifa was standing with her friends, pulling faces, gesticulating and laughing. She always liked to joke that she was strong and if we fought she would beat me. Aysha was walking towards a large truck discharging bright green plantains but on seeing me she ran towards me, holding my hand. She told me she had been 'saving serious' and would soon be able to buy her hand held sewing machine. She said she would try and come to the Spot later but now she had to work.

'I will do it mummy, I will soon do it' she said, full of hope.

I watched her run back to the truck, towards the work that would eventually bring her closer to her dream of owning the sewing machine.

Shy Nurah and the dignified Rebecca, both with their babies, who were growing fast, said they would join us soon. They just had to buy 'chop'. I noticed Nurah had a plaster over her left cheek.

I asked Latifa to get in the car. They had known me a long time now. Surely they could trust me? She giggled and laughed, and eventually got into the car. It was literally one-minute drive from the Tree to the Spot but she constantly ducked down laughing out loud when she saw any of her friends walking past carrying their loads atop their heads. As we entered the Spot Gifty actually gave me a smile and within minutes the volume on the tinny radio was suddenly reduced! There were two other men in the small rectangular space, the first seemed to be a sleeping drunk and the second an impeccably dressed young man in a pin striped suit, with tie, cufflinks and tie pin and of course our friend Cheiko on the wall.

Once in The Spot, alone without her peers, Latifa seemed very shy. Gone was her boisterous cockiness. She constantly looked down at the ground, only raising her face to glance at me bashfully, smile and look down again. I asked the man in the pinstriped suit if he could translate for me. He told me his name was Martin and that he worked as an accountant for a large bank in Accra. The banking sector in Ghana has been growing enormously in recent years with many new banks entering the market opening branches all over the country and providing much needed employment, loans and mortgages for the growing private housing market. But all this new economic activity bypassed the kayayo girls.

Latifa said she had been in Accra for six months and that she had come down to Accra with her older sister, whose name was Rayina.

Looking at Latifa once again she appeared even younger than when I had first seen her in the Spot some weeks ago. She was pre-pubescent and her breasts had not yet formed so I would guess she was not older than about twelve. When I asked her if people were bad to her in Accra she said 'no', even though I knew this was not the case. She then averted her face and looked down at the floor. However Martin, the accountant, attempted to explain her cryptic answer fully.

'For them verbal assault is so common it just seems

part of their everyday life, like washing or sleeping, they don't actually notice it. They take verbal and even physical abuse as part of their job.'

Then Martin mentioned what I was later to hear over and over again from the kayayo. That often their customers did not pay them for their work.

'Sometimes the girls agree a price for carrying the load, say 2 cedis (£1 Sterling) and then once the kayayo has carried the load to the destination and packed it into their customer's car, the customer will then only pay them 1 cedi or 50psws, or sometimes nothing at all. The girl will be powerless to do anything about it.'

Martin spoke to Latifa and she agreed. She told me that many times the customers didn't pay them.

Martin also went on to point out, as the kayayo themselves had told me, that wherever they sit or sleep they are moved on. They have an itinerant existence, not only do they not have a home, but even the tiny patch of ground where they want to lay and rest cannot be safeguarded.

I asked Latifa where she slept, and she said she slept in a room with many other girls.

'How many?'

'There are so many I can't count.'

Before Latifa had said she slept in front of shops in the market. All this confusion made me realize I must find an interpreter. I mentioned that problem to Martin and he told me that for them, Twi was only a business language. Anything you talk about with any deeper meaning will not be understood. I asked Latifa, who was very slowly sipping her Coke, eager to make it last as long as possible, if she missed her parents and family. She sat quietly and tears welled up in her enormous possum like eyes.

'I want to go back to the village. But there is no money there so I have to be here. I want to see my mother and sisters. I used to ring my parents in the village but somebody, he stole my phone when I was sleeping.'

She held up her Coke to see how much was left. I told her to drink on, if she wanted I would buy her another one. The drunk kept swaying from side to side as he slept on the wobbly plastic chair. He kept veering precariously too much over to the left where we were seated and I kept thinking any minute he was going to topple over, but always just within seconds of it happening he grunted and appeared to straighten up. Dribble was trickling down from his mouth.

I asked Latifa where she stored all her personal belongings. She told me 'in a bucket', she also went on to say that herself, unlike the other girls in her group, did not walk round soliciting work.

'I sit under a tree. If someone wants me to carry their load they will come and get me. Many times they call me from their car or taxi.'

The sun's rays seeped into the darkened shack, illuminating millions of dust particles in its beams, and lighting up with its spotlights various dingy corners in our rectangular patch. Places best kept in darkness. Some of the dribble from the drunk's mouth caught the rays and sparkled. Cars and taxis could be heard driving outside, but within our little cocoon they seemed miles away. On the radio which had been turned down quite low, I could hear a news announcement, 'a tsunami and subsequent earthquake had struck the coast somewhere in Indonesia, hundreds were missing'. I had never heard the word 'tsunami' before, and wondered what it was.

Just then the bamboo curtain swished and Nurah and Rebecca brushed through with their babies on their backs. With them was Aysha, her arms still decorated beautifully with the henna tattoos. As the two older girls entered they quickly untied their infants, sitting them down onto the broken tiled floor. Then all three of them sat down and remained quiet, looking at me with expectant eyes. I knew they couldn't wait to get their drinks. Gifty appeared, looking at us vacantly, as if she was just waiting for us to tell her what to do next. She brought back the Fanta and Sprite with no emotion, a completely blank expression on her face.

I asked both girls again about how difficult it was for them to wash, noticing once again the long strip of plaster on Nurah's face. She looked at the other three girls as if asking permission to speak. They remained quiet, Latifa looking at the ground, Aysha cleaning her nails and Rebecca looking up at Cheiko.

'We bathe in the public bathhouse down the street here,' and she pointed in that direction, 'It's plenty (very) crowded. So many women go there, that many of us, we have to bath in the street in front of everyone as there is no room left inside. We have to pay a lot of money for the bucket of water and we even have to bring our own bucket and soap. It is shameful to bathe in the street in front of men. The bathhouse is next to the open gutter and many times it smells.'

I had indeed seen this many times as I often used to drive past the bathhouse. Girls standing almost naked in the street covered in white soapsuds, babies would be sitting in buckets and bowls half way into the street, and cars would hoot for them to move over. Many women desperately were trying to bathe while still wearing some clothes to hide their shame from all the onlookers. Once bath time was over the remaining water was used for the laundry, yet I doubted there was any water left for rinsing. They then had to tie their now clean babies onto their backs, pile their wet washing into their tahilis and walk back to the rectangular patch of dirt which they called home. Here they would attempt to hitch bits of string between the shop front and other poles, so the washing would hang diagonally and horizontally over the few square feet in which they slept, dripping on them the whole night. Rebecca looked at me in a way that told me she had something more to say.

'When we want to go to the toilet they make us pay again, 30psa for toilet and 10psws for the paper, if we want to urine we have to pay 20psws. Sometimes we have to queue long time to use the toilet.'

I was keen to find out about their finances, how they ever managed to save a pesawa in this environment. I asked the young girl Latifa how much she spent on food a day. She looked towards Martin, who was beginning to look decidedly incongruous in his pin stripe suit. She spoke in a thin, girlish voice.

'I spend about Gh1.50 or Gh2 cedis a day (75 pence-£1 Sterling). I buy porridge or rice in the morning, it is 50psws, (25 pence Sterling) then rice for lunch again 50psws and in the evening I buy banku or kenke. Every day I must give 1 cedi to a lady who saves for me.'

I asked her who this lady was. Latifa's large black liquid eyes darted around before she spoke.

'She is a lady who saves for us, she writes it in a book.'

'Can you trust this lady?'

'Yes, she always gives us our money.'

Aysha, just finishing her fingernails and always keen to talk about such matters added, gesticulating with her decorated palms to emphasis her point,

'Yes the lady who keeps our money she can be trusted. It is good for us to give the money to her as then we don't spend it.'

I asked them if they had ever considered putting their money in a bank, if you save the bank will give you some on top.

At this they all roared with laughter, except Aysha who said, looking at Martin, keen for him to translate.

'Mummy, we can't go to the bank, we can't speak Twi and they won't take our money, it is too small to go in the bank.'

I guessed she was referring to the fact that they only put in one cedi a day, but I reminded them of the proverb I often heard repeated in Ghana,

'Small drops make might oceans.'

Again they all roared with laughter, including Gifty who had been sitting on a table nearby. The drunk momentarily stirred, opened his eyes as if in shock and went back to sleep. I told them, and Martin the accountant who knew about these things backed me up, that there were many different kinds of banks. In Ghana there was a women's bank especially for women like them. They didn't seem convinced and as time went on I noticed they were very stubborn about entering anything that was considered part of the mainstream. They trusted their own people, their own ancient ways of doing things. Those ways had evolved over the years and were finely tuned and adapted to their precarious ways of life. Yet I couldn't help thinking that keeping their money in a bank would safeguard them from the almost daily and weekly thefts that affected them. Also, contrary to what they had just said, I had read reports where the kayayo had stated they were sometimes afraid of giving their money to 'susu' operators as they had heard that they had at times run off with their savings money.

It appeared all the kayayo's savings arrangements operated outside any formal banking structures. One publication noted that the kayayo's savings took two forms, which were the adashi and susu. In the susu system the kayayo give their savings usually on a daily basis to an informal banker, say for thirty days. The kayayo was given a card and the 'susu man or woman' had a corresponding card upon which the savings were tallied. At the end of this fixed period the 'banker' paid the girls back the lump sum minus a charge for the security provided. The adashie system was described as a savings scheme 'arranged within the kayayo community itself' and was a form of 'rotating box credit'. Within this system groups of between ten to twenty women saved a set amount daily, giving it to the girl whose turn it was to act as 'treasurer'. For example, if ten girls saved one cedi each for ten days, that would be ten cedis per day. After ten days the hundred cedis (£50 Sterling) collected will be paid out to one (or sometimes two) girls in the group in accordance with the turn taking rules of the group. In this way, sometime during the year each girl will get her 'turn' and receive enough money to purchase the goods needed to return home. Furthermore, it was noted that the adashie system was also used as a way to protect the kayayo from the consequences of loss of income in the case of sickness or any legal disputes which may be taken to the police. For example, a bout of sickness will allow a kayayo girl to move higher up the queue for her turn to receive the funds. It was noted that the adashie system was in fact a 'self-organised' medical insurance scheme. However, when talking to the kayayo about this they always referred to the adashie system described above as 'Susu', and I have consequently referred to all savings schemes described likewise.

Latifa held up her drink, which was now empty, and she turned her chair, laying her head on Aysha's lap, resting her legs and letting them hang over the other chair. Aysha started to play with Latifa's hair. It looked endearing. I asked if they had known each other a long time. Latifa giggled, looking up at me as she lay on

Aysha's lap, she covered her face as she smiled widely and looked the other way, leaving her friend to answer.

'We were born together, we come from the same village, we grow together.'

'What's the name of the village?'

'Bandugu'

'Isn't that the village that Nurah and Rebecca come from?' I said, looking over at them both.

'Yes, we all live there.'

Rebecca, with her strong arms, was gathering up crying baby Madihah from the tiled floor, and she quickly pulled out her breast to quieten her. She looked at me, smiling confidently as if she was about to reveal some enchanting secret.

'Yes, I'm from Bandugu too, all of us we are from the same village.'

She laughed again and said to the others,

'She didn't know, Mummy didn't know we were all from the same hometown.'

The seated drunk suddenly woke up and looked around, wide eyed. The girls glanced at each other and giggled, covering their mouths with their hands. He stood up abruptly, as he did so a rancid odour wafted from his direction, then, just as quickly, he swished through the bamboo curtain into the bright sunlight outside.

I was keen to find out more about how they earned their living and saved. For the kayayo saving is their primary aim. Many times they would tell me, 'we suffer to save'.

Aysha showed a great maturity and was extremely articulate despite her tender years. She explained how she started up when she arrived in Accra.

'When I came to Accra I had to buy a metal bowl. To be a kayayo you must have a tahili. I had to buy my bowl and it cost GhC11 (£6 Sterling) so I had to pay for it small small, as mummy, I did not have even a pesawa. I paid for it Gh1 (50 pence Sterling) every week and after about 10 weeks the bowl was mine.'

This appeared to be the way that most girls acquired their bowls on arriving in Accra, using hire purchase or credit. I asked how much they were paid for their arduous backbreaking work. Were they paid by distance or weight?

Martin explained and the girls agreed that there were no exact payments. He said most of the time the girls were cheated and had to work for much less payment than they should rightly receive. This was because they had no bargaining power. They were powerless and people knew this. They knew that the kayayo could do nothing about how they were treated, so they exploited this. The kayayo were just mute and were obliged to accept any payment they were given.

What he said reminded me of a blog I once read on the internet from a British Ghanaian girl who had gone to her home country for a visit.

'When I was back in Ghana I would occasionally go to Medina Market in Accra with my mum and I remember seeing them every time. I often wondered why they weren't in school, why they were doing what they do and why they didn't bargain what was paid to them. My mum would lament about their plight and each time she patronized their service she would ask them why they were doing what they did. Unlike my mum, most patrons of the kayayo's services were not so considerate and didn't think twice about having them carry twice their weight. This is a very sensitive topic to me, because the way I see it, a twist of fate, and I could have become one.'

I watched Aysha slowly unravel a piece of cotton thread from Latifa's hair. Baby Madihah had now been quietened by her feed and lay asleep, her mother's nipple still in her half opened mouth. Rebecca pulled it out and efficiently pushed her breast back into her bra. Gifty came and collected up the empty bottles. She didn't wipe the table and small pools of liquid in varying colours floated on it. I discerned a tall dark figure through the bamboo curtain, and heard a melodic intonation. It reminded me very much of the Arabic language, a kind of guttural sound. The voice was strong. Resonant. Deep. Suddenly we saw long fingers gripping some bamboo strands, pulling them to one side about two thirds of the way up the doorway. We sat watching. All of us were absorbed in our own private thoughts. A face peeped through. Confident. Bright. Passionate. It was Mahab with baby Adnan on her back. She strode over, and embraced me with her long arms. She apologized for not coming before. She had been helping to unload a truck full of yams that had arrived from the town Kintampo close to the northern region. She had had to walk far so it had taken her a long time to get back. I ordered some more drinks and she drank eagerly. She was hot and thirsty. We again sat for some minutes lost in our thoughts. I again noticed the plaster on Nurah's cheek.

I asked her what had happened to her face. Her jovial expression vanished. She fell silent. Martin asked her again. She looked down at the floor. She avoided my gaze. Rebecca, dignified and as always seemingly unflappable, answered the question her friend could not.

'Last night a man came to our group and he tried to lie with Nurah, he tried to lie on top of Nurah and she pushed him and shouted. He pulled her hair and her face rubbed on the ground. The ground it scratched Nurah's face. It happened where we were sleeping.'

'What happened, did you take the man to the police?'

'We beat him, we beat him hard but he got free and ran away, we couldn't catch him.'

'Was her face badly cut? Nurah was still looking at the ground.

Rebecca murmured something to her friend, and Nurah pulled off the plaster, which revealed a very large graze across her face, which had been treated with gentian violet. She continued to look at the ground as if ashamed. Rebecca added,

'We took her to the hospital this morning and they made us pay five cedis. We put our money together and paid.'

I admired Rebecca for the way she gently and tactfully handled this sensitive topic. She could have been a professional psychologist in a court room, such was her composure and discretion.

Martin then went on to tell me that they were often sexually abused but they didn't like to talk about it. They felt ashamed to mention such things. He went on to add that in addition to the injuries from sexual assault they also often got injured in the numerous fights that broke out between them. He said they fought and quarrelled amongst themselves a lot. I guessed this might probably be the case but to date they had always said no whenever I had asked them about this. He told me he had personally had to separate fighting kayayo girls on two occasions, which I believed as I had often seen fights breaking out between women in Accra which had to be separated by bystanders.

'They are very tribalistic and often if there is a disagreement between two different tribes then their co-tribe members join in the affray. Also, if two girls from two different villages start to fight a similar pattern occurs.'

I wanted to know and had asked the girls several times what happened when they were pregnant. They always said that they 'went back to the village' when they thought 'the baby will come'. In Accra hospital costs for pregnancy and birth would be yet another cost for the kayayo. Martin told me he had actually witnessed one kayayo girl starting to give birth by the side of the road.

'She was lying there and her friends were behind. At first they couldn't find a taxi that would agree to take them to the hospital. Taxis often don't want to take them in their cars, they think they are dirty and they usually can't afford to pay the fare.'

'What happened in the end?

'In the end we persuaded the taxi to take her to the hospital, but the taxi made the girls pay for the taxi before they started the journey. They clubbed together and paid for the taxi and hospital bills.'

It had been a long stint today in the Spot. I was beginning to find out more about how the kayayo earned and saved, but needed to know more. Martin told me that his family, who lived just yards away, had allowed a kayayo woman and her children to come and live in their family compound. He told me she had been through great hardship and her baby had almost died. He wanted me to meet her as he was keen to help me, as were many others, with the book. Although many people in Accra were extremely cruel to the girls, just as many felt the utmost pity for them, and wanted to help in any way they could. I agreed to meet Martin the next evening.

I walked with Latifa, Mahab, Aysha and Rebecca back to the tree. Rebecca told me that Nurah would be travelling to her village the next day, and I wished her a safe journey and looked forward to seeing her again. She told me she would be taking back money for her siblings' school fees and a mobile phone for her father. She would also take some cloth for her sister.

While walking along we saw a very young kayayo girl, looking only about nine or ten years old, sitting against a wall with a friend, crocheting. I had never seen anyone in Ghana doing this before. I asked her through Rebecca how she had learned. She told us that she had 'learned herself.'

'What are you making?' I asked

'I am making a skirt but I only have a little wool left.'

She then asked me if I could buy her some more wool.

'Where do you buy it?'

'I will show you the shop now,' she said enthusiastically.

We followed her into the market where we found a small converted shipping container selling wool and other 'needlecraft' items such as thread, rolls of different decorative edgings for dresses, needles, and other such items. She was using yellow wool so I bought her two small rolls of this colour. She thanked me and skipped off with her friend, vanishing quickly into the dark hidden nooks of the market.

It was Halloween night. The larger shops in Accra were full of witches hats, masks and pumpkins. Accra's growing middle classes and their families, those living on the smart housing estates, with their cars parked neatly on their driveways, seemed a million miles away from the daily lives of the people in this area.

I had arranged to meet Martin at the Spot at 5.30pm. When I met him he told me that the woman he had wanted me to meet had gone out as 'she needed to work' but he assured me she would be back by eight. I came back later and we made our way to his house. We walked down a darkened alley just two feet wide, and soon came to a compound house. We entered the compound. It was dimly lit, with shafts of yellow light creeping from underneath the doors, which led into the occupants' various rooms. An old lady was sitting in a rocking chair in the middle of the compound floor. Some children were playing in a corner, sitting together on the bare concrete. I was then introduced to Salamatu, who was also sitting on the floor of the inner courtyard of the compound, together with two of her children. She told me she was from the Malugu area, a Mamprusi speaker, and as was the norm didn't know her age. Surprisingly, she didn't know the age of her middle daughter, whom we thought looked about nine years old. She told me she had been in Accra for about eight months. She seemed older than most of the very young kayayo I had met so I presumed she must have been coming and going between Accra and Malugu for some years. She started to tell me how her young baby, now suckling on her breast, had become very ill.

'She was vomiting and had running stomach.'
'Did you go to the doctor?'
'No.'

The kayayo, like most poorer Ghanaians don't normally go the doctor in the first instance but rather to what is known as a 'chemical store' where cheaper generic versions of medicines and local herbal concoctions are sold, often by unqualified people or laymen. There had recently been a lot of counterfeit medicines flooding into Ghana from both Nigeria and India. One recent swoop on a pharmacy in Nigeria found that a high proportion of the medicines on the shelves were fake. The Ghanaian government had stated that it would soon be introducing a scheme whereby one could check the validity of medicines by making a simple check by text on your mobile phone.

Salamatu went on to tell me that the medicines the 'chemical seller' sold her 'didn't work' and Shaheeda, her baby daughter, continued to deteriorate quickly. The fever was rising fast. She took her baby to the Bilal

Polyclinic, and the medical professionals there, quickly realizing the severity of the condition, told her to go to the Korle Bu Teaching Hospital, the largest and best equipped hospital in Ghana. Shaheeda was subsequently admitted for ten days and had to be fed by drips. Luckily they did not ask for prior payment but presented her with a bill for Gh50cedis (£25 Sterling), which was well beyond her ability to pay. Martin's father, who was also now sitting with our group amidst the murky light of the compound, told me he had hired the taxi to get her to the hospital.

Martin told me that even before going to the chemical store, Salamatu had attempted to self-medicate her baby by putting shea butter on cotton wool, melting the butter and pushing this into the child's anus, thinking that the heat of the butter would penetrate the child's stomach and cure her. According to Mr Martin Senior, Martin's father in whose compound she stayed, she was 'severely reprimanded' by the medical authorities for carrying out this practice. I asked Salamatu how she paid the bill.

'I didn't have plenty money like that to pay the bill. The other girls from my village they helped me to pay.'

She told me that she now had to pay this money back to the association of the kayayo group from which she had borrowed.

'I will not be able to leave Accra and return home until I have paid back the money, if I try to leave here before giving back the money they will tell everyone I ran away and I didn't pay. It would bring me shame.'

Mr Martin Senior told me there was no official documentation for this money and it was given as a matter of trust. Salamatu told me she had five children, three of whom were with her in Accra. The two boys were in the village and the older boy was the only one of her children who went to school. She said she sent money home to pay his school fees. Leila, the 'nine year-old' daughter, and her twelve year-old daughter also lived with her and her baby in Accra. These girls did not therefore go to school but rather worked with their mother carrying loads. However, she told me her daughters, being smaller, carried much smaller loads than she did and they had smaller bowls. The mother had to carry her baby on her back in addition to the load.

When I asked her if she had ever been to school she said she had only had a few years of very elementary education.

I realized that the entire time I had been talking to Salamatu she had never raised her eyes once to look at me, she had been looking down at the ground. Compared to many of the kayayo who were quite loud and boisterous she was self-effacing and had the look of a woman who had suffered too many hard knocks and had thus just resigned herself to being a victim and condemned. I felt a lot of pity for her, sitting there on the cold stone floor, one baby at her breast the other lying across her lap. She had been taken in off the streets by the people in the compound out of pity, according to what Mr Martin Senior said.

'You get to know them in the area, maybe they carry for you, they may come and wash clothes, she also used to fetch water from our compound….you must as men of God do something to improve the fate of those you come in contact with.'

He went on to say that he had wanted to 'take her out of the market' and put her in the compound. She was sleeping in the market with all her three kids. Martin Senior said the compound floor was better than the market floor as, he said,

'They are packed there more than you can see in a tin of sardines.'

When I asked if she had a room at the compound, Mr Martin looked embarrassed, and told me that Salamatu and her children slept in the open. I didn't know if she was charged for sleeping on the compound floor but she did do some chores in exchange. Mr Martin said that when they cooked they often gave her and the children food.

'Many people in Accra said Salamatu and her daughters should go back but they like it here.'

I told Mr Martin Senior that most of the kayayo I had spoken to said they missed their villages. He disagreed with this. We did however both agree on one thing and that was that they liked Accra in as much as they could earn more money here than they could ever hope to earn in the village. He started to joke that the kayayo could even buy things those living in Accra could not afford to buy. He explained why.

'A normal Accra resident would have to pay rent, electricity bills, water and gas bills, school fees, transport to and from work, this would be either trotro fares or their own car, which would need petrol and which could take up to 'half of your salary.' The kayayo, on the other hand, slept anywhere near their place of work so they had no transport costs, rental or utility outgoings as did most other Accra residents, so they could save everything. He said they even 'don't care what they eat' and added the main reason Salamatu's baby got ill was 'because of malnutrition'.

I remembered what the doctor had told me some time earlier, how the babies were often malnourished and suffered from anaemia and other illnesses as a result.

Mr Martin Senior told me that 'when they travel back to the north'. They go in a big bus that leaves from a place just around the corner from his house. He said the bus goes quite often, not because they travel home often, usually they only go home once a year, but because he said, 'there are just so many of them'. He told me I would be surprised if I got onto one of these buses and saw the number of things they were taking back. He gave examples: mattresses, zinc roofing sheets, bikes, radios and so on.

I saw that Salamatu was tired. It was getting late. Her twelve year-old daughter, Rasna, was immaculately dressed, her hair beautifully braided. She was plump and her skin gleamed. She could have been any little girl in Paris, New York or London. She looked stunning. It was a credit to this poor woman that she could bring up such beautiful kids in such appalling circumstances. My heart went out to her. She said her husband was in 'the north.' I was interested to find out what all these husbands did. I said goodbye to Mr Martin Senior and Salamatu and Martin Junior accompanied me to my car. I drove home thinking of poor Salamatu and her three daughters.

Chapter Four

Searching for Dagomba

It was now mid-November and the weather was getting hotter, the harmattan would soon be arriving. The harmattan is a wind that blows down from the Sahara during the West African winter, bringing with it fine clouds of dust. This dust at times can be so severe it can seriously limit visibility, costing airlines millions of dollars in cancelled and diverted flights. For those responsible for cleaning the house it is a nightmare, and can cover a house in fine dust in a matter of minutes.

It had now been almost three months since I first started talking to the kayayo at Tonga market. Yet still, finding the seemingly inaccessible and remote Debele market, in order to meet some of its purported ten thousand plus kayayo inhabitants, had eluded me. Surveys and research had suggested that approximately eighty seven per cent of the of the city's kayayo inhabitants lived in central Accra which included Debele and Abusia markets, and the areas of Kantamanto, and Tudu.

A friend had introduced to me a young graduate called Salifu, also from the Dagomba tribe, who was interested in helping me. If I wanted to speak to any of the kayayo from this tribe, which seemed the only other main tribe from which the kayayo came, I needed someone who spoke the language. Today I would try yet again to reach downtown Accra and attempt to locate Debele market. My first attempt had been curtailed by the Ghana police under the watchful eye of Bishop Duncan Williams.

I set off early, driving across the overhead bridge. Again the life size cut out of the Bishop towered above me. I drove on down, past an assortment of crumbling colonial buildings interspersed with the newly renovated. Each was testament to a different era, the former to Ghana's long post-independence decline, the latter to its recent economic boom and revival. It had been estimated by Xinhua Chinese News Agency that Ghana's real GDP growth rate reached over 14 per cent in 2011, making it one of the fastest growing economies in sub-saharan Africa and indeed the world. However, as one professor at the University of Ghana recently pointed out to me, this was not evenly distributed, with vast wealth and extreme poverty running side by side. Not long after the overhead I took the wrong turning, and was stopped by the police.

'Where's your license?'

I handed it over and got the usual spin that it had 'expired' even though the date stamped on the front meant if was valid for a further three years. Yet again, the policeman pointed to some obscure figures on the back of the card, hardly visible to the naked eye, similar to three security digits on a the back of a credit card.

'It's these numbers you need to look at,' he said, pointing with long delicate fingers.

I did not have the time or the will to argue.

'I'm really sorry,' I told him, 'It's my fault, I'm really sorry, what shall I do?'

He smiled broadly.

'You, can give me some money for iced water, I'm thirsty.'

I gave him five cedis and drove on. Obviously, far more than was needed for iced water. But then everybody knew that 'iced water' was just a euphemism for 'as much as possible.' Within five minutes of driving I was stopped again. It was the same story. I told him I was sorry. 'I know I'm bad.' I should know better. Was there anything I could do? I coughed up another five cedis. It was getting late. Salifu would be waiting. I turned another corner and was stopped again.

I had had enough. I was forced to listen yet another time to the mantra about my 'expired' license. This time I changed my tone. I told the policeman that I had been stopped by his 'colleagues' round the corner, twice within the last five minutes and had given them all the loose change I had. I now had run out of money.

He gave me a knowing smile, squeezed my hand affectionately, and said,

'Don't worry then madam, drive on.'

I did. As quickly as possible. It was some minutes later that I drew up outside the main post office. I could see Salifu standing patiently under the clock tower of the clock that no longer worked. On seeing me, he approached, smiling broadly. He was relatively short for a northerner, and his hair was shaved down almost to his scalp. A large brown printed kaftan concealed a stocky frame. His nose was long and angular and his forehead was quite prominent, casting shadows over his deep set eyes. I was now hot, flustered and in a bad mood after my three encounters with the Ghana police in less than fifteen minutes. I no longer felt in the mood to walk around downtown Accra trying to locate the kayayo in the searing heat.

But I did, and some ten minutes later, we came across three little girls asleep in their bowls at an empty doorway near to the headquarters of the Bank of Ghana. It was around 11am and I was loath to wake them but Salifu gave them a gentle nudge. They woke up very slowly and sleepily, rubbing their eyes, confused as to why these complete strangers wanted to talk to them. They looked very young, around thirteen or fourteen, maybe a little younger. They told Salifu they had decided to come here to sleep as they had been walking around since about five in the morning but there had been no work. They were tired and they couldn't go on any longer. Since the previous evening they had eaten no food. The doorway was deserted. The shop closed down so they could sleep there, concealed, with no shopkeeper to move them on.

Salifu wanted to find out where the girls were from. When he first started speaking to the girls they giggled and hid their faces in their hands. The girls spoke Dagomba and two of them, childhood friends, Aysha and Ekima, were from the village of Bulipe. The other girl was from the village of Kunube. Both villages were near the Tamale area from where Salifu also came. We asked their ages, but like all the kayayo before them, they had no idea.

The Dagomba tribe were spread across a large area of Northern Ghana centred around Tamale and Yendi. The Mossi-Dagomba states were considered some of the earliest of the great West African empires which began around the 12th century. Many who have examined the language and culture of Dagbon believe their descendents were from Arabia rather than Africa and indeed the language of Dagbani has many words which take their origin from Arabic. The widespread use of Arabic names was also promoted by the Wangara and Mande traders from the northwest trade route in present day Mali and Hausa traders from the north east trade route in present day Northern Nigeria. However, even today where the widespread use of Arabic names among the mainly Sunni Islamic Dagomba is almost universal, traditional names are still often used alongside these. The Dagomba are known to possess a very sophisticated oral tradition based around drums and other musical instruments. Until very recently most Dagomba history has been performed by drummers and musicians acting as professional historians.

According to this tradition the history of the Dagomba was revealed. The origins of Dagbon can be traced to a man named Tohadzie, also known as the 'Red Hunter'. For his bravery in ridding the village of a wild beast he was rewarded with a Malian princess who bore him many sons. One of these sons, Naa Gbewaah, migrated in the thirteenth century to present day Northern Ghana where he established the Greater Kingdom of Dagbon which he ruled until his death. He also gave birth to three sons. One, Tohagu, founded the Mamprusi kingdoms, the other, Mamtabo, the Nanumba Kingdom and the third, Sitobu, the modern Dagomba Kingdom. As a consequence the people of these three kingdoms considered themselves as kin and brothers as they all shared the same ancestor, Naa Gbewaah and a shared language. Today the overlord of the Dagbon Traditional Kingdom is known as the Ya Naa, which translates literally as the 'King of Absolute Power'. His court and administrative power is based in Yendi, which has been called the 'largest village in West Africa'.

All the girls in this cramped dark doorway were wearing the regulation flip-flops. Their feet were dry and worn, their thin legs scarred by insect bites. There was another girl in the doorway. She remained still, fast asleep in her bowl despite our talking. She had covered her face with a cloth to keep away the flies and the shafts of sunlight, which entered seemingly by stealth into our darkened little alcove.

Salifu was a university graduate, now doing his Masters in Economics at the University of Ghana. A young, good looking man, that these girls could never dream of meeting or talking to under normal circumstances. A gulf as wide as the oceans separated them socially.

Partly because of this they were extremely shy of him. They were enthralled by his attention and he knew it. They continued to hide their faces in their hands and look down at the ground, smiling and giggling bashfully despite Salifu's pleas with them not to. Yet I could see they were happy to meet someone in Accra from their tribe. It never ceased to amaze me how happy Ghanaians and Africans become when they meet another from their own area in a strange and far off place. For them it's almost like meeting family.

The girls told me they had only been in Accra for two days. This was also their first time in the city. They had never left their village before. I could see one of the little girls staring across the road wide eyed, her mouth slightly open. She said something to Salifu in their language, Dagbani. He told me they were afraid of the policeman. He was carrying a gun. They had never seen a gun before.

Suddenly another kayayo girl walked into our shady alcove, plonked down her tahili, sat down on top of it, covered her face with a cloth and appeared to fall asleep within seconds. She didn't greet us and none of the other girls seemed to know her. She was probably in a hurry to 'bag' a shady spot quickly before it was taken. Such tiny patches of dirt seem like gold to the kayayo. These were places where they could sit, rest and eat without being harassed.

We sat there in silence for a while, watching the world pass by. Most people walked by and didn't see us. They almost stepped over you, but never saw you. They were seeing the world at a higher level both figuratively and literally. Sitting down on the pavement next to these girls with the busy lunchtime office workers of central Accra rushing past, you developed a feeling of what it must be like to be a person living on the street. Those people racing past have a purpose, a home to go back to at night, buses to catch. They have safety, security, possessions, a door they can lock at the end of the day; if they complain, people listen. Sitting with these girls, putting myself in their shoes for just an hour, you saw the world going on around you in a different light. As a club of which you could never be a member, however hard you tried. You were doomed always to live on the fringes of life. You got the impression you could curl up and die here and no one would notice. As we sat there a middle-aged man glanced down at us, an old-fashioned archetypal disciplinarian Ghanaian teacher. He pointed his finger and shouted at the girls in Twi.

'Answer their questions! Do as you're told!'

We continued to gaze at the sun-drenched technicolour world beyond the shade of our alcove. Aysha and Ekima were sitting back to back in the same bowl.

We asked them where they lived. They told us at Debele market. 'Oh my God,' I thought. At last, we may have found out exactly how we can locate the place.

'Could you take us there?'

Little Ekima told us,

'It is far from here...you need to take a trotro, and to walk... it is far.'

Ekima finished speaking, then bowed her head and covered her face with her hands. She was so shy. They were both so innocent, so young. She rearranged her position, laying her head on her childhood friend's lap. Her friend caressed and stroked her hair. They gazed into each other's eyes and smiled, catching Salifu's glance they again covered their faces with embarrassment. Salifu continued to joke with them in their language and they giggled more and more, still hiding their faces.

As we all sat huddled together in the semi-darkness

a girl called out from across the street. It was another kayayo - two or three of them were walking past a department store opposite.

'That's my older sister,' said Aysha, 'I have two sisters here with me in Accra.'

The word 'sister' (and 'brother') is often used in Ghana to refer to friends, cousins, distant relatives and older colleagues so I could not be sure if it was in fact her biological sister. I asked her if they were from the same mother and same father as herself, and she said one of the sisters was and the other was from the second wife.

Salifu then took it upon himself to do some of his own research. He asked the girls if their parents knew they were coming down to Accra. They said yes and that their parents wanted them to come down here to bring back some money, as they said this they started once again to bend over and cover their faces, giggling.

I could see the shock on Salifu's face. He looked at me, aghast.

'Their parents actually know they are here, how can a parent send such young girls down to Accra on their own, it's so dangerous.'

I found it hard to believe that Salifu, like most other people in Accra, knew so little about their lives. Not only had he been surrounded by them for all of his twenty-five years, he was also from the Dagomba tribe, which was the tribe from which the highest proportion of kayayo purportedly came from. They really were from a hidden world. They were around everyone's legs as they stepped over them on Accra's streets but were unseen. Salifu also did not believe it when the kayayo said they preferred their villages, that they wanted to go back to the village. He then asked them if they had the money to go back home today would they go?

'Yes' they replied in unison.

'Then if I give you the money now will you go?'

'No,' and they all looked at the floor again and laughed.

One of the drawbacks of interviewing and doing research is that often people tell you what they expect you want to hear rather than the truth. One has to pry beneath this. Maybe the kayayo feel ashamed to admit they prefer Accra to their villages, that the very act of doing this would seem to them disloyal. With almost every kayayo and every group I had spoken to over the year in which I was carrying out the research, not one kayayo girl ever told me that she preferred Accra to living in the village. I felt that when they told Salifu they wouldn't go back it was because they had travelled so far to get here to earn the money they desperately needed. They needed to stay in Accra to earn money, not because they liked it. Many economic migrants detest the conditions in which they live and miss their families, but they tolerate it because they need the financial rewards. It is a temporary means to an end. All the kayayo girls agreed on one thing. This was they could never make the amount of money they were making now back in their villages.

Ekima and Aysha realized that they must soon get up again to start walking around and looking for work. It was now almost 1pm and the sun was high in the sky. Sweltering hot.

'Do you catch the trotro back to Debele market?'

'We don't have money and if we go home in the trotro, we might miss the extra work we can find when walking home. If we go on the trotro we won't have that chance. But still it is far to walk from here to Debele market.'

Salifu and I bought them some food; rice, meat and vegetables together with a drink and went on our way. I doubted we would ever see them again, as they didn't always sit in the same place. They had no phones.

They were just three little girls wandering the streets of a large metropolis.

Chapter Five

Terror in Tonga

It had been some weeks since I had seen Rebecca, Nurah, Latifa, Mahab and Aysha and as I drove past the mango tree early one Monday morning, I came to a halt and called out. I had with me a large vat of peanut butter, in Ghana called groundnut paste, and many loaves of bread, plus a couple of knives. Although groundnut paste is a common locally produced food in Ghana it is not normally used on bread but rather put into soups and stews. As the kayayo were generally unable to cook I thought I could show them other ways it could be eaten. It was so nutritious, full of protein, which they often lacked. Protein deficiency, which leads to a kwashikor, a disease related to malnutrition, was common among the very poor in Ghana. Groundnut paste was an easy and cheap way of gaining this protein.

On seeing me they jumped off their bowls and quickly surrounded my car. Amongst this large crowd of about twenty-five I spotted Rebecca with baby Madihah on her back. She approached me, smiling broadly.

'We no see you long time,' she stared serenely at me, saying no more.

'Where are Latifa and Mahab?'

'They are working, they carry plantains for a lady in the market.'

I broke off pieces of bread and spread the thick brown paste on it and gave some to Rebecca. She broke some off and gave a piece to baby Madihah. They loved it. Then pandemonium broke out. What seemed like scores of girls were grabbing the bread, knives and peanut butter, woofing it down at great speed before anyone else could get a hold of it. People across the street and other passers-by were beginning to look across quizzically at this outbreak of raucousness. I told the girls I would come later, by 4pm, but I think many didn't hear me, so busy were they with the food.

When I arrived back that afternoon things had changed drastically. Instead of the usual hesitation and refusals to come in the car, everyone was now attempting to squeeze in there at once! It was difficult to control them. Everyone was pushing, pulling and laughing. Rebecca came as she could help me with the English. When we got to the drinking spot we saw Gifty sitting outside. On seeing us she jumped up.

'I thought you had travelled,' she called across as we were getting out the car. 'I no see you for a long time'.

I told Gifty I had been busy, but indeed I hoped to soon be travelling to the girls' hometown. Then myself, Rebecca, Aysha and Latifa, sat around the table in the middle of the darkened shack. I realized I was once again in the position of not having a good interpreter. Before entering I had seen a few men sitting outside the spot in the street playing draughts. I went to ask them if they knew of anyone who could speak Mamprusi, and if they knew anything about the elusive 'watchman' who was supposed to work near to the Methodist Church, whom I had heard spoke fluent English and Mamprusi and whom I had yet to find.

The church was just one hundred metres away and they told me they would 'go find him.' The girls and I sat in silence for a few minutes. I looked through the gaps of the swishing bamboo curtain across at Black Volta House. As usual lots of noise and shouting was coming from that direction. I looked up at Cheiko on the wall. I quickly averted my gaze from her smile. I glanced over at Rebecca sitting still and serene with Madihah on her breast. She caught my eye, the corner of her mouth turned up in a half smile. She then continued to look down at her daughter. Gifty sat in the corner, looking straight ahead, her face expressionless. Suddenly the bamboo curtain swished.

A very tall man in his early to mid-thirties rushed in, followed closely by the man who had been playing draughts.

'This is the watchman,' he announced triumphantly.

I had been expecting some ancient, doddery, old northern man. The type who, after hearing your question, takes about five minutes to formulate an answer. How wrong I was. George was young, smartly dressed and seemed extremely articulate. He was extremely tall and athletic, with legs and arms longer than I had ever seen in my life. He was fair in complexion and seemed constantly to have a jovial expression dancing across his face. His eyes twinkled. His voice was quite high pitched for a man of his size and it had a kind of warble, as if something was constantly stuck at the back of his throat. He told me that he had heard through the grapevine that 'a certain lady had been looking for him,' and that he had been expecting to meet me for some time.

The man who had been playing draughts continued to linger in the shack, looking at me as if I had forgotten to do something. He had an intense look in his eyes and kept shuffling awkwardly from side to side. I gave him his 'dash', a small tip for going to get the watchman. He quickly went back to his draughts.

George sat down confidently as if he had known us all for years, and gathered up Rebecca's daughter from her arms, putting baby Madihah on his lap. Unlike with me, she seemed quite happy to be with him, this large stranger. She continued to eye me warily from

George's lap. Anytime I approached her she would scream. I was beginning to take it quite personally! Rebecca looked once again annoyed that I had brought in someone else to interpret and would not rely on her English skills.

George seemed immediately at ease with the girls and I could see they liked him. I could sense the relief, the ease and familiarity they felt with being with someone from 'their area'. This also made me realize how uncomfortable they must feel living in Accra. To be constantly surrounded by the Twi speaking people, those from the south who looked down on them. It was as if George was their long lost brother, whom they had known all their life. They seemed so relaxed with him. I glanced over at Rebecca. Today she looked radiant in a beautiful green skirt and top with matching headscarf. Aysha, who I felt was the most talkative and dynamic of the girls, despite her tender years, wore a white top and long flower-pattern skirt. Today she looked amazing. Her hands and lower arms were still intricately decorated. The drinks arrived and we immediately fell into conversation.

I asked Aysha where she had got her hands designed. She informed me proudly that it had been at Nima, the large shantytown in the centre of Accra, not far from where we were sitting now. She described how it was done in great detail, pausing to ensure that George had understood her completely before going on further. Her plump young arms seared through the air, from left to right, rising and falling to accentuate the movements of the tattooist. She clapped her hands together when she had finished a particularly important part of her description. I felt she was describing a complex mechanical process rather than a decoration, so intense was the detail in which she spoke. In her own language she seemed so articulate. Her intonation, the way she used her hands to emphasize her story. She was obviously extremely intelligent and I couldn't help thinking what a waste of talent for her to be here on the streets. Rebecca sat, as always, still. If she moved it was in a slow deliberate manner. Nothing was rash about her. She knew where she stood in the world, no one could challenge this. Her dignity was unassuming but strong.

I had been hearing about how the kayayo took certain drugs to dull the often relentless pain associated with their work. In one of the rare studies done on the kayayo mention was made of the injurious consequences of 'head load carrying'. It stated that the kayayo often self-medicate with specific drugs designed to 'numb their occupational pain,' to enable them to continue working. Indeed they stated that the use of drugs is so endemic among the kayayo that a certain drug used to deaden nerve endings was referred to by the kayayo as 'even the old lady can play ball'.

Aysha raised her intricately decorated hands and opened her pale palms, where the design was more noticeable.

'When we have pain we take doctor's medicine and local medicine. We get many pains in our shoulders and necks. We take medicine for this, if we don't take the medicine sometimes we can't work and we lose money.'

'What medicine do you take?'

I could see that Rebecca was about to speak but was drowned out by the more articulate and younger Aysha.

'We take F-Pack.'

I knew F-Pack, it was a very strong, locally produced pain killer which was also very cheap.

Then Aysha revealed something really shocking that until then I had known nothing about.

'We also have to give medicine to the babies,

especially at night, as they disturb the other girls if they cry too much, the other girls they cannot sleep.'

Rebecca, who leaned back on her chair, putting her legs up on one another, as if fatigued, added,

'Sometimes they cry when we are walking, they cry if they are hot or in the rain when we have to walk, if we give them the medicine they sleep and it is better.'

'What is the name of the medicine?'

'I don't know the name but the man in the chemical store he give it to us, we say we want the medicine that makes the baby sleep.'

Later I read stated in one report how the kayayo, in order to please their roommates and customers, 'had to resort to drugging their infants in order to keep them quiet'. It appeared that it was quite a common practice. Yet the dangers were obvious. Giving them inappropriate dosages and drugs that could lead to overdose or even death was a very real possibility.

I thought it would be a good idea if I spent some time talking to the local chemical sellers and pharmacies to find out more about these things. It was to these people that the majority of the poorer people went in times of illness. They would also have a much clearer picture of the types of drugs that were commonly taken by the kayayo. The doctor was only seen as a last resort.

Suddenly I could hear the scraping of metal pots against concrete, then a cacophony of shouting, high notes of women, hurried angry baritones of men. We all jumped up simultaneously in order to peek through the bamboo curtain. Gifty joined us, straining her neck to bypass our shoulders. There had been another domestic eruption at Black Volta house. A lady had been cooking a giant vat of black-eyed peas and a man, in a fit of rage, had pushed over the whole container, which was now spilling out onto the road. The reddish mush was slowly easing its way along the slight slope, like volcanic lava. The aroma of the red palm oil gushed up into the air. We retreated back into our darkened cave and resumed our conversation. We were now becoming used to the daily dramas of our near neighbours. The novelty value was wearing off.

I wanted to know more about the alleged fights that I had been hearing so much about. When George asked them, with baby Madihah endearingly looking up at him from her seated position on his lap, her eyes like large concentric circles, they unanimously said yes, and then proceeded to tell him excitedly about these in their language. Yet when I was with them they had always said 'no' to this question and insisted that it never happened. I realized George was going to be a pot of gold for me and I would now start to learn much more about the kayayo.

George started to translate what they had been saying.

There were now so many kayayo in Accra, he explained. As a result there was too much competition for work. If, for example, a kayayo thinks that she should have carried a particular load, maybe because she felt she was stronger or it was her 'turn', and another had 'pushed in' and taken it for herself, they will come up to the girl and push the load off her head and then try and snatch the load for themselves.

Rebecca, who had been sitting patiently listening to her eloquent friend Aysha, now saw her chance to speak.

'It is always the other kayayo who snatch the loads. This is what makes us fight each other.'

She smiled gently and her eyes glittered as the sun tried to squeeze towards us through the cracks in the wood, even little Madihah seemed pleased her mother had got a turn to speak, in the midst of the more confident Aysha's talk. She jumped excitedly up and down on George's lap, looking across the table at her mother. She dropped her kenke on the floor. Both Aysha and Rebecca bent down simultaneously to pick up the broken pieces. Rebecca started to talk again.

'Sometimes it is a big load, a big truck will come from Kumasi full of plantains or a truck will come from Kintampo with yams. Then the kayayo are hired as a group to carry the entire load. So all the girls in our group, or from our village, will carry them together. Then they will start to argue over who is taking what. Some think they should get more money for their load than others because their load was heavier. Then they start to fight.'

Aysha started to look anxious, breathing deeply and fidgeting in her chair. She then caressed baby Madiha's head with her decorated hands and said,

'Yes, there are plenty fights.'

There was a short pause, while we listened to the ongoing performance unfolding at Black Volta house across the road. Latifa, who until now had said nothing, got up and peered through the tattered tassels of the bamboo curtain. Across the road more people had now gathered, the spilt beans were transplanting themselves diagonally and crosswise across the road being transported mainly on the soles of people's shoes.

After some minutes the girls again started talking energetically with George. I asked George what they were saying. He was saying how they are angry when men come to them at night. Just recently a man came to them and tried to have sex with Nurah. He hurt her face.

Rebecca said, surprisingly with a suggestion of a smile on her face,

'A man comes and he doesn't inform us he is coming.'

Aysha interjected and looked at me, pointing towards her forehead.

'These men are wrong in the head, they don't have girlfriends.'

Rebecca continued.

'They come to where we sleep in the middle of the night, and take their clothes off and lie next to us quietly, while we are sleeping. Then they will try to have sex with us. Sometimes if the girl wakes up and shouts the watchman will come and the other kayayo girls around too.'

Aysha then interrupted.

'They will come, and they will beat the man.'

There was a short lull in the conversation. Latifa looked bored, she picked up her bottle, holding it to the light, estimating how much was left. She caught me watching her and laughed, covering her mouth with her hands. Rebecca and Aysha both stared at me intensely with their deep-set eyes. Aysha scanned my eyes as if looking for signs of any judgements,

'But mummy, we will never let the man do, we will never let him do that to us.'

Rebecca was about to talk, but once again Aysha beat her to it.

'Sometimes in areas where there are not a lot of people, they can get raped as there are not many people to help if they shout out. This happens if they separate themselves.'

'What do you mean by that?'

'You see…' Rebecca started to speak in her gracious and noble manner, her hands held together gently in her lap. Then Aysha rushed to finish off her sentence, instinctively knowing what her childhood friend would say.

'Those girls who don't live in our groups.'

Rebecca looked irritated by her friend's constant

interruptions, but remained composed, not wanting to make a fuss.

'We cannot help or protect them,' Aysha continued, 'If someone tries to do something bad to them, they are alone'

'But why do they not stay with their group?'

'Sometimes they have run away from their village, sometimes their parents want them to marry old men, and if they run away the men, they will come down to Accra and find them.'

There was a pause. Rebecca glanced at me as if asking permission to speak. In her restrained and unflappable manner she added,

'And if they find them they will take them back.'

Aysha rushed in.

'Also, sometimes if there is an argument in the group, one girl will leave and say she doesn't want to stay with us anymore.'

A short film made about the lives of the kayayo by a local Ghanaian in association with the Peace Corps and an NGO vividly portrayed this predicament a predicament in which many girls on Accra's streets found themselves.

A young kayayo girl finds herself alone on the streets of Accra. She meets a much older man in the market who offers her a space to sleep in his room. She is raped and coerced into a sexually exploitative relationship. She feels trapped and also feels she cannot leave. On returning to her village several months later she falls ill. She is diagnosed with HIV and soon dies in her hut surrounded by her family. The film was actually made to be shown to girls in the northern villages as an 'antidote' so to speak, to the stories of wealth and fortune that the kayayo girls who have already been to the cities bring back with them. It was thought the film might deter some girls from following their friends and peers down to the capital. The film, as had been mentioned in the government policy document before it, recognized the growing significance of 'kayayo' in Ghana's urban society, referring to it now as a 'subculture'. This is what I had been noticing for many years; that the kayayo existed within Ghanaian society but formed their own unique society and culture within it.

The smell of red palm oil wafted into the shack from the lava flow of red mush slithering across the road outside. I looked over at George. His posture was upright and erect, his shoulders at severe right angles to his long, lean neck. His seemingly longer than average arms stretched out across the back of an adjacent chair and onto another. He looked over as if preparing to speak. A kind of intensity overcame him; he pulled up his seat, our circle immediately becoming more intimate.

'It has happened that when they are sleeping someone will come and snatch the child.'

Little Madihah had now left George and was back with her mother, fast asleep, her head buried in her mother's breast. Latifa had been getting up on and off her seat. She was a restless girl. Her looks reminded me of a baby gazelle but so did her behaviour. She never stopped moving and found it difficult to keep still, her large round eyes also constantly darted around as if sensing danger. Aysha glanced across at me, agitated.

'They say when this happens you will never get your baby again.'

Rebecca nodded in agreement, looking towards George.

I asked why they snatched the children, thinking it could be a child trafficking ring.

Aysha's placed her elbows on the table, her hands clasped with her chin resting upon them. She too was listening intently.

'They use the babies for juju,' George said.

'What is juju?'

George put his hands onto the grubby plastic table. He squeezed them together hard, so hard it made him wince.

'It is a type of magic, they believe if they use certain people or body parts this will make them rich.'

George and the girls laughed as he said this. Gifty, sitting on the wooden bench, near the tattered bamboo curtain, nodded in agreement. She, as ever, looked miserable.

George, whose voice now had a hushed air, said,

'There is a belief that if a snake swallows a baby the snake will vomit money.'

To many people such ideas will probably seem far-fetched, but many people in Ghana and indeed Africa do still believe these things and it is not only among the illiterate.

Ghanaian newspapers abound with stories of people found trading in body parts, in the hope of improving their finances, love lives or educational achievement. A young schoolboy was murdered and cut into pieces in the town of Winneba, the suspects admitting they had killed the boy to sell his head for 'ritual purposes'. There was some years ago a spate of serial killings of hunchbacks, as it was believed using their body parts and blood would help you to 'get rich quick'. A young man was found dead in a pool of blood in Nima, Accra's largest and most notorious shantytown, in what became known as an 'internet fraud' or 'sakawa' related murder.

Traditional magic now seems to be fusing with the new technology of the digital age in the form of sakawa. The word 'sika aduro' in Twi means 'blood money medicine' and it expresses the widely held belief in Ghana that it is possible to get rich quick through magic. Magic requires sacrifice and the bigger the sacrifice the bigger the likely rewards. This belief increasingly is being recycled and reapplied to the digital age in the form of sakawa or internet fraud.

This type of fraud is mainly carried out by young men who seem to enjoy spending their entire lives hanging out in the capital's internet cafés. The belief exists, and is now growing, that it is possible to spiritually compel those they defraud, those people in Europe and other places half way across the world, with 'sika aduro'. After making a 'friend' on the internet it is believed that by making sacrifices you will be able to spiritually force this person to send you money. It is a bizarre example of how ancient traditions and digital technology can amalgamate into amazing new forms.

I had thus too discovered that the main motivation for snatching the kayayo babies was not for child trafficking but rather sakawa and 'sika aduro', the trade in body parts associated with juju. Basically, it is the desire to 'get rich quick' through supernatural means.

I looked up at Gifty. She had dozed off yet again and was asleep, balancing on the long wooden bench that had been pushed up against the wall. Her two children had returned from school, the son sitting on the floor reading a book and the girl chatting outside the doorway with a friend. I knew Gifty was just a worker at the Spot, she did not own it, and I guessed she lived locally and it was a handy job for her.

The interior of the Spot was now hushed due to the subject matter, making the noise from outside even more pronounced. I wished I could just go outside and tell them to shut up. George then told us of the day he had seen a kayayo child abducted. He told us the incident had occurred at Tonga Market about two years ago.

'I am a night watchman near to the Methodist Church around the corner, so most nights I patrol the area. One night while doing so outside the church near the entrance to the market, I saw a man park his car just outside the market entrance and walk in. He walked around where the kayayo were sleeping and snatched a baby that was lying near its mother. Luckily someone saw him and shouted. People started to chase him and he ran with the baby. In the end he just threw the baby on the floor as he was running and got to his car and drove off. The baby was injured but recovered.'

We could hear the singing from the Methodist Church. The wailing of the muezzin from the nearby mosque. The shouting from Black Volta house across the road. Gifty continued to sleep on the wooden bench, snoring softy. I gave her son the money for the drinks. He smiled at all of us as we left and settled down in his corner once again with his book. It was Harry Potter.

George and I said goodbye to the girls and they disappeared into the cavernous market. George took my number. We agreed to meet the next week.

George rang me a week later and we met as usual outside the Methodist Church. We walked down to the mango tree. Late rays of sun cast dappled reddish light beneath its branches. As we strolled I was surprised to see once again the little 'crochet' girl sitting in the same place. She was holding her crochet and the hook. When she saw George and I coming towards her she jumped up, ran towards us, and then stood next to us silently. She didn't speak at all. She held up her band of yellow crochet. I said she had done well but that I could see she had run out of wool.

'Would you like some more?'

She nodded, smiling up at me with her large endearing eyes. She told us her name was Martha and that she came from a village in the Mamprusi region called Sugu. We walked to the shipping container shop.

'What colour would you like now?'

'Red.'

She took the wool and again skipped off, and disappeared into a narrow alley.

Rebecca and the other girls were nowhere to be seen. The shady rectangular patch beneath the tree's boughs was devoid of life today. George and I decided to walk down towards the bathhouse to see if any of the girls were there. As we turned the corner we saw Gifty sitting outside the Spot. On seeing us she swished back in through the bamboo curtain getting ready for us to enter. I called through that we were not coming today and she looked quite upset. Her son, aged twelve, was sitting on a chair outside still buried in his book, and his sister was playing ampe with some other girls in the middle of the street. As we strolled past Black Volta house I peeked in. Surprisingly, all seemed quiet, but one lady who was cooking over a coal pot in the compound waved at us.

We kept on walking down the street. It was already dark, and teeming with people, all at various stages in their evening's preparations. Some were cooking in the street, others brushing their teeth, a handful were already eating, some just returning from work. I could see large numbers of kayayo down the other the end of the street. Shadowy outlines of slender black bodies covered in frothy white soap suds were standing in their tahilis' their precious metal bowls which for them acted as a sleeping and seating device, a bath, a washing machine, and carrying vessel which provided their entire livelihood. Indeed for them it was a most treasured possession and one that they could not do without. Babies were also standing and sitting in their mothers' bowls being washed and scrubbed. There were so many girls and bowls that they were spilling out of the bathhouse en masse, taking up well over half of the adjacent road. All this was making it difficult for cars to pass. Tiny shacks just a few feet wide housed any number of businesses at the side of this road from hairdressers, barbers, seamstresses, internet cafés and drinking spots. In front of these businesses, others had erected temporary stalls consisting of rickety wooden tables, selling foodstuffs and drinks. This narrowed the road still further. A large 4x4 car attempted to thread down the lane slowly, trying to avoid hitting people and stalls.

Its headlights briefly illuminated some naked kayayo bathing in their tahilis, who ducked and dived, attempting vainly to escape the light.

I saw a few I knew. Industrious Aysha suddenly appeared out of the darkness, dripping with water. It was the first time I had seen her without a scarf. We looked around for Rebecca but Aysha said she had already left. We turned to retrace our tracks. Ahead, two towering graceful kayayo girls glided effortlessly before us, their outlines formed within the bright beams of a car's headlights. They walked majestically, their long gracious arms at right angles to their hips, as they held on to their overloaded bowls. The long tassels from their scarves dangled and swished down their backs. They looked incredibly beautiful. The spotlight now moved. The car passed. They were now like us. Walking in darkness.

We reached the crossroads. On one corner was Black Volta House, opposite was 'the Spot'. Opposite Black Volta House on the other side of the narrow road was the mosque. Opposite the mosque, a short way from the corner, was the Methodist Church, some yards from there sat the Blue House, with its ancient mango tree. It was a small, intimate world.

As George and I continued to walk in semi-darkness we entered Tonga Market. It then became darker. The shops, so full and bustling during the day, were now shut. They were windowless, and the metal gates that acted as their shop fronts were securely padlocked. It was pitch dark with just one or two single 40-watt bulbs dangling in the distance from bits of rusted wire. They cast eerie patches of yellow light, illuminating scenes that should best be kept in darkness. Shadowy outlines of hundreds of young kayayo girls and their babies could just be discerned in the dim light. I had never before seen so many kayayo in one place, there were not even any spaces left on the cracked pavements. Many were lying asleep, some were sitting and lying in their metal bowls. We briefly turned round. We could see that countless numbers were still making their way back from the bathhouse to their 'cement patches'. Many had babies strapped to their backs. For a few seconds a spotlight fell on them, and for what seemed a fleeting moment we saw them in a haze of dazzling radiance. They were laughing and talking amongst themselves. The car's spotlight shifted. Just as quickly the image was again enveloped in darkness. The car drove on, its headlights now illuminating the children and babies lying in the mud on pieces of cardboard ahead of us. Small fires had been lit in various places, creating a red warm glow for a few feet around their perimeters. We walked deeper into the seething market that covered a several square miles.

Suddenly we came to a very high wall, at least four metres high. Sacks of black charcoal were piled high against it, rising into the night sky. In the darkness they looked like the outlines of small hills. We continued to walk along the wall's edge. I was feeling claustrophobic.

Suddenly, we were confronted by a large, high

metal gate in the wall. This served as the main entrance to the inner-market, which was surrounded by the four metre high walls. We entered. We then turned left and were now walking along the other side of this towering barrier. It was now pitch dark and we used the light from our mobile phones to illuminate the ground before us. After a few minutes we came to a narrow alleyway. Flanking one side of this was a row of about ten warehouse type shops. They were closed their black metal gates now securely bolted. Outside, huge sacks of maize flour were piled high. In the distance a yellow 40-watt bulb cast a smoky light over a large group of kayayo girls. They were squeezed along a narrow cement ledge that ran along the face of the shop fronts. The ledge was only about four feet wide and then a step led down to the dirt track. The dirt track between the narrow ledge, on which the girls slept and the high wall was about three feet.

   I soon discovered that this alley was 'home' to the mango tree girls. It was where they laid their heads at night. The place reeked with the stench of perspiration and also the smoky retch of urine. Sickly, emaciated babies with swollen bellies ran around half naked. Some of the kayayo girls turned round to smile at me as they hung up their evening's washing. They were not permitted to bathe, or wash their clothes in this narrow alley. This had to be done some walk away, down at the bathhouse. They could not cook either.

   I looked down and immediately before me on the ledge I could see Rebecca and Mahab putting clean nappies onto Madihah and Adnan. It was the first time I had seen them without a scarf. They smiled broadly. I got the feeling that they, like many of us the world over, were experiencing that familiar reaction we all have when having guests for the first time to our home. I felt they were saying, 'welcome to my home but sorry it's not that grand and in a bit of a mess'. I had the feeling that they were worried in case I didn't like their home and were feeling uncomfortable. Or maybe they were ashamed that I was seeing how terrible the place was where they lived. But they were doting and courteous hosts. Mahab ran to buy me a sachet water to drink. Rebecca found George and myself a bowl to sit on and placed it upside down on the ledge. Rebecca, aware of our need for home comforts, placed a small piece of cloth over the bowls to prevent us from soiling our clothes.

In the distance, further down at the other end of the locked up shops, I spotted Latifa and Aysha with their young friends, chatting and laughing and getting ready for bed. Mahab started to hang up her washing. Mahab's baby, Adnan, was playing with a piece of cardboard on the stone floor. In this wretched narrow alley they tried to live as normal life as possible. I saw Rebecca twisting up the piece of cling film or polythene in which she kept a few teaspoons of baby powder for Madihah and putting it into the scratched empty jar of Vaseline petroleum jelly in which she kept her few other toiletries.

In Ghana it is possible to buy almost anything in tiny quantities, as many people live a hand to mouth existence buying everything on a daily basis. From a normal bag of sugar, which we buy in the supermarket, and a tin of cocoa a Ghanaian lady can make her living. She will wrap two or three teaspoons of sugar in a piece of cling film, twist it at the top to seal it and then sell these in conjunction with other equally small bags of chocolate powder. From a small tin of cocoa and a bag of sugar she could make up to a hundred tiny portions and make enough profit for the day to feed her family. It may be only two or three cedis, maybe a little more, but she is able to survive. The same goes for rice, baby powder, margarine, in fact almost anything will be divided and sold in twisted up bits of cling film. Colgate toothpaste and Blueband margarine is sold in tiny sachets by the manufacturers. A common profession for many Ghanaian ladies is to buy a tray of eggs, a tub of Blueband, tea, sugar and tinned milk with a few onions and tomatoes and make fried egg sandwiches and tea by the roadside, which people buy for breakfast or even in the evenings. They use either the coal pot or a small gas cylinder and a 'camping' gas ring. I always use these and one lady I knew well explained how she started at 5.30am and finished at 8.30am. During these few hours she could make as much as 10 cedis, which is about £5.00. She then had the rest of the day to do a different job. The women of Ghana are so hardworking and industrious.

As I sat there, I was doing mathematical equations, trying to work out how many girls could squeeze into so many square centimetres of concrete slab. Baby Adnan suddenly gave out a piecing wail. Madihah, in an attempt to grab the piece of cardboard, had got hold of his cheek and was squeezing and pulling it hard. Rebecca gave Adnan back to Mahab and swooped Madihah up from the floor, offering her the breast. All was quiet again and the small boy now had the 'toy' to himself.

Rebecca explained,

'We cannot lie lengthways on this slab as there is not room, we have to lay like this.'

She moved and lay down to show me the direction they slept.

She then shifted to the horizontal position along the slab.

'But when we lay like this, the rest of our legs and feet cannot fit so they have to hang off the ledge.'

I loved the way she explained it in a matter of fact

way, as if she was describing how she made a cake.

It looked very uncomfortable. Just a few doors down I noticed that a middle-aged couple from the south were locking up their shop for the night. They told me their car was parked outside and they were off home. Part of Ghana's growing middle class. They were quite an ordinary married couple, not particularly rich, not particularly poor but among all this degradation, poverty and illiteracy they seemed positively affluent and privileged. These were the last shop owners to leave and now all the girls could get ready to sleep. It was around 9pm. Now that all the remnants of daytime normality had disappeared, the place took on an eerie quality, like a hideout for the wretched and dispossessed. It reminded me of something out of a Dickensian novel.

The whole place was littered with the yellow plastic containers that were used for storing water. The actual awning that was meant to protect them from the rain consisted of a narrow piece of rusted corrugated iron with holes. A dingy bulb, suspended on dodgy wiring, descended from it.

Latifa and Aysha had now come back to join us. They were pushing and chasing each other, giggling with excitement that these seemingly important strangers had come to visit their home. Aysha seemed always to revert back to the child she in fact was whenever she was with Latifa. Her articulate eloquence and precocious maturity vanished. Latifa told me, glancing at her friend first,

'At night there are many ants and they bite us. They are very painful.'

Both girls burst into uncontrollable giggles.

George came to the rescue. He told me that these are the large soldier ants that 'roam around in packs.' He went on to say, 'they bite serious'.

I could see malaria-carrying mosquitoes were buzzing in swarms everywhere - they almost formed like a haze hanging over the place, there were so many of them. I finished my water and Rebecca considerately came to take the empty sachet away for me. The wall had now been entirely obliterated by wet washing, making the place seem even more claustrophobic and clustered. Many babies were crying. There was a putrid, pungent smell in the air. There was no wind or breeze and it was stifling. George pointed to the many large black shiny cockroaches scuttling around in the dark and Mahab said that these, together with the rats, disturbed their sleep.

'They run over us at night. They come out when we sleep. They crawl over us, it is not nice.'

As the shops around were warehouses full of corn and flour, many rats and other insects fed on it. Thus rodents and insects were everywhere. We sat silently for a minute or two. Aysha had started to braid Latifa's hair, the younger girl's head now resting in her lap. Babies Adnan and Madihah were now sleeping peacefully together on a piece of sacking on the floor, looking like twins entwined together in the foetal position. Rebecca sat back languorously, leaning on the sacks of corn flour behind her. She appeared happy and content here with her childhood friends in this narrow alley.

Suddenly we heard shouting. Three ferocious, heavy looking guys, wearing thick gold chains, real gangster looking types, approached us angrily. It was an older man, flouted on either side by two younger what seemed like 'lackeys'. He rushed towards Rebecca, who was at that time the only person talking to us, grabbed hold of her and threw her against the wall. She fell over, hitting her head badly. She looked up and remained where she fell as if she was afraid to move.

She looked truly terrified and made no attempt to defend herself from the abuse. There was absolute terror and panic in her eyes. The middle-aged man was screaming and waving his arms around and the other girls started to retreat uneasily. I asked George hurriedly what was going on.

'The man is saying he takes care of the girls and we just can't walk in here without getting his permission.'

George also looked very worried and this was making me feel even more frightened. I often tried to gauge the seriousness of situations by studying the faces of those who really knew what was going on and I didn't like the look of this at all. The other girls were all now backed up against the opposite wall and corner. I suggested hurriedly to George that we make a run for it and get out through the nearby gates, which were just yards from us, although we couldn't see them. Then I remembered that when the shopkeepers were locking up a man had come to tell us that he was locking the main gate, but at the time I hadn't taken much notice as I was so busy writing. The gates were locked and I had no idea how to get out. I slowly realized we were trapped within the inner market with these heavies and the girls. I really started to feel uneasy and I could see the girls were utterly petrified.

Just as suddenly the man started to walk away from the scene and told us to leave. As we followed them the girls, now all standing, were backed up against the padlocked shop fronts. I could see that many of them, including Latifa and Aysha, were pressed up silently in the darkness against the bars. A scary, awful feeling came over me. The man says this is his alley, and he takes care of the girls. Does this mean that these girls who are locked in at night are like his prisoners, and that he has complete power over them, which meant he and his lackeys could come in here at any time and do what they liked? It very much seemed as if this was the case.

We continued to follow the three 'protectors' in the pitch darkness. I was scared and disorientated. I hadn't a clue where I was. We felt as if we were being frogmarched out of 'his territory'. As we moved further into the enveloping darkness I started to discern tiny wooden shacks dimly lit inside by candles and sometimes the light of a mobile phone. The smell of marijuana peppered the air. Inside the shacks lots of men, some with women, were sitting playing cards, dominoes, smoking 'wee' (marijuana) and drinking apeteshi which is a kind of locally brewed gin. I realized the girls were literally surrounded by a whole colony of low life men who could just walk into their caged alley at night and do whatever they wanted. The kayayo couldn't even escape, they couldn't even complain. Who would believe them? If they did complain they would be ejected from the market and where would they then sleep? For me it was too painful to contemplate.

After some minutes I saw the lights of the Methodist church in the distance and although the darkness and narrow alleys had disorientated me I was actually in fact quite close to home, to my familiar territory.

It had for me been a trip to Sodom and Gomorrah. I walked home in the darkness and lay down in my bed and sobbed.

Chapter Six

The Chief

The next day I set off from Medina, a northern suburb of Accra, towards Kejetia. I had arranged to meet George at the Methodist church. As I neared Tetteh Quashie Interchange, named after the man who first introduced cocoa into Ghana from the island of Fernando Po, my stomach clenched as I saw the dreaded vertical arm lifts of the police signalling me to stop. I quickly thought of an excuse to get away. Ghanaians are very respectful of death and the dying, some say more than the living. I would tell them one of my 'relatives' was at death's door.

'Can I see your license?'

I handed it over.

'Where's your triangle and fire extinguisher?'

I had left them at home.

'Then you will have to pay a fine or go court.'

I reluctantly handed them over the money and then regretted it. I started to feign desperation and told them I needed the money. A relative of mine was 'very sick' in hospital, I was on my way there now, I had to pay the hospital fees. I prepared my speech.

'How can you be so callous taking the money which is meant for paying for a dying lady's hospital bills....it is wicked!' I said indignantly.

They suddenly became overcome with guilt. They stood like scolded children who have just realized they have done something dreadfully wrong. They then gingerly handed me back the bribe money in a very slow manner, just in case I decided once again to 'give them a bit back' as recognition for their noble gesture of returning their 'bribe'. Well, I didn't give them anything back again. I just quickly drove off before they could think of anything else I was supposedly doing wrong.

As I continued to drive along the six-lane highway glimpsing the beautiful hotels and luxury flats which flanked it, I spotted the latest giant poster of Bishop Duncan Williams looming ahead. On it was as always his face and adjacent to this was a large image of a roaring lion, its mouth wide open, displaying its formidable canine teeth.

'WAR CRY, JOIN US FOR 3 DAYS OF PRAYERS AND FASTING AT ACTION CHAPEL.'

I was imagining the queues and traffic jams along the Spintex road of all those flocking to attend.

I continued driving. I went past 37 Military Hospital, then through the Nima shantytown towards Kejetia. I parked and looked around for George, who was standing in the street near the Methodist church. We sat on a wooden bench on the pavement opposite. I told him about the police problems en route. He said he was sorry but he looked preoccupied and worried. I asked him if anything was wrong. He told me that someone had been killed in Tonga earlier that day. Two men had been fighting over one of the kayayo girls. They had fought with knives and one had been stabbed and killed. This had now heightened the overall tension in the market and had led to the chief of the area announcing that he wanted to rid the market of the kayayo girls 'once and for all'.

All Ghana lands are presided over by a traditional chief and they had to be consulted before anything could be carried out on that land and also in the case of any disputes. As Accra is the traditional home of the Ga tribe I presumed the chief would be a Ga, even though many of the people who now inhabited the market were from the North of Ghana. George went on to tell me that it had been a man named Shagba who had gone to the Chief to 'plead with him' to change his mind about 'ejecting' the girls from the market. At a much later date in my research I counted well over two thousand kayayo in the market, so it would have been indeed a huge job to get them out. The chief had listened to his pleas and decided to allow the girls to stay. Ironically, Shagba was the man who had come screaming at us the night before, the self-appointed 'boss and protector' of the kayayo girls. George suggested we should visit the chief. Once he knew about us and what we were doing, Shagba would no longer be able to 'stop' us.

Over the next few months I spoke to many Ghanaians about the incident the previous evening when Rebecca was assaulted. They told me that Shagba, as I had also thought, was 'probably looking to get money'. I have seen this tactic so many times in Ghana. People make a huge fuss about something in order to frighten and intimidate you and then suggest that if a 'small sum' is paid then 'everything will be alright'. The person at the receiving end is usually so frightened by the end of it that he or she coughs up just to keep the peace. It is a tactic used widely by the Ghana police.

So it was on Farmers Day, a public holiday to honour the country's farmers, always at the start of December, that George and I found ourselves standing outside the chief's house in Tonga market. It looked a squat non-descript type of building, much like any other. There were no redeeming features to distinguish it. As we entered through the small doorway we encountered a large open compound with many doors leading into different rooms. The compound was shady as there were several trees growing inside it. Many people seemed to be going in and out of various rooms. They took little notice of us so I got the impression the place was like a constant thoroughfare with people coming and going to visit the chief for any number of problems. George had told me earlier that a 'gift would be expected' and I had bought some money with me for this. I have always disliked going to see Ghanaian chiefs, with their protocol and longwinded ways of doing things. Just to say hello normally takes about twenty minutes and 'how are you' an hour and that's before you even start to get down to business. However, George had insisted that we went ahead with this visit, despite my reluctance, as he said, 'we wouldn't be able to walk about the market freely without their permission'. He said we needed to walk about without any harassment. Once again he reminded me that finishing the book was 'very important'.

As we entered the chief's section of the compound, we saw seven or eight men sitting on small stools in a semi-circle. They were dressed in the full national costumes of the northern tribes with all the regalia and looked spectacular. George prostrated himself flat on the floor beneath them in the customary greeting. In the northern region there must be utmost respect for the chief, and the tradition is still very much alive. For the next five minutes or so there continued to be more bowing and clapping. I wondered how long it would go on for. I thought the chief and his elders were most probably from the Dagomba tribe but I later learnt they were from a different tribe to George and the kayayo. They were, in fact, Hausa. This was the main language spoken in Accra's sprawling shantytown Nima. Many tribes, especially from the north and even other parts of West Africa live in Nima but for some reason Hausa is the lingua franca in that area and its surrounding environs, like Maamobi, and Kotobabi. It was mainly the 'assistant' chief who did most of the talking today perhaps because he was more proficient in English. He was silent for a moment then said,

'The man who looks after the girls in the market sees them as his sisters, he says he gets angry when he sees people going near them at night because of the problem of the babies.'

'What do you mean by that?'

'It has been happening in the market that men prowl around at night and have been taking the girls' babies. The men come in cars and then drive off with the babies they snatch. That's why the man 'protects' the girls. There are many girls in the market who do not have a watchmen like Shagba to protect them.'

The chief then went on to explain why they had initially decided to 'sack' the kayayo from the market. He told me,

'The male youths in the area came to see me with their representative. This was because they wanted to ask my permission to sack the kayayo from the market. The youths said, 'because the girls disturb too much'. The reasons they gave me were many.'

'What were the reasons?'

'The reasons were that they didn't keep the gutter clean and threw rubbish in it. They also threw their rubbish everywhere, and lastly one of the main problems was the fighting. The girls fight a lot and it's a lot of trouble to separate them. Often it may start off as a row between two girls but then others join in and it becomes a massive brawl and then it's up to the local boys to sort it out. These fights are between girls of the same tribe.'

There was silence once again for a few minutes. I didn't know what to say and kept quiet. I looked over at George and he avoided making eye contact. We continued to sit. All of a sudden the main chief came to life. He adjusted himself in his seat and prepared to speak. All eyes were on him and we continued to sit in silence for about another minute. Waiting. And waiting.

'But I have now settled the matter and I have decided to allow the kayayo to stay. I have spoken to the kayayo's leader.'

I had no idea who the 'kayayo's leader' was, and I was hoping he was not referring to Shagba. I wanted to find out more about Shagba and pretended I couldn't remember the name of the man who came to 'plead' on the kayayo's behalf, was it Waga? Shada?

'His name is Shagba. He works for a rubbish collection company and he is in charge of the rubbish and cleaning up the market.'

I asked one more question about health. What could be done to help the girls with healthcare? The assistant chief once again took over,

'There is a hospital at Tonga market. If the girls have health insurance they can probably be treated there free, but I am not sure.'

I wondered how many girls had health insurance. Did they even know about it? I would have to find this out. I thanked the chief, and they continued to look at me. They didn't seem to give that knowing glance or feeling that it was time to go. I gave the chief the money and some of the others looked at me also, so I handed out some more money to a few others and left. George was giving me admonishing looks as if to suggest I was embarrassing him by not giving them sufficient money.

We once again found ourselves standing in the bright sunlight outside. It was still quite early and George said he had to rush back to work as he had 'sneaked out' especially for this meeting. I watched him weave his way through the crowds to the edge of the market until he disappeared around the corner.

Chapter Seven

The Rubbish Dump

George had rung several times asking when we could go again to talk to the girls. He repeated that the book was 'very important' and thus we must not allow it to fall by the wayside. I told George we had to meet Shagba, to find out more about all the things that I had been hearing about him. So it was some days later, as I watched the large red sun slowly sink below the rusted corrugated iron rooftops of Kejetia, that George and I entered Tonga market. He told me we would go to Shagba's office. We walked deeper and deeper into the centre of this dilapidated, ramshackle rectangle towards the central area, which was locked at night. High walls surrounded this central inner-core of the market and there were two or three 'gaps' through which you could enter which had gates that were locked at night. We entered through one of these gaps, and eventually reached an area where three or four massive rubbish skips were parked. They were piled high, almost to breaking point, with garbage. What appeared in the distance to be tall stick-like men holding long hoes stood high above us. They were on top of the skips adding and spreading more rubbish across them. Other men down below heaved up the rubbish to those at the top. The place stank of putrid rotten vegetables and other foodstuffs.

    We were literally surrounded by rubbish on all three sides. On the fourth side was a small corrugated iron roofed shack. Leaning against the shack was a small wooden bench. Three men were sitting on it. George also joined the men and sat down on the bench. I guessed this would be the place we would be waiting for Shagba. I sat down on a plastic chair, which had been lying around. I started talking to the second man on the bench. He was a middle aged, amiable man and he told me his name was Amuba. As always we started talking about the kayayo. He told me that twenty-five years ago there were no kayayo in Accra, none of them travelled south. Amuba went on to tell me that,

'Fathers don't like them coming to Accra they don't want them to give birth.'

Amuba and the other men sitting around were adamant. They even spoke in unison, like a chorus when they said the main reason why the kayayo come to Accra was due to,

'The mothers.'

I couldn't imagine why it was only mothers but later when travelling north I would hear this opinion repeated over and over again.

'The government built free schools in the north but the mothers don't want their daughters to go.'

'What was the main problem for the girls in Accra?'

Again a chorus.

'Shelter...where to lay their head at night.'

Then Amuba continued.

'This brings most of the other problems, the problems of theft, rape and the taking of the babies.'

I sat and looked up at the tall stick-like men continuing to load rubbish onto the skips towering above us. The sky was now turning a brilliant shade of red with the setting sun, and their shapes were silhouetted against this dazzling background.

I started thinking that it was quite amusing that Shagba's 'office' was in fact on a rubbish dump. He was surrounded on all sides by the stuff. The whole ambience and odours of the place were quite befitting for his job description of 'rubbish supervisor'. There were a lot of hard, rough looking characters around.

They also resembled the type of people I saw him surrounded by the night Rebecca was assaulted. The red sun had now disappeared behind the burnt amber rooftops and dark shadows started to fill the corners. I couldn't see much now. My senses were overcome by the stench. While waiting there I was getting impatient, and asked George when Shagba would be arriving. He said,

'But he's already here!'

And he pointed to the third man on the bench who until this time had just sat silently, while the other two, Amuba and his friend, and George had been chatting away. I thought to myself why didn't you tell me before? Why didn't you introduce me? Shagba sat at the end of the bench. Sullen, silent, not making eye contact with anyone. I couldn't believe this was the same man, who with his lackeys had terrorized us so much some nights before. Although he seemed quiet and reserved, his demeanour in fact appeared to conceal a kind of morose and psychotic nature. I tried to include Shagba in the general conversation, as I was eager not to get into his disfavour. I asked him directly what HE thought was the main problem for the kayayo in the market. He gave me a one-word answer.

'Shelter.'

I then asked him about the problem of the snatched babies. He said nothing but the others spoke for him. The man sitting next to Amuba commented that it had happened on four occasions in the market over the last couple of years. Each time they had been lucky to get the babies back. Shagba continued to stay silent, looking down crazily at the middle distance, seeming to focus on some invisible object. He seemed to be staring wildly into space and looked like any minute he could lose control. The other two men continued the conversation without him. They told me, and I think

Shagba vaguely nodded, that most of the snatchings took place between midnight and 2am.

'Men usually come around and make out they are doing something in the market, like they are occupied on some chore, and while they are doing this they quietly try to pick up the baby and run away... luckily each time someone has seen it and they chase the man... Once they managed to catch the man and took him to the police station. The man they caught was not normal.'

I wasn't sure what they meant by that but I guessed he was probably mentally challenged in some way.

'On the other three occasions they did not catch them, but the men just dropped the babies, the babies were not badly injured and recovered.'

This matched the story that George had told me of the one occasion he had witnessed an incident.

'Why do you think they try to take the babies?'

'We are not sure.'

The men then went on to tell me more.

'Anything to do with the head porters he (they nodded toward Shagba) is in charge, if they are sick, if they have to go to court...the police can call him even at midnight...even at 1 or 2am.'

I asked them what the police usually called him about, thinking that this meeting was supposed to have been a meeting with Shagba and his role in the market, yet it was now his colleagues that were doing all the talking and answering questions on his behalf.

'It is usually about the kayayo fighting. Just some short time ago a man was killed here in the market. It was because he was fighting with another northern man over a kayayo girl. The fighting between the kayayo is usually because of work. They get so exhausted and stressed so the slightest thing, they just lash out. It often involves issues like lack of work, money. They flare up quickly.'

The man on top of the skip was now leaning against his long pole, which was almost at right angles to his shoulder. He cocked up one leg and bent it at the knee. The silhouette now resembled two long sticks, one balancing against the other in the darkening, purple-black sky. As I sat there gazing up at him, I could sense the three men on the bench watching me.

'He stays up there well into the night filling the skips.' said one.

'The company will come and collect the rubbish skips away in the night,' added the other

The two men on the bench were very jovial and started chatting to George in their language. Shagba remained morose, silent. He looked like he was angry about something, probably about me asking him questions. I tried to be friendlier, asking him who he worked for, although I already knew.

'The rubbish company. I am the supervisor for the refuse collection in the market.'

He was obviously very proud of his job and the status it gave him to bully around everyone else in the market, particularly the kayayo girls. I took an interest in his sparkling white T-shirt, which he wore with an equally dazzling pair of white trousers. Both looked quite incongrous amidst the backdrop of rubbish mounds and filth. The T-shirt was emblazoned with the logo:

MALARIA CONTROL PROGRAM

He continued to sit there saying nothing. I thought it was time to go. I walked some of the way home with George and then we parted, going in our respective directions.

The days drifted by in a haze of heat and dust. Almost two weeks had now passed since that terrible night when Rebecca had been assaulted. Since then I had not seen her. I was worried and decided I must go and visit her, I also wanted to spend some time with the girls to get an idea of how their days unfolded. For that reason I decided I would go to their sleeping area early the next morning.

It was around 5am and I was entering Tonga in darkness. A solitary man stood urinating in the open gutter. I was thinking it was next to these gutters that the kayayo and their children had to sleep, eat and carry out their daily activities. As I turned the corner and walked to the iron gate that was locked at night I passed many seemingly lifeless bodies still asleep, adults, small children and babies, some naked or half naked as they had rolled out of their covers during the night. They were all lined up in rows, just 'like sardines in a can' as Mr Martin Senior had said. Some girls began to sit up, rubbing their eyes, picking up their clothes, which had gone astray during the night, and wrapping themselves around with them to keep out the chill of the dawn. Some had lit small fires with wood, perhaps to boil water for tea or porridge or for washing themselves. When I reached the place where most of the mango tree girls slept I found the gate was still locked. I had come very early as I thought most of them got up and left very early, but I had misjudged in my zeal. Through the iron bars of the bolted gate I could see that a few of them were already up, and were walking around in the half darkness. As before I got this creepy feeling that they were not locked in there for safety. They were locked in there with hordes of low life men who could basically do with them as they wished. All sorts of undesirables peopled this market - petty thieves, drug addicts, and other criminals.

On seeing me some of the girls came up to the gate, poking their heads through the bars. Some were still half asleep. Eventually a dodgy looking character with a huge spliff hanging out of his mouth came and opened the gates. When I spoke to him he just grunted. He looked completely out of his head. Rebecca was not around and it was difficult for me to explain what I wanted to do, as she was the only girl who could speak English. I saw Aysha and asked her to show me where Rebecca was. I found her sleeping on a cement floor with scores of other girls in a dirty warehouse full of grain sacks. The girls had been sleeping in between the sacks. Other girls were sleeping on the ground outside. As many girls as you could imagine were packed onto the available floor space on the ledge outside the warehouse. Rebecca came to the door. She was still half asleep, her scarf was off and her hair looked a mess. Other girls also slowly started to gather at the door, emerging from the darkness of the interior, their eyes squinting at the new rays of the sun. The building had no windows and was as dark as a dungeon inside. On seeing me Rebecca looked worried, in fact terrified. Instead of her usual wide grin she looked down at the floor, and would not look at my face, would not even look at my eyes. She wouldn't answer when I spoke to her. I was perturbed and her behaviour was indeed very uncharacteristic. The other girls said,

'Rebecca won't talk to you.'

Then Rebecca, still looking at the floor and not raising her head said quietly,

'They told me if I talk to you they will beat me and that I cannot live in the market again.'

I realized Shagba and his lackeys had threatened her. The image during my meeting with him some nights before with his crazed expression amidst the mountains of rubbish flashed in my head. I started to realize the girls were being treated like caged animals, constantly beaten and threatened by their 'keeper' or 'protector', Shagba. They were threatened and bullied in the market not just by Shagba but also by other market women and men. As I walked out of the market early that morning I felt so sad and worried for these girls. I felt sad when I recalled the terrible look on Rebecca's face, the fear she had of being banished from the market, to be sent away from her village sisters, those she had grown up with since her birth. If she couldn't live in the market with them, where would she go? It was only by being together as a village unit that they were able to maintain a modicum of protection for each other in this dangerous environment. If Rebecca could not live in this market with her 'siblings' she could no longer earn the money that allowed her to buy the basic necessities. For her this market offered opportunity, wealth. It was hard to imagine this awful place could mean so much to so many people. Sadly in a world of extreme poverty, it did.

That same evening I was waiting outside the Spot in my car for George. We had planned to walk around the market to carry out some interviews. Suddenly a head appeared at my side window, beaming. It was Rebecca and she had little Madihah, as always, on her back. She had now changed completely from this morning. I told her to come and sit in the car. Inside the car it was cool, relatively quiet and we could talk better in a more comfortable environment, and besides it kept out all the putrid smells welling up from the adjacent drain. She sat next to me with baby Madihah on her lap, still eyeing me warily but now with a slight smile as if she was now teasing me or playing a game. I noticed something.

Little Madihah, who was so tiny and petite, had a massive bump and cut on her forehead. It was bloodied. I asked Rebecca what had happened.

'I left Madihah with my junior sister to look after while I went to carry things but she didn't look after her properly.'

I asked how old her sister was?

'I don't know but she is about eight years.'

Again this was evidence of what I guessed had been happening. Young children, who shouldn't be left on the streets in the first place, were being left to care for infants, while their teenage mothers went off to work to try to earn a living.

While buying tomatoes in the market the other day, I had seen a beautiful baby lying asleep in front of an adjacent shop. The baby was completely alone. I asked the tomato lady if it was her baby, not noticing at the time that she already had one strapped to her back. She said, 'No!' and then started to complain to me about the girl who had just come and left the baby lying there on its own, and walked off. I asked her if it was one of the kayayo girls.

'Yes!'

She went on,

'That's what they've been doing, they don't look after their babies and just leave them all over the market.' She added,

'Look at the baby, it's dirty, can you see my baby?'

She turned her back so I could see her son more fully.

'See how clean he is, you see this is the reason the babies go missing, they leave the babies anyhow, they even leave them with small children to care for them who are not much older than the babies.'

I had actually seen children much younger than seven or eight looking after infants, sometimes they looked no older than five or six, often carrying babies on their backs that weighed only a little less than themselves. I felt, and others had also mentioned this, that many of the young kayayo who were used to living in remote communites 'where the whole village was your family' did not appreciate or understand the dangers of city life. For them the market seemed like an extension of their village, and in many ways it was- they lived with those from the communities they had left behind, and they I believe, continued to act as if they were still there, thus leaving minors and babies thinking others would 'watch over them'.

I asked Rebecca if she had been to the doctor with Madihah's injured forehead. She told me she hadn't. She didn't have money. I told her we should go now and we drove the short distance to the Polyclinic at the market. Madihah was seen by a duty doctor, who examined her head injury. We then went to a nurse who applied a dressing and told Rebecca to bring Madihah back the following day. I left the car in the Polyclinic car park and we walked through the market together. The lights were on and place was bustling. We stood talking for some minutes. Beside us was a brightly lit wooden kiosk, a barbershop. Its walls were adorned with pictures and photos of lots of different hairstyles. I could see David Beckham's face, his blond highlights rippling through his hair.

I felt someone tapping me from behind.

I quickly turned and found little Martha behind me. She had her crochet. She now had two stripes, red and yellow. She held up the work proudly to show me.

'You need another colour,' I said and we went to the same shop we always went to. 'What colour do you want this time?' I asked her.

'Blue.'

She took the wool and ran back to her shop front.

Rebecca smiled.

'The skirt will look beautiful when it is finished.'

Rebecca and I stood for some time in silence. Baby Madihah, her head now covered in a fresh white bandage, looked content and happy tied to her mother's back. We walked together back to the car and drove back to the Spot. After a while Rebecca started to speak.

She told me why she hadn't been able to speak to me in the morning when I had come to the warehouse. She was sorry and it pained her to see me sad. Then she proceeded to tell me what had happened.

'After you left that night, after he pushed me, he came back. He came back insulting me and threatening me with a stick saying to me that if he sees me talking to you again he will beat me and not allow me to sleep in the market again, as if he owns the market.'

George then arrived, pushing his head against the side window of the car. He jumped in and sat at the back. He also added that he had seen Shagba 'beating the girls with sticks.' I was wondering whether when he did this the girls still had babies strapped to their backs. He could hit a baby's head and either badly injure the infant or even kill it. Rebecca went on,

'The girls, they always complain about that (the beatings). He thinks that because he's 'taking care' of us, he can just beat us whenever he likes.'

George looked at me.

'He doesn't feed or clothe them, how is he taking care of them, just because he's from the same tribe, Mamprusi, even his hometown girls they complain that he beats them.'

I asked George what he meant by that.

The girls from his hometown, those from his own village - apparently there were five girls from his home village living in the market.

Little Madihah, with her bloodied swollen forehead now covered in a crisp white bandage, started slowly to drift off to sleep, secure, warm and happy in her mother's arms. She was blissfully unaware of her poverty and also the contempt with which everyone around viewed herself and her mother. She was only wearing a T-shirt and had a bare bum.

I started to delve deeper into the character of Shagba. Rebecca was telling me that he often made them give him money for 'projects' he was supposedly doing in the market.

'He tells us we have to contribute the money and if we don't he will beat us.'

'Do you give him the money?'

'Sometimes we do, sometimes we don't.'

From what I could deduce, Shagba probably felt a deep-seated resentment towards the kayayo when he was unable to extract the money from them which he mistakenly believed he deserved as their 'protector.' He then took out this anger on the girls, using any flimsy excuse he could think of to beat them. Even though he always gave other reasons for his beatings, most commonly usually 'fighting', he was in fact beating them because he couldn't extract the money he wished. Rebecca went on to say,

'Even if we are in a group and we are just talking, he rushes towards us with a stick and starts shouting, 'stop this fighting' and then starts beating us.'

We continued sitting in the car. Darkness now surrounded us. The dim flames of candles and kerosene lamps outside flickered. The electric lights had all gone out some time ago. It was 'lights off' as the Ghanaians refer to the almost daily power cuts that plagued the country. In the darkness we caught fleeting glimpses of other kayayo on their way back from the public bathhouse at the end of the road. Piles of wet washing were balancing on their heads and babies were strapped to their backs. Rebecca continued.

'I contributed money before, also Aysha, Nurah and Mahab, we have all given him money before, he told us he was going to use the money to maintain the market.'

Rebecca smiled, looking over at me.
'He has two girlfriends who are kayayo.'
'Is he already married?'
'Yes.'
'I know the girls who are Shagba's girlfriends. They are very young.'

It was getting late and Rebecca said she had to leave. She got out of the car into the darkness and strapped a now sleeping Madihah to her back. She walked back to her shop front. I drove back to my flat. George walked back to his room.

Chapter Eight

Poppy and the 'Old Lady'

The harmattan winds had arrived in Accra, wrapping the city in a film of fine sand, blown southwards from the Sahara. People and buildings were seen blurred, as if through a gossamer haze. Throats became itchy. Eyes became red and noses became blocked from the constant drizzle of fine dust falling on the city.

George had rung me several times over the past month. He told me that some other kayayo girls in the market were eager to meet and talk to me. My schedule of work, school runs, and meeting with the other kayayo girls from Bandugu village meant my time was constrained. In the end, however, both the girls' and George's persistence paid off and eventually we all met up. As always, 'the Spot' was the venue of necessity if not exactly choice!

On approaching our now regular meeting place, I ran abruptly into George standing outside. He told me the girls would soon be arriving and that I should wait inside. I took my place in the darkened corner and ordered a Sprite. I had nothing to do but stare at the walls. Cheiko was as usual smiling down at me. As always her fixed mechanical smile displayed a fine set of iridescent white teeth.

I finished my Sprite but George had still not arrived. I rang him and he assured me he would 'soon be coming'. After another ten minutes he arrived with four kayayo women. We asked the girls their ages, but as usual they had no idea. The young girl, whose name was Lashida, I guessed perhaps was around fifteen. She sat silently, appearing completely bemused by what was happening around her. There was an older lady with all except one of her front teeth missing. I never learnt her name that day as George insisted on referring to her as 'the old lady'. I asked George how old he thought she may be, and he said, 'forty-two!' I thought to myself how can she be an 'old lady' at only forty-two? What do you call someone of eighty-two? Another woman, who told me her name was Mamuna, was probably in her mid to late twenties. She sat as still and motionless as a statue. Lastly there was a woman who also looked in her mid-twenties, slightly plump and thick set, who was quite gregarious and talkative. She was the obvious spokesperson of the four. Her name was Poppy. She was so eager to talk. She had been waiting a long time. George started to translate.

'Poppy told me she had four children. All were back in the village, a six year-old, a five year-old and twins of three years. She told me her husband too was in the village.'

I asked her why she had come to Accra?

'We come down from the north because of suffering. There we can go a year without even using toothpaste. Usually when we farm we get paid in food not cash.'

'How did your husband feel about you coming to Accra? Was he angry you left the village?'

'My husband is happy I'm here because I bring back money for food and clothes. At home, in the north sometimes my children they even had to go without clothes, they had no clothes at all and were naked.'

I asked her how she herself met her husband. Was it an arranged marriage?

'My parents brought a man and told me to marry him.'

'Do you like your husband?'

'Because of the children I have to force and like, there is nothing else I can do.'

Mamuna continued to sit still, her eyes gazing into nothingness. Lashida, the young girl gave me a shy smile. I changed my leg position crossing them over in opposite directions to dry off the perspiration.

I asked Poppy if she had attended school. I was surprised by her reaction, which was so different from many of the other kayayo girls. With the other girls, despite many of them wishing to go to school, they appeared resigned to their fate, and they seemed calmly to accept the inevitable. Poppy, however, was different.

She suddenly became very emotional. Her voice started to break as if she was choking back tears.

'Mummy, when I think about school it pains me too much. We (my brothers and sisters) really wanted to continue school but our parents didn't have the money so we had to stop. When I think about not going to school I can't sleep at night. That is why now I want to work hard so that my children can go to school.'

Choking back tears, and bending her head to hide these from me she mumbled between sobs,

'Because when I see things I cannot know I feel pain.'

I understood she meant that when she saw writing she could not read or understand, this made her sad. Although primary education is free in the Northern Ghana, it is still often difficult for parents to send their children to school due to the cost of text and exercise books, school uniform, PE kit and other such items. I remembered the civil servant I had spoken to at the government ministry, she had also mentioned this problem and stated that the government had set up some pilot schools where poor children were given a capitation grant to purchase the necessary items to enable them to attend school. There had also been a school feeding programme whereby children from poor families could get free school meals. However, these measures were limited and many families just like Poppy's still fell outside the net.

We sat in silence for a while and I asked Gifty to bring some more drinks. Gifty, unsure of what to do, looked at Poppy with a dazed expression. Lashida, Mamuna and the forty two year-old 'old lady,' as George insisted on calling her, also sat silently. All six of us sat nestled together, listening to the traffic going by outside.

After a few more minutes Poppy began to speak again. She told me she had left school at Primary 2, perhaps when she was around six or seven years, and Lashida at Primary 3 a year later. Mamuna and Kadima had never attended school. Kadima suddenly gave me a wide toothless grin, nodding her head, making sure I knew that she was in agreement with the general consensus.

I had heard there had been schemes in Accra which had attempted to get the kayayo back once again into full time education. However it appeared that most of these had failed. Some surveys had suggested that this was due to the fact that for the kayayo, the need for money was so great that income generation was in direct competition with time they needed to spend on education. A report conducted by the OAU and UN Children's fund on Africa's Children, entitled, 'Africa's Future' mentions the inevitability of children working in Africa due to the survival requirements of low-income families. In fact, legislation already existed which prohibited children under the age of fifteen working in Ghana. Another report into children's work in Nigeria also commented that 'added to the arduous tasks they are forced to do, the added stress of trying to escape official detection would do little to increase the child's welfare'. It would also leave them wide open to the extortionate practises of minor officials who would demand bribes and other services to turn a blind eye. The kayayo have before complained that minor Accra Metropolitan Authority (AMA) officials demand toll and other 'taxes' from them. Under these circumstances the survey into the kayayo concluded that is 'seems unlikely that girl children will disappear from the economic scene in Ghana'. Instead they suggested various policy initiatives such as providing education outside working hours on a 'drop in' basis, which would run alongside other adult education initiatives. These could be offered near to their places of work.

Poppy and her friends seemed to reiterate the report's conclusions.

'We would like to go to school, but because of work we can't go to school now.'

Like almost all the kayayo I had met to date this group operated their own 'susu' savings schemes. Poppy told me proudly how her group of ten girls saved one cedi each every day. Each day the 'treasurer' would collect a total of Gh10. They then saved this amount for twenty-one days. The susu money would then be divided into three with each girl receiving Gh70 cedis each. Poppy said that currently she was the treasurer of the susu group, and that when she got her Gh70 cedis, which 'will not be long now' she would use the money to buy uniforms, books and shoes for her children to go to school.

'My children go to school so I have to buy their books and uniforms,' she said with such pride.

I asked what the others were planning to buy. George translated and said the 'old lady' wanted to buy roofing sheets.

'My hut in the north it only has a grass roof so I am saving to buy some iron (zinc) sheets for the roof.'

She smiled and gave me yet again a broad toothless grin, simultaneously nodding her head.

Poppy chirped in.

'I am also saving to buy roofing sheets but first I have to get the money for my children to go to school.'

Lashida, the younger girl, said she was saving for clothes and T-shirts and added also that she wanted to buy a sewing machine. Mamuna smiled at me, but didn't let me know what she wanted to buy. She was a very quiet woman who hardly spoke or moved. When I looked at her I kept wondering what she was thinking, she seemed wrapped up in some invisible world.

'I also want to buy a sewing machine,' interjected Poppy.

She smiled and again said,

'But first my children, my children. They must go to school. They must not be like me.'

I thought to myself that no, your children will not see and not know, they will see and understand.

They all had lots of plans for their future. Things to improve their homes, the education of their children, business possibilities to bring in more income. They were like mothers the world over.

The stench wafting up from the open gutter outside the Spot was beginning to become overwhelming, my clothes were sticking to me, and as dusk fell thousands of mosquitoes were starting to emerge. It was getting dark and it was time to leave. Poppy, the 'old lady,' Lashida and Mamuna had to go and bathe and prepare to sleep. George had to rush back to his second job of night watchman at another place across the road from the Methodist church. George had two jobs, a day job and a night job. This meant that literally he was working for twenty-four hours. He could usually snatch a few hours sleep during the night shift and that kept him going.

For a long time I had wanted to talk to the market women and shop keepers at Tonga. They saw and spent their time with the kayayo more than anyone else. How did they see the problem? What was their relationship with the kayayo like? As I walked one hot afternoon through the market alone I stopped to talk to a lady, Gladys, who owned a provisions store in the market. I sat on a chair, which she had placed on the small rectangular patch of broken tiled floor in front of her shop. I asked her what she knew about the kayayo in the market. She replied angrily.

'They don't respect and they are very dirty and lazy. They scatter all their rubbish all over the place and besides that they don't look after their babies at all.'

'What do you mean by that?'

'They often leave their babies with other small children to look after, often the other children are about three or four years only. They can't look after their babies I am telling you, the babies are crying and hungry, and thirsty. We, the women in the market, we feel pity for the children and we feed their children.'

She then pointed furiously to a ragged four or five year-old child walking past carrying a baby and exclaimed,

'Look, look, you see it's just like I told you.'

I had also noticed this a lot in the market but had just assumed that the mother was somewhere in the vicinity, but it increasingly seemed this was not the case. Gladys then went on to tell me that her colleague's shop next door was closed most of the time, so the space was free and empty. Because of this, she said the kayayo congregated there even during the day.

'They eat and throw all their food stuffs around on the floor and when I tell them to pick it up they insult me.... now if I see them there and they refuse to go I throw a bucket of water on them.'

I asked her how they reacted when she did this and she told me again crossly that they insulted her.

A strong gust of wind came suddenly driving the dust up in angry spirals, into the eyes of those around. People begin to rub and cover their eyes with their hands. I couldn't seem to stop Gladys, she went on telling me more and more.

'Also they defecate in the gutter.... the problem is they don't want us to teach them how to be neat or clean.'

I asked her about the fighting, was it true that there were many fights between the kayayo?

'Fights?'

Gladys held her hands up to her head in mock despair.

'I am telling you when they start to fight there is nothing you can do to separate them until they stop fighting, sometimes more than twenty plus will be fighting, they fight as if they don't know each other. They fight as if they don't come from the same region. ...and three months ago one girl had a boyfriend that was not from her tribe, the boy rather was from Accra. When her tribespeople got to hear about it they wanted the girl back, there was a fight with knives and the wrong person was killed.'

She was obviously referring to the murder George had first told me about which had also been brought up when I visited the chief at Tonga market. I asked Gladys if she knew anything about the rapes that I had heard about. Her voice then dropped in tone and became less angry.

'Yes, this often happens with the kayayo who work in restaurants and help food sellers. They often sleep in the chop (eating) bars at night, and then it is here the girls are being raped, sometimes trotro drivers let them sleep in their bus.'

However Gladys told me that this didn't happen so much to those who slept outside due to the fact that they were always in large groups. This was what Rebecca and the other girls from the mango tree had also told me. If a man came to them, together they would beat him and drive him away.

Soon after Gladys had to start work again. Customers were arriving at her shop and I could see she was busy. I said goodbye and told her I would try to pass by again. She wrote down her number and told me if I needed anything to ring her.

I met George again about a week later at the Methodist church at the southern end of Tonga market. I could discern his lofty frame far in the distance walking towards me, his steps seemed like those of a giant. We were going to meet Poppy and her friends once again. As I passed by the mango tree on my way to the Spot I could see a few of the Bandugu girls sitting beneath its shade. As usual the patterns of the leaves above danced in shadows across their faces, swaying gently with the ebb and flow of the wind. In the distance I could see a kayayo girl struggling to carry a massive load. She was bending her knees intermittently to ease the weight from her shoulders. As I got closer I saw that it was Rebecca. Perspiration was streaming down her face. Baby Madihah, asleep on her back, was also drenched both in her own and her mother's sweat. She panted, she couldn't talk, the load was paining her back, it was paining her neck. She struggled on past me. She was bearing the weight.

As I entered the Spot I saw that Gifty looked more miserable than I had ever before seen her. It was even beginning to make me feel depressed. Her son, Kwaku, was lying asleep on one of the benches. George had gone to fetch Poppy and her friends and I sat alone with her. She looked sullen. She didn't want to talk. Yet I felt I should make conversation, perhaps I could help her or find out what was wrong. I asked her where she lived.

'Dansoman,' she said with a resigned air. I was amazed. It was one of the furthest suburbs that you could possibly get from the Spot. With the traffic in Accra it would take hours to get from there to Kejetia every morning.

'What time do you get up in the morning?'

I get up at 4.30am, prepare food then I catch the trotro at 5.30am. Normally I reach here at 7.30am. That gives time for children to buy some breakfast outside, then they walk to school.'

The density of traffic in Accra meant many people were forced to leave home before 5am when it was still dark in order to reach work sometime between seven and eight. Most offices, banks and restaurants opened at 8am. When I lived in the outer suburbs of Accra I also had to do the same. The same goes for the return journey, many people not reaching home until between 7.30am and 9am or even later. It was a life of work and sleep. There was not much time left for leisure.

Gifty then went on to tell me that almost all her salary was spent on trotro fares, which I could well believe and I suggested that she look for a job nearer to Dansoman where she lived. She looked miserable.

'The money they pay me here is too small.'

I really felt really sorry for her. She was in a predicament where her job meant most of her meagre earnings went on transport. I avoided looking up at the wall. I didn't want to see anyone smiling today.

Suddenly, Poppy burst through the swishing bamboo curtain beaming broadly. She ran across to me, holding me tightly. She was plump, energetic and full of life. She seemed so happy we wanted to talk to her and seemed to love meeting us. She was followed in by her friends, the 'old lady' Kadima, the young silent girl Lashida, and the even more silent Mamuna. This time

Mamuna had her son, Mohammed, with her. He was wearing a crisp, bright yellow Power Ranger suit.

Gifty got up slowly and sullenly to get the drinks.

I wanted to find out about how they spent their money. Ghanaians always talk about how one shouldn't waste money, every pesawa was important. I asked Poppy, if she thought any of her friends wasted money on unnecessary things. Her information and her opinions gushed out at lightning speed.

'Yes, I know a girl, sometimes the girl buy meat and they also buy sweet things...anything she see, she buy and so she will see in small time the money will finish and then she will say she wants to borrow from me.'

'Did they think buying meat was a waste?'

'Yes', Poppy added, 'it does not fill your stomach and it costs (expensive).'

George, placing his gigantic hands together behind his head, was nodding in agreement with Poppy. He placed his feet up on a nearby chair.

She continued talking about what for her, and indeed many kayayo, was sacrilege, the wasting of money that should be saved to take back home.

'If you buy unnecessary things you can't get money to get back home and here is not our hometown. We came here for a purpose, for something else and it is not for meat and toffee.'

Kadima, the forty-two year-old kayayo senior citizen was again grinning and nodding. Mamuna stayed motionless and as always Lashida smiled tentatively, as if she was unsure whether at any moment she should be smiling in agreement or frowning with disapproval.

I was eager to know what type of 'unnecessary' sweet things they bought. What were they?

George translated officiously, as if he had just uncovered a momentous crime.

'They buy fan milk ice cream sachets, hack cough sweets and chewing gum,' he announced, as if these were major contraband.

All these items cost below 30 pence. Hacks would cost about 5 pence, chewing gum 10 pence and a sachet of yoghurt ice cream around 15 pence. Yet for the kayayo even these were seen as luxuries they could ill afford, so much so that by buying them you risked scorn and accusations of 'money wasting' from your peers and neighbours. I was having visions of kayayo girls having to buy hacks and chewing gum in secret.

Mamuna was continuing to sit motionless, her face an empty canvas. I could never decipher her thoughts or mood. I wanted to find out more about her and George asked her how long she had been coming to Accra. Her answer was slow and deliberate, as if even to talk was a struggle.

'My husband died when I was pregnant with my fifth child, a boy. He died about two years ago. The sickness it came and catch him and then it was one month and then he die. I cannot now marry again because I have already born five. Three of my children are with me here. Two girls and the boy who is about one year.'

She then ceased to talk and once again sat motionless, staring ahead at no fixed point.

The conversation once again turned to the problem of saving money in Accra. Poppy said that often they should earn more money but she said that their customers sometimes 'were wicked' and didn't pay them the agreed price.

'If we tell them to pay the right money the madams tell us we are bad girls'.

'They get us to carry and then don't pay us properly, they cheat us.'

Did other incidents often prevent them saving as

much as they wanted? I knew in Ghana constant demands from relatives can often eat into any plans for personal expenditure and savings. Many Ghanaians had told me that the demands of the extended family acted as a 'rope around your neck', curtailing your ability to save, invest and even look after your own family properly. It had been concluded from a continent wide survey that arguments within the extended family over financial and related matters frustrated and hindered enterprise and inventiveness. Successful individuals feared jealous relatives who would often try to put an end to their accomplishments, especially if they did not receive what they believed was 'their share' of the loot.

Examples abound. A neighbour who worked as a nurse in the UK regularly sent money back from her hard earned salary to her three nephews. This went on for over fifteen years until my neighbour felt that, now as fully grown adults, they should be in a position to fend for themselves. Instead of being grateful for all the help they had received over the years they were angry that she had 'cut them off' and broke into her house (while she was still working in the UK), taking everything. Successful Ghanaians can often find themselves in a Catch 22 situation. If they do not redistribute their earnings and profits amongst their extended family and even 'friends' they risk their wrath which, as just seen above, can often destroy their businesses, homes or even lives. If they do succumb, and redistribute as tradition dictates, they risk thwarting the little success they have made as any money needed to reinvest for further business growth evaporates. This common phenomenon in Ghana is now called the 'Ghanaian Ph.D' the acronym meaning 'Pull Him Down'. Some successful Ghanaians I know deal with this situation by cutting themselves off from their families, rarely visiting their villages as they know their pockets will be emptied. The kayayo girls also were classic victims of the 'Ghanaian Ph.D'. Almost their entire earnings were redistributed amongst their kin. I have often thought that if these girls, who were so enterprising and resourceful, had used their hard earned savings for investment many would now all be running successful businesses. Yet I know they would fear returning to their villages empty handed. I looked across the table and saw Poppy's tormented expression. She also began to tell me that it was difficult for them to save due to the repeated demands from friends and relatives in the village to send money back.

She desperately tried to explain her predicament. She looked angry and frustrated.

'Sometimes it's difficult, because when I start to save a little money I hear that something has happened in my hometown, so I have to send money there.'

'What kinds of things happen?'

'If one of our family member or our friends marry it cost us.'

'Why?'

'Because when a family member marries you have to buy Geisha soap, cloth, sandals, perfume and a handbag,'

Geisha soap is a brand of soap, cheap in cost, sold locally in Ghana.

'And then if your friends marry you have to buy them a bucket and you have to send them about Gh10 to Gh20 cedis (£5-10 Sterling).'

Poppy continued.

'When there is a death in the village it cost us so much, we have to send many things.'

I saw Mamuna look at me as if she wanted to speak. I think the unfairness of it all even moved her, she who was always so still, so passive. When she spoke she half closed her eyes, as if she needed to close off the world around her to put all her energies into what she needed to say.

'Yes so if no one dies for one or two years we can save, one year I managed to save a lot as nobody died in the village.'

Mamuna looked exhausted and she kept rubbing her eyes, and holding her head in her hands as if trying hard not to fall asleep. As I sat there looking at her I couldn't help thinking that she looked resigned to her fate, as if life could dish up no more shocks for her. She had no alternative but to accept what life doled out.

Poppy was again desperate to tell me something, this time her look was not anguished but a little softer.

'But mummy, if nothing happens we can save and take things back like cooking pots, eating bowls and sometimes even sewing machines.'

The women told me that is was now 'so easy' to send money to the village from the market where they lived as a bus left for their area every week so they were able to send the money up with a friend. Also the advent of the mobile phone had now made it much easier for those in the villages to contact relatives they knew living and working in Accra; they could now be rung day and night by any number of friends, relatives, neighbours and acquaintances, requesting money or other things to be sent back.

Poppy had more to say on this subject, she was so energetic.

'But mummy, it's not just weddings and death, sickness is also a big problem for us.'

Again Mamuna stirred from her silent reverie. Her son Mohammed, his handsome head now buried deep within the folds of her emaciated breasts, was fast asleep.

'If our mothers or fathers are sick we have to send money to them too, boys don't look after their parents so the responsibility always falls on us...sometimes you will come here for one year and you will not be able to save any money, not even Gh30 cedis to save, but some years it is good and you can save.'

For the first time Kadima spoke.

'The people in the village, they worry us and ask for plenty money.'

She went on to say that this was especially so during the strong harmattan season because the dust is strong and cold.

Poppy looked like she was about to burst, she couldn't wait to tell me more and more.

'They will ask for money, they say they have to go to hospital, they say they are sick, but sometimes it's just when they don't have money to spend, they will say they are sick, this makes us very angry, so we don't always send them money every time they ask, only when it is very critical.'

I have never come across people who managed to save, survive and even prosper in such conditions. The kayayo lived on meagre subsistence wages. On top of that was the fact that many of their more unscrupulous customers either did not pay them at all or drove off paying them only half of what they had agreed. If this was not enough their small savings and earnings were often stolen from them while they were sleeping. Furthermore, hard earned susu savings often had to be broken into to pay for bouts of sickness and hospitalization. They were frequently bullied by market officials into paying for various 'projects' which appeared not to exist. Now I am starting to realize even on top of all this, further demands were making their way down to them from their villages. I wondered how they ever managed to save anything. The poor girls seemed to be exploited by everyone. Everyone wanted a share of their tiny daily pay packets. It was like the loaves and the fishes.

All four women had now been sitting motionless for some minutes. They were no longer with me. Their minds had temporarily travelled back to their villages. George used the lull in the conversation to ask me, in his warbling tones, when the book would be published? He wanted to come to England. Could I help him get a visa?

Suddenly Poppy once again looked angry. Another thought had just crossed her mind. Another injustice. Again it was the people from her village that were disturbing her peace of mind.

'Even when we go home we have to give lots of money to the other villagers. If we don't they will talk about us.'

I knew what she meant as I had experienced it myself, along with countless other Ghanaians but I acted as if I didn't know. I wanted her to tell me in her own words.

'When we go back to the village, *all* the villagers come out to greet you, so that when you see them you have to give them something. They say to us, 'God will bless you because you have travelled and have come back and given something to us.''

'How much do you usually give them?'

'Sometimes I give them Gh1 cedi sometimes 50psws, but there are many and the money I have to give becomes plenty'.

There was another pause in the conversation. Gifty was sitting on the plastic chair staring into space. Maybe she was calculating how she could make ends meet this week. George was sitting there tapping his elongated fingers impatiently on the table. I thought that maybe he was planning his trip to Europe. He again clasped his hands behind his head. He looked thoughtful. His brows were deeply furrowed, his lips were tightly squeezed together. Then full of resentment he pronounced,

'It's terrible they will take all your money, it's not good to go there (to the village) too often.'

Because of the extended family system in Ghana those with any money are expected to help those without. In many respects this can be a good system for those without have a safety net, but not unlike our own social security system in the west, there are many in Ghana who will just abuse the system and do nothing, living off the backs of those, like the poor kayayo, who are prepared to work hard. Almost all Ghanaians I know redistribute their money to their poorer relatives.

I always remember a report I read in a book many years ago that summed up the Ghanaians ability to look after each other in times of hardship. It was 1982. The country was going through one its worst droughts in human memory and there was near starvation on the streets of Accra. Shops were empty. Things could not have been any worse than in that year. Yet not long after, things did get gravely worse. Neighbouring Nigeria, in a frenzy of xenophobia, expelled more than 1.3 million Ghanaian migrant workers from their country. They arrived back in Ghana en masse. Also starving and penniless, many of them had not even been paid. The report went on to recount how the 'famine watchers' in the western media were preparing to descend en masse on the small West African nation in preparation to film the unfolding tragedy. Western relief agencies were also drawing up emergency plans to erect feeding camps. Yet almost before all this could be done,

'The deportees had disappeared, absorbed back into their extended families like spilt milk into a new sponge. What was potentially the greatest single disaster in Ghana's history was defused even before foreign donors or government policy makers could figure out what to do about it.'

This gives testament to the extraordinary ability of Ghanaians to pull together in times of hardship to help one another out. It is this inherent ability that allows young girls like the kayayo to survive and even prosper in an environment in which many of us would perish.

We all got up to leave and I paid Gifty. Poppy saw my phone and sang out,

'Oh you have a hello hello.'

I had been hearing them called this way by many of the kayayo before.

'I used to have 'hello hello' but it got stolen.'

I think almost every kayayo girl I have met to date has had her phone stolen. But they got up, and they soldiered on. They had no choice.

As usual Poppy beamed and gave me a bear hug before she marched off back to her chores. For some reason whenever I saw Poppy rushing towards me I always thought of the childhood nursery rhyme character of 'Old Mother Hubbard'. I can still visualize the picture from my old story book of a plump women in a tattered dress with her sleeves rolled up, peering into an empty cupboard with her hungry brood seated beneath her. You got the impression this plump woman in the book, despite her predicament, would always manage to provide for her children, due to her determination and ingenuity. This was how I always saw Poppy. I could picture her dreams. Her dreams of sending her children to school, the happiness of seeing them smartly dressed in their uniforms, polished shoes and books on their backs. It was this dream that motivated her to get through this hell with her head held high. Despite the degrading circumstances in which she lived on the street, despite the sneers and insults from those around her, deep in her heart, there was a treasure. Her children were achieving.

I watched all four of them walk off into the distance. Kadima was bent on improvements to her home. As she fell softly to sleep she dreamed of her small hut in the north with its shiny new roof. What about young Lashida? Did she imagine arriving in her village adorned with the latest fashions from Accra? All her peers would admire her. What about Mamuna? Did she long for a year without weddings, births and deaths? Dreams of the kayayo.

I decided to walk back home through the market. Perhaps I would be able to talk to some more shop or stall holders about their opinions of the kayayo girls. I had to soldier through in the intense heat, perspiration was dripping down my back and face. I passed by a tiny tailoring shop. Inside a wizened old man sat. He was staring blankly outside, and as I passed he smiled at me and we began to converse. The man introduced himself as Issah. He was a tall, slim man, as were most northerners, and he had a long, thin face with high cheekbones and sunken cheeks. He spoke with a marked stutter that made it difficult to follow what he was saying.

He seemed very concerned and keen to talk about the kayayo and their problems. He told me what I had already assumed, that he was from the north, and a Dagomba and said immediately that the main problem leading to so many young girls ending up in Accra was due to the fact that in the north they only work for a season, and that after the rainy season there was no work.

'I know that because I'm a northerner,' he stammered.

'D-d-down here they can earn a lot of money, a day say they can make Gh5-7 cedi (£2.50-3.50 Sterling) a day.'

He started to say something else and his stammer became very bad, he broke off and waited, resuming after several seconds.

'S-S-S-Sometimes the girls used to work as maids in p-people's houses, people would come around the market and say they were looking for a worker. It could be in a shop, a r-r-restaurant, and specifically a house maid in a private house...then the girls would follow them to the house and sometimes the k-k-kayayo don't come back for the family to see them again.....this h-happens once in a while. Now the girls are more v-vigilant, so if someone say they want a worker other people will go with the kayayo to check, but these days the kayayo don't want to work inside the house as a maid.'

Then I remembered the day, a long time ago now, when I had first asked the mango tree girls to come in my car and how they had refused, and I was so puzzled.

'B-B-But sometimes the kayayo can meet a good lady and they will treat them like family and when it is time for the girl to go to her hometown they will buy goods for them.'

I asked Issah if he thought the kayayo girls coming to Accra seemed to be getting younger and younger all the time and Issah agreed with me.

'Now you s-s-s-see the girls are beginning to grow up in the streets in an all women environment, the baby boys, once they reach four or five, they are sent back to the village...you see when I see them I used to c-c-cry, they are too small and if they meet a wicked woman they will give them plenty work and if you don't finish it early they will whip or cane you, and if the girl cries they will s-s-s-sack her.'

Again the stuttering prevented Issah from continuing. He stopped for a short while, gazing at the people walking past his shop.

'Because it is an all women environment they are preyed upon by men. s-s-s-Sometimes in the night you see the b-b-boys around disturbing them, the boys come and talk. Some will follow the boys. In the dead of night, about midnight or 1am when you pass at the back of the shops you won't see anyone. Some of the kayayo take a boyfriend and the boyfriends take them in the corner of the market which is lonely and dark.'

'Are the boys mainly from their own tribe?'

Issah nodded his head in agreement.

'Most southerners can't speak Dagbani and most of the girls can't talk Twi well, so usually they mix with people from their tribe. The boys often don't get work and the girls give them money.'

Issah and I sat for a while longer. He told me that whenever I wanted to talk to him about the kayayo I could come to his shop.

I left Issah and continued to walk through the market. The heat was intense. Blistering. I turned the corner into Springstrap Road and walked home.

The next time we met Poppy and her friends it was one evening about a week later. This time we didn't go to 'the Spot' but rather to their 'shop front', their home in Accra.

As George and I entered the market it was already dark. The lights had gone off in Accra once again. Faint yellow light arose from what seemed like thousands of minute flickering flames arising from small tin containers of kerosene. These makeshift lamps were placed on tables lining either side of the narrow tracks. Each lamp cast a warm amber flush on the shiny perspiring faces surrounding it, on the people busy at work, cooking, serving and eating food from the roadside stalls. The familiar aroma of sickly sweet fried plantains crowded the air.

By now it was almost 9pm, and some of the girls

were already asleep on the bits of cloth they used to carry their babies around in during the day. I saw about four or five tiny babies asleep in one small doorway, one was still lying next to his mum, breastfeeding. Although it was quite late, some toddlers and small children were still running around, and when they saw George and I they ran towards us shouting and shrieking, grabbing each other playfully with their arms around each other's necks.

Eventually we arrived at the Springstrap Road end of the market, to the shop front that Poppy and the girls from her village called 'home.' As we approached and greeted them, some of those who were already lying down looked up at us, smiling from the floor on which they slept. The shop front was pleasant. They had been lucky. It had a broken tiled floor that was immaculately clean. The doors of the shop were emblazoned with a painting of a Colonel Saunders like figure advertising, 'American Rice Master Rice'. Railings surrounded the patch of ground on which they slept. This could be shut at night with the gate, but as the railings were only waist high it would still be easy for someone to bend or step over them to steal or harass the girls if they so wanted. It would also have been just as easy to put a hand through the large gaps in the railings to steal or molest.

There were about twenty girls in this shop front, and like Poppy they were all Mamprusi. Poppy had not yet arrived back from the bathhouse. After some time we started talking to Mamuna who was sitting on an empty white plastic paint pot. She was sitting with her two young daughters, Rasna who was around eight and Aba who was perhaps eleven. They were all eating fufu and groundnut soup from the same bowl placed on the concrete floor of their 'living room.' Mamuna's son, Mohammed, was fast asleep, further behind near the shop door, as usual in his yellow Power-Rangers suit.

Some other girls within the group brought George and I two empty paint pots on which to sit. As I sat there watching them eat I wondered if they ever managed to save the food that was left over. I asked Mamuna.

'We try to save food for the next day but whatever food we try and save the rats come and eat it.'

I asked them why they didn't cover the food and put it inside one of the plastic containers. Then they could seal it tight and the rats then wouldn't be able to get it. They told me they didn't cover the food because when they did this the 'food spoils'. They told me the food 'changed colour and tasted bitter'. They felt rather that if the wind 'was blowing' on the food it would not spoil. They told me there was a small wooden table pushed against the railings of the shop front so they would put their food under there.

They also told me, as had other groups I had spoken to, that the rats, 'walked on their legs' but because they were so tired they didn't wake up, because they,

'Slept like a dead person because of the work.'

But they told me that when the rats walked on their heads they did wake up. The girls then added that at night,

'The rats urinate on us, they urinate on the clothes we are wearing.'

They told me sometimes it seemed like 'rain', but then they realized that it was the rat urinating on them. I asked them about the scorpions. Just then, through a tunnel of heavy darkness illuminated on either side by flickering yellow light, I could see a figure rushing toward me' the light was jumping across its body as it moved quickly in and out of its faint radiance. The hurried movements appeared odd amidst the general nocturnal languor of this market. People dozing, the sleeping bodies, chores carried out in slow heavy gestures. As the figure approached I could see it was Poppy. Following closely behind her was the old lady, her slow deliberate movements more in tune with the current nocturnal ambience. She was heavily laden down with the day's laundry balancing precariously on her head. They were returning from the bathhouse, which was near to the other end of the market by the Spot.

Poppy beamed and hugged me and sat down on another empty paint pot. She was happy. She told me the susu money would soon mature and then she could take her share of the money back to the north for her children's uniforms and books. George appeared to be writing down some calculations on a piece of scrap paper. The old lady started to unload the washing. She hung it carefully over the railings surrounding their concrete patch. I told Poppy we had been talking about the scorpions in the market.

'Yes they are here. There are many of them in the market. Large black ones, but I haven't been bitten by one cos I sleep plenty.'

'What about the cockroaches?'

Manuna and Poppy and young Lashida, who had been sitting silently until now, laughed.

'The cockroaches and the bed bugs are like family, so they sleep with you as a family, but the bed bugs suck our blood.'

In the darkness some way ahead and beneath a flickering yellow flame I could just make out four young kayayo girls sitting on their paint pots. They were braiding each other's hair. Silence descended for a short while upon our group. I was thinking about my forthcoming trip to the north. I had wanted to travel up there for some time. But as yet I had not managed to find someone to accompany me. When Nurah had left I wasn't ready. I had now started to think that I had no alternative but to travel there alone. I would tell Poppy that I would soon be travelling to their village. Perhaps she could help.

Suddenly George looked up from his calculations, which he had been doing under the feeble light of the kerosene lamp. He was rubbing his chin between his thumb and forefinger, as if deep in thought.

'We will soon have to start to apply for a passport,' he warbled, 'because I have to be ready for when the book comes.'

Ignoring George, I returned to my planned statement. I told Poppy and the other girls that I would soon be travelling to Poppy's village. There was general laughter. Not the normal raucous laughter. Everyone was too tired for that.

'What is the name of your village?'

'Wialu... but you would never be able to find my village, it is too far away, there is no road,' Poppy said, perplexed.

I assured her I would and she and the others laughed even more.

The mango tree girls, Rebecca and her friends, had also said the same. I would prove them wrong.

Again Mamuna was starting to fall asleep as she struggled to stay upright on her paint pot. Her eyes were involuntarily closing. Despite their tiredness I could see they enjoyed us coming to listen to them. Drops of water were now falling from the wet clothes hanging on the railings. A small stream of water was making its way across the broken tiled floor. I glanced over at young Lashida. Our eyes moved involuntarily towards a fleeting illumination of a lone bathing kayayo girl appearing suddenly out of the darkness into the headlights of a passing taxi. She bent to hide her shame. The vision just as quickly vanished. We sat again in darkness.

I watched Mamuna dozing off on her paint pot and listened to the soft snores of other sleeping kayayo girls in the group. As I regarded the mushrooming rivulets of water which were now forming across the broken tiled floor, I decided it was time to move.

As George and I turned the corner into Springstrap Road we fell upon a scuffle. As always crowds were gathering momentum, intervening on behalf of the side that they believed were most aggrieved. A young woman was accusing a man of taking her money and not paying it back. It would probably go on for hours, transforming itself into a veritable modern day TV court drama played out on Accra's streets. George soon sauntered off to his favourite fast food stall to eat rice and stew. I strolled down the road to my apartment. Thinking.

Two days later I received a phone call from George. He told me he had heard that something bad had happened to Poppy. I had to go to work at the school, but spent the whole day worried. What an earth could have happened? I met him later that evening at the Spot and we walked towards Poppy's shop front. Not far from there we came across little Martha sitting with her friends. She ran towards me, held my hand and asked me to wait. She ran to what I assumed to be her shop front and came back with the crochet. Now she had completed three stripes in red and yellow and blue. She needed more wool. The container shop was nearby so we went with her and bought her more.

'What colour would you like this time?' I asked.
'Green.'
She ran off with the wool, her crochet and the hook.
Then George and I walked over to the 'American Rice Master' shop front where the girls lived. It was unusually quiet. The girls were sitting around listlessly,

as if all the strength that had kept them living through this Armageddon had been sucked out. They stared into space. On seeing Poppy I noticed her eyes were red and swollen. She did not run towards me. She did not jump up and hug me. What had happened?

Poppy explained to George, who translated. Someone had come in the night and stolen all the susu money the girls had saved. George explained to me that they had only had two days left to go before it 'matured' and all three girls including Poppy would have received their Gh70 cedis (£35 Sterling).

I asked what exactly had happened. Unusually, Poppy was not the first to speak. Young Lashida explained that Poppy had tied the money into the folds of her skirt. I knew that many women in the market kept their money this way. When she had woken up that morning she found the money had gone. Then Poppy spoke. She told me, gazing down at the broken tiled floor, her heart also broken.

'The thief he came in the night with scissors and he cut it out, he cut our money out.'

It may seem surprising that thieves can do this without waking them up but if one takes into account their unique circumstances it is not so astonishing. Firstly, they are used to activity and movement around them as they all sleep on top of each other so that any unusual movement would not wake them. Secondly, they are just so tired they sleep, as many kayayo had themselves told me before, 'like dead people'.

I could see from Poppy's face that she was absolutely devastated by this great loss. Their savings were their life, the main reason they were in Accra, as they said,

'We suffer to save.'

She had lost not only her own savings but that of all the other ten girls in their susu group. They had planned to divide this susu into three so that each girl would get Gh70 cedis and now she and the other two would get nothing. I asked Poppy how the other girls had reacted to this loss.

'They were angry, they blamed me, they said I should have hidden the money deeper in my clothing, maybe inside my brassiere or panties...now they say me that I have to pay back all the money to them...the money is plenty. It is Gh1800 cedis (almost £100 Sterling).'

'How will you do this?'

'Slowly bit by bit.'

Poppy looked up at me intermittently with her red swollen eyes with a curious, ambivalent expression. Beneath the devastation, deep, deep, deep below, I could discern a faint flickering of an indomitable spirit. That spirit was the kayayo spirit. It was the spirit of all the downtrodden peoples of the world. The spirit that says that we must once again rise up in the face of adversity and soldier on. It was as if her red eyes were telling me, in her own endearing words, as she often did,

'Mummy, I am devastated, I have lost my dream, the treasure in my heart has gone, but soon it will come back again. I will struggle to make it come back.'

As I sat there, I thought of probably the most popular proverb in Ghana, a proverb that is reiterated across the country day after day from the mouths of its citizens, from its billboards, from the bumpers of its taxis and trotros,

'NO CONDITION IS PERMANENT.'

'Yes, Poppy, remember: No condition is permanent.'

Chapter Nine

Dr Azeem

For a long time now I had wanted to visit the Bilal Polyclinic. I had been to see Dr Asamoah at the Tonga Market Polyclinic and he had told me how many of the more serious cases that he dealt with in relation to the kayayo he referred there.

The hospital lay on the edge of Nima, and it did not take me long to drive the short distance from my apartment. On entering the clinic I told them about the book I was writing and asked whether there was a doctor who could help me. They introduced me to Doctor Azeem. He seemed a very confident and busy doctor who was kind enough to make time to talk to me on the spur of the moment. He started by telling me there had been an outbreak of cholera in Accra (which I was completely unaware of) and many of the people being brought in were kayayo from Tonga market. He told me, however, that all the cases had been successfully treated and there had been no deaths. He said they (the kayayo) tended to get things like this because they 'don't take good care of themselves'.

He said one of the major reasons that the kayayo ended up at the clinic was because of what he termed 'incomplete abortions'. I asked him what he meant by this. He said,

'They arrive bleeding and when I ask them what is the problem, what do they think has caused the bleeding, they won't tell me.'

I had heard many times before that any problem of a sexual nature will often be concealed by the kayayo as they are often either are too ashamed or too embarrassed to mention it.

'A few will tell you but most don't.'

I then asked him how they determine what is causing the problem if the girls refuse to explain?

'This often has to be verified through a pelvic scan.'

A nurse knocked on the door, quietly making a request. Dr Azeem, a handsome man with a prominent forehead and eyes that glittered like a cat in the night, quickly and deftly wrote out a prescription, handing it to the nurse as he continued to talk to me.

'For example, one patient who presented herself to me was already three months pregnant. She had taken the medication that induced the abortions. She bled for some time and then the bleeding stopped. At the time she was unaware that the termination had not worked. It was only later that she started to get more pain. She then became weak and ended up being brought to the hospital.'

Dr Azeem went on to say that in extreme cases they arrived at the hospital unconscious often, being rushed there in the middle of the night. He told me that fortunately they had not experienced any deaths from any of these cases, but the girls sometimes had to be rushed to Korle Bu, Accra's major teaching hospital, where they had more and also better equipment.

I said that I would presume that such emergences would necessitate a lot of intervention and how would the kayayo pay for this? He said that the hospital had to treat them 'as paupers', so they didn't pay, but added that sometimes 'they gathered together and paid'. He gave a recent example of one young kayayo girl who had just arrived from the north.

'The baby, who was one-and-a-half years, came in vomiting and with high fever. The girl had only been in Accra a few days. Because the girl was a newcomer the other girls had to contribute and pay for her.'

I asked him what medicine they took to induce the

abortions. He said it was called 'cytotech'. It's normally used as a prostaglandin when people are delayed in labour. Gynaecologists use it to induce labour.

'When the kayayo buy it and take it to induce their own abortions they take no heed of directions.'

'Where do they get it?'

'They are often sold it by 'chemical sellers' or pharmacies employing unqualified people.'

Again there was a knock at the door. Dr Azeem jumped up, walked to the cupboard and handed the nurse some medication. She quickly left the room again, shutting the door behind her.

'They don't know how to take it and just take it anyhow.'

He also said among the kayayo skin diseases were also very common. He told me that some of the diseases he saw them come into the surgery with were 'very strange and unusual.'

'We often have not seen them before so we have to refer them to the dermatologist.'

I told him I had noticed this myself and that the doctor at Tonga Market had also mentioned it.

'But the most common disease is malaria and also diarrhoea.'

He then went on to talk about other issues. The kayayo girls often have a high degree of injuries from assaults. The girls are assaulted by their boyfriends. I recalled what Officer Gyedu had told me in downtown Accra. I asked him about the babies. I said that the girls sometimes told me they were married but I thought this was not always the case. I felt that sometimes the kayayo girls didn't want me to know that they had become pregnant and then had been abandoned by the baby's father.

Dr Azeem then also added that some kayayo came

to Accra with their babies but that many got pregnant while living down here. He told me that some of them are 'too afraid' to take the drug to abort. He explained that medical care for pregnant mothers in Ghana was now free.

'For a year after pregnancy treatment for the mother is free under the health insurance scheme, and for the baby treatment is free for six months after birth.'

I asked him if the kayayo were aware of the National Health Insurance Scheme. He said that most of them didn't have health insurance. He said they knew about health insurance but didn't attach much importance to it.

'Their main aim is to save money quickly. Their mentality is, why should I pay Gh25 cedis (£12.50 Sterling) when I'm not ill, they don't think that will save them money for the rest of the year.'

He also said Typhoid fever was common. When they do the Widdal test on them, it's often very high. Dr Azeem explained that the type of diseases the kayayo got reflected their unhealthy living conditions. He also told me that Sexually Transmitted Diseases were common among the kayayo.

There was another knock at the door and Dr Azeem was this time called out. There was some kind of emergency. I waited for about five minutes and then he returned, smiling broadly. He apologised for all the interruptions but I told him there was no need to apologize. He had been kind enough to talk to me without prior notice. He drank some water and then resumed his discussion.

He told me that many of the kayayo suffered from malnutrition. I asked whether the fact that the girls just ate stodgy food with little or no nourishment would affect their breast milk. He said obviously breast milk was good for the baby, but he added that,

'They don't always know how to attach the baby to the breast and the baby is sucking away and not getting much milk.' He explained that the babies should get a good attachment to the breast - often they just hold the tip of the nipple. As a result the babies are malnourished. He said they often had to send them to the nutritionist for rehabilitation.

I asked him how he determined whether or not the children were malnourished? He said that usually the children would have rashes. They would have a potbelly, which is a characteristic sign of kwashikor. This is the most common form of malnutrition found among the kayayo. Kwashikor is a common disease in Ghana, caused mainly by protein deficiency. The most visible symptoms include swollen belly and changes in skin pigment and hair colour or texture. The other main type of malnutrition you see a lot among the kayayo is called Marasmas.

'Unlike in Kwashikor where patients suffering from the disease are listless, when you are affected by Marasmas patients are still alert, they still have a good appetite and want to eat. When you see a child with Marasmus it may be only a year-old but it will look like an old man or woman. The kayayo patients that arrive here are lethargic and often have sores around their mouths.'

'How is it treated?'

'We send the girl to the nutritionist and they are shown how to feed their babies with good food. We tell them to feed their babies on common types of food that they can easily purchase in the market. Beans, groundnut, millet, sorghum. Sometimes the nutritionist prepares things for them and give them samples.'

The nurse once again opened the door, this time with an anxious look on her face. Doctor Azeem glanced into the corridor and noticed the growing queue of patients outside his surgery. I realized it was time to go and thanked the doctor for taking the time to talk to me. As I left the room the first patient was approaching Dr Azeem's door.

Some days later I was passing a well-known pharmacy that served a large area around Springstrap Road and Kejetia. I was keen to find out about this drug, cytotech, and the extent of the demand for it. I asked the pharmacist, whom I knew vaguely as I had also used this pharmacy myself. She was a qualified pharmacist as were most who work in the reliable stores. She told me she once worked as a pharmacist for 'Boots' in the UK. I told her what the doctor had told me and asked her if she was aware of the drug. She said she was aware that the drug was taken for these purposes but that they didn't stock the drug in her store.

I started to walk back home. I was thinking. I still had not managed to locate or find the infamous Debele market where supposedly the largest number of kayayo in Accra lived. It was troubling me that I seemed to be having so much trouble reaching the place. However, when much later I did eventually find this market what was revealed was a vastly different world to what I had discovered at Tonga market in Kejetia. A world that disclosed even more shocking secrets than what I had already unearthed. But some months still had to pass before I reached them.

Chapter Ten

Hope returns for Poppy

I had been to the market several times over the past few weeks but had not seen Poppy or any of the other girls from the Rice Master Shop.

No doubt they were trudging the streets of Accra, probably in some other location. I was concerned how Poppy was managing. How on earth was she going to pay back all that money, in addition to having to save once again for her own children's needs? I also thought of Rebecca, Latifa, Nurah, and Mahab. Of their troubles and distress. Rebecca was being bullied and threatened by the so-called 'protector' of the kayayo, Shagba. Her daughter, Mahidah, was injured due to being left with a minor. Nurah had been injured due to an attempted rape. Mahab had been bullied and pushed on the streets when we were stopped by the police. I had to go and see them again soon.

It was only two days after Christmas when once again I sat waiting for George on the wooden bench on the opposite side of the road from the Methodist church. As I sat there I could just glimpse inside through the gaps of the half opened doors. The lights were on and many people were inside praying. Like many cities the world over at this time of year Accra was adorned in festive glitter' twinkling fairy lights hung from shop doorways, windows and trees. Shops and kiosks had their ubiquitous 'Christmas boxes' strategically placed to maximize donations. Suddenly another man who had been sitting on the bench got up and the whole thing tumbled over. Me too. Almost simultaneously George approached, once again reminding me that I should always sit in the middle of the bench, not at the ends.

As George and I entered the market it was already dark but still early and the place was full of life. The small dirt track that ran around the perimeter of the market was bursting with loaded carts, taxis and motorbikes. In the distance vehicle headlights were momentarily illuminating groups of children before once again throwing them into darkness. It was as if one were watching the darkened stage of a theatre set, its spotlight randomly lighting up scenes before once again enveloping them in darkness, into oblivion. As if these were scenes that must only be allowed a fleeting glimpse, that one must never be shown the full picture.

One kayayo girl, no more than about fourteen years old, was attempting to put on eyeliner holding a mirror in her hand at angles to catch the erratic light. A taxi, moving round a corner, again briefly shone its beams on a lone girl washing in her bowl. The bowl was balancing on a plank of wood placed across the drain. She believed the darkness would hide her secret. Another girl was sweeping up dust from the broken tiled floor of her shop front with a witches broom. The headlights illuminated the trillions of dust particles dancing around in its rays. Taxis hooted as they drove slowly along in the darkness. Insanitary retching smells wafted up from the open drain. As we entered further some of the younger kayayo girls were swinging on the shop poles, smiling at us as we passed. The wet washing was already being strung up onto bits of string around where they slept, and had already started to drip on those sleeping beneath.

Suddenly I felt a tapping on my back. I turned round. It was little Martha. Whenever I went to the market she always seemed to find me. I imagined she relied on some kind of bush telegraph to send out alerts whenever I was spotted. She held up her crochet for me to see. It now had four stripes: red, yellow, green and blue.

'So many colours,' I said, 'soon you will run out of colours to choose...what colour do you want next?'

'Purple.'

We bought the wool and she darted off to start on her next stripe and colour. I wondered why we were continually seeing so many girls bathing in the street. It seemed quite a lot of girls didn't bother to go down to the bathhouse as they managed to get some water and carry out their daily ablutions near to their shop-fronts. Yet I thought it must also be due to exhaustion. After a long day, yet another walk carrying loads of washing plus your child down to the bathhouse was just one more onerous task. If it could be avoided, why not? Also depending on where you were situated in the market it could be quite far to walk.

George and I continued to walk further into the darkness. Without warning I felt a strong force behind me. Something was around my neck pulling me backwards. I panicked and jolted round abruptly.

It was Poppy giving me a bear hug from behind. I was overjoyed to see her.

'Mummy, we have all missed you, where have you been?'

I also asked her,

'Where have YOU been?'

'Please come with me,' she sang in her melodic, guttural language, 'come please come. I want to show you something.'

We followed quickly behind for several minutes until we came to a 'Tea and Fried Egg Sandwich Stall'. Scores of empty Blue Band margarine tubs flanked its perimeter.

'This is where I work now in the night time...when I finish my kayayo work I come here and do more work.

The owner, this man, he pays me well.'

A tall, thin, wiry man with a goatee beard smiled over to me as he was pouring some tea into a cup.

We sat down on a step. She told me that because of this extra job she had already started to pay back the susu money. She also said in a hushed voice that the other girls didn't know how much she earned.

'I tell them I only earn small so I can pay back the susu money very small, then the rest I save in my private savings. I put these savings in a different bag. This is just for me.'

She told me after some time she would soon get back the money for her children.

'They will no more sack my children from school, I will no longer pay bit by bit.'

It is quite common in Ghana for children to be asked to leave (or get sacked) from school for lack of payment. Many poorer families are forced to pay the school fees weekly or in very small amounts as it comes in. If they miss a week the child will be asked to leave until the next payment is made. The fees for government schools in Ghana are very low but many if not most families struggle to send their children to private schools. They believe the government schools are not good and that private schools will be better for their children. Many of the private schools' fees are also very low and such schools can be found in all neighbourhoods, from shantytowns to middle class areas. It may not always be the case that these schools are superior to the state schools, but as in my own country the belief nevertheless prevails. I glanced at Poppy, her eyes were wide with enthusiasm.

'I am going to pay for my children's school for the whole year. I've never done that before but the tealeaf money, it will help me a lot.'

She rubbed her eyes with her worn out hands.

'They (my children) will only need to wait small and I will find the money for them soon.'

She told me again, so full of delight about her accomplishments. She got up at 5am went to bath and started working, trudging the sweltering dusty streets and carrying back breaking loads most of the day. She finished around six, bathed and started to work at the tea stall around 7pm till around 11pm when she slept.

She told me she had to go to her shop front to fetch something and we could go with her. All along the short route through this teeming market she beamed and hugged me tightly at regular intervals.

As we approached I spotted the Colonel Saunders lookalike on the shop front pointing at us. We sat down on a paint pot inside the railings. Young Lashida and Kadima started talking to George in their language. He thought for a moment and then turned to me.

'The old lady and the small girl, they tell me now there is no work. When they walk they find it hard to get work.'

I asked them what I had heard many times and also read about. Did they think there were too many kayayo?

Suddenly I heard a chorus of 'yes' from all of the three women who were sitting there. This did certainly seem to be a huge problem. A case study done of a large number of kayayo girls by an NGO also found this to be so. What many years ago was quite a reliable job, now seemed no longer to be the case. In the study many kayayo stated that because so many girls were now arriving in Accra, they were having to walk further and further distances to look for work. Comments included,

'There are too many of us (kayayo) in the system and so I have to wait longer to get a customer, times have changed.'

One sixteen year-old commented,

'There are too many girls working as kayayo now, day in and day out more people are coming and making the pay less and less than before.'

Another girl mentioned the high competition for customers between the kayayo. This led to two things. Firstly it encouraged the girls to accept heavier loads for less pay in order to win over customers from rival kayayo, leading ultimately to more injuries and accidents. Secondly, less income and work eventually led to desperation amongst the girls, leading to more fights breaking out between them due to competition over work. One young kayayo girl summed up the situation,

'Our dreams of getting money and buying the needed items are not materializing, this is because we outnumber the jobs.'

On top of this problem of more girls chasing few and fewer jobs, was the added difficulty of those kayayo with infants. It had been noted in some reports how customers generally preferred to hire girls who were not burdened with babies on their backs. This was for two reasons, one economic, one compassionate. Customers felt those already burdened with the weight of an infant (usually up to two years) would be more restricted and less able to carry the heavy weights than those without. Moreover other customers felt pity for the babies who were carried around by their mothers in all weathers. In hot weather many babies got overheated and dehydrated and during the rainy season they got soaked, often being unable to dry out before night time. They consequently went to bed wet and chilled, which could cause pneumonia, especially when so many of them were undernourished.

Ironically, or rather sadly, this 'predicament' has produced yet another dilemma. This was the phenomenon of what has become known as the 'baby kayayo'. Due to the restrictions which infants placed on their mothers' ability to earn income, many kayayo have started to bring down even younger relatives, nieces, younger sisters and cousins to 'babysit' the infants while they are out carrying loads. These babysitters usually range in age from about four to nine years.

This arrangement within the kayayo's social structure, has started to resemble, as was noted in some research, an 'occupational career structure'. It was pointed out that the kayayo themselves exist within an 'occupational chaperoning context' whereby either an older sister, cousin or village acquaintance will accompany the girl down to Accra, ensuring that she works. The older relative or family friend will also 'enforce savings activities on the part of the child in the interest of the family'. The research pointed out, as I had also found that,

'When the kayayo girls have infants these were tended to by young girls between six to eight years who acted as kayayo 'nannies'. These 'nannies' eventually move up the occupational ladder into the kayayo work itself.'

Research has also emphasized the 'high level of social organisation evident among the kayayo'. For example coming to Accra in the first place requires an initial investment on the part of the girl or her family for the cost of travel and the hire purchase of necessary equipment, that being the metal head pan.

Amongst the migrant groups of Accra, being a kayayo is seen as an honourable trade. In fact it could be regarded as a self-employed profession within the informal economic sector. It is a profession which requires an initial investment, albeit small. Furthermore, the kayayo are not viewed necessarily as 'street children'. One report into children and the kayayo concluded,

'On the basis of the evidence collected it would seem inappropriate to consider the kayayo under the category of street children, if street children is taken to mean children who have either been abandoned or have abandoned their families. These children (the kayayo) are deeply embedded in the family structure. They are responsive to their families requirements for cash, obedient in remitting earnings back to parents and expect to return permanently to their family homes.'

In many respects the kayayo could be seen as migrant workers with a unique occupational and social niche. However, whereas in many countries migrant workers tend to be adult men, in the kayayo context they are adolescent girls and female children.

I wanted to find out more about the babysitting arrangements. George and I asked the girls. Poppy told me that Mamuna gave her infant son Mohammed to her 'younger sister' to look after. She pointed to a girl sitting to her left who looked no older than six or seven. Poppy added,

'When we are walking and carrying loads, the little ones will look after the babies. Those that are still (breast) feeding they still carry them on their backs.'

I was unsure of this. Most kayayo babies and children were breastfed until quite an advanced age compared to western standards, generally until eighteen months or sometimes longer. I had seen babies much younger than this being tended by small children in the market. As mentioned earlier I had often presumed the mothers were in the vicinity, within several minutes walking distance but later discovered that this was not always the case. Many were trudging the streets in other parts of Accra. What Poppy had just said suggested something far more worrying. That babies who relied on breast milk for their sustenance were being left the whole day with children who did not know how to feed them properly. This could have led to dehydration and other illnesses.

'Actually we are not happy when we leave our babies with our younger sisters,' Poppy continued.

They told me they would much prefer to work in one place where they could stay with their children, but because they were walking around they couldn't take a toddler with them.

'Sometimes when we come back the baby is injured and we don't know how it happened.' said Mamuna.

I thought of Rebecca's baby, and how her forehead had been bruised and cut.

'Sometimes the cars knock the babies,' said Poppy.

According to the girls this happened only yesterday and the baby had to be taken to hospital. The infant was 'about two' and a small child was 'minding the baby'. They also said that sometimes,

'When the cars hit the babies they (the cars) will run away.'

Near to Lashida was a very young mother, Aysha, who could not have been more than fourteen years. Next to her was 'her babysitter,' a young girl of no more than six years, who was holding a baby of about six months. Three children looking after each other.

I asked the group what they thought could help them. They told me they needed help so that the children could go to school and so they could get a little money and 'buy and sell in one place'. It appeared the itinerant nature of their work hampered their ability to look after their children properly.

I sat there quietly for some time. Watching the wretched and ragged scene before me, I thought how the kayayo world was an exclusively women's world, a community only of women. Being a kayayo, one report concluded, means a 'separation of the community of men and the community of women'. On this tiny patch of stone, sat women in their thirties, with their older female children, women in their twenties with their younger female toddlers and girlish adolescents, often with infants.

Mamuna's son Mohammed was fast asleep. He looked clean, well fed and smart. Today again he was wearing his yellow power ranger suit of shorts and matching T-shirt. Her two daughters, who stood leaning against the shop pole, were looking down at us. I guessed it wouldn't be long before they too got pregnant. It was sad to see this poor woman living alone on the streets with all her family. Yet they looked forward to us coming to talk to them. I think we were probably the only people they had met that took any interest in them.

A young kayayo girl who had been sitting watching us in the doorway started to feed her baby water from a plastic bottle top. Mamuna shared her lump of bread with an infant boy sitting nearby, breaking it into two pieces. Another toddler, called Brahari, was eyeing it watchfully from a distance. He saw his chance, pattered over and grabbed it, leaving the other baby screaming. Poppy came to the rescue, taking the bread and dividing it once more so both children got a piece. Everything was divided into smaller and smaller portions. Nobody was left without. The loaves and the fishes.

The girls now began to tell me things they had 'been seeing' while they slept in the doorway. They told me, as had Rebecca and her friends before them, how men would come and lie in the middle of them.

'When he comes to lie with us we expect he wants to do something....but once we realize he is sleeping with us we shout and he runs away.'

This issue of men quietly coming to sleep amongst the girls during the night was a recurring theme in my discussions with the kayayo. The girls had reacted to this by moving and keeping within tight socially knit groups at all times, especially at night. The way they organized themselves in this way protected them for the most part from the rape and sexual assault that could have easily occurred had they been alone or in pairs. The major challenge was for girls whom for one reason or another were not able to live within this flimsy safety net the girls had woven around themselves. This was especially so for those girls who had to leave their homes due to forced marriage. Poppy also reiterated this.

'If a girl runs away because of forced marriage. They (the relatives) will come to Accra to try to find her.'

I had heard this before, however what Poppy told me next was truly bizarre, adding an astonishing twist to these disturbing events,

'For that reason they will usually try to find the young woman who they know is the girl's best friend and then try to force her to tell them where the girl is, where they can find her. They will then beat the friend severely if she refuses to tell them where the girl who ran away is hiding. Sometimes if they don't find the girl, the friend will have to marry the old man in her place.'

I asked Poppy if she did not have to get back to her tea stall. She told me she wanted to talk more, that she would go back very soon. A toddler just then urinated on the floor, Lashida, sitting nearby, used some unwashed clothes to mop it up. Two little toddlers sat before us, and we observed their tiny backs. They were facing the drain and the road beyond. They, not unlike us behind them, were observing the theatre of night time rituals performed amidst the shifting spotlights of cars. The conversation resumed back to the topic of having to leave the village.

I told them that I had heard how the first and often older wives got neglected in the village. I had heard this often drove their daughters to come to Accra.

Poppy told me that this often happened in her hometown, Wialu. She had a friend. Her name was Azetu. She ran away because of being treated badly by the junior wife and her children. The father stopped providing food for the older wife and her children. Poppy explained.

'What happens in the end is that the older wife is left to look after herself and her children.'

She added vehemently,

'Even if older wife is sick he will not help.'

One girl was sitting on a paint pot dozing, she kept keeling over to one side and just as you thought she was going to topple over she straightened up. Lashida smiled with a worried look on her face. Am I doing the right thing? Should I be smiling now? Kadima, with her one tooth smile, nodded in agreement to the views Poppy had been expressing.

I asked Poppy if many girls were forced to marry much older men.

'This happens a lot and if the girls tell their mothers that they don't want go marry and the parents still continue to force the girls, sometimes they hang themselves.'

She added that she knew girls who had drunk poison and died.

I asked her why the girls resorted to such extreme measures. Why didn't they just run away instead?

'Often they don't get the money to run away so they do that instead.'

Of the reasons cited for 'neglect' many of the girls

gave the reason, 'because my father married another wife.' They told me that polygamous marriage was the norm in the north. They all stated unanimously that once their fathers married second younger wives the children of the first wife, and the first wife herself, were neglected, picked on and often abused by both the husband, the younger wife or wives and their respective children.

I told them that I had heard that traditionally the junior 'co-wives' must look up to and respect the senior wife. Poppy replied that in theory or traditionally that should be the case but 'it's not like that' and the husband usually favours the younger wife and her children.

Poppy looked at me. Both anger and sadness flashed across her face, her tone was brutal,

'The new wife will be terrible to the older wife's children and often they have no alternative than to run away.'

In my subsequent interviews with the kayayo many girls told me similar stories. Their mothers and siblings had just been abandoned or neglected by their fathers. Some had been abused. This usually occurred when the husband took a second, third or fourth younger wife. Although it was not usually cited as the main reason for the kayayo leaving their homes to come to Accra it was definitely a contributing factor.

Their stories reminded me of when some years earlier I had got to know a chief's wife in a village in a remote part of the Upper East region of Ghana. We became quite close friends and she started to tell me about her life, and how the women suffer in Ghana. She had married the chief and had several children. When her first daughter reached the age of about thirteen or fourteen her father decided to marry his own daughter's school classmate. This very young girl also bore him children and the same thing again happened. When the first daughter of his second wife reached a similar tender age he again married her school classmate. This continued until he had four wives.

While staying at the village for a couple of weeks I would meet a quite young girl who would be introduced to me by Elizabeth in a jocular tone as 'my rival, this is my rival'. It went on and as the days passed I would meet another girl. 'This is my second rival,' she would tell me facetiously. They were all her co-wives. I knew her son, who was by this time around twenty-one years old. He was very intelligent, fast and streetwise. Yet he one day confessed to me that he could not read or write and he wept. He said his father had 'brought forth' so many children that it would have been impossible for him look after them properly and send them to school. He told me that when he was young he adored his father and disliked his mother. Yet as he grew he realized how much his mother had scrimped and scraped to send him to school from her own daily meagre earnings. Yet in the end she had been unable to sustain this and he had been forced to leave at a young age. He thought very differently of his father now.

Poppy jumped up hurriedly, announcing that she had to get back to her tea stall. She was happy she had this extra job. I told her very shortly I would be visiting her village. As had done all the girls before her, including herself, she gave me a hesitant look and told me I would not be able to find it. I told her I would but she would have to give me the names of the bigger surrounding villages. She smiled and rolled them off, counting them on her fingers as she did so: Sandema, Tumbilu, Yaya. Then beaming and full of energy as always, she waved goodbye and I watched her disappear into the darkness, the yellow light of the naked flames fringing the track, drifting over her body as she strode along.

Chapter Eleven

Does anyone want a lift?

Because of George's work schedule I always had to meet the girls after 4.30pm, which was becoming increasingly inconvenient for me as this was exactly the time my daughter returned from school. My teaching was now freelance so I could organize time to fit in with any schedule. In the light of this I decided I would go to the market alone one day. I would walk further towards the interior of the market, as I had always tended to hang around its perimeter. Both Poppy and her group and Rebecca and her crowd tended to sit around the fringes of Tonga. Also I wanted to try and find some girls to come with me to the north. I was sure there would be someone around the market to translate for me. I decided to go very early before my teenage daughter even awoke.

I walked to Tonga before dawn. A few people were around, and were starting to carry out their ablutions in the street. I could hear metal buckets and saucepans being scraped across the concrete, taps running which were filling up the buckets and saucepans for the morning wash. The sun had not yet started to rise. As always when I got up at this time I couldn't help having this smug feeling that I would be able to cross at least three things off my 'to do' list even before breakfast.

Christmas had now been and gone. The harmattan winds were now at their height. A shimmering mist of fine dust hung over the scene unwinding before me. Hundreds of young girls and babies were slowly beginning to stir. A young woman was waking up slowly. Rubbing her eyes, she extended her arms, yawning. In the distance were what seemed like miles and miles of coloured cloths stretching as far as the eye could see, below which were humps of various shapes and sizes concealing the sleeping bodies of the kayayo and their families. A few were already awake and were starting to wash their babies in the metal bowls. The water was cold. Cooking fires were lit and this smoke mingled with the sea of harmattan dust creating an unearthly atmosphere as if everything was being viewed though fine chiffon. Some men, coming from their compounds to the right side of the track, walked around in their bathrobes brushing their teeth. Litter was everywhere. Many kayayo were 'brushing' their teeth with the chewing sticks or digbas in their mouths, which they intermittently spat onto the floor as each section of the stick was used up. A huge container truck, carrying thousands of large bright green plantains, had just arrived from the Ashanti region, and it gushed out its load onto road as if in the last stages of maternal labour. Fat, fleshy market women sat around starting to barter over their wares and stick-like kayayo stood around with empty bowls waiting to carry them to various places around the sprawling market and beyond.

I came to a group of girls I had spoken to briefly yesterday who had told me they were going back to the north the following Sunday. They had a positively ornate shop front in which to sleep. It was beautifully tiled with broken tiles in different shades of blue. Surrounding it was a high decorative metal grille that could be locked at night. It was compact and safe. They had been lucky with that spot. Behind them the name of the shop was emblazoned on the wall:

VOLTIC DRINKING WATER

There was a young boy standing nearby, perhaps about eighteen years old, and I asked him if he could speak Mamprusi. He could. He also told me he was a student and could speak English fluently. I asked him if he could help me translate while I spoke to the girls sitting around us.

There were about five of them sitting on the tiles. Others from their group were milling around nearby preparing for the day ahead. I spoke first to Lamya who had been in Accra for one-and-a-half years with her child. She said that she could often make quite a lot of money in Accra getting as much as Gh5-6 cedis (£3 Sterling) a day. She spoke in the guttural language I was now becoming accustomed to hearing, slightly reminiscent of Arabic, and I remembered reading how it was believed that many words from the Dagbani/Mamprusi languages had their origins in the Arabic language. She clapped her hands together, turning her palms upwards as if to emphasize her point. This appeared to be a characteristic mannerism of people from this region.

Lamya's son, who looked between eighteen months to two years, was jumping up and down naked on the narrow track on the other side of the metal grille that separated their home from the road. His body was covered, as was everybody else's, including my own, in a thin film of silky harmattan dust which made his body look paler. He turned and smiled at me. His eyes looked exotic, lined with black khol. Lamya was fair skinned, a light nut brown. More girls started to gather round us as the large red sun started to rise in the sky. Lamya and all the other girls within her group had the distinctive Mamprusi marks of two small vertical lines along their cheeks. I saw another girl with different tribal marks and they told me she was a Gonja. She had small diagonal lines fanning out from the corner of her mouth like rays of the sun. What I realized as I got to know this market better was that not only did tribal groups stick together but each small grouping tended to come from adjoining villages.

As I sat there gazing at the broken tiled floor, which was dark-blue, light-blue, powder-blue and turquoise, Lamya told me that she would soon be going back to her hometown near Walewale and that once the 'money was finished' she would come back again to Tonga. She said she couldn't always take as much money as she wanted because the lorry fare was Gh25 cedis and expensive. I saw that as my cue to offer her and perhaps two or three friends a ride. I told her I too had planned to travel to the north next weekend and if she wanted I could take up to three of them plus their babies and luggage and they could go free. I would also give them an extra Gh50 cedis each. They would then make Gh75 each with the saving on the fare. Many of them would have to trudge the streets for months to save that amount. They then started to come out with funny answers. Funny excuses. All of which were being used as a pretext for not being able to come with me.

Firstly, they said that they wouldn't be coming back so therefore they wouldn't be able to come with me. I said that wasn't a problem and indeed if anyone else from the village wanted a lift back to Accra I could bring them. They seemed unsure, hesitant and wary. The next day I went past and asked again this time they said,

'But you can't take us as you don't know the way to Walewale.'

'But I have been there several times before, I even know a family that lives in a village which is nearby,' I replied.

They still seemed reluctant. I asked the boy in the nearby kiosk if he could persuade them. I told him I would increase the money I was willing to pay them to Gh100, the equivalent of months of trudging the streets just for sitting for several hours in an air conditioned car. However, when I returned a few days later they had yet another excuse waiting. This time they told me that even though I knew the way to Walewale, they and also I didn't know the way to their village from Walewale. I said that wouldn't be a problem as we could ask when we reached Walewale. I went away again, and tried for a second or third time to ask some of the neighbours around if they could persuade them to change their minds.

Eventually I got a positive response from the boy in the kiosk. He phoned me and told me to come down as, he said, 'they have agreed a plan'. He told me that eventually after many hours he had succeeded in persuading them to come but, he added, the only hitch was that I would have to take all seven girls with seven babies!

I said that this would be impossible as there wasn't room. I gave up. I then asked George if he could find out if any kayayo who were planning to go home wanted a lift, they could save their fare and I would pay them Gh100. After a couple of days he came back and told me he had scoured the market but hadn't been able to find anyone. Events were now mirroring all the explanations I had been hearing over the past months. That the kayayo will stick together as a group at all costs to maintain both their safety and solidarity, even if this meant losing precious funds of what was to them the equivalent of months of hard work. Their steadfastness in this regard was overwhelmingly strong, their resolve phenomenal and almost inconceivable when seen against the reality of their living conditions.

It was some days later that the young boy who worked at the kiosk again rang me. This time he informed me that the girls now had a 'new idea' and that I should come to meet them that evening to discuss it. When I arrived at their shop front they were not there and the boy told me they had walked to the inner market to wash their clothes. I waited for some time but they didn't come so I asked the boy, called Paul, to accompany me there. It was pitch black, there were hardly any lights, and the place was dotted with large nondescript mounds covered in tarpaulin. The place appeared to be peppered with what looked like large black humps in the darkness. I could see black cats scuttling in between the mounds and pointed them out to Paul. He told me they were rats. I had never seen rats that huge before, the place was crawling with them and now I understood what the kayayo girls meant when they said the rodents disturbed their sleep at night.

We eventually found Lamya and the other girls in her group, bent double doing the day's laundry hidden among the mounds of tarpaulin. A single solitary light bulb hung precariously from a nearby kiosk, casting a faint amber radiance over them. Barefoot, half naked toddlers were chasing each other, running around their mothers in circles, laughing. Once with them I no longer felt afraid or disorientated. Standing within this tight knit cluster of women, girls and children you became distinctly aware of an invisible umbrella enveloping you from the harshness of the world outside. It was an impenetrable group, which attempted to keep all that which lay outside it at bay. There was an imaginary wall surrounding them.

They were excited and happy. They would all be going home soon and wanted to share their latest plan. Paul translated. I was hoping we wouldn't bump into George this evening. I had a legitimate excuse for using another interpreter during the day but now it was evening I didn't. If we were unlucky enough to collide with him while walking round the market he would think perhaps he had lost his job!

The girls talked animatedly.

'We will give you our mobile number so that once you get to Walewale you can ring us. We would have gone the day before on the bus so we will already be in the village when you arrive.'

The plan was then that they would 'direct me' to their village via the phone. I would then come and see them and give them the money!

I envisaged that their talk would be misinterpreted by the villagers, who would probably start to think that 'this lady' would arrive in their village and give everyone Gh100. I thought it best to leave it. I would have to find another solution to the problem. I said goodbye to Lamya, her friends and their children and as I walked away their solitary group were again swallowed up by the darkness. After that night I never saw them again.

What could I do? I decided the only solution was to go alone. I had driven up there and back before alone, I could do it again. Yet that was many years ago, crime in Ghana was now increasing, there had been stories of hold ups, car jackings. I told George the next day that I planned to go alone. Once in Tamale and Bolgatanga I could find someone to accompany me to the villages. George was adamant that I should not drive up there by myself.

'It is too dangerous', he told me, sounding like something was vibrating and stuck in his throat.

'Don't worry, over the next few days I will find someone who can come with you.'

Some days later while walking around my area I ran into Martin the Banker once again. As usual he was impeccably dressed in a navy suit with matching tie. After the customary greetings I told him about the incidents which had occurred with Lamya and her friends. How I had found it almost impossible to persuade any of them to come with me to the north.

'They are like that, they are told before they come to Accra not to trust anyone except themselves, and there have been reported cases of kidnapping and abductions so they only trust each other.'

I understood what he said. It was only by maintaining this complete separation from the world outside that they were able to guarantee even a modicum of security for themselves amidst the threatening and dangerous world which surrounded them. They did not know who I was. I was a foreigner and looked strange to them. Shaking hands, Martin took his leave. He was on his lunch hour and had to rush back to the bank.

Later on I drove past the tree. Many of the girls were there and I stopped and told them I would be leaving to go to their village in a few days. They all laughed and said for the second or third time now,

'You can't find it, it's too far.'

I asked if anyone wanted to come with me for a drink, for a last chat before I left and as usual there was a stampede with about twenty girls all simultaneously trying to push through the doors. I saw Nurah once again. I had not seen her for some months. She said she had come back on the bus some days ago. Mahab had boarded the same 'kayayo bus' going back. Also little Latifa, the stick-like doe eyed girl with the movements of a baby gazelle, had gone back with her. Latifa had now been replaced by her older sister, Rayina, who looked just like her, only bigger. It was like a never-ending conveyer belt moving swathes of humanity north and south in an endless stream.

Nurah, Rayina, and two other girls joined us. Rebecca and baby Madihah were carrying goods some distance away in downtown Accra. I managed to shut the doors of the car quickly and we drove the forty-five second journey down to the Spot. When we got there we found it was closed. They seemed disappointed, and I told them not to worry that we would find another spot, another drinking place. George was conversing with a man outside his workplace, and on seeing us waved his elongated arms towards us excitedly. He joined us saying we would have to be quick as he needed to get back to work. We drove around for about five minutes and we soon found a much larger, nicer place on the other side of the Kanda Highway, the main high road which separated the Nima slum from the other, better side of town. They fell out the car into the adjacent car park but I had to walk alone into the restaurant with George. The girls cowered outside. They were afraid to come in. George and I continued to sit there alone. It was quite a large eatery and several smartly dressed Ghanaians were sitting there eating and drinking. I was then forced to get up and walk outside again to try one last time to persuade them to enter. Eventually they reluctantly slinked in looking very awkward and very shy. They told me they were not used to being in places full of people not 'of them'. George explained that they felt too shy to be sitting in a place with so many different people. They lingered, sitting hesitantly, perched on the edges of their chairs, looking down at the floor. I asked Nurah, who had just returned from the north, what she had taken back when she had gone. She said she hadn't taken many things because the last time she had gone she took many things.

'What did you take this time then?'

'I took money, I took Gh100 cedis (£50 Sterling) with me.'

As the girls all looked so embarrassed to be sitting in this 'posh' café, we soon left and dropped them off at the tree. They waved goodbye, knowing I could never find their village.

The next day George rang to say I should meet him at Tonga on Sunday as he had found someone who wanted to accompany me to the north. That Sunday I arrived early and sat at the Springstrap Road end of Tonga waiting for him to arrive. I sat near to the shop front of Poppy, Mamuna and her group but this morning their patch was empty. I had no idea where they had gone. Here on Sundays a whole new world appeared. It was different from the weekly daylight world of bustling shops. It was different to the nocturnal night time world, where ancient settlements from the parched north reinvented themselves around the empty storefronts. Now it was the 'Sunday world', a world of mainly shuttered up shops with countless temporary market stalls emerging as if from nowhere. These stalls perched themselves precariously along the side of the drain. Many of the 'villages' that inhabited the nocturnal world had disappeared, vanishing with the rising sun. Yet there were still many that remained, those that were lucky enough to live at a shop where the owners stayed away on the Sabbath.

As I sat there waiting, I started talking to a young man whose makeshift stall was beside me. He was selling plastic carrier bags and take-away cartons in bulk to the fast food sellers and market women. I had forgotten my pen and asked him if he could lend me one. He called a small girl who was sitting around and I heard him tell her, 'oh koh toh pen,' in Twi, or 'go and buy me a pen' and he gave her a coin. I insisted that he take the money for the pen, but he was persistent in his refusal.

He told me he was a senior secondary school student (SSS), eighteen years of age, and that he came to the market on Sundays to earn some extra money to help pay his school fees. He then proudly showed me the books which he always brought with him and which he read when not attending to customers. His name was Norman. We started talking about the kayayo. He said the saddest thing for him was,

'When it is raining and they have no rest from the rain.'

While I was talking to Norman I noticed a kayayo girl and her baby still sleeping on a damp step behind us. In fact they were both in an incredibly deep sleep despite the noise and bustle around them. She was lying directly on the cold, damp concrete without even a thin cloth to protect her from it. Her dry withered breast (she was a young girl) was hanging out and lying on the concrete floor near her baby. The infant had obviously been suckling during the night and had fallen asleep. It was a pathetic and sad scene. They were both dirty and flies were crawling over them. In front of this wretched scene of mother and child were two fat women selling bright green okra.

Norman also noticed this poor girl. He pointed to her.

'See the girl needs a mat to sleep on, but she sleeps on the bare concrete.'

He then went on to tell me something I had never heard before but which I did not find surprising.

'It is in exactly in these situations,' he continued, contemplating the sleeping mother and her child, 'it is exactly in these situations where a mother is sleeping with her baby during the daytime, that the baby can wake up and then toddle off on its own, while the mother continues to sleep deeply, like a dead person.'

Someone approached and bought some takeaway cartons, giving him lots of loose change, which he quickly put into his leather school bag tucked under his seat. He resumed his explanation, continuing to gaze at the sleeping mother.

'Obviously the toddler will get lost and disorientated. And often in these situations the women lose their babies.'

He went on to tell me that if the baby was found it would often then get taken to the police station as the market women had no way of knowing who the mother of the child was. He told me that something like this had happened the previous week.

'A mother was sleeping nearby with her baby during the day and the baby wandered off, the mother and the other kayayo girls had no idea where the baby went. They searched everywhere for the baby and couldn't find it.'

He told me that all the kayayo girls were crying.

'When something happens to one girl all the girls from her village gather together and cry and cry.' He added,

'That's what I love and admire about them, they love themselves (each other) too much.'

He went on to tell me that they 'work and work' and that they become so tired they fall asleep 'anywhere they sit down'. And then while they are sleeping their babies and children run about. I had noticed this a lot in the market. The place was teeming with toddlers and even babies who were often running and walking and sometimes even crawling aimlessly around in the middle of the same tracks where vehicles plied. I have often thought that these infants were at great risk of being run over. Norman told me that it was very easy, as the children were roaming in the market with no supervision for,

'Anybody to come along and just pick it up.'

I could see and understand his point. He went on.

'Babies are always going missing but most usually they are found, market women take the baby back to the mother and then start insulting the mother for not minding her baby properly.'

I asked Norman what the market women say to the kayayo. He told me they tell them,

'Your eyes are not open and you are careless.'

Just then I spotted George sauntering towards in me in the distance. He was late. On seeing me chatting to Norman an expression of mortified alarm appeared across his face as if to say, 'have I lost my job?' This was quickly replaced by a fixed yet defiant smile towards Norman.

By now some of the kayayo who had been hanging around at the adjacent shop front had begun to join in our conversation. George, eager not to give Norman a chance, quickly got stuck in, fearing his well laid out plans for European travel were becoming endangered. I told Norman how I couldn't imagine that, in this huge market where between two or three thousand kayayo lived, they could possibly locate the mother of a lost child. How did they manage to trace her? Norman asked the girls how the market women managed to find the mothers. The girls said,

'The kayayo will give an announcement.'

'How?'

'Representatives of the group from which the missing child belongs will walk around the whole market, visiting each of the 'villages in exile' and telling them 'our child is lost'. They will give them the approximate age of the child, what it looks like and was wearing, so that if any one sees and picks the child they will know where to bring it back, they will tell the whole market at what shop front they can find the child's mother.'

The girls also told Norman and now George that the child will most usually be distressed and crying so people will suspect it is lost. She also told us that sometimes a child can go missing for up to three days but,

'It will come back.'

This conversation then broadened into how the kayayo grieve together as a group. I had not heard anything about this before and I was fascinated. It was further evidence of how close knit they were as a unit. The young girl, no more than fourteen years old, standing at the next shop, told me that three months earlier a young kayayo girl had started to give birth in the market and she was rushed to hospital where she later died. She told me that after the death,

'We all contributed small and then we all gathered together and cried.'

She added,

'Some sick because of overwork, they go to hospital and they die.'

She explained that whenever a kayayo girl dies in the market they buried her in Accra. They did not send the body back to the north. The last time a woman from a certain village died, she said, 'they buried her here.'

Then, she explained, they put her cloth (dress) in a calabash and send it back to her village. Also they will put some soil from the girl's grave into another calabash with more of her clothes.

'As soon as the people in the village see the calabash they know that someone has died and the whole village they gather together and cry.'

The slim young kayayo girl, whose hair had been immaculately and beautifully woven with coloured threads and other ornaments, went on to add that when a kayayo girl died at the market, representatives from all the different village groups, that is from each shop front, walked to the shop front from which the dead girl came. She then told me,

'When they arrive at the dead girl's shop front they kneel down and cry.'

Within an hour or two a representative from every village in the market will be crying outside the dead girls 'home'.'

The girl explained further.

'After this we get two or three men to go round and collect money from every kayayo in the market. This could be Gh1 cedi (50 pence Sterling) or 50psws (25 pence Sterling). This money will help us to buy small land to bury the girl.'

Despite their extreme poverty, the kayayo girls are often able to raise quite large sums of money and achieve remarkable feats, due to their pulling together as a group and facing adversity as a strong social unit. Fifty pesawas or one cedi, may not seem much but with three thousand girls it can amount to £1500 Sterling. She told us,

'After all the kayayo girls in the market have contributed, the money will then be divided into two. The first half will be sent back to her village and the other half will be used to buy the land to bury her in Accra. They normally buy land in an area called Awudome, near to the centre of Accra. The land will normally cost about Gh200 (£100 Sterling).

'However the funeral in the village is much bigger than the one in Accra and can cost Gh1000 cedis (about £500 Sterling) and can even at times cost five times as much.

'They buy pito and millet drinks and brew it for three days. They also need to buy fowls, goats and sheep. Then they have to dance for four days.'

Numerous surveys have drawn attention to the amount of money Ghanaians tend to spend on funerals. It was cited in one report that, 'Eighty per cent of Ghanaians live on around $2(this may be higher now) a day (yet) a funeral costs on average between $2,500–$3,000.' This was especially the case for Akan funerals in the south of Ghana. It went on to state that,

'One of the most serious attitudinal problems to have crept into the Ghanaian society is the insatiable desire to invest in the dead rather than the living. We go to bizarre extents to try to outdo each other in the grandeur of the funerals we organize. We take to task our compatriots who for better sanity or lack of resources try to organize relatively modest funerals, describing their efforts as 'burying their loved ones like fowls'. How can a people that hope to develop their impoverished nation become so obsessed with investment in the dead rather than the living?'

The kayayo too were spending excessive amounts of their hard earned cash, cash, which could better be utilized on education or investment, on funeral rites. Norman seemed to be getting busy with his customers so George and I decided to take our leave. It was already getting late and heating up so we decided to cancel the interviews we had planned for that day. George told me, however, that he had found a lady who wanted to join me on my journey north. She wanted to travel there in order to visit her husband who had been posted there by his company. She would travel with me all the way to Bolgatanga. We went to see her and I arranged to meet her by the mango tree early the next morning by 5am. It was all arranged. At last!

Chapter Twelve

Heading to Bolgatanga

The next morning I got to the mango tree before 5am. I was enjoying the silence and desolation in the street, which within an hour would be once again full of life. It was not long before Roberta arrived loaded up with luggage in the 'Check Check Bags', more commonly known as the 'African Suitcase' or 'Ghana Must Go'. She was a plump, fleshy, woman. Her eyes seemed to be too wide apart, almost on the edges of her perfectly rounded face. Her hair was curled into an old fashioned perm. She had on a knee length pink floral dress with high heeled pink shoes. She wore large framed glasses, the frames also tinged pink. She looked in her early fifties. There was that feeling you get when about to embark on a long journey before dawn. Anticipation. Excitement. We drove through the almost deserted streets of Accra. In the distance I spotted another giant poster of Bishop Duncan Williams and the roaring lion beseeching all to join his '3 Days of Prayers and Fasting.' Like Cheiko on the wall at The Spot he was holding a fixed smile, frozen in time. After about thirty minutes more cars started to appear, and by 6am the traffic jams had started. Outside central Accra the traffic jams begin by 5am. I was glad to be out of Accra by six. Lines of traffic were now coming in the opposite direction. We were on the open road. I felt free and exhilarated. I was soon to be disappointed.

About thirty miles out of Accra I was stopped at a police roadblock. I prepared my act. I wound down the window, holding fast the broadest smile that was technically possible.

'Eti sen?' I asked, 'How are you?'

'Where's your license?' he barked, trying as much as possible to appear intimidating.

I handed it over and as usual he didn't look at the expiry date on the front but pointed to some obscure almost indiscernible numbers on the back saying that I had forgotten to renew my license.

I could see a repressed smirk and then he announced in an irate manner,

'Then the issue will have to be decided by the courts, can you pull over and we will have to take you to the police station.'

He turned his back to me, pretending to survey the land behind. I didn't have time to argue so mouthed the expected euphemism which really means, 'how much do you need to let me go?'

'Sir,' I said, fawning, 'Is there any way I could help you?'

The speed with which he turned round could only be measured in mili-seconds.

He eyed a ten cedi and five cedi note on my dashboard. I offered him five cedis.

'It's not enough,' he barked briskly.

I put it back and I offered him the ten cedi note. It was still 'not enough'. So I gave him the two notes totalling fifteen cedis and as I drove off shouted back at him,

'We are told on Ghana TV to report corrupt police officers such as you!'

He didn't care anymore as he'd got his money, which came to approximately £7.50 (Sterling). I was wondering how many more times I would be stopped on the way to Bolgatanga, usually known as Bolga, as at this rate I'd be bankrupt before I even reached there. People who had lived in Nigeria had told me similar stories. How they would take a lot of cash out for their weekly shop. On their way to the supermarket they were stopped so many times by police officers (and those pretending to be police officers) asking for bribes that by the time they reached the shopping mall, they had no money left. Roberta, sitting to my left, told me that the police had been doing this a lot to trotro and taxi drivers, sometimes taking away their entire daily earnings

After about forty-five minutes of driving through the lush green landscape, I saw in front of me another police roadblock. I felt a tight spasm in my stomach. Not again. As I approached I saw they were busy extorting money from some other poor unfortunate driver, my tension dissipated and we drove on. By the time we had reached the outskirts of Kumasi we had passed six police roadblocks, every time bar the first we were lucky in that they were harassing other drivers. I calculated that we had 'saved' approximately £40 Sterling.

Just outside Kumasi we stopped at the roadside for a breakfast of fried egg sandwich and milky tea. We then continued driving. The landscape was lush, tropical, evocative. Swaying coconut trees, the broad deep green leaves of the banana and plantain trees, and the long arched leaves of the numerous palm oil trees laced their way along the highway. The surrounding vegetation towered above us. It was dense. As you drove down the road you felt claustrophobic as if you were driving in a narrow green tunnel with no end in sight. Along the roadside, women in bright colourful dresses sold the produce of this abundance. Fresh green plantains in massive bundles only just cut from the trees, oranges and tangerines arranged in pyramids of six and twelve, blood red tomatoes, pineapples, mangoes of varying degrees of ripeness and colour, the dark reddish orange of the oil palm tree nuts; almost every village we passed was awash with colour and profusion.

We also noticed another not so appetizing red. It was everywhere. On walls and doors. It was on tree trunks. It was on shops and kiosks. It was even on lamp posts. VODAFONE. Not that long ago the company bought a majority stake in Ghana telecom, and there was some controversy surrounding the sale with allegations of bribery and corruption. As part of their aggressive advertising campaign they had almost covered the entire nation in their logo. Whole villages were now covered in red gloss paint emblazoned with the Vodafone logo. In the Akwapuem Mountains, villages with a unique architectural heritage had been completely obliterated by Vodafone's advertising. It was as if Vodafone, or Virgin or T-Mobile had gone to the Cotswolds region and painted every house and historical monument with their cheap paint and logo. It was horrific and sad to behold. Moreover, the villagers were not paid by Vodafone for allowing the company to use their homes as cheap advertising gimmicks. People informed me the company's officials had told them that their houses would be painted 'for free'. Many villagers didn't have the money to paint their houses, so actually felt that Vodafone was doing them a favour. The company was exploiting people's poverty and ignorance and destroying Ghana's heritage. It was the 'vodafonization' of the Ghanaian countryside.

I continued driving, now angry and annoyed. Why was the beauty of Ghana now covered in red? Roberta and I now hit Kumasi, Ghana's second largest city. It is a crazy, bustling, fast city and the capital of the ancient Ashanti Kingdom. It has the largest market in West Africa. I was terrified we were going to get lost, but we seemed to be doing OK. We got to the heart of the city, which I remembered from years back, but then I couldn't find the way back out to join the road heading north. We had to keep stopping and asking people directions. Everyone was very friendly and helpful. The city had grown unbelievably since my last visit over five years ago, testament to Ghana's general overall development and building boom. In addition to the usual red and yellow signs for Vodafone and MTN (a rival mobile phone company based in South Africa), the city was awash with signs advertising local builders and merchants.

KWASI OPPONG BUILDING MATERIALS
JK ANNAN BLOCKSWORKS

I noticed the city was far, far cleaner than Accra. Foreign visitors to Kumasi in the nineteenth century were often astonished both by its cleanliness and orderliness. They reported clean, wide streets with many carefully planted trees, the houses possessed flushing toilets and all garbage was burned on a systematic basis. The Ashanti had famously defeated the British in some of the numerous wars which had taken place between themselves and the colonial forces during the nineteenth century. During this time it was the famous female Ashanti warrior, Yaa Asantewaa of the Ejisu-Juaben district of the ancient kingdom, who insisted on the final uprising against the British in 1900. In her speech to the Ashanti court she famously pronounced,

'Now I see that some of you (the men) fear going forth to fight for our king. Is it true that the bravery of Ashanti is no more? I cannot believe it. It cannot be! I must say this: If you the men of Ashanti will not go forward then we will. We, the women, will. I shall call upon my fellow women. We will fight. We will fight till the last of us falls in the battlefields.'

It was with this call that she took on the leadership of what was to be ultimately the last Ashanti uprising against the British. On 1st January 1902 the British achieved what the Ashanti army had prevented them from realizing for almost a century and it was on this day that the mighty Ashanti Empire was eventually made a protectorate of the British Crown.

We passed a row of about six kayayo girls. All were sitting in their bowls fast asleep with their heads propped up against a wall. All six had covered their faces with striped hankies to keep out the sun and dust. It looked comical and I wished I had time to fetch my camera from the back of the car. But we were lost. Cars were hooting, people shouting at us to move.

Eventually after spending almost two hours going round in circles we managed to get out of Kumasi. We were now back onto the main road heading north towards Techiman and Kintampo. We drove through the Brong Ahafo Region, which separates the north and south of the country. It was at this this moment that my car decided to start playing up and it continually cut out whenever I accelerated too much, causing me to panic that we were going to be marooned in the middle of nowhere.

Roberta and I now stopped at a roadside kiosk in Kintampo called 'Papaye Fast Food,' emulating the popular Lebanese owned fast food chain found in Accra and Kumasi. After trying to force down a disgustingly tasteless meal of chicken and rice we continued driving towards the north. I could no longer drive fast for fear of the car cutting out and coming to a halt. Despite driving as carefully as I could, it continued to cut out about every twenty minutes or so. We then had to both get out and Roberta held up the bonnet while I pumped the diesel filter. We had to do this regularly and it was slowing us down considerably.

Around us now the landscape generally started to change, the lush towering trees gave way to shorter more scrubby varieties like baobabs and acacias. Banana, plantains and coconut trees now became less common sights, although the giant mango trees, their shape always reminding me of the ancient British oaks, still abounded. Shea nut trees were becoming increasingly common. Neem trees, although also common in the south, could now be seen more clearly here as the density of vegetation changed from lush jungle to open grasslands. The deep green grass of the south was now becoming drier, more yellow. After Kintampo, the last major city before we hit the north, the architecture too began to change. Grass roofs started to become more common and the shapes of houses became less rectangular, and more rounded. The trees were getting sparser and shorter, and as we turned a corner of a hill a wide vista opened up as far as the eye could see. Miles and miles of beige ochre coloured sahelian savannah, dotted with deep green mango and shea nut trees. We were in the North.

The map of colour dazzled the eye. It was the dry season and various hues of yellow, beige and brown now characterized the landscape. The teak trees that lined the roads were shedding their leaves, reminding you of a temperate clime's autumn, almost leaving their branches completely bare. Areas of blackened vegetation could be seen everywhere, tell tale signs of either forest fires or slash and burn agriculture. New vegetation pushed its way back through the blackened cover, now a more brilliant shade of green than you could ever imagine.

We continued driving up through this parched landscape. It was 4.30pm. I was tired. I had been driving for more than eleven hours along some severely potholed roads. Suddenly the sky turned purple, and an immense wind blustered across the road making the car career horizontally, like an empty cardboard box being lifted by a gust. I felt confused. We were in the middle of the dry season, yet rainstorms were looming. Was this evidence of climate change again? I had read in one book that climate change could affect parts of West Africa in a way that would actually make the climate wetter. The storm broke suddenly. Rain banged down on the car. I started to get worried. Images of the recent flash floods raced through my memory. Hundreds dead. Thousands made homeless. Branches broke off the trees with ease like matchsticks and blew across the road. Visibility was now almost zero. The wind was making it impossible to drive in a straight line. I saw a few huts and thought it best to stop for a while. If anything did go wrong at least there would be others around. We saw a few cars crawl past, their headlights on. After about another ten minutes the storm subsided and we resumed our journey. We had now been driving for twelve hours and I doubted we would reach Bolga before dark. Driving after dark now in Ghana is not advised, as there can be hold ups and armed robberies. We crossed the bridge. Beneath us the wide Black Volta River meandered. I rang Salifu, the young university graduate who had accompanied me to interview the Dagomba girls in downtown Accra some months before. He was still on vacation from University and had said he would like to translate for me in Tamale. He had arranged a small guesthouse where we could stay. He told me his friend would meet us and we parked near the main State Transport Corporation bus station to wait for him. The friend would then accompany us to the guesthouse. Salifu's family home was nearby. Roberta and I were waiting for some time. Outside the car it was hot, dusty, raucous. I needed a shower, to eat, to sleep. I was exhausted. I rang the cell phone number that Salifu had given me. His friend answered. I told him the exact location where we are waiting, that we were two women waiting in a red car.

He rang back some minutes later.

'I have found your car. The red Mitsubishi but you are not in it.'

I assured him we were in it. Eventually he saw us and we drove to the hotel. The relief of being able to shower and wash away all the dust was indescribable. Later Salifu arrived and we walked across the road to his house where we were introduced to his parents. On returning to the guesthouse I asked what time breakfast would be served. I wanted to get an early start. The man at reception told me, smiling broadly,

'In this guesthouse breakfast is compulsory.'

I had visions of those refusing breakfast being tied to their dining chairs and having it forced down their throats.

The next morning I awoke early. I switched on the TV. It was a programme called 'Good Morning Jesus'. Pastor Beatrice Asante from Kumasi was gyrating across the screen to the sound of Gospel Music. I turned it off. I decided to go for a walk. Outside the sun was just rising, the sky tinged a pale pink and the narrow dusty streets were deserted save for a few goats and fowls. I needed the peace and tranquillity after the exhausting journey the previous day. I walked around for some time, savouring the peace and desolation that would very soon be broken. I then walked back to the guesthouse. I soon met Roberta in the compound and after our compulsory breakfasts we left for Bolga. After driving a few hours we arrived at 10am. It was here we said our goodbyes. I told her I hoped we would meet again when she returned to Accra.

The hotel was old. Ancient mango trees grew in its courtyard, bestowing much needed shade. For the rest of the day I just rested. Later in the afternoon I went to see if I could offer someone the small job of translating and accompanying me the next day on what would be my long journey to Bandugu and Wialu villages. I would be travelling on very remote roads so was keen to have one or two other people with me. Having a few extra faces in the car would make me feel more reassured. In fact although these deserted long roads did seem more lonely and intimidating on the surface, the likelihood of being held up on them was much less than on the major roads. As someone had pointed out to me earlier, the only people who would be travelling on these roads would be those on their way to and from the villages and they wouldn't have much to steal, meaning most robbers would not be interested to hang around in such places. As it turned out, once out of Bolga the only vehicles I did see, other than my own, were mopeds, bicycles, a few buses and one Vodafone car probably on its way to emblazon its logo on some national monument in a far-flung corner of the country.

At the reception I asked a talkative young girl if she knew of anybody who could speak Mamprusi and English who would like to travel with me for the day. Even though Bolga was not so far from the kayayo girls' villages it was in fact home to a different tribe who spoke Frafra. Most Frafra were Christian whereas most Mamprusi were Moslem. Later, Sandra, the receptionist told me she had found a lady who would come with me the next morning. She also told me there were two, could I take both? I again thought of safety in numbers and said it would be fine.

We left early. Mary, an extremely petite woman, with her hair plaited into cornrows, sat next to me. She had a pleasant air about her, and wide, open, friendly eyes that seemed to smile on their own, without any effort from her. Her friend Faustina sat in the back. Faustina was the exact opposite. She was tall and lanky, her hands huge and elongated. She had a mannish air about her and wisps of hair sprouted from her chin. Her facial expression seemed to be set in stone. Stubborn. Intractable.

As we drove, the vista before us was amazing. There were wide, open spaces, the air was full of a characteristic aromatic woody smell which I always noticed when coming up here. Something similar to sandalwood or patchouli. On the way to Sandama small groups of black and white pigs could be seen eating from rubbish dumps. Light skinned Malians and Nigerians (from Niger) could be seen begging by the roadside, environmental refugees escaping the spreading drought north in the Sahara. Many of the houses in the north, unlike the south, had not been painted (either by themselves or Vodafone) and still retained the colour of the earth from which they were built. The houses and the earth around blended into a parched, brown ochre monochrome.

All along the route, more noticeable in the north as the landscape was not so dense, was the litter of literally thousands of plastic and polythene bags. As the wind blew they hooked on to trees, bushes and other vegetation, blowing like tattered flags in the wind. Flocks of grey speckled wild Guinea Fowl ran intermittently across the road. The meat from this fowl is popular in the north. Shea nut trees were becoming much more common. A man rode by on his bicycle with a live pig strapped to the back of it. The pig was screaming. As the large red sun gathered pace over the horizon we saw groups of children, walking single file along the road to school, their books balancing on their heads. We saw a man whose face was completely covered by the tribal marks of the Frafra, lines going diagonally across his whole face. This scarification is not practised much now and tends to be seen only on older people. The road from Bolga to Sandema was starting to deteriorate; increasingly it was covered with potholes. It was not always easy to spot them in time to slow down and the car kept bashing into them. As we progressed I saw that a lot of the traditional grass roofs were gradually being replaced by shiny new aluminium ones. This was always an indication of increasing prosperity in Africa. I started to wonder if it was the money that the kayayo were bringing back from Accra that was financing this. I remember 'the old lady', Poppy's friend, telling me she was saving to bring some back, and how Mr Martin Senior had said you often saw these roofing sheets tied to the roofs of the buses taking the kayayo back to their villages. I also noticed a lot of people riding shiny new motorbikes. The last time I was in the north, about seven years ago, most people were still riding bicycles. Money was coming from somewhere, but it was not evenly distributed.

As we entered Sandema, each side of the road was flanked with massive neem trees. Neem trees are traditionally used in Ghana to treat malaria. The leaves are boiled and the water from it drunk. It was from this tree that the drug quinine was extracted. Quinine has for many years been one of the main medications used to treat malaria. The road leading to Sandema was regal, majestic. The towering trees joined mid-way across the road shaping a long green tunnel. Many donkeys grazed by the sides of this boulevard. In the north they were used with carts to transport goods or as beasts of burden to carry loads, much like the kayayo girls in the south.

We stopped for breakfast in Sandema. The tribe here was called Bulisa. In the north there were many different tribes and languages can change every few miles. The Bulisa houses looked stunning, built like fortresses, two or three stories high. We pulled up in the town and sat down at a round table outside a small wooden kiosk. I asked for three sandwiches with one fried egg in each. The vendor told me she couldn't fry one egg she only fried two at a time. We kept insisting we only wanted one egg and she wouldn't budge. I couldn't fathom why it took me so long to come up with the solution that she beat and make an omelette with three eggs and then cut this into three pieces, but for some reason it did and this chit chat about the eggs went on for several minutes. She eventually agreed to use three eggs and cut it into three pieces. As I, Mary and Faustina sat under the neem tree munching our much anticipated egg sandwich with milky sweet tea we watched a blurry picture on a TV that had been placed on top of a high table inside the kiosk. On it there appeared to be some kind of riot going on. I heard that a president had stepped down, not far from here really, just on the other side of the Sahara, in Tunisia.

Faustina continually looked sullen. A scowl seemed to be fixed impermeably on her face. She never spoke. A mentally challenged or 'madman' as they are referred to in Ghana approached us. He smiled and waved and said hello, probably not seeing many strangers in this small town. A gang of teenage boys then came up proceeding to punch and throw stones at him, shouting at him to get away. The man ran away, shouting back at them. The teenage boys, the shopkeepers and market ladies were all laughing. The teenage boys looked over at us smugly, as if they had done a good job in driving him away, saving us from certain destruction. I had seen this many times in Ghana, when mentally challenged people were just taunted and abused.

As we continued to sit under the neem tree, the mentally challenged man again slowly started to approach us. A smartly dressed man nearby spoke to us in a reassuring tone.

'Don't worry, so long as I'm sitting here he will not attempt to come near!'

I continued eating my sandwich and tea. I asked the man sitting with us (with the kayayo in mind) whether he thought the people coming back from Accra with money was making a difference to the economy in the north.

'It will not help, but if people get help in the form of new technology for the land it will help more...the money is in the soil.'

He went on to say that the kayayo only go down to Accra to get money for their daily needs. This 'will not develop the economy.'

I glanced again over at the TV. The programme had changed. Displayed across the screen now was an affluent middle class Accra family with two children. The two doting parents were standing either side of their children. Behind them was the shiny new three-bedroom house they had just purchased with a mortgage financed by The Housing Finance Corporation (HFC)...the ad went on to say,

'Open an account with us and within eighteen days you will qualify for a housing loan.'

As I looked around me it all looked so different. Yet despite this poverty in the North, many areas of Ghana were booming, even Tamale itself was now one of the fastest growing towns in West Africa.

We set off again on the dreadful potholed roads and after travelling for many miles at a slow pace we reached the remote town of Tumbilu. We were there confronted by a towering telegraph pole for the MTN mobile phone company. We continued shuttling along the road, now no longer tarmacked. We were now on dirt roads. We reached a large village called Chanchiwe. There was a sign:

ONCHO FREE ZONE

This referred to the disease, onchocerciasis, commonly known as 'river blindness', which is endemic in these areas. Suddenly a huge bus pulled up near a crossroads. It was full to bursting and so much stuff had been tied to the roof that it looked like it was about to topple over. Even people were sitting on the roof. Mary told me the bus was on its way to Accra and I could see many kayayo squashed inside. Were they making their first trip from this desolate area? We drove for another twenty or thirty minutes not seeing a thing. Just sand, scrub and desolation. We passed another old faded sign:

AIDS IS REAL

We had now been driving, albeit slowly, on this appalling road for almost an hour with no sign of any houses, villages or vehicles. I was silently beginning to panic. Never before in Ghana had I driven so long without seeing any sign of humanity. I was beginning to think we were in the middle of nowhere. Suddenly we saw a beautiful Fulani girl in her stunning tribal dress, she was walking alone on the track that had now become our road. We then also saw a herd of cattle, with a solitary male herder. I stopped the car to talk to her and she ran for it into the bushes. She disappeared. This led Faustina to mouth her first words that day.

'She is afraid, she thinks we are going to grab her and take her away somewhere, we are strangers to her. That's how the kayayo girls are, they are afraid of strangers and stick to themselves.'

We drove through a cloud of dust, the road had now become soft sand, we saw another old and battered sign:

WORLD VISION: WEST MAMPRUSI
DEVELOPMENT PROGRAMME

Well, I thought, at least we were in the Mamprusi area. A characteristic of the more remote poor areas of

Africa and Ghana was that the only activity you tended to see around was that carried out by NGOs. Amidst all this desolation and wilderness I was surprised to see yet another MTN pole, near the village of Yaya. After soldiering on for about another thirty minutes, despite the constant reassurances from villages that 'Bandugu was not far' we eventually reached the place.

It was a neat, clean village, spread out on a gentle slope that rose from the small track. The buildings were of a traditional structure and architecture and almost all had grass roofs. There were many trees around giving much needed shade.

I felt a bit odd walking in; the village was much bigger than I had imagined (I had imagined maybe just a few huts) and I wondered if I would be able to find Rebecca's parents, Latifa and her family, Nurah's parents and family. Their names were quite common and I guessed there might be quite a few Latifas and Nurahs around. Yet first, as custom and protocol demanded, we had to visit the village chief, to greet him and let him know the reason we had come to the village. It was always customary to bring a gift so I had bought some money, a lot of it in small change as I knew that almost everyone I spoke to would want a 'gift' and I remembered what Poppy had said. When you arrive back home, EVERYONE comes out to greet you in the expectation of getting a 'dash'.

Mary told him about the book I was writing, and that we knew Nurah, Latifa, and Rebecca and Mahab. Suddenly I saw a beautiful, tall, strong young woman running towards me, some distance away. It was Mahab! Suddenly my fear of having to leave the village without identifying the people I had come to see vanished. She was one of the first girls I had met under the mango tree in Accra. She looked in a state of shock and disbelief. She kept shaking her head, covering her shocked wide-open mouth.

'How did you find us?' she screamed.

I think Mahab thought their village was far too remote for anyone except themselves to know about or even find. She continued to look at me, shouting, 'hey!' shaking her head with disbelief and clapping her hands simultaneously. I knew Latifa was at the village and I asked Mahab if she was around. I was told that the man who had been observing us from the foot of a large mango tree nearby was Latifa's father. He was a tall, strong, quite handsome man, looking in his forties. He was wearing the long ankle length kaftan, common in this area. He had a gentle but confident manner, his confidence was tinged with a sense of pride and dignity. The people held on to their sense of dignity at all costs, however wretched their lives became, and I could see the wide smile, so characteristic of Latifa and her sister, on his face. Faces from Accra being redrawn on faces in villages hundreds of miles away.

I asked Latifa's father about his daughter. Was he not worried that his young daughter who looked no more than twelve years old was roaming around and sleeping out in the open in a big city? He replied,

'In the name of almighty God anytime she is there I am not afraid.'

He told me they had heard about the sakawa, the organized crime syndicates but went on to say,

'You can even sit in your house and someone can attack you. We give all to God.'

I asked Latifa's father how many children he had. He told me he had eleven children with two wives. Then darling little Latifa arrived. I could see her coming towards my car, we greeted and I gave her a big hug. She seemed very shy and probably like Mahab, could not believe that I was actually there. She looked a little worried. Perhaps she thought I had arrived in the village to report on her antics in Accra? I felt like the school board man who we all used to fear when I was a kid, the man that let your parents know about all what went on when they were not around. All I needed was a clipboard and a pen. She was no more the boisterous, mischievous Latifa who would, surrounded by her peers, beckon me from the roadside. Her long delicate spindly arms and legs still reminded me of a baby gazelle, and she could not look me in the eye, only smile at the ground.

Soon after I was told that a girl who had been leaning against a tree, with her hands holding onto the overhead branches was Rebecca's sister. She resembled Rebecca a lot and I could see her features in her sister's face. In most cases I didn't need to be introduced as I could see the family resemblance immediately. She stood, swinging from side to side, holding on to the branch, just smiling at me. Then I realized that these apparently rootless girls, who were treated as homeless vagabonds in Accra, had a beautiful village, where they were cherished and surrounded by their loved ones. Here these girls were looked up to. Here strangers couldn't treat them with contempt. Here they belonged.

More and more people started to gather on the dagbala, a type of wooden seat, under the mango tree. Latifa's mother had now come down, and like nearly all women of childbearing age in this region had a recent new arrival strapped to her back, a baby of about four months. The baby had moved round to her hip and was pulling her left breast into his mouth. These mothers seemed to constantly have one breast hanging out of their blouses almost all of the day, satisfying the demands of their babies. Latifa's mother was a short, dark woman. She seemed confused and bewildered by the whole carry on. She didn't seem to know what was going on, why I was there, how I knew Latifa. Maybe she thought I was someone from the government inspecting her children. Why was her daughter in Accra and not at school? Due to their semi-illegal status on the city's streets the kayayo tended to get frightened of any person who represent officialdom. Latifa, a little girl, thought I had come to report on her antics in the town; her mother thought that maybe she would be in trouble for allowing her daughter to go to Accra, Latifa's father excused himself by putting all in the hands of God. There were a lot of mixed emotions at play.

The crowds around us were becoming too much and I asked if I could talk to Latifa's mother alone, perhaps in her house. Mary and Faustina could translate. I told them that I wanted to go to Latifa's mother's house alone. I didn't know how this was translated, but we were followed to her house, which was up a gently rising slope, by an even bigger crowd of about thirty people, many of them children. Instead of the homely living room conversation that I had envisaged we were followed into the compound by this same huge crowd who duly surrounded us on all sides, laughing wildly when things I said were translated. I think Latifa's mother was under the impression I wanted to see where she lived. The heat was rising to unbearable temperatures.

I asked Latifa's mother in front of our now large audience how Latifa's money from Accra helped the family. She told me she had five children and Latifa was the oldest, she also said that she wanted all her children to go to school. At the moment, it was only the two boys who went to school.

'I use some of Latifa's money to send the two boys to school.'

Although primary school was free in the north she still needed money to buy books, stationary, uniforms. I told her that it was also good to send girls to school and added that in my own country girls were now out performing boys in many subjects.

'It's not like that in Ghana,' she said, looking confused.

I asked her that if she had plenty of money what would she like to do?

She said she would use the money for farming and trade. Many kayayo had told me that they would like to do trade, but I wondered if it was really beyond their reach? Wasn't it rather that they didn't know how to start, how to pool resources to achieve it? Yet they were able to pool and manage their own resources efficiently when they participated in susu and other savings schemes.

One of the main policy recommendations of one report into the kayayo suggested that 'drop in' centres which were currently provided for the mainstream population for literacy purposes should also be provided near to the kayayo's places of work. These, in addition to basic literacy programmes, could provide 'business education' along with measures that could improve the kayayo's access to the formal banking system. It also recommended the provision of low cost credit systems that would enable the girls to purchase any equipment that may be needed to improve their skills and income. The report interestingly stated that the proven track records of the kayayo's rigid adherence to their own savings schemes suggested that such credit schemes 'would be most unlikely to run aground due to non-payment'. I also deeply felt that if they were pointed in the right direction and given appropriate support the kayayo would be able to climb much higher up the skills ladder and become very astute entrepreneurs. They always seemed to use their savings for basic survival needs, especially cooking pots and clothes rather than trying to reinvest it. Latifa's mother went on to say that,

'I want to trade but I have no money, if they built factories and work here we wouldn't go anywhere.'

I knew The Body Shop had an outlet in Northern Ghana where local women processed shea butter; if only more companies could come to the area to process and manufacture their raw materials then the mass exodus of the region's young females may be at least abated to some extent.

Mahab kept disappearing for five or ten minutes and then reappearing, eyes still wide with disbelief, shaking her head and clapping her hands. I think she will remember and be talking about this day for years to come.

I walked towards to the dagbala positioned at the bottom of the mango tree near to where my car was parked. I was not given the privacy I strived with Latifa's mother, but anyway I guessed that to be able to really get her confidence would have taken weeks or even months.

We sat under the shade for some minutes. A short while after another woman arrived. She was a handsome middleaged woman, dressed beautifully in a green kaftan dress with matching scarf. She had an air of gentle calmness about her. She was dignified with a regal air. She told me her name was Memonatu. She was Nurah's mother. I was not surprised as her manner and gentleness was so similar to that of Nurah. She spoke to me about her daughter.

'She was attending school but because of financial problems she stopped. She was by then grown enough. She went to school for five years.'

When I asked her if she was worried that her daughter was in Accra she said she was not worried but happy that she was there. She told me that Nurah was about sixteen or seventeen. She told me she had eight children and four of them were at school. Of these four two were girls and two boys.

'Nurah's money also helps with the school.'

An old weatherworn man with leathery skin sat next to Memonatu on the dagbala. He sat still, gazing vacantly into the distance. His eyes looked glazed as if covered by cataracts. I was told he was Rebecca's father. He looked old enough to be her grandfather, even great grandfather, and I remembered the stories of Elizabeth and her husband marrying her daughter's classmates. I asked him about Rebecca.

'She was at school but unfortunately she got pregnant in Tamale.'

I asked him when she would come back to Bandugu. He told me he was not sure when she would be coming back.

My cell phone rang. It was my son in London wanting to know where I had put the scissors! One good thing about having giant telegraph poles dotting this wilderness was that now most places were within the reach of cell phones. Rebecca, Nurah, Latifa and her sister, Aysha and Mahab could ring home and talk to their families. Even though their phones were often stolen they could borrow a friend's phone and ring anytime.

The village chief then appeared once again and sat down on the dagbala. I wanted to ask him about the life of the kayayo girls in the village. He told me in his language, that when they were growing up, during the dry season, which was now, there was no work or money so they had go to Accra to work and buy the things they needed. He told me,

'They suffer down there, that's why they come back.'

'What type of jobs do the kayayo usually do in the

village?'

He told me that they usually did farming. They helped with the rice harvest and cowpea harvest, but other than that there was little for them to do. Once the harvesting was finished there was no work.

The chief conceded that sometimes during the dry season the people in his village did go hungry, especially when there was not enough rain. He then told me, as I later heard from an NGO officer in Bolga, that even when it did rain during the rainy season, it often caused damage.

'Floods have now started to come and it destroys our crops.'

I had remembered reading in one publication that due to the frequency and severity of flooding in some parts of the northern region, certain tribespeople would need to permanently relocate.

Realizing that most of the young girls travelled to Accra during the dry season as there was no work, I asked him what the men did during this time?

'During this time, many of the men are engaged in building and also repairing the houses and grain stores. They do this by using mud, or mud mixed with cement, in the traditional way.'

I had seen this being done on my journey up to the village. We all continued to sit together under the protective shade of the neem tree looking out to the horizon. Some of us were on the dagbala, others were seated on logs strewn around nearby. A boy climbed a tree to get a bird's eye view of us all.

'What is a normal average working day in the village?' I asked the chief.

'After breakfast, they leave to travel to their farms between six and seven. Some of the farms are far, some are not far.'

Mary kept reminding me that time was beating us.

We had to get to the next village and back to Bolga before dark. Whenever I glanced up, I could see her anxious face gazing at me. We said goodbye to the chief and left them all under the tree. I offered the chief some money and after that quite a few others gathered round. By the time I left the village, I had given money to so many people that I had lost count and I had become considerably poorer. Faustina was sullen faced and had still not hardly uttered a word. I had the impression she was not enjoying our trip to the villages. I was later to find out why.

We continued to drive along the now sandy track. The hatchback door of my car would not shut properly and the car was consequently becoming full of red dust. We were literally covered with it from head to toe, and were constantly coughing due to the irritation it was causing at the back of our throats. Today I wasn't having so much trouble with the car cutting out all the time as I could only drive very slowly and therefore could not accelerate. The tarred road had ended at Sandema, the electricity at Tumbilu. We were now on the way to Wialu, Poppy's village. The road had now deteriorated to the point where we could only go about fifteen miles an hour. Dust was getting in my eyes, making them sore. I asked Faustina if she was OK and I got the usual nod with a sullen face. I had seen no other traffic coming in either direction for a long time, making me feel that it was only people (or a person) like me that would be foolish enough to travel on this road and it would be at our peril! I could imagine the sign. 'Those who venture beyond this point do so at their own risk!' I had only myself to blame. I also saw very few people walking along. The distance between villages was vast.

We eventually reached Wialu. The first thing I noticed was a small wooden table set up on the side of one of the tracks. It was selling phone credit. There were scratch cards for MTN, Vodafone and Zain. I topped up my phone with MTN. We then started to enquire after Poppy's husband. We went straight to the chief's house to get that over and done with. We entered his compound, which was large, comprising of various huts leading off the main central courtyard. These huts would be for the different wives and their families. We entered his small grass roofed adobe hut. Inside a very elderly man was asleep on a mat. His room was full of what appeared to be fetishes of various kinds. As he awoke the men who had led us there lay prostrate before him on the ground, just as George had done at Tonga Market some weeks earlier. They then got up, continuing to bow low, clapping intermittently. I gave him the customary gift of some money before we left.

The village was made up of traditional Mamprusi circular compound houses, many with grass roofs and like many areas in the northern region it was literally covered with the litter of plastic bags, white black and transparent, making the whole village look like a rubbish dump.

After visiting the chief, we were told that Poppy's husband and children were not in the village as she had said, but rather they were in Kumasi where her husband worked as a teacher. I was beginning to wonder if we had got the right village. I hadn't known that Poppy's husband was educated and a teacher but I had noticed she always seemed very proud when mentioning him. She often liked to talk about her husband. I proceeded to read out the names that Poppy had given me and then gave them the names of Poppy's parents. We followed our two elderly guides for some time before eventually arriving at a large compound house. We then said goodbye to the elders and once again I had to dole out money to them as gifts. I now had hardly any money left and hoped we wouldn't meet too many people on the way back.

We sat there and waited for a while. One lady was cooking in a large blackened pot over an open fire in the centre of the compound. Another group of women and girls had their hands submerged in what looked like a massive vat of brown goo. I was told they were making shea nut oil using an age-old traditional method. After some time a very elderly couple appeared in the compound. The old woman had a small child balancing on her hip. We were told these were Poppy's parents. I asked them if we could take some pictures, both for myself and for Poppy. They agreed, continuing to look bemused and bewildered. The village had that deadened feeling that I had noticed in many remote villages of Ghana, where all those with any prospects, energy, or education had long since left, leaving the place abandoned to the old or less able.

They told me that Poppy did not come back to the village often and this made them sad and unhappy. They then added that even when she did come it was not for long.

'How long was it?'

'She comes for one week.'

I thought this was unusual as normally when the kayayo came back to their villages after a stint in Accra they normally stayed for some months, often several. They told me that Poppy's children were with her husband in Kumasi.

The elderly couple, just like the village itself, had this forsaken air about them that blended in with the general atmosphere of the place, as if all their children had grown and gone leaving them only to their memories.

I asked whether the fact that Poppy did not spend

long at the village was because her husband and children were in Kumasi?

'Yes, because he and the children are there she goes there more often.'

'Does her husband come to the village?'

'No he doesn't come much and doesn't bring the grandchildren.'

I asked if she was worried that Poppy was alone sleeping on the streets of Accra?

'No.'

'Why?'

'Because she is with her people.'

'Had Poppy been to school?'

Her mother told me she had completed JSS and SSS. SSS is equivalent to A levels in the UK and takes Ghanaian children up to the age of eighteen or nineteen. I doubted this, as I knew Poppy could not read or write, neither could she speak a word of English. I wondered once again if we were talking about the same person. Did I come all this way, suffer this entire journey just to end up talking to strangers about a person I did not know?

After giving out another load of money to the people in this compound I ran out of small change and had to run back to the 'Vodafone Shop' in the village to buy more credit in order to get more change. I then proceeded to hand out more small notes to a profusion of hands coming towards me. I thought it best to leave soon before I became bankrupt. I noticed Faustina surveying the rubbish all over the village. She became animated and suddenly broke out of her self-imposed silence.

'These villagers, they don't know how to be clean, they are uncivilized.'

Now I knew why for most of this trip she had had this scornful look on her face, she was thinking that she was having to spend time and mix with people who were 'beneath her'. This kind of attitude is common in Ghana, indeed it is common all over the world. Where those from lowly positions who manage to do a 'bit better' and move on, then pour scorn on anyone who prods them with reminders of the origins they would much rather forget.

We drove back to Bolga in a sea of dust. It was blinding our eyes and making us cough. About half way home, amidst a massive cloud of dust that reached a height of about thirty feet, we saw another large bus, which Mary said this time was bringing the kayayo back rather than to Accra. The bus, as had been the one we'd seen earlier, was loaded to the point of tipping over. Many people were lying on the huge piles of grain that had been tied to the top of the bus. The bus stopped and people began to disembark, making their way on foot towards their various villages. I boarded the bus to peep inside. It was pandemonium. I'd never seen such a crowded bus in Ghana and these days in Accra, Kumasi and other large cities this wouldn't be allowed. It was impossible to walk down the central gangway so people were just exiting the bus by climbing out of the windows. Small babies were being passed down the bus from person to person till they reached the exit. Some babies were being handed down through the bus's windows.

After much heat, dust and perspiration we eventually got back to Bolga just as the sun was beginning to set. Mary, Faustina and I were all now coloured a reddish brown from the dust which completely covered us. It took several washes to get it off. Mary and Faustina got down, and for the first time since morning Faustina smiled. Most probably it was from relief!

The next morning I had some appointments with

NGOs. I set off early. I had washed several times but still had not yet managed to eradicate all the dust. I first went to an organization called 'Platform for Development'. They told me that one of the main problems in the north, which was leading to many of its young people ending up on the streets of Accra, was the fact that all the industry in the region had collapsed. There had once been a thriving tomato industry and factory in Bolgatanga, which had been run by the government and set up during the presidency of Kwame Nkrumah. The factory, which was government owned in the 1970s, collapsed in the 1980s due to bad management. Ghana, then called the Gold Coast, was the first African country to win its independence from colonial rule in 1957. Nkrumah had fought for Ghana's independence and had become the country's first president.

They went on to tell me that there were a massive amount of tomatoes grown in the North, but he said dejectedly,

'Who would come and buy them?'

I told him that these days almost all Ghana's tinned tomatoes and tomato puree, which were used daily by every family in the nation, were now imported from Italy. It would be a great idea for someone to set up a tomato processing factory in Bolga.

'Where can we get the money?'

'There are loans.'

I've noticed there is a total lack of vision when taking advantage of especially agricultural opportunities in Ghana. Many people are uninterested in agriculture, seeing it as 'backward'.

'They also tend to pick the tomatoes when they are very ripe,' added Richard the NGO official.

He went on to explain that it was difficult to bring the tomatoes into town from the deep rural areas, the villagers had no cars, and they had to bring them in on a donkey cart; sometimes they would bring them in on a trotro. I thought that if there was a factory established in the area a truck would be able to pick up the tomatoes from the farmers at various collection points in the rural areas and bring them into Bolga or Tamale.

'When the farmers get to the market they can't sell the tomatoes and many of them will rot.'

Richard told me that it was a sad paradox that in a region where seasonal hunger was common, masses of food in the market was rotting uneaten, unable to provide a living for those who grew it. Richard said there had also been a meat industry, and there had been a factory, but this too had collapsed.

Were there any other industries in the north?

He said there was shea nut production in the Northern, Upper East and Upper West Regions but they had sent the factory to Accra. Richard continually kept talking about how the government wouldn't do anything, but I told him that individuals could also do something.

I mentioned onions and he said these were 'good' as they could be stored. Onions were more durable. I also mentioned the countless mango trees that dotted the countryside of the entire northern region. Most of these mangoes too ended up rotting under the trees from which they had fallen. It was a terrible waste.

He concluded by saying that the only thing that would minimize the kayayo heading south was if the government could attract foreign investment to the area to create jobs. I asked him why he thought so many girls left their homes to go to kayayo and not boys.

'Boys are more resistant to the poverty, their needs are not plenty. They don't need so many things, clothes, shoes, cooking stuff.'

I gazed out of the window for some time. NGO and

other government office workers, many of them bright, highly educated young people were standing around in groups, chatting under the shade of the multitude of neem trees surrounding the enclosure.

I asked another Ghanaian man in the office why he thought so many of the kayayo went to Accra, and he said he believed that both girls and boys went down there for 'greener pastures', but the reason why more girls went down there was that they are more able to do the jobs available. He went on to say that they were fast approaching the season where they saw famine-like conditions in the north.

I thanked everyone for taking the time to talk to me and then made my way across town to another office building. It took me some time to locate it and several times I was sent in the wrong direction. I started to feel tired and hungry so went for an early lunch before proceeding on my search.

I then spoke with Kevin Aggrey at the Agency for Environmental Progress. He told me the issue of unemployment was a headache for both private and public organizations and in the north the problem was more severe. This was because past governments had neglected the development in the three northern regions. He also pointed out another problem that had also been mentioned the previous day by the Chief of Bandugu and that was the problem of perennial and recurring natural disasters. In the dry season there were bush fires and in the wet season there were floods.

'Where were the floods mostly concentrated?'

'There has been a lot of flooding around the settlements along the White and Black Volta rivers.'

He explained that this was because of the 'spill-over' from neighbouring Burkina Faso. He thought some of the problems were due to climatic changes, as previously there had been no spill-over floods from this country but recently there had been heavy rainfall and the Burkina government had as a result, opened up their dams to prevent flooding in their country. However the unfortunate consequence of this was that it flooded Ghana. He said as a result many of the people who may have decided to go into farming were now changing their minds, and were no longer interested. He elaborated,

'Because of this many parents will entice and push their children to go to the south.'

'Yet,' he added, 'some kayayo go to the south' or run away due to peer pressure.'

'They sometimes go even without their parents being aware they have run away.'

Through the window I could see the sun was slowly starting to set, and it flushed the office with a pink-yellow warmth. Outside an argument was warming up between some market women.

'Also the traditional rites scare the kayayo when they are not fully mature or developed. They are forced to marry outside their age groups. They often even marry people who could be their father or grandfather. They should be eighteen years before they marry.'

I was beginning to realize there were a complex array of reasons why the kayayo were going south in increasing numbers. At the heart of it I believed was the lack of any investment or opportunities in the area. There was literally nothing they could do. Climatic changes and pressure from the west were making it even more difficult for villages to make a living from agriculture. Annual flooding was leading many to abandon farming all together, making them more reliant on the migrant labour of their mostly female children.

I asked Mr Aggrey what he would do if he had the money and the remit to change things in the north?

He said he would try to change the mind-set of the opinion leaders and chiefs in the region, and bring on board opinion leaders, chiefs and assembly members.

'We try to educate them using many of our key role women in society. This illustrates to them what women can achieve if given the opportunity. If the chiefs say 'Ok we are willing to change but we don't have money', we as the NGO come in to provide finance and assistance to enable girls to go to school.'

Mr Aggrey leaned back in his seat, drank some water and commenced again.

'Because it has been the practice over a very long time to subjugate women, they now find it hard to change their views, for example in family meetings girls are not allowed to talk...women don't talk in family meetings, but our NGO continues to educate and many of them are changing.'

We sat for a minute or two looking out into the street below. It was full of traders, bicycles, motorbikes, a tapestry of sound and colour.

'Because of this oppressive life that many of the kayayo in the north endure, when they see their friends come back with one or two million (old money) cedis after being in Accra for several months they find it very enticing.'

I asked Mr Aggrey about female circumcision as this was an area I had not really dealt with. He said that the majority of girls who are over twelve in the northern region would have been circumcised. However, he said that on the whole most of the tribes now in the northern region have 'stopped this practice' but not in its entirety.

The conversation went back to the same problem which was the lack of overall development in the region. He said that,

'Unfortunately the traditional perception in Ghana is

that agriculture is not business. They look at farming as a peasant activity, but not as a money making activity.'

This does very much seem to be the case in Ghana.

'I still maintain though that we could achieve a lot of things by changing people's mind-sets, as the traditional cultural practises are limiting us.'

I thanked Mr Aggrey for taking the time to talk to me on these issues and I walked back to my hotel. The next morning I would be driving back to Tamale, where I would stay again another night and go to the Dagomba villages to talk to the kayayo and their parents there. Were there any differences? Were the conditions in Dagomba any different to those in Mamprusi? Why did the Dagomba and Mamprusi not mix in Accra when they spoke the same language and were from the same area? I hoped tomorrow to find out more.

When I got back to the hotel reception I asked how much breakfast would be the next morning, as until now I had bought breakfast outside at kiosks thinking it would be cheaper. She told me that breakfast was free.

'Oh, you mean it is included in the price of the room.'

'Yes, it's free.'

Was this just another way of saying breakfast was compulsory?

Chapter Thirteen

Tamale

The next morning I drove down to Tamale. It was a short drive and in just over two hours I was there. I remembered the direction to the previous hotel where I had stayed and went to book in there. I was becoming disillusioned. I was utterly exhausted from the trip I had done. My car appeared to be on its last legs. It was the hottest time of the year. I had two more villages I wanted to visit of some kayayo girls I had met in Accra but I could not find or locate these on the map. It had been planned that Salifu would accompany me on this trip, acting as my translator. On arrival at the hotel I rang to tell him that I didn't think I could continue. I was tired, I couldn't find the girl's villages and the thought of enduring yet another trip like the one I had just completed to Bandugu and Wialu would finish me off. I said it was best that the next day I travel back to Accra and come back to Tamale at a later date once I had got to know another group of Dagomba girls well.

Salifu spent a long time trying to persuade me to change my mind. He was going through maps and ringing friends trying to locate some NGO offices in Tamale that I had wanted to visit. I was quite touched with the way he was so eager that I didn't lose heart. Eventually he told me that he had located the whereabouts of the NGO. I had read that a man working there had done a lot of work with the kayayo. I did eventually agree to go with Salifu, still feeling disillusioned and tired, and I was sure once we got there he would have either 'travelled' as you frequently hear in Ghana or left his employment.

We arrived at the office a short time later, in a leafy

residential suburb. The watchman, or gatekeeper, slowly opened the large creaky metal gate.

'Is Mr Siedu Suamani there?'

He told me that he had gone out but that I shouldn't worry, he would call and tell him to come. I couldn't believe my luck!

We were led into the reception where we waited only for about five minutes. A very tall, slim man appeared before me and shook my hand. It was Seidu Sumani. He had a strong presence about him. His eyes were extremely bloodshot which made them difficult to distinguish. He was very animated and was keen to talk to me about the kayayo. I had the impression he had been waiting for me for many years. He had a story to tell.

'Why do you think the kayayo are travelling south in ever increasing numbers?'

'People say it's poverty but I think this is only one aspect. When we were kids girls didn't go south for kayayo. During our time things were better. We are now moving into the developed world and people's needs are many. For example in my day there was no electricity, we could only use a lantern with shea butter. Now everyone needs money for mobile phones.'

He also pointed to the soil.

'Years ago one got more yield from the soil because the land was more fertile.'

He went on to another issue.

'Some of the girls want to marry but before they marry they need to buy cooking utensils. Yet even though some are already married they still go. It has become a habit.'

Seidu, rubbing his sore eyes, which were most probably the result of the strong harmattan, added that it would now be very difficult to eradicate going to kayayo.

'When they come back to the village they only tell the good side. The girls say they don't like it down there but they keep going. They get boyfriends down there. Many get pregnant and some try to get abortions. Often they don't know who the father is.'

He continued to rub his eyes. I started to cough. The Saharan dust in Tamale was too severe. I could see the familiar fine film of dust covering everything in the office. During the harmattan it is almost impossible to eliminate however many times you dust and clean your house. Seidu continued.

'Going to kayayo in the south definitely has lots of downsides, but it's not a problem you can stop unless you have jobs in the north.'

He told me he had heard that some boys go down to do 'male kayayo', collecting scrap metal using trollies instead of the metal head pan. He said the girls didn't like living in the market but they did like living on their own. There they did not have to abide by the discipline of the village.

An Italian volunteer appeared. She was a young woman in her early twenties. Seidu looked at her and then at me and smiled.

'I have seen so many of them come and go over my years working here.'

How long had he worked there?

'Over twenty years.'

As we were on the subject of discipline the Italian volunteer added her thoughts.

'When you live in the village the whole village are your parents.'

This reminded me of a proverb I used to read in essays of Nigerian college pupils.

'It takes a whole village to properly raise a child.'

Seidu then mentioned something I was to hear over and over again both in the Dagomba villages and in

Accra.

'It is the mothers who push them to go. The fathers don't push them. They (the mothers) will tell you in front of your face that they don't want their daughter to go but behind closed doors they will tell them to go. The fathers don't push them.

'They can learn sewing, but then if all the girls in the village learn sewing how much can they earn?'

I shared Seidu's sentiments on this. For years and years I had seen NGOs and other 'projects' aiming to improve the lives of women and girls in Ghana. Always they 'teach them how to sew'. The economy can only support so many seamstresses. Indeed of late handmade clothes were now much less in demand due to the influx of donated clothes from abroad that were sold so cheaply all over Ghana. The other occupation that was always a mainstay would be hairdressing. These were both service industries. Surely there were other things they could do that would also boost the productivity of the country? Most food in Ghana was imported so local food production would be a good investment.

However, above all Seidu did stress to me that the girls didn't actually like being in Accra. He believed truly that they preferred the village. He looked across at me, perturbed.

'But the season is 'lean' so what can they do?'

He then added,

'Generally men don't want to marry girls who have been to kayayo. They demand an HIV test.'

He said he knew of one married girl from Dagomba, Lookyaha, who went down to Accra to do kayayo and then she got pregnant. The marriage broke down. He went on to say that for relationships 'going to kayayo is very bad'.

I told him how I had learnt how the kayayo tended to live and stay within tightly knit groups in Accra, this protected them from sexual assault, rape and other dangerous incidents.

'Yes', he said, 'those that stayed in the groups were more protected to some extent. But there were also many who needed to hide for one reason or another. It was these girls who were more in danger. They stayed in northern men's cubicles in the market. The men told the girls to stay in their cubicles.'

I thought of the little shacks and cubicles I had passed the night Rebecca was assaulted. Of how I saw some women and girls sitting in them together with the men.

'They tell them you will not get malaria, outside there is much malaria, or they will give the girls other excuses, rain, people stealing their things. The girls get enticed.'

The Italian volunteer, Sylvia, also commented that northern men like to have 'quite a few girlfriends', something that I've noticed in Ghana generally.

Seidu then said anxiously,

'I'm not moving forward, I can't see what the government can do to tackle this problem, only if they provide more jobs here.'

He drew the curtains to keep out the sun's rays.

He went on to say that when the girls went to kayayo their status changed.

'When they come back they feel superior to those who haven't gone. They feel more superior than their friends. It's like their friends and the other people in the village haven't seen anything.'

He added that the flip side of this was that some of the boys said they didn't like the girls who went to kayayo and wouldn't marry them. He said if he were a young man he would prefer to marry a non-kayayo.

Later I was to hear George mouth the same sentiment. I asked him why?

'Because if she has already done kayayo she could go back to Accra at any time and bring sickness. There are some girls who don't do kayayo at all. It all depends on the parents. There are certain areas in Dagomba where traditionally a lot of kayayo come from. Karaga is the highest but also Tolon and Kumbungu.'

Sylvia, the volunteer added,

'You can always tell the ones who have been to kayayo. They stick out a mile. They dress differently.'

'How do they dress?

'They wear jeans, tight fitting skirts and skimpy tops, things like that.'

Also she said,

'Many don't want to go to Accra alone so they ask their friends to come.'

This was the evidence of the peer pressure leading to young girls leaving home. It could also explain why younger and younger girls, even of four and five years old, were now appearing on Accra's streets to act as 'kayayo babysitters'. Many would be persuaded to come down by their older sisters and other relatives.

Suddenly Seidu looked more upbeat, more optimistic. He said he had one 'good idea' of how to stop the kayayo. We all listened intently.

'They don't walk to Accra. They go on the bus or trotro. When they go they go in groups. When they get to Tamale they fill the vehicles going south. I would stop the car and arrest the driver. That would stop them going south. Then the girls wouldn't come to Tamale to board the bus for Accra.'

Another person who had been standing until then suddenly asked Seidu,

'Are you sure that would work, what about their human rights?'

He agreed that it would be an infringement of

human rights, but that it may stop them nevertheless.

'You said in your day there were no kayayo, no young girls going south, when do you think it started and why?'

'The kayayo started around the time of the Guinea Fowl war. This was the war between the Dagomba and Kokumba. After the war many people didn't have homes. The kayayo itself didn't start from Tamale, it started around the Bimbilla area where the war lasted for three months. Many people were killed and many villages destroyed. It was called the Guinea Fowl war because it purportedly started over a quarrel in the market square over a Guinea fowl.'

Seidu believed that this was the root cause of the problems they had today. He said he remembered in the late 1980s 'there used to be these Zambara people from Niger.'

'They used to do this job. In Accra you wouldn't see any northerners doing this job. It was always the Zambara.'

He added that he didn't think the Zambara actually decided to stop but that when the northerners, Dagomba and Mamprusi, started to arrive in Accra, the Zambara just went away.

It was an interesting idea. It was different from the opinions I had thus far been hearing, that the kayayo started due to the collapse of agriculture, rice especially in the north. This collapse was mainly a result of decisions made in western countries by the World Bank and IMF to restrict agricultural subsidies as a condition for economic assistance. It had also been noted that the recent floods in the northern region, which left many homeless, had made the 'kayayo problem' even worse, contributing to far more people than ever moving to the large cities of Kumasi and Accra. Climate change had also been cited. In fact as in most scenarios the overall reason was most probably influenced by all these factors. Seidu was obviously very concerned and worried about the exodus of young women from his region. He felt helpless to provide a solution. He kept saying,

'I feel bad, I feel very very bad.'

After this interview with Seidu I felt re-invigorated. My disillusionment and tiredness had been swept away. Sylvia and Seidu had suggested that I should go to visit some villages in the Kumbungu district. It wasn't that far from Tamale and many young girls went to kayayo from this area. While having lunch at a local Indian restaurant Salifu and I perused the map. He pointed out some villages we could head for the next day.

Next morning after a hurried breakfast we headed off. I was imagining it would be another long nightmare journey like I had done just two days previously to the Mamprusi villages. Salifu had pointed them out on the map and said they were not far from Tamale, but I wasn't convinced. I had come to the conclusion now that if there was no pain there was no gain. Yet I was wrong. After driving for less than half-an-hour on a smooth tarmacked road, we arrived in the capital of the Kumbungu district. It was a small place. Most of the houses were of the traditional adobe and mud structures with grass roofs. The ubiquitous neem, mango, shea and teak trees were dotted everywhere. The familiar aromatic woody smell overwhelmed my senses, hitting me as the breeze caressed my skin. I could not help noticing, although noticing is the wrong word as it immediately slapped you in the face and jarred your senses, that Vodaphone and MTN were here in force. Almost the entire village was covered in the trademark red gloss paint of Vodafone and the yellow of MTN. Home after home, small shop after small shop, kiosk after kiosk, all had been quickly sloshed over with cheap, red paint. Even lamp posts and trees had not been spared. Salifu became angry, saying they were taking advantage of poor people.

'They cannot afford to paint their houses so the company paints them for free, but they are in fact taking advantage of their poverty and getting free advertising. Not only that, the company is destroying our heritage and architecture.'

At the heart of the village was a giant Vodafone telegraph pole, towering over everyone like some Big Brother nightmare.

Some of the men from the village started talking to Salifu about Vodafone.

'The company asked us to do the digging so they could erect this antennae.'

They pointed to the pole, angrily.

'They promised us if we did the digging that we would be retained by the company to do further work, however once we had finished, the other work did not materialize.'

Such was the scale and intensity of the 'redness' of Kumbungu that Salifu told me he had personally renamed it 'Vodafone Village'.

From the district capital we drove a short way on an untarred road to the village of Walankadi. The village was clean and spread out over a wide area, with large areas of trees and grassland between each compound house. We could hear the gentle swishing of the neem trees , as the wind rustled their leaves and branches and sent wafts of the unforgettable woody aroma towards me. It was magical. The whole village had an ethereal quality as if you were watching something that had been pulled out of the daily reality of life. It stood still, timeless. The plumes of long grasses shimmered as they swayed gently in the wind. We could not see many people around. By this time many had left the village 'to go to farm.' In the distance, sitting on a dagbala, beneath a mango tree I could see a girl. Salifu approached and asked if we could talk to her. Her name was Hejer. She didn't know her age, but she looked between fourteen and sixteen years. She appeared very dour and serious. She continued sitting under the tree with an air of nonchalance, we could have been her sisters or from the moon. Either wouldn't have mattered to her, so detached did she seem. She had a name tattooed on her forehead, she said it was the name of her brother. Many kayayo girls have tattoos on their forehead, sometimes they will be names, other times a shape, symbol or insignia. She said she was not married. She was carrying a baby on her lap that she said was someone else's daughter. She was wearing an orange and white striped T-shirt, and a long wrap around skirt made from local cloth. Around her head she wore a sea blue scarf, which dangled quite far down her back. Her eyes were small and deep set, her mouth full and wide. Her skin was coated in the pale, powdery dust of harmattan. We sat for some time. She was chatting to Salifu forlornly. Her expression never changed.

Not long after a very tall, slim man arrived. Many of the people of this region tended to be very tall and slim, which differs from the south of Ghana where people tended to be shorter and more stoutly built. The man, who was most probably in his fifties, was wearing a snazzy, loud, blue and yellow checked suit. He seemed as if he had just stepped out of a blues club in 1960s New Orleans. I imagined him holding a shiny brass trombone. He looked stately, with an air of authority that you wouldn't like to challenge. Perhaps this came from the confidence of being a member of a society which revered both age and maleness, meaning that most people, save his peers, were obliged to treat him and all he said with unquestioning obedience and respect. We greeted him and informed him of why we had come. Surprisingly, neither Salifu nor anyone we met mentioned that we should go and visit the chief, so I just kept quiet not wishing to jolt anyone's memory. This tall man turned out to be Hejer's father, and he told us that Hejer had already been to Accra to work as kayayo on two occasions. Hejer nodded and then smiled faintly. This was the first time her expression changed.

I asked her father what he felt about this. The answers he gave and indeed his tone and attitude towards 'going to kayayo', were dramatically different from the voices and opinions we had heard at the previous villages two days earlier. He spoke in a gruff, deep, gritty voice that reminded me of a metal chair being dragged along concrete.

'I feel bad about my daughter going to Accra. When they are there they are not under any supervision and their lifestyle changes. If they were here we could teach them and imbibe them with their traditions and tribe and also show them good behaviour.'

Another man now arrived. Extraordinarily tall and slim, he had on an emerald green suit and was wearing, as was almost everyone in the village, flip-flops. Slowly a small crowd gathered around us, some coming on foot, others on bicycles. But it was nothing like the wild attention we had received at Rebecca's village. I was wondering if this had to do with the fact it was quite near to Tamale and they were more used to seeing strangers. Bandugu and Wialu were very remote and inaccessible and most probably did not receive many visitors. This could have explained the difference.

I approached two little boys, around two or three years, smiling and they screamed and ran away. The tall man in the green suit joined in the general conversation. He told me that one of the village girls had gone to Accra and had 'come back mad'. He said,

'She went mad when she was down there and had to be brought home.'

A few more men had joined us now and seemed to be very involved and interested in the conversation that was going on. Hejer still did not say much and I remembered what Mr Aggrey had told me two days earlier about girls not being allowed to talk in family meetings, and also what I learned from other northern women on my second and subsequent trip to the north about how, 'women are not supposed to talk'. Another man started to speak. He had a complaining tone in his voice and an angry expression on his face. I looked in the distance. The grasses and trees were swaying, the shimmering sunlight was embracing them, it looked like paradise. This man also had a gritty, throaty voice and a thin goatee beard was hanging from his chin.

'They go to Accra and all they bring back is clothes and cooking pots.'

Other men were now mumbling in agreement. Hejer continued to sit there. Silent.

'Us fathers, we are not in agreement of our girls going there.'

I remembered this very much confirmed what Seidu in Tamale had told me the day before.

'But we find it difficult to stop them. They (the girls) and their mothers plan it without our knowledge.'

The man was holding a shiny, new mobile phone and I was wondering if it contained a Vodafone SIM card.

Another man joined our crowd – tall and slim with deep-set eyes, also characteristic of this region. His added to the general symphony of complaints.

'They don't even bring money home, especially those who are not married but want to get married, all they bring home is cooking utensils.'

But this was what tradition dictated they buy before marriage. It was what they had to buy, for them it was a necessity.

According to traditional Dagomaba rites, both mother and daughter were expected to form a procession on their wedding day. Other girls walked behind them holding their pots and cooking utensils, the greater and grander the procession the higher status the girl and her family received. There was an immense pressure on the girls to acquire these pots, bowls and utensils.

Hejer now started to speak. She said it was true that the girls mainly brought back cooking utensils, but they also brought money to pay for their siblings' school fees.

I asked them why they all kept buying cooking utensils. How many pots and pans did they need?

I didn't get a straight answer. Hejer only told me that on the last two occasions that she had been to Accra she had brought back bowls and clothes. Her father said she was 'about fourteen years' which meant she probably first went to Accra when she was around thirteen, yet she was already buying the items she needed for her wedding. I asked her what she would bring back the next time she went to Accra.

'I will bring back bowls, clothes and money, but the last time I went I didn't bring back money.'

I was told by some of the men that a girl had just yesterday 'run away' and gone to kayayo without telling anybody. Another girl, called Leila, who was now sitting with Hejer said that she had been to Accra several times and slept outside the market. A third girl, Awubu, now in our little group under the tree, said she worked as a kayayo in Kumasi, one of the busiest and largest market towns in West Africa. I asked them all as a group why they went to kayayo.

'We want to buy things for ourselves, the things we need, and we can't get money to buy them here.'

It seemed so simple really, isn't that why everyone migrates to wealthier areas than their own? I wanted to find out how a girl's status and the way she is viewed by others in the village changes after she had 'done kayayo' as this was one of the issues that Seidu Sumani had mentioned in Tamale. I asked them if the other girls looked up to them when they returned from Accra or Kumasi?

'We buy new clothes and they are nice. The other girls in the village, they come to us and beg us to buy our clothes, but we won't sell them to the girls because the clothes are nice.'

It's worth noting here that when leaflets appear at our doors in the west asking us to donate clothes 'for Africa' these are the very same clothes that end up on the backs of the kayayo and other poor Africans. Once they reach Africa, they are sold in huge vacuumed packed bundles to market men and women dealing in second hand or 'home use' clothes. They are then sold on Accra's streets from between 20 pence to up to £5 depending on the quality and type of clothes. Shoes especially go for a high price and I am constantly arguing with the street vendors that a pair of second hand shoes from Primark that they were selling for up to £7 or £8 I can actually buy at a lower price new directly from the shops in Europe. The second hand clothes business is huge in Ghana and indeed the rest of Africa. It has led to the decimation of especially the male tailoring industry. Men, particularly, no longer bother to get shirts, trousers and suits made as they traditionally did. They can buy them now more cheaply from the markets. Women still tended to prefer having traditional dresses made locally, so it had not had such a devastating effect on female seamstresses. However, the second hand clothes business does provide a lot of employment and income for countless numbers of people in Ghana and this has probably compensated to a large extent for the loss of employment in the tailoring sector. That is also why most Ghanaians look like a million dollars wherever they go, often adorned in expensive designer labels from Europe that they pick up for less than a dollar.

Lost in thought for a moment, I came slowly back to the here and now. The girls looked at me, waiting for me to pay attention, they wanted to tell me more.

'If we could get work here we wouldn't go to Accra.'

'What type of work would you like to be able to do here in the Dagomba area?'

'Any work,' they replied.

I asked them how much money did they generally earn in Accra?

'Sometimes we earn a lot of money, sometimes we don't earn much. It's not regular.'

I asked them what they most like about living in Accra. I got the usual reply.

'We are only there for the money, we are not looking for anything.'

Hejer, then looking tired, laid her arms in Awubu's lap and Awubu laid her head on Hejer's shoulder. Childhood friends from birth, all that they had ever experienced they had done so together. They reminded me of the two little Dagomba girls, Aysha and Ekima that Salifu and I had met in the doorway near the main post office in downtown Accra many months ago now. They were also holding and leaning on to each other, overwhelmed by their first weeks in a big, strange city. They had also come from a village just like this.

I asked them if they were ever maltreated in Accra.

They said that mostly the southern people there don't 'worry them', but some do beat them and push them. They told me that if you don't interact with a lot of people you 'won't get problems'.

'Sometimes men come to us and tell us they love us, and if we don't agree to have sex with them they beat us.'

Two women walked past balancing large heavy metal buckets full of water on their heads. They stopped to greet us. These were older married women. As they passed the men around said these two women too had been to Accra to work as kayayo. In fact some studies have maintained that almost every northern woman, those from the three northern regions of the Upper West, Upper East and Northern Region, will some time in their lives go to Accra to work as kayayo.

An animated conversation now began in Dagbani between all the people around me. The girls started giggling and laughing uncontrollably, bending over from the waist, holding their arms out stretched before them, clapping. They fell on each other. I had no idea what they were talking about. Yussef, one of the men in the group who was married, starting talking again about the subject of how the kayayo 'connive' with their mothers to run away to Accra.

'When the girls come back, they (the mothers) use some of the girls' money to buy sewing machines. Then the girls learn how to sew, but they still go to Accra again. They say the sewing will not give them the same money they can get in Accra. But in Accra you have to pay for bath, pay for water. Here it is free.'

Someone then commented that the traditional industries and skills that they learnt like sewing and hairdressing couldn't compete with the potential earning power of the kayayo work in Accra.

I remembered what Seidu had said about the men

not wanting to marry a girl who had been to kayayo and I wanted to find out more about this.

Adnan, the man in the emerald green suit, said,

'In this village almost all the girls and ladies who have married have been to kayayo in Accra, so we don't have a choice when it comes to marriage. If we don't marry them, who will we marry? All the young ladies who have got married have been to Accra once, twice or more. When they go they change their lifestyle.'

'How?'

'It changes in the way they respect. The way they respect their parents changes and also the way they respect their brothers and sisters changes.'

A man whose name was Hussein and who had been sitting on a bike joined in.

'They used to wash their siblings' clothes but now they don't because they think they are big, but if they stay in the village again for some time then they revert back.'

He and the others sat for some time, they all looked as if they were deep in thought, their brows furrowed.

'The air in Accra is different to the air here, so when they breathe the air in Accra all changes.'

The 'southern jazz singer' in the blue and yellow checked suit also said,

'When they come back they have grown fat so they feel they are big even though they are still small.'

The other men nodded and the girls laughed. Salifu was smiling. Another man verified what the man in the checked suit had just said.

'Awabu here (he pointed at the young girl) used to be very lean (slim). Then she went to Kumasi. She's now grown fat so when she meets her age mates she feels she is above them.'

Fatness in Ghana, especially traditionally, was not

viewed in the same way as in the west. Being fat carried with it connotations of wealth and good living.

It was as if each statement added fuel to the argument, stirring the fire. They had more and more to say, each time they became more vibrant. The girls sat listening, smiling. A tall, lanky man called Mohammed straightened himself ready to talk, pausing for a moment to make sure everyone was listening.

'Some of them when they go their dressing changes and they dress like men, they wear trousers and jeans. As a woman you should dress like a lady and not wear trousers like a man.'

He went on to say, as had the others, that the men and especially the elders in the village didn't like it but they were powerless to do anything about it. Another person complained,

'And some of them don't cover their hair.'

The Dagombas, as Muslims, traditionally must cover their hair and in the villages and towns of Dagomba they do. However, once in Accra they come under the influence of a more western culture and some start emulating the dress codes and styles of those in the big city. The man in the snazzy blue and yellow suit again contributed,

'Most of these things, if there were here, they wouldn't have learnt. They have to respect their husband and be submissive to their husbands.'

This led Mohammed, with his long lean arms stretched out and his palms wide open, to glance at both Salifu and I with a helpless look on his face. It was as if he was saying through his manner, what can we do? There are forces stronger than us.

I thought of Chinua Achebe's novel 'When Things Fall Apart'. How the ancient traditions and customs that had held the protagonist Okonkwo's village and society together for millenniums had become derided and ridiculed in the face of the white man's ways. How these customs and values, which were in fact the tribe's nuts and bolts, had become loosened and unstuck. The same was happening in this village too. Other greater forces outside their control were leading to kayayo: bureaucratic decisions in the west, climate change.

'The girls come back and call the men 'farmers', this is an insult and the girls now think they are above the men.'

All the girls, Hussein who was sitting on the bike next to us, and everyone in the group including Salifu roared with laughter. It took them some time to calm down. The term 'farmer' would be used by the kayayo as a term of abuse, saying that the villagers are illiterate, 'bush', they don't know the real world. Generally in Ghana everything from the village is 'bush', unsophisticated, illiterate, backward; the city represents opportunity, advancement, wealth and sophistication.

The raucous laughter gradually died down. In fact the subject did have serious overtones. The breakdown, whether good or bad, of the traditional social fabric of the village. Sobriety returned. The subject of marriage now emerged. Hussein, who was wearing jeans and a light blue buttoned up shirt, began to speak,

'In most marriages now they fight a lot because of kayayo, because the wives come back and don't respect their husbands. In the process of fighting (arguing) they leave the house and go back to Accra and take the children. Because of this new behaviour, there is no respect, they still feel big, the husbands beat them and they run away.'

I was thinking that this had serious implications. The women ran away to the city with their children. The knock on effect of this would inevitably be that whole families and children would live and be brought up on the street. No values. No rules. No education. No home. It was horrific.

The little group around the tree all then started to shout and argue amongst themselves as if I was no longer there. After some time I asked the men standing around that if they didn't like the girls going to Accra why didn't they buy the items necessary for marriage as this seemed to be one of the main reasons the girls went there.

'It is very expensive to marry a woman in this village, the marriage rites alone can cost 4 million old (£200 Stering) money.'

Not long ago Ghana 'downsized' for want of a better word, its currency. It had started to become unmanageable. Inflation was rampant and the equivalent of £100 Sterling was 2 million cedis. Credit cards were not used much so people would often have to carry cash of ten, twenty, even up to 100 million cedis. Denominations were small and it was not unusual to see people walking out of banks with suitcases and rucksacks full of money. Not surprisingly thieves and robbers had a field day. So 1 million cedis became 100 cedis and ten million became ten thousand and so on. However, many people still talk in the old currency and it can get very confusing. Instead of paying saying Gh5 cedis (say £2.50 Sterling) for some apples, they will insist on maintaining the old style and saying 500 cedis, which in the new currency is £250!

'So,' Hussein continued, 'So you cannot add the burden of buying utensils, so the woman has to contribute.'

We heard a roar of a machine, and two men arrived on a motorbike. They greeted us.

'Dasebaa'

Everyone answered in a chant,

'Naaaa'

This spirited conversation never seemed to come to an end, the complaints were innumerable, unfortunately they were all coming from the men, the girls didn't get a chance to speak, and it was only later on my second trip, that I had time to talk to some women privately. They were more educated and thus voiced their views vehemently. The next complaint was,

'The mothers insult their daughters, they say, look at your friend she has bought all of these thing and why don't you go. The mothers know that immediately they bring back those things they are ready for marriage.'

In Dagomba tradition there is a social stigma attached to girls if they do not marry at the conventional age and this stigma is always extended to the parents of the girl, particularly the mothers. A girl will also lose potential suitors if she remains unmarried after attaining the customary marriageable age. This must explain why the mothers put so much pressure on their daughters to go to kayayo to bring back the necessary goods.

A young boy had climbed a tree and sat there silently surveying all below him. His knees were bent at right angles resting on the branches. He was covered in white powdery dust. I asked them, as I had asked many others if they thought there was any way of stopping kayayo.

'You can't stop it for now, there is no way you can stop it. It is because they look up to friends that they go...I would make sure my daughter is very close to her older sister so she can mentor her,' said the man in the snazzy suit.

Hussein decided that it was time to go, he waved a cheery farewell and rode off on his bicycle with an air as if to say 'what can you do?' It seemed that young girls going to kayayo were challenging the customs of traditional marriage and also the traditional rites of respect to elders and siblings. Conventional ways of dress and behaviour were also changing. The social fabric of the village was being torn asunder. Not only that, marriage breakdown was leading to whole families being brought up on the streets of Accra.

As I walked through the village I saw a lot of building was going on. This was the dry season. No farming was being done. It was time to redecorate, repair and refurbish their homes. A whole group of young men were engaged in this communal village labour. Some sat atop a wall, others were rolling up a mud-like mixture into balls, throwing them up to those on the wall, who then fashioned them into the shape of the wall.

I strolled through the village. A building that looked like it had once served as a community centre stood among some trees. It now looked abandoned. Maybe it had been built by an NGO. They had left and the place was now no longer used. Yet another example of how people coming from the west perceive people's needs in Africa through the distorted lens of their own cultural biases. It was now midday and very hot. In the distance, through a haze of chiffon I could see some tall wiry men cycling towards the junction. Our group had now scattered. Salifu had disappeared. He had gone to look for the lady whose daughter had run away the previous day.

I turned a corner and a party or celebration of some sort was going on. A new baby had just arrived and all the women in the village had come together to celebrate. I walked into a large compound, big pots were cooking over fires and hundreds of enamel bowls and cooking pots were strewn across the floor. All were identical - white enamel with a flowered pattern on the front. The women wore brightly coloured clothes. The colours and the patterns seemed even more intense against the monochrome hues of beiges, ochres and browns of their surroundings. Outside this large adobe compound house, I could see giant neem trees through the gauzy haze. Scores of bicycles were parked underneath and some men were standing there chatting. Because of the haze they seemed further away. Less real. A silence filled the air.

Back inside the compound, I was led by some of the women into a hut leading off the main courtyard. As I entered, I was confronted by a large wooden cabinet with glass doors. It was crammed with identical white enamel pots of various sizes. All had the same flowery pattern on the front. A man was holding a tiny baby, its skin was very pale, in fact almost white, compared to the other dark skins around and I guessed it had just been born. His mother was sitting on a stool nearby. As the infant was being held by one man, another was slowly attempting to cut off the baby boy's foreskin. He was using a penknife. Below the baby was a small plastic bowl full of water that had now turned red from the blood dripping into it. The baby was curling up his little legs, screaming. Once the circumcision was over the men covered the head of the baby's penis with pounded cola nut. This they said would stop the bleeding. They then wrapped the baby and gave it to his mother. She held him at her breast and he soon ceased to cry.

I went back out into the bright sunshine of the compound. It had been dark inside the hut and it took some time for my eyes to adjust. As I walked around I saw many young women walking with numerous cooking pots balanced on their heads. Some had two or three balanced one on top of the other, others had five or six balancing in a tower. Without exception, they were all decorated in the same identical flowery pattern. They were definitely a status symbol in the village. It appeared the more you had, the more regard you received. I saw Hussein again on his bicycle and he jumped off and came over to me.

The women wanted me to take their photos, which I did. Someone came to me. They told me they had, 'found the lady'. I saw Salifu in the distance and he approached and introduced me to her. Her name was Rashida, she was calm and looked like she was in her forties. She wore a very long black shawl wrapped several times around her head. Yellow and white flowers were embroidered on it. Her whole face seemed to be contorted into an expression of constant anxiety. The space between her brows, just above the bridge of her wide nose was furrowed. I asked her about her daughter, also called Rashida.

'I went to town yesterday morning and when I came back Rashida had gone. Rashida went to Accra alone. She didn't go with the other girls.'

'How old is she?'

'She is about twelve or thirteen,'

I asked if she had any other children. She told us she had two more. I noticed that Hussein and Mohammed were following us everywhere we went and I thought after some time that they were probably hoping they would get some kind of payment or gift when it was time to go.

Did she have any co-wives?

'I am the first wife, but altogether there are three of us.'

Rashida seemed a very quiet, humble woman. She told me there had been no neglect of Rashida.

'I sell rice in the market. The money from this I use to look after my children so it doesn't matter if my husband doesn't give me money. It is me alone that provides the money for my children so there is no neglect.'

I remembered what some of the girls had told me in

Accra. That once their fathers took second, third and fourth younger wives they would not only neglect their first wives and children but often abandon them altogether. Rashida's mother continued her story,

'I felt very sad when I found out Rashida had gone to Accra, had I known she was planning to go I would not have allowed it. When the girls come from Accra they don't tell the people in the village any bad stories, they don't tell us where they sleep. It's only the other people who go to Accra and see where the kayayo sleep that tell us how horrible the place is.'

I noticed her hands, they were tough, weatherworn and chapped, testament to a hard life of manual labour. As we were sitting there, Rashida's mother seemed so worried she hardly seemed to know where she was. A man came out. He was a tall elderly man. He stood there, looking at Salifu and myself, and also Rashida's mother, who was sitting in a plastic chair under a neem tree. He waved his finger, looking down at us like a school headmaster.

'We don't like the girls going to kayayo'.

He then laughed and walked away. Just then a large, brand new shining Toyota Land Cruiser pulled up and parked under the tree. There were no roads, it just drove on the baked earth around the village. It appeared that the people piling out of the car were important dignitaries of some sort. African 'Big Men', with big cars, big salaries, big houses, big families and big wives. They had all the trappings to let you know and not forget that they were rich, influential. You attempted to cross them at your peril. Those who were wise kept in with them at all costs, by doing so they ensured their safety and that of their families. That was definitely the feeling that came across as they piled out of their cars, probably from some 'big job' in Accra. All were wearing their national costumes. Despite their western education, cars and the modernity in which they lived in the city, they loved to come home to their village and steep themselves in the traditions of their birth. All the 'big men' strolled off to join the other males who were sitting under the tree.

Rashida's mum continued to sit in the middle of some waste ground, silently on her plastic chair. From a distance she almost looked like a statue. She was so still and hushed. Dead leaves whirled around her in the wind, translucent willowy grasses swayed from side to side. I eyed her through gossamer.

'Do you think the girls can be stopped?'

'The only way you can stop them is to engage them in a trade.'

She lifted her hands and rubbed her eyes that had been hit by the dust blown up by the wind.

'It is difficult for all of them to change. If they saw that some of their friends were making it up here they would copy. It must start with one person. If one makes it the others will follow.'

I agreed with Rashida's mum. If there were good role models, it would only take a few to turn the tide. If only there were better ways for them to make money. She sat for some time and then continued to talk. Worry was etched all over her face.

'I worry so much every day, but I don't know how to tell her to come back. I can't call her because Rashida doesn't have a phone. It will be only if Rashida calls someone else in the village.'

I did feel sorry for this woman and I told her that when I got to Accra I would try to locate her daughter. I knew most of the Dagomba girls lived in Dcbele Market. When I had time I would go there. I looked more closely at the ground, I hadn't noticed before because of the grass but the entire ground was covered in peanut shells. I had heard that this was one of the staple crops of the area. Again, another older man approached us. I think word had got round and everyone wanted to come and give his or her opinion or idea on the 'problem'.

'We have to try to form an association to stop them going,' this elderly man suggested

'What do you suggest?'

'Tailoring and sewing.'

Oh no! How many tailors and seamstresses can one village support? I thought to myself.

'There is also an association to make clay pots', he added, 'if there were more things like that the girls wouldn't go.'

The man then moved onto the familiar topic of blaming everything on 'the mothers.'

'If a mother says she is not aware that her daughter plans to go to Accra she is lying.'

Rashida's mum heard this but continued to sit silently.

'Often it is the mothers who give them the lorry fare to go, but they will then tell you that the girl has gone and she didn't know about it. It's the things they bring back that creates the rivalry between the mums in the village. Also, our own cultural practices are to blame. When a married women gives birth to her first child, she must go back to her parents for some time, to her own village. The women use this as an opportunity to run away. They run back to Accra with the baby.'

The village was indeed falling apart. I wondered if it could now be ever be put back together as it once was. Most probably it wouldn't. A new form would develop. It would be only a fusion of abandoned fragments. Some ancient, others recent from alien and unfamiliar origins. It would be a hasty structure. The new parts would not bond to form unyielding joints as it once did. Yet like all such constructions it would get by, it would limp along. But it would never function as it once did.

Chapter Fourteen

Exodus

Back in Accra, I had rested for several days after my trip to the north. I was completely exhausted both mentally and physically. I was keen to see Rebecca, Nurah and Aysha, both to prove them wrong (I had got there and you said I never would) and also to show them the fantastic pictures I had managed to catch of their family and the village. When next driving my daughter to school I stopped at the mango tree. The little world beneath its dappled shade always seemed so magical and intimate. It was as if the tree itself was breathing, the movements of its shadows caressing and encasing the girls within its boughs.

When I stopped the car only a few girls were there. Rebecca and Nurah were still around and on spotting me they leapt from their upturned bowls, which were shimmering and reflecting the rays of the early morning sun. Babies Romatsu and Madihah were both tied to their backs. They had been in the middle of eating their breakfast. I did feel slightly smug that I had proved them wrong and couldn't help saying to Rebecca,

'See, I told you so.'

She just looked at me with a dumbfounded expression. I then held up the camera and showed them the pictures. Both girls were overjoyed, but in their restrained and dignified way, there was no squealing and shouting out. Rather they quietly and gently pointed to the familiar faces that unfolded before them on the small screen. Nurah looked transfixed when looking at the pictures of her mother. Rebecca seemed mesmerized when looking at the pictures of her father. She seemed very proud of him. She held the camera gazing at his photo with a whimsical air. I told them I would get the picture printed and give them all copies aware that these would probably be the first and last they may ever have of their families.

It was now February and the weather seemed to be heating up as the days passed. For some time I had planned to walk around the whole of Tonga market to try and gauge the number of kayayo girls that were actually living there. Also I wanted to try and understand how the tribal and village groups arranged themselves. Was there any pattern? How many girls were there on average in each group? How many different tribes were represented among them?

It was evening and once again I was sitting on the wooden bench opposite the Methodist church waiting for George. The white building, so incongruous amidst the drabness that surrounded it, was glittering from the glare of its own lights. George arrived soon after and sat down on the bench with an expression that told me he had something important to announce. He declared that he would be travelling to his hometown the following week, as he had 'to sort out his marriage.' He told me he had found a girl whom he wanted to marry and then said,

'I just need to born one child and then no need to worry anymore.'

For him, and indeed any Ghanaian man or woman at his age, which was about mid-thirties, it was of utmost importance to bear children. If not tongues would begin to wag. I asked him why he didn't think of marrying one of the kayayo girls and then he said no, he wouldn't marry any of them.

'Why?'

'Their eyes are wide open and their mouths too wide.'

I asked him what he meant by this,

'They themselves are alone here in Accra and they say things they are not supposed to say if they were with their parents.'

This kind of attitude, that the girls have slipped away from the net of the socializing influence of the tribe and family and thus have, 'turned wild' echoed what I had heard from both from Seidu Sumani in Tamale and the elders in the Dagomba village of Walankadi.

As we entered the market, with the small mosque on one corner and the Methodist church on the other, we came across our first group of kayayo girls. The group was quite large, and they had spread themselves out across several shop fronts. They told us they were from the village of Naboya and that they were from the Mamprusi tribe. In total the girls from this village numbered approximately thirty-five, although this would probably vary from month to month as some left and more arrived. Many of these girls also had babies but we didn't count them.

It's worth noting that each shop front is generally no more than two or three metres wide, with either bare cement or if lucky a broken tiled floor. This floor space jutted out from the shop door by no more than two or three metres. Some of these shop fronts consisted of just a series of steps leading up to the doorway, which was elevated about a metre above ground level. Those girls unfortunate enough to occupy these doorways had to attempt to sleep balancing on a step no wider than about twenty to thirty centimetres wide. They could then only usually sleep on their sides. If they had attempted to sleep on their backs half their body would hang over the step making it extremely uncomfortable to sleep. For those with babies sleeping on the steps was even more precarious. Many wedged their babies between themselves and the step so the babies would not roll over in the night, meaning they slept literally balancing on just several centimetres of space. Not only that, at the bottom of the steps was an open drain about a metre deep by half a metre or so wide, which meant if any of them rolled over during the night they could fall into the drain. Some girls had placed various narrow planks of wood across parts of the drain to prevent this, but not all of it was covered.

All the girls from this village were unfortunate in that their 'home' or sleeping space was made up of such steps, with a much wider step being situated at the top. Most of the girls in this group slept on the wider top step, which went along the breadth of four to five shop fronts.

As George and I walked further into the interior the heavy smell of ripe plantains being fried once again hit me in strong wafts depending on which way the wind blew, this mingled with the less desirable smell of old smoky urine welling up from the drain. The whole market was awash with smells, most of them undesirable. Aromas of frying fish also moved around in waves on the wind.

Suddenly the lights went out. 'Lights off again in Accra.' Moans and sighs of disappointment reverberated around. The surroundings were abruptly thrown into heavy darkness. Mobile phone screens and the quivering flickers of flames from kerosene lamps now were the only sources of light. After passing this large group of girls and babies from Naboya, we found another smaller group huddled together on a minute broken tiled shop front. They were around ten in number. They told us they were from the village of Zunezu, which was beyond Wialu (Poppy's village). I wondered if it was possible to find a village even more remote than Poppy's village. We then spoke to another small group of girls living in the adjacent shop front, who said they had travelled down from a village known as Nakpo. On some of the steps naked babies were already sleeping on bits of cloth and cardboard. Other half clad toddlers sat on the empty paint pots that were balancing on the narrow planks of wood positioned across the open drains.

Darkness enveloped the market. It was so dark at times I had to shine the light from my mobile phone onto my Michael Essian Ghana School exercise book to see what I was writing. As we continued walking, we noticed that many of the shops, some of which had been made out of empty iron shipping containers, others comprising of wooden shacks or permanent 'blocked' buildings, had now been bolted up for the night. However, not all these shops had 'shop fronts' as such. Many had not managed or got round to constructing a cement or tiled patch in front of their buildings and therefore the kayayo could not use these as sleeping areas. We ran into a shop unloading hundreds of disposable nappies from a truck parked outside. Most people in Ghana now used these nappies. Planks of wood had been placed intermittently over the long gutters to enable ease of access from the road to the shop. They acted like a type of bridge.

Suddenly the fruity tang of freshly peeled oranges punched my nostrils, it was a welcome relief from the heavier more odorous aromas wafting around. I did not want the scent to go away. As we continued round talking to the various groups we noticed that many of the kayayo had still not returned to their shop fronts. George commented that many of the girls wouldn't return until the owner had closed and gone home for the day, and suggested that due to this we should come later in the evening the next time we visited. I felt sad that many of these girls who had finished their work, and also their nightly ablutions and laundry could still not return 'home', and were forced to hang around the market until the shop or stall owner had left. If they did dare to arrive before the shop had closed they were likely to be insulted and shouted at.

We now passed another group of girls from the village of Nakbalu. In all, about thirty-five girls and their infants shared this shop front of about five to six shops and its adjacent drain. These girls were also Mamprusi. Until now all the girls we had met had been from the Mamprusi tribe. I was told Nakbalu was beyond Wialu which also meant it must have been an extremely remote place. Many of the girls in this group had 'gone to bath', but those remaining assured us that 'in small time they will come'. We passed small fires made with charcoal glowing in front of the now darkened shop fronts. They smouldered warm and red in the surrounding murkiness. Sparks snapped off from the fire and blew away in the wind. They reminded me of fireflies hovering in the night. I asked the girls what they were cooking. They told me 'yams and cow meat' and I wondered if any of their neighbours had been gossiping about them 'wasting their money on meat'. As we walked along the tracks many groups of kayayo were passing us, chatting and laughing amongst themselves. Many were on their way to the bathhouse, their metal bowls or tahilis full of the day's washing. Giant yellow plastic containers once used to hold cooking oil, now being used as water containers, were piled up high by the side of the tracks. Motorbikes drove past slowly in the darkness, their solitary shafts of light tossing spotlights on the various scenes of wretchedness around. It looked surreal in the darkness.

The orchestra of sound resonated behind us, the high notes of the kayayo calling out and laughing, the baritones of the car and motorbike engines, the trumpets of the car horns, the screeching violins of the babies' wails. The cacophony of sounds and smells of this market overwhelmed your senses.

We almost stepped on another group of girls lying in the darkness. They told us they were Mamprusi girls from the village of Doni. There were about twenty-eight plus their babies and they seemed worried that we had come to 'count them'. George assured them we were not census officials and that we were writing a book about them. The next 'village' we saw was called Minka, which we were told was near to the town of Wangli. There were many girls from this village, which seemed more to resemble a small town and they occupied shop fronts on both sides of the road. The girls at this shop front seemed quite fortunate compared with many of the others we had just seen. Their patch was clean and the floor had been laid with broken tiles. It also had an iron fence all around it on which the kayayo girls could hang their clothes at night. A beautiful little baby of about nine months by the name of Kookhaya sat in the middle of the tiled floor. There were just so many infants and toddlers around. It was like a kindergarten. The girls' 'check check' bags, or 'African suitcases' containing all their possessions were piled up, one on top of the other in the corner of the shop front. I could see how easy it would be for thieves to come and just take away their things in the night while they were sleeping. They could just lean over and help themselves to anything they wanted. This space, just like all the others, was littered with empty plastic paint pots used for storage. They also doubled up as seats. As we sat in this clean, compact area we watched the shadowy outlines of others walking past in the darkness, often barely visible. One kayayo girl on the other side of the road was standing on a step calling out to her friend. She lost her balance and fell, her load crashing down on top of her. Others ran forward to help.

This activity, the noises and reverberations, odours, whiffs and pongs, shaped what was the nocturnal life of this market. A life that appeared only at dusk, as did many of its kayayo inhabitants. The market reminded me of a forest habitat which takes on a different life as the sun withdraws, its nighttime inhabitants only feeling safe enough to venture out when the other daylight dwellers departed.

The candles and tiny kerosene lamps flicker in the distant darkness, sometimes casting a shimmering glow onto the faces of those huddled around. I can see many of what have come to be known as 'baby kayayo,' these are girls between the ages of about five and eight. They are walking around in pairs, sometimes in groups of three. They stop and stand, chat and laugh in groups as they wander around the market. We now have reached the end of this track and turn right onto another.

On this new track the number of kayayo girls was immense. There were about one hundred girls occupying a number of shop fronts on each side of the track. They were from the village Shakbalu. I was beginning to wonder what percentage of these villages' female inhabitants occupied this market at any one time. I am sure that for some of the villages it could be as much as fifty per cent or even more meaning therefore that about half of the villages' female citizens had left. Piles of rubbish lay around, lots of discarded cardboard boxes were piled high, and the place was strewn with empty plastic water sachets. Some naked kayayo girls, covered in white soapy suds, were washing in their bowls in full view of passers-by. They tried to finish as quickly as possible, aware of the prying eyes. They were scrubbing themselves with the Ghanaian traditional sponge that resembles a thin, elongated fishing net. We reached Springstrap Road and we were now at the other end of the market. A television had been placed outside a shop and many people including the kayayo gathered round to watch. Small children and 'baby kayayo' were dancing to the music. George and I had reached the end of the track and had now covered two of the four tracks that surrounded the inner core of the market. George said he was hungry and rushed off to his fast food stall for rice and stew. We agreed we would meet tomorrow to cover the remaining two outer tracks of the market.

The next evening, while sitting in the darkness on the wooden bench opposite the Methodist Church I was preoccupied with the previous night's events. All the groups of girls we had met that evening had been from the Mamprusi tribe. I had not met any Dagomba. Why was this? Did the kayayo separate themselves according to their tribal allegiances? Did neither tribe, despite being from similar geographical area and sharing similar dialects, interact at all with each other? It was definitely beginning to seem like this. It was also becoming apparent that not only did the kayayo divide themselves along tribal lines, they also very much grouped themselves together according to the village from which they came. All the groups I had met the previous evening were grouped according to their village of their birth. Even the positioning of the groups within the market mirrored the regions from which they originated. I now realized that if I wanted to meet kayayo from the other main tribe, I would eventually have to go to the notorious Debele market.

I stared across the road. In the surrounding darkness the church appeared like a fusion of light. A bright star in a sea of gloom. Tonight, instead of the usual stream of mismatched sounds, melodic hymns, hymns I remembered from my school days long ago, sang out through the windows.

Oh come all ye faithful
Joyful and triumphant

I was transported back to my old school, sitting cross-legged on a polished wooden floor. Mrs Ellwood, our form teacher, stood by, looking down sternly at us.

In the midst of this George arrived, rushing across the road, late as usual. As he approached, darkness unexpectedly encased us. The church, with its glittering lights, was obliterated. Lights out. The hymns ceased. Groans of disappointment could once again be heard from those standing nearby. Silence then ensued.

So two hours later than the previous day, George and I once again entered the market in darkness. This evening we planned to cover the two remaining tracks that formed the perimeter of this commercial hub. We hoped that most girls would now be at their shop fronts, it being that much later. We met our first group of girls. They were from the town of Walewale, a sizeable market town on the way to Bolgatanga. Several of them were bunched round an ice-cream tub. It was filled with rice and they were all eating from it with their fingers. They were balancing on a narrow strip of pavement between a wall and the drain. Some were braiding each other's hair.

We passed another shop called 'Big Brother Rice'. Seven girls were sitting at this shop's frontage. They were all eating in the darkness, their wet washing strung up above them on bits of string. Their metal bowls were turned on their sides, leant against a wall. Again, the only light was from the few passing cars, which illuminated them intermittently. I was reminded of the ghost train of my childhood, as you rode in the darkness, sudden forbidding scenes, scenes you would rather not see, flared up before you. The cars had to drive slowly in order to avoid running down any stray child or group with protruded too much into the road.

We turned off the main dirt track road into a path. This road was completely in darkness and followed the perimeter of the central market. Sacks of charcoal were piled up high into the night sky, resembling black hills when seen from a distance. It created a kind of ghostly skyline. As we continued walking the gloom increased and we could now only see faint outlines of things. We saw vague shadows of clumps of girls and babies, huddled together. Such was the darkness, that the solitary lights of the mobile phones being held by various kayayo, were now the only indication that certain shop fronts were 'inhabited'. We made out a small group of humanity nestled together on the left side of the track. An older kayayo woman was among them and she had a huge growth on her neck. Most of them were now lying on their cloths or bits of cardboard ready to go to sleep for the night. This group was from the village of Dabakpi in the Mamprusi region. They were what I called a 'lucky group' as they had a clean, tidy shop front with a tiled floor and a fence around. In this group there were about twenty girls. This track was littered all over with discarded rubbish and I wondered where Shagba and his refuse collectors were tonight.

In the next doorway were some other women from the same village. This whole batch of shop fronts, which comprised three or four shops, was tiled and surrounded by wire mesh. Suddenly, I saw Rebecca. She was standing around talking to some other girls nearby. We almost collided in the shadows surrounding us. They were encased in the yellow glow of the naked flame of an adjacent kerosene lamp. Baby Madihah was not with her. She was wearing tight black jeans and a Lurex top, which I'm sure would have greatly pleased the elders in her village, had they seen it. I imagined her being accused of 'dressing like a man' by her village kinsmen. She greeted George and I in her characteristic quiet and dignified way, smiling serenely. She then continued talking to her friends.

Immediately in front of this row of shop fronts, which housed the female inhabitants of yet another village in exile, a lady had set up a table on a low stool. Next to the table she had placed a coal pot on which was burning charcoal. On the table she had put out various tins of Milo, condensed milk, sugar, coffee, tea bags, a tray of eggs, some loaves of bread, and 'salad' consisting of a plastic bowl of chopped up tomato, onion and salt. Herself, and her sole means of livelihood, which had been arranged in an orderly manner before her, were both shrouded in the saffron radiance reflected from the exposed flame that flickered beneath her face on the table. The warm light caressed her cheeks and brow bone, revealing a beautiful countenance. From this stall she made and sold sandwiches of fried Spanish omelette and tea or coffee for passers-by, including myself. From such a tiny 'business' she could probably make as much as Gh10 cedis (£5 Sterling) in an evening.

We came to another shop. This was situated well back from the drain giving the girls a large sleeping area of about thirty feet long between the drain and the road on one side and the shop front on the other. They did not therefore need to balance precariously on steps or narrow strips of pavement. Many girls in this shop front were sitting on their empty paint pots. Another girl sat doing her washing in her metal bowl. They told us they came from the village of Bowa, near Walewale. As we gradually progressed up this track in obscurity, the girls and babies multiplied. What seemed like hundreds of adolescent girls and their babies and younger sisters were sleeping on the dirty pavements and shop fronts. On the other side of the road was another group of girls we almost missed, they being in almost total darkness. They were also from the village of Bowa. In the distance, through the darkness, the orange embers of a charcoal fire glowed. We continued walking.

The next group of girls we found sleeping outside a shipping container that had been cut in half and transformed into a kiosk. It was painted entirely in red and emblazoned with the ubiquitous Vodafone logo. The patch in front of this 'shop' was surrounded by the type of wire mesh you find at the front of rabbit hutches. Inside another ragged group of girls slept. They said they were from Bubogipu, yet another Mamprusi village. Yet still I had not come across any one group of Dagomba girls and this reinforced what I had been thinking earlier, that the girls seemed to settle according to tribal allegiance.

In the distance and darkness we could vaguely make out yet another contour of vague human forms, like a large hump on the pavement. The only light we now had was from our mobile phones. We shone the light from our phone onto the bulge. On sensing the light a few of them stirred. As the light further illuminated the group, we noticed several naked babies sleeping next to their mothers on a piece of cardboard on the pavement. One was still sucking his mother breasts. I saw two more toddlers sitting alone in the middle of the road, either side of a metal saucepan. They were dipping in their hands and taking out rice. It was dangerous as if a car or motorbike had come along they may not have seen them and they would have been run over. George and I picked them up and took them back to their group. Their mothers were sleeping.

It was not long after this that George and I passed by the metal gates that locked the central area of the market. It was these gates that had locked us in the night Rebecca had been assaulted by the so-called 'kayayo minder' Shagba. It was also behind these gates that Rebecca and her group usually slept. Despite being late the gates were still not locked so we walked in. We saw some of the girls from Bandugu milling around, carrying out their nightly rituals. To my surprise I spotted the little gazelle Latifa, who told me she had returned to Accra only yesterday. She looked even more skinny and bony than before, her possum eyes glittered in the darkness reflecting the light from our mobile phones. She leant up against the towering wall, smiling tentatively at me, as if she was unsure of how she should behave. As she was alone with us without the backup of her peers, her usual shyness gripped her. Yet it was not long before the other girls on spotting us, ran over. They jumped up and clapped as they approached. I started showing them the recent photos I had taken in their village, the faint light of the camera now shining on their faces as they looked down at the lens. They were quite amazed to see their 'entire village' paraded before them on this small contraption, as each picture flashed up they were calling out the names and pointing at the people they recognized. The familiar faces they had known since childhood.

Then, out of the blue, the stoned gatekeeper appeared, with the customary spliff hanging out of his mouth. He told us, in his slow and sluggish manner, that we had to leave as he was locking the gates. As we left, the girls stood pressed against the cold metal, their heads wedged between the bars, watching George and I disappear into the darkness.

When we got to the end of this track we came to the corner where, some weeks earlier, I had spoken to the tomato seller. She had been complaining to me, as a baby had been left lying alone behind her stall. She had told me angrily how the kayayo did not care for their babies properly. During the day this corner was bustling with activity and commerce. But this evening, under the cover of darkness the same patch took on a vastly different hue. On this corner lay an enormous group of about fifty or sixty girls in addition to the babies and toddlers and 'baby' kayayo.

The girls slept in front of about eight or nine shops which curved round the corner into the next street. The girls took up part of one street, the rounded end /corner and then part of an adjoining street. The whole place was cluttered with empty paint pots, metal bowls, check bags and was completely criss-crossed with washing lines sagging under the weight of the night's wet washing. They told us they were from the village of Litusu.

We soldiered on then glimpsed some high steps coming up directly from a drain. There were about four or five steps in all where many kayayo were sleeping. It was a miracle they didn't topple over into the drain below, as the steps were very narrow, barely twenty centimetres wide. Some were laying half on one step and half on another. It looked very uncomfortable.

We now turned right again back onto the main track. The number of kayayo girls we saw sleeping outside began to increase. All of a sudden the lights came back on. Indistinct shapes once again took on human forms. Suddenly a surge of cheers rang out from all around. Light had returned! We walked on now at a quicker pace as we no longer had to tread carefully. The number of kayayo milling around increased tremendously. What was particularly noticeable around here was the number of 'baby kayayo' or very young kayayo girls between the ages of four and five to about nine or ten years. I asked some of the 'older' girls, mostly in their teens, if these small girls actually carried heavy loads as they looked too small. I imagined that if they carried loads like the older girls it would probably break their necks. They told me,

'No, these girls look after the babies.'

This confirmed to me what I had been hearing but until then had still not been sure of. The fact was that small children even as young as four or five were being brought south now by the already under-aged kayayo girls to look after infants between the ages of one month to two years.

I squeezed one small girl's cheek, and about twenty of them jumped up in unison clapping, cheering and laughing. I did it again, and the crowd increased more. Then they wanted me to do it again and yet more small girls crowded round and it started to get out of hand. It became like a game.

The first doorway on this new lane housed girls from the village of Duduli. They were all Mamprusi. There were about twenty girls and babies in this doorway. As we continued to progress along the dirt tracks lined with shabby, rickety wooden kiosks now lit by light bulbs of varying colours the number of 'villages in exile' started to multiply. Paint pots now were sky high, metal bowls littered the road, huddles of girls were hidden behind lines and lines of wet washing tied to poles on either side of the shop fronts in which they slept. We passed the 'village' of Pepiculu, now emptied of forty of its young female inhabitants. Next to this village laid the village of Limpolo, with over thirty of its inhabitants lying huddled beneath a kiosk emblazoned with a logo advertising 'Indomie Noodles'. Next to this, in front of a 'Big Jones Rice Master' kiosk, lay the girls and babies from Makali village, twenty-eight in all. Next to that was the town of Nyanti, where around forty girls lay in front of a kiosk emblazoned with vivid colours advertising 'Blue Band Margarine'.

In the next doorway were girls from Ligani village. I spotted one lying asleep on the bare cement floor, with nothing under her to protect her from the cold, nor over her to give warmth. Another two young girls about ten or eleven years old sat braiding each other's hair in the dim light. It went on and on and on. On and on and on. Village after village after village. Each in its own small doorway. Each forming its own small tight knit microcosm in this far off land. We reached the last corner. About another two hundred girls were sleeping here, mainly from the village of Shoslu. I would estimate that in total, and given the fact that we had not counted the many girls that slept in the central market area and also that many of them were missing probably still bathing, there should be between two and three thousand kayayo girls living in Tonga market alone.

I now began to realize why people had told me that is was so easy to find the girls in a huge city such as Accra, even though they had no address, except a doorway. I remember Officer Gyedu telling me,

'They can find them...they know how to find them.'

Before mobile phones, facebook, email and google maps, people from villages like Bandugu and Wialu could within a short time trace their loved ones amid the teeming millions through their own 'bush telegraph' system: word of mouth, kinship, clan and tribal loyalties that reached back over millenniums. It was incredible.

It was breathtaking what I had seen. Whole regions and villages emptied of their female inhabitants. A constant stream of them endlessly coming and going, recreating their homes and villages thousands of miles away.

I began to realize that Tonga market represented the Mamprusi region in exile. It was the exile of its young women, female children and babies. Each doorway represented a microcosm of the village back home. It was as if each village in the northern regions was again reproducing itself in the city. In the Upper East region Wialu laid adjacent to Bandugu, in the market Wialu's doorway laid nearby to Bandugu's doorway. Each village and the small intimate world associated with it was again reinvented and recreated in a far-flung region. But this newly created region was different to the one that had been left behind in one important aspect.

It contained no menfolk. No males. It was a world consisting and made up entirely of women.

Chapter Fifteen

A day in the life of a Kayayo

I had now estimated the number of girls in the market. It had been far more than I had ever imagined. I had also realized that they were all from one tribe, Mamprusi, and that they arranged themselves in this 'rectangle' of bustling commerce which was Tonga Market, according to their own private village groups. Yet I still hadn't really learned what a normal working day for them was like. How did a 'normal' day for them unfold? I had heard about the backbreaking work, the heat, the rain, the insults and their inability to even be able to rest for a few moments. Yet I needed to experience this myself as I went around with them, as they carried their loads from place to place, as they bore the weight of their loads.

I had spoken to Nurah and Rebecca about this and we had arranged to meet under the mango tree at 6am one morning. When I got there I was shocked. The tree had almost disappeared. It had been pruned and cut back almost to its trunk. It no longer provided the much-needed shade onto the pavement beneath. The patch beneath its once thick boughs was deserted. Neither Rebecca nor Nurah were there. I decided to go to the warehouse where they last had been sleeping. When I got there Rebecca was just waking, so I decided to go back to the now slimmed down tree and wait. After the trouble with Shagba I did not want to be hanging around the area and be seen. I was in fact in his 'territory'. Outside the perimeter of the market, on the main road, he had no jurisdiction or at least I hoped not.

I arrived at the mango tree and sat under it with

some of the other girls from Bandugu, who had already arrived. There were now four of them, all sitting on their upturned bowls. As the tree no longer offered shade some of the girls had shifted to the adjacent corner a few yards away. After a short time Rebecca and Nurah arrived with Madihah and Romatsu on their backs and both sat down on the empty plastic paint pots. I asked Nurah what she carried in her pot. She told me it was medicine for Romatsu. This included a small 'twist' of baby powder and-a-half used tube of cream, which I had bought to treat Romatsu's sores many months ago. Nurah then went off to buy nappies. She soon came back and handed one new disposable nappy to Rebecca. They told me the nappies cost 30pws or 50psws (between 15-25 pence Sterling). Many of the girls were cleaning their teeth with the chewing stick, the dibga, spitting it out in sections.

The domestic morning activities continued next to the 'Guinness is Good for You' emblazoned kiosk beside which they sat. Two more girls sauntered over with their babies and sat down. A little later entrepreneurial Aysha came over carrying her empty bowl. The decorations on her hands had now faded. There were seven girls, five with babies, now sitting outside the kiosk which was in fact, a quarter of a shipping container which had been converted to make a shop. I had no idea what the kiosk sold when it was open. The girls were all sitting inside their bowls, with many of the babies climbing over them. Today, all the babies were wearing minute identical plastic shoes of the same design. Nurah told me graciously how they had bought the shoes in the market for only 50psws (25 pence). We tried more and more to cramp under the awning of the brown and cream coloured 'Guinness' kiosk, desperately trying to hug the shade, as the sun was attempting to thrust its rays towards us more and more. Little Romatsu, Nurah's baby, was playing with a piece of cardboard she had found. Yet more girls now wandered over to join our expanding group.

I was now coming to realize how this unit worked. When they had finished a job they may come back to the tree and touch base, rest for a while, chat to any other girls who may also be there before going off once again to another job. Sometimes there could be as many as fourteen or twenty girls here, other times just two or three. Generally there was continuity. Normally at any one time some of the group would be there. Those from Bandugu village knew that if at any time during the day they needed to rest, share food or chat, this patch under the tree would always be available. Girls were leaving and re-joining the group all day. It seemed to be one of the few places where all the girls from Bandugu could congregate without being harassed and I had always had the impression, until today, that the 'The Blue House' from which the tree grew was deserted as I had never witnessed any soul either going in or out of the property, and at night when passing I never once noticed any lights from inside the building. I believed they had been lucky in that they had found a 'spot' where they could not be disturbed or moved on. Today, however, all this seemed to have changed.

As I sat there I suddenly noticed little Latifa walking past with a massive load of charcoal on her head, her 'madam', the woman whose load it was, strolling behind her. She attempted to nod and smile at me but the load was so heavy she could hardly move her head. Perspiration was streaming down her forehead and face like spring water. As she walked on I observed her bony frame, the way she constantly had to bend her knee to transfer the weight from her shoulders. I kept thinking any minute the massive load would break her tiny back.

I looked back at the group, and saw that Latifa's sister Rayina had joined us. She was holding a mobile phone from which Joy FM, a local Ghana radio station, was broadcasting. I listened, and learnt that the previous day the Egyptian President Hosni Mubarak had stepped down. Rayina abruptly changed the channel preventing me from gaining more details of the story. Music was now playing. She was dancing to the rhythm. Aysha joined Rayina and also started to dance. Other girls were now starting to tie their babies to their backs, picking up their empty bowls. They were going off to find work. They headed towards the centre of the market. One girl, whose name was Kookaya, looked very sick. Her arm was heavily bandaged. I asked what had happened. Rebecca told me that the previous day she had cut her arm badly on glass while she was carrying her load. I remembered Doctor Asamoah at the nearby polyclinic mentioning to me this very same problem.

'The arm had to be stitched, it cost altogether 15 cedis,' Rebecca reported miserably

'How did she pay for this?

Rebecca glanced over to check on baby Madihah who was now fighting with Romatsu over the piece of cardboard.

'We had to use the susu money...now we have to save more before we can use the susu money to buy our things.'

It was most probably not Kookaya's 'turn' to receive the susu money. However, sickness will allow you to bring forward your turn. In this way the susu savings schemes provided life saving insurance in times of dire need. Added to this was the kayayo 'death benefit scheme' whereby representatives of all kayayo in the market collected from their village groups to contribute to funeral and other costs for the dead girl. It was because of these communal efforts that the girls, despite their dire poverty, could sometimes afford things such as hospital and funeral fees, costs that other more prosperous people in the community struggled to meet.

While all this was going on the girls were breastfeeding their babies intermittently. Aysha stopped dancing and started to collect coins from the girls around, she was going to buy food for the older girls who were currently busy with their babies. I also gave her money to buy food for me; fried egg and 'tealeaf'. She soon came back swinging a large black polythene carrier bag, inside this were eight smaller black plastic bags and about eight sachets of water. Inside each little bag was a little portion of rice with some pepper sauce, it had cost each of them 50pws (25 pence Sterling). They had also each paid 10psw (5 pence Sterling) for the water that, together with 30psws for the nappies, came to Gh1 cedi, which was about 50 pence. It was still only about 8am. If they had to buy water to bathe, go to the toilet and buy toilet paper this would have been another 50-80psws or even one cedi. That's Gh2 cedis, about £1.00 (Sterling) even before breakfast. I was not sure if they washed both in the morning and evening. If they did the expense would mount up.

Out of the blue, two girls jumped up and joined Rayina who was still dancing to the tune ringing out from her mobile phone. Now three of them were dancing as the sun gradually gained momentum in the turquoise sky. Its rays, now gaining strength, were trying more desperately to harass us as we were simultaneously trying harder to escape, continuing to push deeper and deeper under the narrow awnings. It was merciless in its quest to attack us and I thought of how the kayayo have to use similar tactics against the rain.

All the girls, bar those dancing, were now eating their meagre portions of rice, sharing it with their babies. They pushed the rice into their babies' mouths with their fingers. Rebecca put Madihah into her bowl and I went to feed her myself. On seeing me approach she screamed. Nothing changes!

Now the number of girls under the awning of 'The Guinness is Good for You' kiosk had risen to ten. They constantly came and went. Sat down. Chatted. Went. Another then came. Another went. It went on. Some who had gone earlier now passed, their tahilis full of the heavy loads their customers, smart office ladies getting in a quick shop before starting work, had asked them to carry. The office ladies marched behind them. The girls called out across the street to our little group as they passed, being careful not to turn their heads quickly. Most were carrying loads of vegetables and other provisions such as rice, cooking oil and yams. The weekly shop.

Almost an hour had passed since I first arrived, but many girls were still sitting around. Yet more girls arrived with their black plastic bags full of cooked rice. The morning's breakfast. They discussed what they had paid. Some paid 50pws some paid 40pws. For them 10pws (5 pence Sterling) would make a difference, with that they could buy a sachet of water. I remember how so many of the poor in Accra hit the roof when the price of sachet water went up from 5pws to 10pws. It was such a small amount, literally 2 pence, but for people on these incomes, who will by all means have to buy at least three or four of these sachet waters a day, it made a difference.

We were now all sitting in front of the kiosk, on some on the planks of wood that had been placed over the open gutter, the same open gutter that I had several times witnessed men urinating into. Nurah had put her metal bowl onto a plank of wood and Romastu was sitting in it. The sun was getting hot and we were all perspiring profusely. I was having to suck my tea through a hole in a black plastic bag and it was too hot. People were walking past ignoring our little group, as if we were invisible. I suppose in a way we were, unless you looked down onto the pavement you wouldn't notice us. Just as I was thinking this an older man spotted us, he saw me and then came over and started shouting at the kayayo.

'Why are you not going to school?'

No one took any notice of him, they just continued eating their breakfast.

'They take the abuse as part of their job,' as Martin the banker had said some months ago, 'They don't even hear it.'

Just then another girl, her baby securely fastened in her cloth, jumped up abruptly and went off to work carrying her empty bowl. She returned walking past about five minutes later with a big load of shopping on her head. Another smart lady in an office suit was walking behind her. She transported the huge load to her customer's car, almost stumbling on a stone as she did so and packed it neatly into the boot. She came back and sat with the group for a few more minutes and then went back into the market to look for another customer.

Rebecca continued to sit on her paint pot containing Madihah's powder and cream. She put Madihah back in the bowl and the baby looked at me again and started wailing. Nurah's baby, Romatsu, smiled and looked over at me, still playing with her 'cream biscuits' cardboard wrapper. Latifa's sister, Rayina, started to sing a traditional song from the village. Some minutes earlier the mobile phone battery had died putting an end to the music. I often wondered where they charged their phones and learnt that they usually asked a shop or kiosk owner whom they knew to do this for them. Rayina continued to sing and then all the others joined in. It was melodic and enchanting to listen to, far better than the rap music from Rayina's mobile phone! It seemed so nice, sitting in the shade of the Guinness kiosk outside, eating breakfast and listening to this song. We were the lowest of the low, sitting at the side of the gutter but, in many respects, there was happiness. They had each other, their beautiful babies. They had their dreams, which eventually materialized, albeit often more slowly than anticipated. They had their village, where they belonged and were loved. Here was temporary. Transient. A means to an end.

Little Madihah was now really tucking into the remainder of the rice inside the black plastic bag. She put her hands in by herself and was pulling it out in big handfuls, she then pushed it into her tiny mouth. Another girl arrived with a few more sachets of water. Nurah got one and started to feed Romatsu the water from a hole at the top. Romatsu sucked furiously. Another girl who had left some minutes ago now passed, her bowl piled high with yams. She constantly had to bend due to the weight. Rivulets of perspiration streamed down her face, and her tiny baby, strapped to her back, squinted as the sun's rays hit his eyes.

The owner of the 'Guinness is Good for You' kiosk arrived, a plump middle aged women in a dark brown dress. All the girls suddenly seemed to panic, jumping up and shifting their babies, their bowls and their half-eaten breakfasts to the exterior of an adjoining kiosk, which was still closed. As we did this, the lady opened her kiosk and started to set up her stall. She threw them a contemptuous look as if they were vermin. She didn't bother to greet them or acknowledge them in any way. The girls seemed unperturbed. For them this was just an occupational hazard. She continued tossing poisonous glances in our direction. She looked annoyed because we were still sitting near her stall. She started to get her eggs from the iron shipping-container and laid them according to their sizes onto the table she had erected outside.

We were now sitting outside another shipping container which had been cut into a quarter of its original size. This one was painted red with 'vodafone' written on the front. I also had no idea what this container was used for. It wasn't long after that I noticed the girls again looking anxious and worried. Once again they jumped up and quickly moved their bowls and babies, this time across the street outside the side wall of the Blue House. A tall young man arrived, probably in his early thirties, and he gave them an equally intimidating look. He opened his kiosk, which was full of light bulbs or varying colours and sizes, plugs adaptors, rolls of electrical wire and other electronic accessories. He shouted across to one of the girls, and waved his arms furiously. He was telling them to come and pick up their rubbish.

I was starting to get an inkling of what it was like to be a kayayo girl on Accra's streets. Twice within twenty minutes we had been forced to pack up our food, drink, babies and stools and move to a different place. They had to interrupt their breakfast, their babies' feeds. Sometimes other kayayo have told me that they were absolutely exhausted, yet whenever they tried to sit down people shouted at them to move on. They went from doorway to doorway, gutter to gutter, never finding peace. Nevertheless they seemed to take it all with a pinch of salt as the girls often told me,

'That's how they are, there is nothing we can do about it.'

They accepted their fate.

Three kayayo including Nurah and baby Romatsu now got up and started tying their babies to their backs. They all walked off together. They told me they were going to Nima to do 'washing clothes'. I had often heard of the 'Washers of Nima' and how the people who washed your clothes there were renowned for making them unbelievably clean. The girls told me they could earn between Gh5 (2.50 Sterling) to Gh8 cedis (£4.00 Sterling) for a morning of washing clothes. Most people in Ghana did hand washing and those that could afford would send the washing out to be done by professional washers. As I stood watching Rebecca and Nurah recede into the distance, yet more overloaded kayayo girls struggled past me, their customers strolling along beside them as they made their way to the cars and packed in the goods. The egg seller, now to our left, gave our group another derisive glance and continued to arrange her eggs. The sun was now high in the sky, merciless in its heat.

Another week passed. It was now almost the end of February and the months were slipping past quickly. As I now no longer had a car, I walked to Tonga most mornings to buy my groceries. As I entered, there were some girls sitting on their bowls under the now bare tree. Mahab, who had been so surprised some weeks ago when I had arrived out of the blue at Bundugu, was now back with her baby. She and Adnan looked well and rested. Mahab told me proudly in her deep resonant voice, and Rebecca translated, how her brother was now making money because of the bicycle she had taken back with her to the village.

'Now he can travel far to the town and there he is learning to be a car mechanic. Sometimes he fixes the cars and the people they give him money. He say me he will pay me back the money for the bicycle when he get more.'

Mahab told me that this time she wanted to save for roofing sheets to put on her family house. This made me remember Kadima, the kayayo's forty-two year-old 'senior citizen' and I wondered how far she had got with saving for these.

'The roof of my house leaks, and when wind comes sometimes it blows the grass so I want a metal roof on my house in the village.'

This led young Aysha who was sitting nearby to tell me about the progress she had made in saving for her sewing machine.

'Mummy I now have only another ten cedis to save and I can buy the machine. The lady in the shop is keeping it for me, and I have already given her most of the money. I don't want to keep the money with me because I might lose it or someone can steal it.'

She wanted me to come with her to the shop to see her beloved sewing machine but I didn't have time. I promised I would come another time.

I asked, Mahab jokingly if she wanted to be 'my kayayo' and she accompanied me into the market. We first got to the 'cold store,' a small shop with two deep freezers selling frozen meat and fish. It was a precarious livelihood due to the constant power cuts. Generally the power was not off long enough for the frozen goods to completely defrost, but if that did happen shopkeepers and cold-store owners could potentially lose all their stock. The relentless power cuts or 'Lights Off' as it was known locally made life for Accra's poor and rapidly growing middle class even more insecure and unstable. Small businesses such as hairdressers, internet cafés, welders, mechanics, corn mills, seamstresses, and a plethora of other enterprises often had to shut down their businesses for hours on end, sometimes whole days because of the cuts. The larger companies could afford generators, but for those struggling to make ends meet, for those who tried hardest to make their small mark in the world for the benefit of themselves and their families, power outages forced many to teeter on the edge.

I asked the shopkeeper for two kilos of chicken legs while Mahab and Latifa stood next to me, chatting. The shopkeeper, a skinny woman wearing an orange polka-dot dress, glanced over at them and unable to use her blood covered hands to point, jutted out her chin scornfully in their direction. She looked down her nose at them and said to me offensively,

'Are these with you?'

I think she expected me to say, 'no' and she would then have duly started shouting and cursing at them to go away. As I didn't, she handed me my chicken, rubbing her bloodied hands on a nearby cloth. I continued walking, buying fruit and vegetables and putting them in Mahab's bowl. Each time I did this she bent her knees to lower the bowl down to my level. Her long arms were strong and muscular. I couldn't help thinking that for shoppers, the kayayo acted as 'human supermarket trollies'. Instead of wheeling your trolley to your car you take the kayayo. As I walked around the market I saw busy office women in suits coming to shop after work just like me, all with kayayo girls by their side.

Walking home some ten minutes later I stumbled across a scuffle brewing in front of me. I felt wary at first. An elderly man of about seventy years was physically trying to restrain his wife, who was flailing from side to side like a trout on a fishhook, with some difficulty. The woman was holding an empty bottle of mineral water, and shouting at two or three kayayo standing nearby. I asked what the problem was.

'I have just cleaned my part of the drain (which was the drain in front of her stall where she had been selling fried yams) and she (she pointed furiously at the kayayo) came along and threw her bottle in my drain. Why doesn't she throw the bottle in her part of the drain?'

The two kayayo were obviously hurling insults at the woman in their language as this could be discerned by their tone, body language, and the war-like expressions on the girls' faces. The man continued to hold his arms tightly around his wife's waist to prevent what would most probably have become another kayayo 'battle' which would necessitate passers-by to break up. I realized that the ferocity of this woman's response over the littering of 'her drain' was out of balance and I couldn't help thinking that the resentment now being shown towards these two girls was a calculable indicator of the general animosity and anger that had been simmering for months throughout the market. All it needed was a spark to ignite the raging fire. I had been noticing this type of smouldering anger a lot in the market recently. Yet to be fair, one has also to look at the problem from the shopkeepers' point of view. It cannot be pleasant when arriving at your shop premises, to be every morning confronted with a horde of girls and their babies, so tightly packed across the floor, that it was even difficult to open your door. In addition, most usually the previous night's washing would be strung up, several layers thick. Not only that, during shop opening hours the kayayo often hung around outside outlets, blocking the entrance for customers. The shopkeepers felt in turn that the kayayo were harassing their customers. Quite a few times when I had been to shops, the owners would ask me sneeringly,

'Is she with you?'

Shopkeepers habitually shouted and chased away the girls, telling them to leave their customers alone.

On top of all this were the frequent fights which erupted between the girls, leaving it up to the market dwellers to separate. The girls were living in a place not only where they were not wanted but amongst people who actively disliked and resented them. This in turn caused the kayayo to feel even more insecure about their status both in the market and the city in general. It was a state of mutual hostility that could very easily flare up one day.

It had been some time since I had seen George and I guessed he was having trouble finding a wife. I wondered how much longer it would be before he returned. Not having him around meant it was difficult to have any meaningful conversations with the girls. So it was a relief when some days later I received a phone call from him saying that he was back in Accra. He told me he had indeed found a wife. She worked in a restaurant he had been frequenting in his local area. He said he liked this lady and said also that,

'Because I am handsome small (just a little bit handsome)...she liked me too.'

He had been to see her parents, and all had been agreed. He said he wanted to get married before his trip to England for the book launch, because it 'would help with the visa.'

He was also asking me if he could be on the cover of the book and I had to remind him that the book was being written about the kayayo and not George Abugah.

Later that day I strolled alone through the market. I walked up to the Ricemaster shop but could see no sign of Poppy and her friends. The shop was open. They obviously would not be welcome and would return only under the cover of darkness. Yet I could see their 'landlady'.

She resembled an ancient matriarch. She was a large

old lady wearing huge glasses. She sat on a very high stool at the back of her shop, so high that the top of her head almost hit the ceiling. The seat of the stool could only be reached by climbing some steps. The resulting image combined elements of the surreal and the comic. Cornflake boxes, Blue Band tubs, pale pink toilet rolls and Nescafé containers granted her a colourful backdrop. The numerous fluorescent bulbs afforded no subtle hues and she was cast, along with her technicoloured stage set, in dazzling lights that reflected onto the shiny perspiration covering her corpulent frame. She sat still and motionless with a fixed expression of solemnity, not even appearing to blink. This shop was her world, her fiefdom. She had reigned over it from her position of elevation for decades, and you got the feeling she would continue to do so until the day of her death.

I was a little hesitant at first when approaching her. I told her I was writing a book about the kayayo and I would be interested in hearing her views. I knew some kayayo girls slept outside her shop during the evening. On hearing the word 'kayayo' she shifted from side to side on her throne, as if wanting to get comfortable for what was to be a lengthy soliloquy. Like most people she had strong opinions on the subject.

'Do the kayayo bother you at all?'

'Yes they do bother me, they go to the toilet in the gutter and drop it in front of my shop. When they are sleeping at night and they feel like going to the toilet, they just do it in the gutter. They will not bother to walk to the proper toilet.'

She also added,

'They even put their children's toilet in the gutter.'

She started to complain that they didn't want to pay the money to bathe at the bathhouse. She became incensed.

'So they start making fires outside my shop and boiling water to bath. Even they don't bathe properly, they just wash under their armpits.'

I asked her if this was the case why didn't she just tell them to go?

'If I tell them to go they won't go, after I go home they will just come back and then I see them again here when I arrive in the morning. Sometimes if they don't get up I throw water on them.'

The matriarch ceased her speech. She once again sat motionless for some minutes. She let out a deep sigh and resumed.

'And you know more and more are coming, every day more arrive.'

As she was speaking a storm started to break, the wind blew up clouds of dust, the sky turned purple black, the coconut trees, tall above the shops on the distant horizon began to bend.

'But sometimes I want to weep when I see them. They are carrying loads and they are not strong enough, they do not eat enough and they are not strong. To carry a heavy load you have to be strong.'

The rain now started to fall, slowly at first but then after one or two minutes it lashed down. People in the market started to rush for cover. The matriarch stirred again.

'Look at them!' she shouted gruffly, pointing with a heavily bejewelled hand, 'look at them, they are running now with their loads to go and sleep on their verandas.'

I looked across and saw the frail, stick-like kayayo through the grey chiffon mist of rain. They were running, one arm holding onto their loads as they went.

'I've seen many frail kayayo girls fall down carrying heavy loads,' she added now more softly, 'They don't eat well, they are not strong, they would rather save the money than eat, they want to take the money home.'

Mini-waterfalls now gushed from the eaves attached to the rusted, corrugated iron roofs' the same roofs that the kayayo slept under at night. The wind was now lashing the rain against me at an incredible speed as I stood on the shop's terrace, and even though I was well under the awning I was becoming drenched. I started to feel cold. I was picturing them. Poppy, 'the old lady' Kadima, Mamuna and her children and young Lashida, huddled in this shop front standing half the night in the rain. The matriarch stared sleepily into the downpour. I ventured, hesitantly, to get her to talk more.

'You know the people don't like giving the kayayo with babies heavy loads. They feel pity for the babies. If you have a baby it is more difficult to find work, so the girls go back and bring their younger 'sisters' to mind the babies.'

We sat again still for some time. The strong winds were blowing walls of water in criss-cross patterns, this way and that, around the market like whispering tornados. The matriarch suddenly appeared to become more angry.

'I know one child, one babysitter who sleeps here. She is very beautiful, very very beautiful. She told me that her 'older sister' came to the village to take her out of school so that she could come down here to babysit for her.'

She started to wave her index finger furiously at me.

'I told the kayayo not to bring the girl down here, I told her to allow the girl to go to school.'

I glanced across the dirt road. I could see the other dimly lit shops through the indignant grey rain. People were standing in long lines. Motionless. They resembled mannequins in shop windows. They no longer seemed human. Gradually the angry rain dwindled. The outraged wind receded. The wrathful deluge transformed to drizzle, and no longer assailed those who sought refuge. The sky lightened, the coconut trees wavered just vaguely.

The towering matriarch continued to sit motionlessly. I told her I was leaving but she didn't stir from her trance. I left.

As I walked home through the market great lakes had now appeared in the dips and dimples of the dirt tracks. The kayayo now waded through them unperturbed. They all wore flip-flops so their shoes would dry off in minutes.

I was thinking about what the matriarch had told me. That kayayo girls were going back north and actually pulling children out of school so they could come to Accra to live and work on the streets. Babysitting the kayayo's children now seemed more important than going to school. I wondered how many other young children had actually been plucked from their classrooms, classrooms and education that were provided free of charge, to come down to live this horrific life on the streets.

Chapter Sixteen

'We Are Like Cows, We Sleep Standing Up'

Since returning from the north I had not seen Poppy and the other girls from the Rice Master Shop: Mamuna and her children, the 'old lady' Kadima, and young Lashida. I was keen to find Poppy to tell her the good news that I had met her parents and also show her the photos I had taken of them. I was also eager to find out how far she had got in paying off the debt resulting from the stolen susu money. This had been taken from her while she had been sleeping during the night. Last time we met, with the help of an extra night job she had been making good progress.

I rang George and asked him if he could locate Poppy and arrange for us to meet the next evening at the Spot. He rang back later and said they would come there. The next evening I parked my (now borrowed) car outside the Spot and waited for them to come. It was now March, right in the middle of the hot season. Accra was sweltering. I preferred for the moment to sit inside my car. Inside my car I could revel in the wintry ambience of the air-conditioning. With the windows rolled up I could keep out the villainous odours in addition to the aggravating mosquitoes. It was as if my car was a barrier enabling me to sidestep the barbaric conditions outside

A face appeared at my window. Unexpectedly it was Rebecca and not Poppy. She had baby Madihah asleep on her back. She jumped in. She began to tell me excitedly how Aysha had managed to buy her sewing machine. She would be leaving for the north very soon. I told Rebecca that I wondered when she would be going back, now all the girls, Nurah, Mahab, Latifa and now Aysha had gone. She just smiled and lifted her shoulders to signify she didn't know. Then Rebecca bent down, she wanted to show me something she had wrapped in her cloth. She pulled out what looked a like piece of paper. When she held it in front of me I saw it was the picture of her father I had taken at the village. When I had given the girls the printed photos she had not been around and they promised to pass it on to her.

She just sat there looking at the picture and smiling to herself in her quiet unassuming manner. She looked up at me, the lights from outside reflecting in her piercing dark eyes.

'My father has been to school and he speaks English, did he speak to you in English?' she asked, once again looking at me with a strange mixture of pride and dignity.

'He spoke to me in Dagbani,' I added, 'Your father is very handsome and he resembles you a lot.'

I then told her how I had met her sister.

'When I saw your sister leaning against the tree near the dagbala she didn't even have to introduce herself, she looked so like you I knew immediately it was your sister.'

As I quietly watched her again looking down at the picture of her father I heard a faint tapping at the door.

Yet no face was at the window. I looked down. It was Martha with her crochet. Her bush telegraph and radar system had beamed out my exact location like a sat nav. She held up the crochet at the car window. I asked Rebecca to ask her which colour she now wanted.

'Pink'

She jumped in the car with Rebecca and myself and we quickly drove to the shop to buy the wool. Rebecca went in with her. As always she became jubilant and running off at great speed, she quickly disappeared into the crowd. We then drove back to our parking space outside the Spot.

I sat for some time staring out of the window. George's face then appeared beaming at the side window. He got in and started chatting excitedly about the things he would need for his forthcoming wedding and also the lack of money he had to buy them. Then yet another face appeared at my right side window, it was Gifty, the passive, long-suffering waitress at the Spot. She had a brand new hairdo, she was smiling and looked much happier. She announced to us all cheerfully, that she would be leaving her job next week as she had found a better one. The job here, she added, pointing at the dingy drinking spot we now all knew so well, didn't pay well and with her two children she just couldn't make ends meet.

Rebecca smiled.

'I am very happy for you, Gifty,' she said, 'You have tried.'

'Did you find a job in Dansoman near where you live?' I asked hopefully

'Yes, it's near to my home so I don't have to travel with my children any longer, they can go to school near my home.'

That was great for her and we said our goodbyes. Rebecca too decided it was time to leave. She got out of the car, tying her daughter once more to her back and disappeared, like Martha, into the darkness. I continued waiting; even with the windows wound up you could still hear a lot of noise coming from outside, not least the noise from the Spot's radio.

George's conversation had now turned to the familiar subjects of European travel and visa applications. He thought he might go to Italy as he had heard you could earn money there picking tomatoes.

After a few more minutes another face could be seen peering through the side window in the darkness. It was Poppy. I told her to jump in.

'Ooooh,' she said shivering as she climbed in, 'It's cold.'

Turning down the air-conditioning, I asked her how she was. I couldn't wait to tell her I had 'found' her village. She had also believed that I would never be able to find the place and in many respects I didn't blame her. It was so remote. She sat down next to me, rubbing her hands together. They were rough and weatherworn. She had the air of a young woman who worked unbelievably hard, thick set and strong. I asked her about the susu money. Immediately she livened up.

'I pay back plenty money. I pay back some of the money to the girls every week. I have been lucky with the tealeaf money ...the man there helps me a lot......I have also been working there on Sundays...I also manage to save my own money in another bag but I don't tell the other girls about this as they will say me that I have to give all to them first. The money in the other bag is for my children's school. I have saved Gh30 cedis (£15 Sterling) for the school.'

Poppy was a nifty saver, budgeting for her debt and leaving enough aside for pressing needs.

It was amazing and a credit to her ability and hard work how she had managed to bounce back financially in such a short time. She smiled at me proudly and I could sense she knew how much I admired her.

I then went on to tell Poppy the good news. I had reached her village of Wialu, and I recited the villages I had passed on the way, the same villages she had mentioned several weeks earlier. She squealed with excitement and disbelief, leaning forward on the front seat to hug me. I told her I had met her parents, and she hugged me again. I triumphantly pulled out the prints of them and gave them to her. There was a strange reaction. Instead of the smiles and shrieks I had envisaged, which I had got from the Bandugu girls when giving them the prints of their loved ones, I was hit by a deafening silence. Poppy looked at the picture of the two elderly people, frozen in time, standing stiffly beside their hut. As she stared at the photo she shook her head slowly. I was worried.

'I know these people, but they are not my mum and dad, they live some few yards from my house, but they are not my mum and dad.'

I asked myself had I travelled all that way only to meet strangers? I had given her name and her parents' names to the villagers and I had been taken to the hut of an old couple I had been led to believe were her parents. I told this old couple that I knew Poppy and they had told me she was their daughter. I recalled now that while talking to this couple I even then had had a feeling that something was amiss, but just couldn't put my finger on it. It just goes to show how confusing life can at times be. Maybe they also had a daughter called Poppy who lived in Accra, but we both had been talking about two completely different people. I showed her some more snaps and she recognised the people, calling out their names as she saw them.

I said to myself, 'Well at least I got the right village,' but I was bitterly disappointed, especially so when I realized how upset Poppy was about the whole thing. However, I was in no hurry to go back there again to rectify the mistake, especially as the trip had put the nail in the coffin for my car and I hadn't the money now to repair it.

Poppy said she had to go back to her tealeaf job and she rushed off into the darkness, into the bowels of the market.

A few days later I was on my way yet again to meet

George outside the Methodist church. I had just finished teaching English to a young Korean girl. We had been sharing jokes about police stops and she had told me how the police had threatened to arrest her father's friend for 'wearing sandals' in the car. I was late and decided to take a short cut through a gap in the hedge that ran through the centre of the road. Conveniently the police were waiting at the other side.

'Why did you do a U-turn there? It is not allowed.'

'I didn't see any sign saying that.'

'Come with me, I will show you.'

I was frogmarched to a small sign, almost concealed by foliage, which said 'no U-turns.'

'So come with us to the police station, you are under arrest!'

I told him I wasn't feeling well. I had malaria, which was true although I had started to feel a bit better.

'It doesn't matter, come with me.'

I had to drive to the station, and was told to sit on a wooden bench. I decided to play up my illness to maximum effect and lay down on the bench. A woman police officer who had been standing behind a counter asked me why I was lying down.

'I'm sorry I'm very ill, I can't sit up.'

She then turned to the police officer who had brought me in and shouted at him in English.

'Why did you bring in this lady when she is sick, can't you see that she is sick?'

The officer said, apologetically that he hadn't realized I was ill, he hadn't known.

The female officer then told me to go home. She was kind and sympathetic.

The officer who had just ten minutes earlier arrested me on Hospital Road, Tema, then accompanied me back to my car. He told me,

'So we have considered your plight and not gone on to charge you so you must consider me.'

In other words he meant, 'consider giving me some money'. I told him I didn't have any money but if I saw him again next time I'd give him some. That seemed to satisfy him and he gave me a firm, friendly handshake and we said our goodbyes.

I rang George and told him that I'd been stopped by the police and that I would be late. On my way back to Accra I got caught up in horrendous traffic approaching the Tema Motorway so I turned round back down Hospital Road and cut through Sakumono. Driving up the Spintex Road I passed the gigantic Action Chapel, with its pair of giant hands clasped together in prayer at the grand entrance, yet here of all places I didn't see any life size pictures of Bishop Duncan Williams nor the lion. I arrived at Kejetia much later than I had planned. I parked the car and rushed to sit in the middle of the wooden bench opposite the Methodist church. I sat there waiting for George. For the first time in living memory that night, as I sat down, the church was in darkness and silence. No lights twinkled and glittered. No speaking in tongues. No hymns that filled me with childhood memories. This evening I had not wanted to come. I felt ill and nauseous, but I had to continue. As George had said, 'the book was very important.'

After some few more minutes of waiting I saw the now familiar lofty figure running down the road. I got up and we walked down to the market entrance. As I was already ill, the smell of the market as we entered made me want to throw up. As we walked along I spotted Poppy's tealeaf stall ahead, lit up with a bare bulb hanging from a wire that had been extended from the shack behind it. In the distance she resembled a soldier ant. I could see her running backwards and forwards, pouring, stirring, taking money and giving change. As we passed we called out, and she ran over and hugged me as she always did, quickly telling me she was 'busy right now' but would come up to the shop front soon. I got to the shop front feeling even more ill.

Mamuna was sitting on a bucket, feeding baby Mohammed. Today he wasn't wearing his yellow power ranger suit, although some minutes later I caught sight of it hanging wet from the railings with the rest of the day's wash. I could see some of Kadima's tin roofing sheets tucked away in the corner, she was buying them bit by bit, ready to take back to her village, to put a new roof on her hut. She noticed me observing them and gave me a proud, knowing smile.

Although tonight the lights were on, the kayayo girls still managed to find hidden dark corners between containers or shacks, in which to bath. Now after talking to the ancient matriarch I realized why so many girls preferred to bathe near their shop fronts. Who could blame then? Most people would not like to trudge half a mile to bathe after working a long day at work. They, like us, preferred to bathe near to where they slept. A roaming headlight from a taxi moved and illuminated a nameless naked body. It bent modestly to hide its shame. Its moments of tenuous privacy had been intruded on. For the kayayo, even their clandestine bathing becomes a spectacle for public consumption, headlights rushing over scenes not meant for unrestricted viewing. It creates a surreal scene of teeming wretched humanity, creative in their struggle for survival.

We sat down on some buckets and both Mamuna and the 'old lady' Kadima showed me some marks on their legs.

'Sometimes we wake up in the mornings and find blood on our legs where the rats have chopped them in the night. The rats chop (eat) our legs.'

Kadima added,

'If we see the rats we chase them into the gutters. We will try to kill the rats, we hit them hard over the head with our bowls.'

I remembered the night I had spoken to Lamya and her friends in the dark depths of the market's interior. How I had mistaken the giant rats for cats. They were horrific.

We sat there for some time. The thought of the rats gnawing at the girls legs at night made me shiver. George was talking to a man in the shop next door. He always looked so well turned out, so smart and I never really understood how he could do it on such a meagre salary. Perhaps he rummaged for hours in the sprawling second hand markets to find the best designer labels.

I then sat thinking for some minutes and I remembered the conversation I had had some months before with Dr Azeem. I remembered he told me the awful story about how at times the kayayo girls would arrive at the hospital unconscious due to incomplete abortions. I wanted to find out more about this from the girls and other health matters relating to pregnancy.

I asked them if it was usual that many girls in the market were often not aware when their babies would be due or when they would give birth? The old lady, Kadima, unusually gave her opinion on this subject. She had just finished hanging the wet clothes onto the railing, which were now already starting to drip onto the floor on which we sat.

'The people they don't know when they will give birth, they do not know the date and sometimes they will go into labour in the market, even when carrying their load, and they will have to be taken to hospital.'

I remembered what Martin had told me about this. How he had witnessed a kayayo girl about to give birth by the side of the road, and how he had not being able to find a taxi who would agree to take the girl to hospital. Mamuna told me that if a girl gave birth in the market, the other kayayo would rally round together to send her back to the north, as they 'don't want you to sleep here with a newborn.'

I also asked them whether they gave their babies medicine to sleep.

Mamuna spoke.

'Yes, at times we give them medicine. If they cry too much in the night it disturbs our neighbours who sleep nearby.'

'Where do you buy the medicine?'

'We buy it from the chemical store, the chemical store near to the market. When the babies drink the medicine they sleep plenty.'

'Do you go for check-ups when you are pregnant?' I asked, increasingly feeling that I was going to throw up any minute. But I soldiered on.

Then both the 'old lady', Mamuna and some of the other girls around, including young Lashida told me that many girls will never go for a check-up when they are pregnant. They will see this, as with taking out health insurance, as unnecessary expenditure, money that could be otherwise saved. The girls cannot see the long term benefit of paying the Gh25 cedis that would ensure and provide free health insurance for the whole year. The health insurance would also cover their check-ups for pregnancy.

Young Lashida added,

'A few girls do go for check-up, they do go for check-up when they are pregnant.'

I asked them if they knew about the drug cytotech that Dr Azeem had mentioned. They told me,

'Sometimes we hear that people go to Bilal polyclinic about that but we haven't seen it.'

As we sat there leaning against the shop front, we watched two large white goats head butting each other as they fought it out in the middle of the dirt track. As they continued, Manuna and the other Wialu girls started to tell me how their boyfriends treated them badly.

Just then I saw a familiar figure rushing out of the darkness towards us - it was Poppy on a short break from the tealeaf stall. She sat down panting, out of breath, but eager as ever to get immersed in the conversation. Mamuna went on to say that she knew many girls who got boyfriends here in Accra. The old lady nodded in agreement. Lashida wondered whether she should agree or not. She kept quiet, her eyes looking around for signals as to the general consensus.

Poppy saw the short lull in the conversation as an opportunity to have her say on the matter. Glancing over at me, she said,

'When they get pregnant, the men they run away. I have a friend called Mayama who got pregnant in the market. It was with a man kayayo'.

I wondered how they managed to spend any private time at all with their boyfriends, the place was so crowded I couldn't imagine anyone even getting the chance to spend time alone here, let alone being able to sleep together.

Poppy continued.

'They find dark corners, empty kiosks and shipping containers, any dark places.' she said adding seconds later that,

'Only those with a lot of money could afford to pay for a room in a hotel, you will have to spend Gh15 cedis (£7.50) just to rent the room for four hours.'

In Ghana renting rooms by the hour is the norm in many hotels, where people go to spend time with their partners, often surreptitiously.

I was thinking about what Poppy had said. Tonga market was full of empty, putrid, dark corners. I felt sad for these girls when I realized that for them, even love and romance was a hurried affair that had to be done hastily and perfunctorily in squalid, dirty corners on sacks of charcoal or standing up in dark dingy kiosks, measuring no more than one square metre. Or perhaps their love consisted of no more than a few minutes in the back of a grubby trotro or taxi carried out amidst the knowing glances and sneers of male workmates? Then Poppy elaborated on the usual consequence of such liaisons.

'But when the girl gets pregnant the man is not helping her, she normally goes home to her parents to give birth. After giving birth and when she comes back to the market, the man he will come to see her again, he will want to have sex with her again, and if the girl refuse a fight will come.'

Then Mamuna said,

'But some girls when they come back they get pregnant again.'

I remember going to see the civil servant at the Ministry, how she explained that the initial problem of the kayayo was becoming more complex and difficult to solve. They were giving birth on the streets and a whole new generation of children were growing up living along the sidewalks. Poppy then went on to tell me that if the girl stayed in Accra and saw the man around,

'The man will say he is not responsible for the baby and he will tell the mother to go away.' She added,

'While the child is growing up the man does not normally take any interest, but by the time the child is about six years he will more often than not want to take the child back, especially if it is a boy. It is only later, when the mother has looked after the child for many years, after this, if he then sees his child in the market he will say to his friends 'look at this child, this child is mine'. But he will never ever want to look after it.'

Many women have told me stories like this in Ghana. That the man is not willing to take over the burden and responsibility of looking after the child, but very willing to use the child for his own self-aggrandizement when showing off in front of his friends and peers.

Poppy told me it was then, 'when the child is more grown', that there will often be a dispute over custody of the child, especially if it is a boy. This will mean that the father and mother will have to visit the chief's palace to resolve the situation. Usually the chief will make the father pay a small amount of compensation to the mother. This will be, according to Mamuna and Poppy, for 'her pains in bringing up the child', for example, giving birth, for the periods of sickness the mother has had to deal with and paying for food and clothing and all the other things she has had to bear as a mother. Poppy said the parents will go and say to the chief,

'Look, we looked after our daughter and her baby when she was pregnant, and we pay the hospital bills and the baby will grow, so if you want the child you have to give us compensation.'

Moreover they would always go to the chief first and only then, only if a resolution could not be reached, would they go to the police.

As we sat there watching the headlights snake up the dirt tracks, one of the babies sitting next to me started chewing the handles of my bag. I picked her up and she dribbled all over my face and mouth. I remembered the cholera epidemic that Doctor Azeem had told me about some time ago and about the numerous cases which were from this market, and I realized I should be more careful.

As the subject had got on to boyfriends and how they treated them I decided to delve more into this issue. I asked them if the boys ever tried to extort money from them, by threatening them, for example.

'Some girls give money to their boyfriends, and the boyfriends will not pay the money back, and he will beat the girl if she demands the money back.'

I thought of the scuffle some nights ago. That too was over a similar issue.

'Yes it happens that if you don't give them money they will force you to sleep with them,' said Poppy angrily.

I wondered if this was just a euphemism for rape. But I didn't delve further.

The girls were in a no win situation, they were exploited by their customers who often either refused to pay them their agreed fee or if they were unlucky, not at all. Their kinsfolk were constantly making financial demands on them, often for dubious and unconvincing reasons. Their hard earned savings were regularly stolen, and even those people allotted to 'protect' them, those like Shagba the market's rubbish collector, abused and exploited them. I asked Poppy, who had told me some time ago that she knew Shagba, if she had been hearing of him lately. Were there any more reports about him?

I was surprised when she told me that Shagba had got married only a few days ago. I told her that I had heard he was already married.

'Yes it's true,' she said, 'He is already married so this will be his second wife.'

Then Poppy confirmed what Rebecca had already told me some time ago, that Shagba in addition to his own wife, also had several other girlfriends from amongst the kayayo. He had married one of these girls earlier this week, whom I was told by Poppy was very young. George laughed and said we should have gatecrashed his wedding.

I asked Poppy if she had ever seen Shagba beating the girls?

'Yes, he does beat us at times.'

This led George to also add that,

'I have witnessed him beating the girls with my own eyes.'

I was increasingly feeling like I wanted to throw up. I told George that we would have to abandon the interviews. He then said,

'If you want to vomit, then vomit and be free.'

Following his advice I duly put my fingers down my throat and threw up about four times into the stinking gutter.

It took me some time until I felt well again. I sat there for some minutes, observing the girls and George chatting away as if I were no longer there. After a few more minutes I started to feel a bit better, but I was still very weak, so went back to the last topic, which was Shagba. Unusually Poppy started to look outraged. A savage look shrouded her normal sunny countenance. She started to talk with passion, gesticulating violently with her hands.

'Shagba is very wicked! Every Saturday all the kayayo girls in the market have to give twenty pesawas to him, if you don't, he beats you.'

Twenty pesawas may not sound a lot but if this is multiplied by two or three thousand it will be a substantial amount. An amount of money he most probably puts in his pocket. Mamuna then also jumped up abruptly from her bucket, holding baby Mohammed who was still suckling from her breast. She was also enraged. Her eyes filled with hatred.

'Yes, one day,' she said, 'He beat my child, my

older daughter, when I refused to give him the twenty pesawas.'

This small amount of money could have provided a small bag of porridge or koko for a girl or her baby. Even though the amount was minute it would be a significant sum for many of the kayayo. It is still possible to buy a small portion of koko millet porridge for 20 pesawas. Apparently, Shagba had originally asked the girls to pay one cedi per week each so that if 'any problem arose in the market he could solve it'. It seemed this was reduced amidst protests from the girls. According to the girls he got up very early on Saturdays in order to complete his rounds. It seemed the girls collected twenty pesawas from each other and handed it over to him as a lump sum for each village group. This made his 'collection' quicker and more efficient.

Kadima, who had been nodding in agreement, also added that when the kayayo man was murdered late last year, Shagba ordered all the kayayo girls in the market to contribute Gh2 cedis (£1.00 Sterling) each so it could be used to 'solve the matter'. This would have amounted to an incredible sum. However in the end, Kadima added, a local MP or assembly man, who was also from the north, met all the costs and told Shagba to give the money back to the girls. But he did not do this and kept the money for himself.

One girl who was sitting near our group, a young girl who only looked about seven years old, got up and walked over to a group of young boys, carrying her small empty plastic paint bucket with her. She was wearing only a pink swimming costume, which was probably doubling up as her night clothes. The boys were walking round the market selling water by the bucket. Soon after a lot of shouting broke out and the girl got slapped by one of the teenage boys selling the water. The little girl began to cry. More people went over and a big shouting match ensued. The shouting got worse and this led the girl's mother to run over towards the affray, leaving her tiny baby behind in the dirt. The baby was also crying and tried to crawl towards his mother, almost falling in the gutter as he did so. The shouting reached a crescendo and then George got up and went over to find out what was happening. Some few minutes later he returned. The boys had said someone had earlier tried to take water without paying and had run off. So to make sure it didn't happen again they had slapped the next person and used them as an example. I watched the crying girl return to the adjacent shop front with her mum. The mother sat down on a piece of cardboard leaning against the railings, which were covered as were the railings at our shop front, with damp clothes. Her daughter snuggled up in her lap. Her mother was caressing her hair and mumbling to her softly. Soon after the tiny girl was fast asleep.

When I asked them if they preferred living in Accra to the village I once again got more information about how things we take for granted in the west are seen very differently amidst their poverty. They told me that what they have seen 'here is better than there' (the village). There (in the village) they couldn't even get any money and even if 'we get small money' the parents used it. In the village they also couldn't buy the food they liked. They could never eat meat.

'The parents will say to you that as a young girl you want to buy food and meat on top. So in the north you will not get good food to eat.'

I realized that in many ways 'meat' and 'food' were seen as different. Food is what you eat to survive, to fill your belly. Meat was too expensive to be seen as something that sustained you, it was rather seen as an expensive luxury and definitely not for everyday use. For many kayayo even bread was a luxury. As we were on the topic of food I asked them about the way they ate in the village. I had watched Nigerian Hausa films where the father had eaten first and then only after he had finished would his leftovers be given to his wife or wives and children, usually in that order. Was this true?

They told me that if you were in a room and the father came, you have to serve the father first, then the brothers and only then do you eat. In a place with little food, that must mean the girls and women get very little indeed. A wife must cook for her husband and serve him separately. Then you go and eat with your children. The wife and children never eat with the father.

'Why is that?'

'Husbands say if you eat with your wife it will spoil you.'

I asked them what they meant by this.

The girls told me that when a man and woman ate together the woman could mention certain words that could spoil the husband's spirit.

'What spirit?'

'The spirit that the man uses to protect himself during war.'

I had also heard that men should 'not talk too much with their wives', meaning that they shouldn't be too friendly to their wives as the wives may then see them as soft and may try to take advantage.

'She will start to grow horns,' I have heard them say.

I asked them what they knew about sakawa. Lashida started to tell me about this. She was a very handsome girl, tall, strong and athletic looking. A small round face framed glittering, deep set eyes. She wore a striped red T-shirt and black jeans. She had a confident air, unlike poor Mamuna sitting next to her.

'They say that sakawa people leave nice things lying around to deliberately attract you. This could be money or a mobile phone. When you see it, you want to take it and so when you pick it up it will turn into a fowl or goat. Then when it is time to slaughter it for meat it will change back into a human being and then it will vomit money.'

I could tell the importance the girls attached to sakawa and how they feared it by the pregnant hush that now permeated the atmosphere in our huddled circle. They watched and listened intently to whoever was talking, their faces serious and concerned. They told me they had heard about sakawa boys coming to take people away but it hadn't happened to them. I asked them was this not perhaps the reason some girls were frightened to come to the north with me in my car?

'They were afraid of you because they don't know you. You look strange to them. They don't know if you are a good person or a bad person, and they don't know if you will take them away. There are people who take them away, they just hear stories.'

Poppy added,

'We don't see the sakawa people with our eyes so they don't know if I am one of them or not.'

I remembered the first time I had stopped to ask the Bandugu girls under the tree to get in my car. How young Latifa, was shaking her head and waving her hands, saying,

'No, sakawa, sakawa.'

The girls were quiet, hushed, their minds had now retreated back to their villages. They were remembering the ancient superstitions in which they were steeped. Poppy began to tell me about the 'night bird'.

'What is this?'

'It is a kind of bird that cries in the night.'

'What does it do?'

'When the bird cries, small children, under one or two years they will faint, so we pour water over them so that they will come back.'

They told me that in the north they burn a concoction so that the smoke will send the bird away.

'What do you call this type of bird?'

'Bad bird.'

When I looked over at Mamuna she had fallen asleep on her bucket, her back and head propped against the wall on which she had been leaning. Baby Mohammed was in her lap, her nipple still in his opened mouth. Many of the other groups around had also fallen into a deep slumber. We said our goodbyes.

It was almost two weeks before I went to the market again. Two days earlier, news had broken of the Japanese Tsunami. As we entered the market early that Sunday morning people were gathering outside a shop in front of the TV. They watched, still stunned by the scenes of horror unfolding on the screen. As we walked along I saw young Aysha. She ran towards me excitedly.

'Mummy I am going back to the village tomorrow morning on the bus. I have my sewing machine. It is now with me.'

She pulled my hand.

'Please, please come and see it. I want you to see it,'

George and I walked the short distance to where the mango tree girls slept. We entered and there on top on some sacks of corn, sat the sewing machine only very slightly illuminated within the darkness of the warehouse. I had been hearing about it for so long, that it now appeared to possess a personality of its own, as if it had imbibed the months of Aysha's angst and anxiety. It was if the sewing machine was embarrassed for all the desperation it had caused and sat there quietly attempting to play down its importance.

Aysha sat down next to it and turned the hand held wheel at the side. Her face was full of delight and wonder. I told her she had worked so hard, she must be so proud of herself. We hugged and I said goodbye. She reminded me earnestly that when she returned she would save and buy another machine so that eventually she would have her own tailoring shop employing several people. I knew that one day she would.

Minutes later George and I were approaching Poppy's 'house', the cosy shop front surrounded by two feet high railings. It was early Sunday morning and rain was still falling. They were all pushed up against the metal shop front and their belongings had been pushed as far back as possible towards the shop door, but despite this many of their things were soaked. In this little group today there were about ten girls, including one girl who was still lying fast asleep on the floor despite it being wet, two babies with runny noses and two very young girls of about eight or nine. As we sat there I could hear quite a lot of hacking coughs. I asked how they had coped with last night's storm and massive downpour. They told me that at about 3am they all had to get up and stand huddled in the dark as far as possible under the awning, which came out about one metre. As the rain had not stopped, they had been obliged to stand in this way for the entire night. Poppy complained, tired and wretched,

'We are like cows we have to sleep standing up,'

The girls were absolutely soaked. The small awning that protruded from the shop front provided little by way of protection from the elements. Most storms in Ghana were accompanied by lashing winds, which blew the deluges of water against walls and through any open windows as it had also done in my house the previous evening. The girls, all damp, cold and tired, said,

'The rain beats us and it feels very cold, and when it rains then water comes around our legs and all our clothes get wet, the wind that comes before the rain blows dust in our eyes and we can't see.'

The 'road' along which they slept was in fact just a dirt track so when the wind came it raised up the dust often in whirlwinds blowing dust, grit and litter all over them.

I wanted to try to focus on something else that would take our minds away from this misery. Some weeks before I had given Poppy a beautiful red shalwar kameez. I asked her if she still had it. Did it fit? She got it out of a thick plastic bag and said she wanted to wear it. It seemed to be the only item of clothing she had that wasn't wet. The old lady, Kadima, held up a cloth and she changed behind it. When she emerged and stood before us she was transformed. Now she was a bejewelled Asian princess. She looked stunning and beautiful. George asked me if people got cold in Pakistan wearing only this thin type of dress, and I told him that there it was hot, just like Ghana. As she walked around the sequined dress glimmered and twinkled. It was conspicuous in the way it stood out against the drabness of our surroundings. I watched Poppy in the distance, as she ambled around on the dirt tracks and she positively glowed in her shimmering gown. George commented,

'Wow if she had bought that in a boutique it would cost ooh...'

Rain was still falling softly, rows of shoes were neatly placed outside the shop pavement showing respect even for this narrow patch of concrete which for them represented 'home'. A tall kayayo girl, very striking, who looked about twenty years old and who was wearing lurex leggings under her skirt sat down and joined our group. A toddler had put both his legs into a plastic bag and was jumping along the dirt track, like he was a competitor in the old fashioned sack race I used to play at school many decades ago. A radio could be heard in the background. It was the BBC. Latino music was playing and it sounded very incongruous in this setting, it changed to Chinese music and sounded even more misplaced. Then commentator announced,

'The BBC takes you on a cultural discovery tour. I'm Harriet Gilbert, listen to BBC worldwide podcasts...'

Poppy told me she had now managed to save another Gh30 cedis (approximately £15). Her savings now totalled Gh 60 cedis (£30 Sterling). She still had to pay back some of the susu money, but it would have to wait. The most important thing was to buy the uniforms, books and other things necessary to send her children to school. She added that now Kadima had got her roofing sheets they planned to go home, back to Wialu the next day. The bus would be leaving in the morning. She told me she had also got the lorry (bus fare) in addition to this GH60 cedis (£30 Sterling).

She then jumped up, full of enthusiasm.

'Wait!' she said, 'I will show you.'

She started to rummage inside a large plastic bag, the same bag that minutes earlier she had pulled out her shalwar kameez. She continued for some minutes. As the seconds passed her facial expressions began changing, from impatience to concern. From concern to unease. From unease to anxiety. From anxiety to distress and then alarm. She began to talk fretfully, agitatedly. This agitation began to infect others in the group. Soon all were talking in tense, loud bursts, words emerging in loud thunderous claps. Within minutes the atmosphere had transformed. I asked George what was going on. He also looked anxious, telling me that Poppy couldn't find her money, and lorry fare. It continued like this for another fifteen minutes until it was obvious the money was not going to be found. Most probably it had once again been stolen.

Poppy eventually gave up her searching and looked up towards me. On seeing her face my heart broke. The pain was too much for anyone to bear. Images of the soldier ant, running back and forth at the tealeaf stall, passed before me. I put my arm around her squeezing her tight. She burst into uncontrollable sobs. Other girls started to cry. I remembered Norman, 'they cry together, they love themselves'. Poppy's sobs were like none I had heard in my life before. The came deep from inside her soul, the sound echoed and resonated for the months and years of suffering, toil, and agony of her life. As I held her shaking and convulsing body, tears also began to run down my face. I realized I would have to help her. I had never wanted to get too involved in their lives, but this was different. I told George to tell her not to worry; her money would be replaced. I left the weeping Poppy by the patch of cement that was her home. As I reached the end of the track, I turned and saw her bent body covered in brilliant crimson amongst the grey sacks of old clothes and other belongings. It was still raining.

George and I got to the cashpoint and sucked out the money directly from its account in a rich far off land, where babies do not sleep and grow up in the streets and children do not die needlessly. Within an hour, we were back. Poppy had her lost money plus a bit more. Her children would go to school. I told her we would come and see her tomorrow morning before she boarded the bus.

It was dawn the next day and there was a heavy mist hanging over the city. George and I entered the market and walked to Poppy's shop front. She and the 'old lady' Kadima, were sitting alone by the side of the track waiting for us. Both women were overloaded. Kadima with her iron roof sheets balancing precariously on her head, walked behind us as we marched down the track in single file. On arrival the bus was so overloaded it looked as if would topple over. On the same bus, through the back window I glimpsed Aysha. She too was on the same bus, together with her precious sewing machine.

Kadima's precious roofing sheets were tied onto the roof and both she and Poppy boarded the bus. In a short while the bus creaked off slowly back to the dried up and impoverished northern villages of Ghana. Poppy waved, the bus turned. She was on her way. Her children *would* go to school. They would never 'see and not know.'

Chapter Seventeen

The Runaway Girls

I had started to become obsessed with finding and visiting Debele market. For almost a year now I had been hearing about this infamous, sprawling market. It was one of the largest markets in Accra and the one with the highest number of kayayo. Yet although I had been living in Accra for almost fifteen years, I had yet to locate it. It was not as if it was inaccessible, a market with numerous transport links in the middle of a city could not be called this. Rather it was off the beaten track. For the majority of Accra's residents, it did not lie on any major transport routes, and nothing else was there except the market. So unless you had reason to go there, you could live in Accra for your whole life and not even know it existed.

I was determined to find it at all costs. Next morning I caught the trotro to down town Accra. This was also another place that people didn't go much now. Downtown Accra dates back to the colonial era. For much of the last century it was this area that was known and seen as central Accra, the main hub. However, due to the rapid economic development and building boom Ghana had been experiencing since the beginning of the 21st century, the city had been expanding rapidly, to the extent that the ancient core had increasingly become abandoned as more and more people moved into the newer, more affluent suburbs. Yet, as in many abandoned inner city areas the world over, due to land pressure, tentative attempts at renovation were starting to spring up.

After alighting from the trotro, and sweating profusely I asked a passer by the directions to Debele market. They pointed at an entrance to what seemed to be some kind of covered area. Once in there I asked,

'Is this Debele Market?'

'No, they replied, 'just keep walking through this market and ask again.'

Massive bundles of second hand clothes, packed in tightly vacuumed polythene bundles, were strewn around, waiting to be opened. They had arrived, courtesy of donations from citizens as far afield as Korea, China, United States and Great Britain. As I walked on, the bales were being ripped open, their contents spewing out onto the tracks and alleys around. People pushed and shoved to get the best deals, market women bought up blouses, skirts and dresses, for as little as 25-50 pence then went to resell them in other parts of Accra for treble or quadruple the price. As usual I couldn't resist a bargain and bought two blouses for 30 pence each from 'Marks and Spencer' and 'New Look.'

I continued to walk. And walk. I kept asking and was always told,

'Oh koh straight –keep going straight.'

I passed a small table selling millet porridge and korsay, a staple food of the north. I bought a small portion of the porridge which they poured into a black polythene bag, knotting it at the top, and three or four korsay, which were small cakes made from mashed up black eye beans and fried, something like falafel. I put them in my bag to eat later when I found a place to relax.

I was getting further and further away from the main part of downtown Accra and had no idea in which direction I was going. The market was dark, full of narrow alleys. I was becoming disorientated and worried I would get lost. I asked a women sitting on her empty stall,

'Where is Debele Market?'

She warned me,

'Be careful it's not a nice place there!'

I thought to myself, this place is not very nice either, how much worse could it get?

I could see what she meant. I've been to some bad areas in Accra over the years, yet the more I walked deeper into this area, the worse it seemed to get. The people, especially the men, looked really rough. Typical low-life types. I had a feeling I wanted to get out of the place, yet it was now so far to walk back and I had no idea how much longer I would have to walk forward that I started feeling trapped, like I was in a maze that I couldn't get out of. Suddenly I spotted a quite 'normal' looking person, an elderly man wearing nice trousers, a shirt and tie, and some preppy glasses. I guessed he could probably speak English. I told him I was writing a book about the kayayo girls and was looking for someone who could translate for me. He told me he would find someone and then disappeared for a short while, reappearing with a man, quite frightening in appearance, his whole face covered in the extensive scarification of the Frafra tribe from Bolgatanga. His eyes were red and bloodshot, his speech was slurred and his breath smelt of alcohol even though it was still only 7.30 in the morning. The elderly man said,

'He will go with you to the market and find someone to help you.'

The man with the red eyes said I had to pay him for this so I arranged to give him five cedis. While the elderly man had been away I had used the opportunity to sit down and eat my porridge. I was famished and feeling dizzy. I saw three ladies sitting on a wooden bench so sat down, made a hole in my polythene bag and stated to suck out the sweet millet tinged with crushed ginger. After a couple of minutes they got up, the bench toppled over, I stumbled and all my porridge splattered over the floor. A chorus then rang in the air, all the people surrounding me cried, 'Oh, sorry!' in unison.

It was not long after that I saw a tall, middle-aged woman standing opposite me holding a fresh bag of porridge. She had gone quickly, on seeing my 'misfortune,' to buy me another one and refused to take any payment for it.

The red-eyed man was looking impatient, so I followed him to Debele market. We seemed to be winding in alleyways for about twenty minutes. On looking at him more closely, I realized that some of his scars were not only tribal, he also had a massive scar from the corner of his left eye that went right across his face, as if he had been in a knife fight. I had no idea where we were going, and we went through what seemed to be various sections of the market reserved for particular products. We walked through a whole section selling kenke, another whole section which only seemed to be selling pink fleshy pigs trotters lined up in pairs and covered in flies, another large section selling all types of fish and their various innards. I started to wonder where an earth we were going, and was thinking that I wouldn't want to walk in any dark alleys at night with anyone this guy recommended. Eventually we reached an open patch, you could even see the sky and clouds, a welcome sight after being holed up in this claustrophobic souk for almost an hour.

This patch was in fact a trotro station. Buses and trotros were parked in their allotted places, and there were about at least one hundred kayayo girls sitting across the pavement on upturned bowls between the parked vehicles. Many of these kayayo would be waiting for buses and trotros to arrive in order to carry either passengers' luggage or produce bought down from the interior. I was told that we were in Abusia market trotro station and Debele Market adjoined this. On arriving the red eyed man introduced me to a kayayo girl whom he said could speak English, but after talking to her I realized it was very rudimentary, and only consisted of a few isolated words. I asked a person nearby and he explained to the red eyed, drunk Frafra man in Twi that I needed someone who could speak fluent Dagomba and English. There were some people sitting in the ticket inspector's office and I asked in there if anyone could help me. One man, who was sitting at an ancient wooden desk, told me he was a Dagomba and his name was Osama. He seemed to be able to speak English quite well, so I guessed he would be able to help me.

By now many of the kayayo girls had begun to congregate around us, wondering why this strange lady who appeared suddenly from nowhere should have such an interest in them. The crowd started to gather momentum, I was getting tired and the heat was intense. I felt I had achieved enough for one day. I had identified my next 'patch' and I had found a new interpreter, and I had walked at least two miles in the intense heat. I decided I would go home and return the next morning. But how was I to get home? I'd never find my way back through that labyrinth. I jumped onto a trotro that was parked in one of the bays. Eventually I was dropped off somewhere near the Circle roundabout, and I wearily made my way home from there.

The next morning I went once again to Abusia trotro station. This time I was armed with a huge map of the northern region, which I had folded in my bag. I caught the tro tro and got off at the same stop but this time, rather than go directly into the same market, I was told

I could reach Abusia market by walking along the adjacent railway tracks. At least they went in a straight line and I wouldn't get lost. The tracks were teeming with people, some just walking along, like me, others had arranged various second hand (or home use as they were called in Ghana) clothes on pieces of plastic for sale, others were selling vegetables and cheap pirated CDs and videos from Nigeria. All were laid out along the tracks, on pieces of plastic or cloth. I didn't know if any trains actually came along here, they would definitely have to go very slowly if they did.

What I did notice, was the number of resident 'preachers' lined up along the tracks at regular intervals. They had a microphone and speakers, both of which were attached to long electric cables plugged into kiosks situated in a market that ran along the side of the railroad tracks. And always, they had in their possession their bible, into which they glanced regularly. They preached the whole day at the top of their voices, which often became hoarse and gritty due to the constant overuse of their vocal cords. Sometimes this was interspersed by gospel music. The noise was overwhelming and I often wondered why nobody ever complained. This could be seen all over Accra and indeed Ghana. Sometimes a preacher would board a trotro and preach for the entire journey at the top of his voice. If it was a long distance vehicle then you were really in trouble and may be forced to listen for hours without any hope of escape, unless you wanted to alight in the middle of a remote highway. Today the preacher I saw was a polio victim, a cripple. He sang and lamented to the sound of heavy vibrating music. I walked another hundred meters or so. I saw another preacher. He was immersed in his own solemn soliloquy.

After walking for about fifteen minutes I was once

again told to turn left into the same market I had used the previous day, and was obliged to follow the same route. Once again I had to walk through the pig's trotters area, the fish and flies area, the kenke area, and the smells were making me retch. I vowed this would be the last time I would take this route. Near the end of the market were some more preachers, this time they were in a group of three, each playing a different instrument, one on the organ, one on the guitar and a third on the drums. All this was amplified by two enormous loudspeakers that had been placed either side of them. Some of the women in the market had left their stalls and were now dancing furiously to the music. We reached the trotro station. 'Fresh' air, space and less noise, I was glad to get out of the market. It was suffocating.

However when I reached the market this time and located Osama he told me that I wouldn't be able to speak to the kayayo without first getting the permission of the local chief. We would therefore have to go and see him first to get 'clearing'. I did not want a situation again like Shagba so I followed him for what seemed ages in the heat, up and down narrow alleys. By now I was exhausted, I just couldn't continue. In the end I had to tell him I couldn't walk any further and that I wanted to go back. He told me 'not to worry' he would call him to come. He then disappeared and I never saw him again for several weeks.

Back at the trotro station I asked some other people if I could talk to the girls, and they said I had to get permission from the ticketing officer, the ticketing officer then said I needed to get the permission of someone else. It went on like this for about two or three minutes. In the end a man called Lameen Baba came to my rescue. He seemed more articulate and educated than most of the people around and spoke very good

English.

I told Lameen that I wanted to find a group of girls from a village, which was not far from Tamale. My last trip, which had taken days of driving on very bad roads, had ruined my car, and I needed to find a village that I could reach easily by public transport. For this reason I had bought a giant map of Ghana. We then went outside and laid the map out on the pavement. The girls started to crowd around and we were asking them the names of their villages while at the same time trying to locate them on the map. I was squatting down and it was becoming quite uncomfortable until a girl offered me a place on her upturned bowl.

Many of the villages the girls were calling out could not be located on the map, being too small and remote. We continued like this for a while, and not long after we found a girl from the village of Nisanu just outside Tamale. Her name was Waharama. She didn't seem very old, only about thirteen, and she was with another girl from the same village called Shafarma. I asked the other girl, who looked slightly older, her age. She shrugged her shoulders, opened out her palms and looked at me as if to say,

'How the hell am I supposed to know, what a stupid question!'

None of them seem to show any shyness or shame about not knowing their ages, as they would if they had to admit they could not read or write. I think for them, not knowing their age is a given, like they are female. They probably assumed everybody else also didn't know their own age either.

Waharama was extremely beautiful; her slender, delicate body was as black as ebony. Her skin glowed and her large cat like eyes shimmered. She was also extremely shy. Shafarma was a little plumper and fairer skinned.

Beyond our circle, which was now all squatting in a large circle on the pavement, I glimpsed many kayayo through the gaps in the legs of the girls pushing firmly against us. They were sitting in small groups wedged between the parked buses, trotros and taxis. They sat on their upturned bowls, their legs splayed, clutching their skirts between their legs for modesty, chewing bits of coconut, drinking millet porridge while occasionally spitting out bits of used up chewing stick onto the floor. I could see striped T-shirts, turquoise skirts, polka dot skirts and bright yellow skirts all with matching or mismatching scarves and tops. It was a sea of colour. Whenever drivers needed to come in or out of their parking bays the kayayo had to quickly stand up, pick up their bowls and other belongings and move to another location.

Two other girls, Salima and Menamatu, were then introduced to us by Shafarma and Waharama. They told us that they were also from the same village of Nisanu near to Tamale. Menamatu looked very young, no more than eleven years old. She was a lot shorter and smaller than the others and seemed just like a child. Salima was slim, and she had a long, thin oval face. They joined our circle, bringing their upturned bowls to sit on and we started to chat. It was difficult, as the crowds had now transformed into eager spectators, surrounding and pressing against us on all sides. The sun was beating down and there was no shade. All of us were perspiring profusely. Lameen was constantly mopping up the beads of sweat forming on his forehead with a crisp white handkerchief. I asked them if they liked being here in Accra. They gazed at each other with a resigned look. Safarma turned her palms outward and clapped her hands together, then she and Salima smiled, sneaking a glance at Lameen and myself.

'No, we do not like it. We come here only for

business and to make money.'

'What do you use your money to buy?' I asked, thinking I already knew what the answer would be. I was sure cooking pots would be in the equation somewhere.

'We want to buy cooking pots. Also, Waharama wants to buy a sewing machine.'

For a long time I had been thinking how the kayayo could progress economically if they could be given help even in very basic business skills. For example they could be shown how to pool their savings to invest in their own small businesses. Their earnings could then again be reinvested into their other projects. Before long they could be running larger, more lucrative businesses. They were so hard working and capable. Their track records of saving together and pooling their meagre resources, amidst unimaginable obstacles, was proof that they could attain this goal with only a little direction. I told them about my ideas and explained how they could very easily be running their own businesses if only they received help and direction. They seemed interested but vaguely confused as if it was an unattainable dream. Sharfarma, the oldest, answered for them,

'We want but we don't know how to do.'

I then asked them if they were shown how to invest and do bigger and different types of businesses would they be interested?

'Yes if they show us how to do we will do.'

I then went on to a different subject.

'Were you not afraid to come to a big city like Accra, so far from your homes?'

They told me they were not afraid because when they came here they already knew a lot of people from their village so they just went there, they went to their village in exile.

The crowd was getting larger and larger by the minute. People were pushing closer and closer. Everyone was oozing with sweat in the intense heat. I realized it would be better next time if we found a quieter more private place and I asked Lameen if it would be possible to sit in the ticket office next time. He replied that it would be fine. It was always a constant problem finding an appropriate place to sit away from crowds of friends and onlookers.

This time going home was easy, I jumped in a trotro going to Circle and then went home from there. Nothing more had been said regarding obtaining the chief's permission so I left it at that, hoping it would not be brought up again.

It was a few days later when I found myself once again driving down to Debele market early one Monday morning. I had arranged to borrow a friend's car for the remainder of my time in Ghana. In the distance towering high above me, I discerned the now recurring image of Duncan Williams standing next to the roaring lion. I had kind of memorized part of the route while on the trotro some days before and now just had to ask directions only towards the end of the journey. The traffic on the narrow roads was making driving hazardous. Also there were many 'male kayayo carts'. These were small carts on wheels that the men pulled along behind them. Many people were walking between the slow moving traffic. I saw one woman almost get crushed between two vehicles. She screamed out, but wasn't hurt. I saw huge trucks arriving from the north, over-ripe tomatoes spilling over, and I suddenly remembered what one man had said about them being too ripe when they were picked. Many of them ending up rotting on the market floors while people went hungry.

I then saw police ahead signalling at the side of the

road and today I definitely did not want to be stopped and delayed. I pretended I hadn't seen them and drove on amongst the traffic not looking left or right, just focussing on the middle distance. I was just breathing a sigh of relief that I had this time managed to dodge them, when another emerged from behind a hedge. He had a furious look on his face and I knew I was in for it.

'Why did you drive past when that police officer behind was stopping you?'

I had no idea how to react, I'd been caught red handed. What I said next put me even deeper into trouble, but I couldn't stop myself from being sarcastic.

'I'm sorry, sir, but I didn't want to stop as I'd run out of money.'

His face contorted into an expression of utter disbelief and astonishment tinged by righteous anger.

'HOW DARE YOU INSINUATE THE GHANA POLICE TAKE BRIBES,' he roared.

'COME WITH ME.'

I had no idea how I was going to get out of this one. As I sat there in the dingy police station reception, I racked my brains. I started to tell them about an attack I had suffered by armed robbers (which was true) that had occurred sometime previously, and how I had become badly injured. They became intrigued by the story.

'You have really suffered madam, it was very terrible.'

After hearing such awful things, they probably felt guilty about putting me through any more ordeals. They bid me farewell and said they prayed that from now on I would be safe. They accompanied me to my car. As I was starting the engine, they were looking a little perturbed.

'Madam, can you give us some money for iced water?'

This seemed hilarious in the light of what they had just said, but I was in no mood for another showdown so gave them each some small sum of money, which by this time they couldn't complain about! I proceeded to drive on through the harsh and unmelodious sounds of the market.

I met Lameen at a large, modern furniture shop. Its headquarters, a large gleaming, modern building, looked completely out of place amidst all the surrounding shabbiness. We then attempted to drive to the trotro station, situated deep inside the market. It was very difficult to drive through the teeming crowds, and I kept thinking I would knock someone over. We drove at a snail's pace. We eventually reached the station, with me vowing next time never to bring my car but rather walk. I was surprised to see that even at this early hour there were already about one hundred kayayo in the station, sitting idly on their bowls. Many were eating breakfast.

Lameen and I entered the dingy ticket office. Here we had a proper chair to sit on and even a fan! Pure luxury. I spotted Shafarma outside and on seeing us she entered. It was always hard to locate the girls at Abusia. According to Lameen they didn't really have a special 'spot' where they congregated, as did the girls at Tonga Market. I asked Shafarma if she had a phone, as this would be helpful when we wanted to locate them. She then told me that she had once had a phone but had given it to her father.

I was keen to find out where the girls slept during the night. I asked Shafarma and she told me she had a room that she shared with others. I guessed this must be unusual. I wanted to find out where the majority of them slept at night. I explained to Shafarma and asked again. Where in the market did they all sleep together? She seemed confused and didn't continue to speak. Did

Lameen or any of the other people around know where the Dagomba girls of Debele market slept? Was there not a central place like at Tonga, where all or many could be found at any one time? We asked other girls outside and they all told us they slept in rooms. Then Lameen told me that most of the girls at Debele did not sleep outside. Yet I still maintained there must be some places where they slept outside, all the kayayo I had met since I had arrived in Accra slept outside.

This was later to be one the biggest revelations of my study. That was when I realized that the lives of the Dagomba girls of Debele market and the Mamprusi girls of Tonga Market were in many ways very different.

Debele market itself differed also in many ways to Tonga, in size, layout and history. Firstly it was a lot larger. I did not really know where the boundaries started and finished. It was amorphous, with no clearly delineated roads or tracks. This differed remarkably to Tonga which was contained within a compact square, its outer perimeter circumvented by roads and inner perimeter by the dirt track along which the kayayo slept at night. Tonga could easily be walked around within an hour but Debele was a maze of tracks and alleys seemingly leading nowhere except to more tracks and alleys. Tonga market consisted of solid constructions, colonial buildings dating back to the nineteenth century, albeit that shacks had been built around them at places. Debele seemed to consist almost entirely of shacks, hastily constructed from bits of plywood and corrugated iron. There were no roads as such, not even proper dirt roads such as ran round the inner perimeter of Tonga. Just tiny alleys, barely a metre wide, then hundreds and thousands of shacks and then more tiny alleys. No motorized transport would be able to penetrate most of this market. There were also no properly constructed drains surrounding the dwellings. As was the case at Tonga, often water and other effluent just ran in streams from the shacks directly onto the alleys where people sat and walked. At Tonga, although the majority of drains were open, they were about two feet deep which kept most of the effluent from running along where people sat and walked.

Shafarma was still the only girl who had arrived, so Lameen went out to locate the others. Alone without her friends all merriment and bravado was lost. She now sat silently, gazing before her at no particular object. Once Lameen was gone, I could too only sit silently and smile at Shafarma, and I realized how much I depended on these translators to be able to do my work. I kept thinking how nice it was to be able to sit in the ticket office with the fan, and not be pouring with sweat under the cruel sun outside. Grubby calendars that had been donated by various local companies hung on the walls. A plastic kettle, used for washing before prayers, was by the door, and there was a large wooden trunk up against the wall on which Shafarma was sitting. A phone was plugged in, and was lying on the floor, charging.

I was suffering from a bad migraine as I had not eaten breakfast, and was finding it difficult to keep going. I went to buy a coke and asked Shafarma if she wanted one.

'No, it's too cold.'

They didn't like the chilled drinks. They were unused to them. Being brought up in a village with no electricity, they hadn't experienced it before. A few minutes later, still sitting in the ticket office now drinking my coke, I noticed a lot of shouting was beginning to erupt outside. A small scuffle broke out. The other men in the ticket office told me some kayayo were arguing and 'fighting' over a metal bowl.

Something about someone trying to take someone else's head pan.

Lameen soon returned with little Salima following silently behind him. She looked bemused and sat immediately down next to Shafarma as if she was just doing what was expected of her, like an obedient child. She stared into space, not making any eye contact. Shafarma pulled her arms behind her back, catching her fists and pulling backwards to stretch. A few seconds later Waharama and Menamatu arrived. They sat down together on the wooden trunk.

We started to chat and I asked Shafarma how she had decided to come to Accra. Did her parents agree that she should come? She giggled.

'I dodged.'

All the girls roared with laughter uncontrollably.

'What do you mean by that?'

'I ran away.'

'What happened?'

'That morning I put on three dresses, one on top of the other, so that my mum would not see any bags of clothes and become suspicious. Then as I always do every morning I go to the riverside to fetch water so when I got to the riverside I told my friends that I wanted to go to the toilet and come.'

At this all three girls burst out laughing once again, holding on to their sides and falling on each other.

'After I went to the bush to go to the toilet I told my best friend, only my best friend, none of the others, to talk to my mother. I told her to tell my mother after some hours that I had gone to Accra. Then it would be too late for them to come and find me and bring me back...when I got to Accra I rang my mother...but there was much trouble in the house.'

'Why...what happened?'

'My dad was very angry, and he told my mum to

leave the house.'

The father suspected that his wife had been colluding with his daughter to get her to Accra.

'So I call my dad and I told my dad to go to my best friend who would explain how I ran away into the bush.'

I asked Shafarma why her dad thought her mother had planned it.

'Because first when I told my dad I wanted to go to Accra he forbade me to come so when I came he think my mother told me to come.'

I asked Shafarma and the others why didn't ALL girls come to Accra, although it did seem as if the majority came, they told me that,

'Some girls…their fathers don't want them to come so some girls they obey their fathers and don't run away.'

While I was writing in my notebook the girls came over to stare. They looked with wonder at the squiggles and patterns I made on the paper. They, as had been described so aptly before by a young kayayo woman in Tonga, 'were seeing but not knowing'. It had been noted in some research that traditionally the Dagomba have not shown that much interest in education, especially the western type. If education was to be given, boys tended to go to the Quranic school in the village which was seen as a 'valid and less dangerous' alternative. Also, while teaching in Nima, Accra's most famous shantytown, I was often told by my adult pupils, sometimes tearfully, how they had been sent to a Quranic school by their parents where they could only learn Arabic. This meant they were unable to advance within the mainstream education system, which was entirely in English.

Then it was now Waharama's turn to tell me how she escaped her village and arrived hundreds of miles away here in this big city. As always she giggled. The men in the ticket office kept turning round to listen, sometimes joining in the conversation. I was starting to get fed up as I felt this made the girls less inclined to open up. It also stopped the girls from talking about more personal things.

Waharama told me that she too 'ran away', and again all four girls began giggling. It was almost as if 'coming to kayayo' in Accra had become a rite of passage for the northern region girls of Ghana. Something they must all do at some time in their lives.

'Someone bought a bag of rice from my mother but hadn't paid. So I went to that person and told them my mother had sent me to collect the money for the rice, but this was not true. Then I used this money for the 'lorry fare' (trotro fare) to Accra. When I got the money I ran as fast as I could to the junction near my village and I got the car to Tamale.'

'Did you come with anyone else?'

'No, I came alone.'

'Where did you stay when you got to Accra?'

'I met another kayayo girl on the bus and when we got to Accra I follow the girl to go and bath. When we got to the bathhouse the girls say me I can go stay in her room... but when I wake up in the morning the girl was gone and I was alone so I went to the 'abroad' and sat outside the shop in the car park for a long time, then I saw a girl from my village pass by and I went to her.'

I asked Waharama what she meant by 'the abroad', where was 'the abroad'?

'It is the big, shiny shop that sell the furniture, people here call it 'the abroad', if you go there it is like going to 'the abroad' as people say that is how the shops are there.'

'Where?'

'In 'the abroad.'

Waharama was so beautiful, I could not stop looking at her, her delicate feline features, her ebony skin and the two vertical tribal marks either side of her perfectly formed nose. Her eyes glittered. She was always smiling, bashfully, glancing up at me and then turning away, her hand covering her mouth as she smiled.

I looked at Salima, who was wearing a long cream skirt that was inside out but she seemed unaware of it. She told me that she didn't like being in Accra but loved her village because in her village they have 'Simpa'. This was a local Dagbani dance. She wore tatty black flip-flopss on her cracked and swollen feet and a multi-coloured top made of a clingy lycra material which had three shiny pearl buttons down the front. She sat there with her arms folded, bending over and leaning them on her lap. She had a long, thin face, deep set eyes and high cheekbones. She looked a little awed regarding what was going on but had a sensible air about her and kept composed and focused on what we were saying. A nice girl. She went on to tell me that when she lived with her mum and dad in the village she felt good but here without her parents and her family she didn't; if anything happened what would she do?

Salima, like all kayayo, did not know her age but she only looked about twelve or thirteen. She had not yet even developed breasts. She looked very very young and spoke in a thin, baby-like voice. She told me it was her first time in Accra, and that she had been here for about three months. She informed me that unlike her friends she didn't run away.

'My mother gave me the lorry fare to come to Accra...my mum and dad wanted me to come.'

Because of what I had heard at Walankadi on my last trip to the north, where NGO staff and male village members had blamed 'the mothers' for encouraging the girls to come south, I asked her who had wanted her to come most her mother or her father?

She told me her mother wanted her to come more.

After she told me her mother had given her the fare, I noticed the look on Lameen's face, the similar look of shock and disbelief I had seen on Salifu's face many months ago when learning that parents had sent their young daughters down to Accra to live on the streets. Lameen looked amazed. I was still surprised that people knew so little about these girls' lives, although it was also possible that Lameen knew but was feigning disbelief. I think for most people the kayayo were just there, like the lamp posts and drains, no one ever showed enough interest in them to discover where they really came from, to discover in fact their human stories. Lameen exclaimed,

'How can parents send a small girl like this to Accra and not send her to school...they sent her down alone to Accra she didn't come with anyone.'

She went on to say that her parents didn't argue about her coming to Accra.

'Why did your mum want you to come?' I asked

She told me it was because 'of money'-even to get food for her was a problem. In fact her parents told her to come, she didn't particularly want to come. I asked her if she felt sad being here without her family. She gave me a nervous smile and said she did and told me that she did sometimes think about them. I asked her if she phoned her parents, she told me she didn't have a phone and she never borrowed anyone else's phone. I asked her then, how her parents, as they were the ones to send her down here, contacted her in order to make sure she was well? She told me that if her parents wanted to contact her they called other girls from Nisanu but it was not often. Salima had earlier said she had five older brothers, and Lameen asked Salima if any of her brothers had protested and insisted that they should not send their younger sister alone to Accra. She told us that her brothers did not even know as they 'were all at farm that day'. This showed how things were often done in secret, otherwise such a long difficult journey would have been known and discussed by the family at large. She then added,

'Nobody knew I was going as I was living with my mother-in-law.'

I asked Lameen what she meant. Surely she wasn't married?

Lameen explained that she was referring to her father's second wife. Salima went on to explain that her mother let the second wife 'mind her sometimes.' The two wives didn't live in separate houses but in the same compound house.

The Dagomba practise fostering or bringing up their children with other relatives. However parental ties are not broken and the children relate to a wider kinship group. A sample taken by Christian Oppong revealed that in one area thirty five per cent of the boys and seventeen per cent of the girls lived away from their parents, mostly with their father's siblings. Salima went on to say,

'Till now my real mother does not know I am here.'

Lameen interjected that her mother-in-law would be proud as when Salima came back with all the goods, she would take the credit saying,

'It was I who helped her to go'.

It could be used as rivalry with the first wife. He opened his palms and clapped his hand to show he had finished making his remark. I asked her how come her mother-in-law had been able to instruct her to come to Accra without her real mother's knowledge. She told me that her real mum had travelled to live for some time in another village and it was assumed that no one had told her that her daughter had left for the capital. Salima had only been in Accra for one month and it was her first time. I asked her how she came to Accra, did she come alone?

'Yes I came here alone.'

I asked her once in Accra how did you find Debele market?

'I just asked.'

'How did you find the girls from your village once you were at Debele?' It was such a big place, at least several square miles.

'I just asked.'

Lastly I asked the smallest and youngest of the group, Menamatu, if she had run away. In her tiny, thin, high pitched voice she told me,

'I was living with my mother-in-law because my own mother, she got sick and she went to her village and she died. My mother-in-law didn't mind me (bother about me) she only cared about her own children and sometimes they didn't give me food. I was hungry.'

'How did you run away?'

'One day when I had finished selling the coco porridge in the village, I told my parents I was going to fetch water at the stream and I took a bucket. I left the bucket at the riverside and ran.'

I asked Menamatu how she had hidden her clothes, her small bag with her possessions, but she told me she hadn't brought anything, she only had come in the clothes she was wearing that day.

I looked surprised and Salima, Shafarma and Waharama started to laugh. I asked her where she had got the money for the fare. She told me that when she was farming, she would save shea nuts every day. When it amounted to a bag she sold the bag.

I asked if her parents would be worried. Had they called her? She said her parents hadn't called and that none of the other kayayo had told her that her parents had called. She hadn't spoken to them since the day she left.

Lameen and I left the ticket office to go. We arranged to meet the girls again soon. When I eventually got back to my car I found that as usual people had parked behind me and I couldn't get out. A big truck had also parked across the exit road, which was used by all the trotro's and buses, so we are all trapped. There was confusion and a lot of shouting, so many people were pushing and shoving, bowls of foodstuffs were everywhere, as were the smells and flies and heat and dust. It all got too much. We eventually got to the main road and so many people were trying to weave their way through the maze of traffic that a lady almost got wedged in between my car and a truck and screamed out. I had driven in Ghana for fourteen years but I had never seen anything like this.

It was about a week later that I arrived again at the ticket office. I had parked my car at 'The Abroad' and had run out of petrol. This time I walked through the market after meeting Lameen on the main road. The market only had narrow tracks but this didn't stop huge container trucks from trying to drive down them going within centimetres of pedestrians. The tracks and 'pavements' around Debele and Abusia were awash with rotting fruit and vegetables, and with the rain that was now pouring down, the whole area became like a skating rink. The place was like a death trap, trucks, vans, taxis, male kayayo carts all trying to push their way through. The vehicles were not going fast but the danger of falling in front of one or being crushed between two was very great. Lameen noticed the look of fear on my face and said,

'That's why I always tell you to come in the car.'

A male kayayo cart came past at speed and I almost

got knocked down. Just walking along here for ten minutes made me understand now why so many of the kayayo I had met suffered constant injuries, just from walking around.

I was relieved to walk into the ticket office. The number of phones now being charged on the floor had increased tremendously. Adapters were plugged into more adapters and wires covered the whole floor. Sometimes as many as ten phones were being charged from one socket. There were four sockets in the small office. Osama, the man I had met initially at Debele, suddenly sauntered into the office. I had not seen him for some weeks. He announced with a broad smile that he had travelled to Tamale as his mother had died, and he had just that day returned and that was the reason I hadn't been seeing him. I told him I was sorry, and he continued to smile broadly and asked if he could have some of my biscuits. He took a whole wad of them and then left after plugging in his phone.

It wasn't long before Lameen arrived back with the girls. As always they were tagging along in single file behind him. I was still eating my biscuits and drink as I hadn't had time to eat breakfast and I didn't want the hunger to spark off another migraine. Lameen told the girls that I was very hungry and they started to laugh.

'How can you be hungry and eat biscuit, that's not food, you have to eat rice or koko!'

Waharama was limping and her foot was swollen. She said that yesterday she had been carrying a heavy load and a car had knocked her foot, the car had been going quite fast but refused to stop. Local tradition dictates that such drivers should stop to take their injured victims to hospital and then pay for any treatment. However, as many people, especially taxi and trotro drivers, lived on such precariously low incomes the temptation was to drive on, ignoring the injured victim. I asked her if she had been to the hospital.

'No I didn't have money and the hospital is far, but my foot, it will get better soon.'

She smiled and hobbled out of the office to buy iced water.

I was interested to find out about the rooms where they lived. I asked Salima if she shared a room and how many she shared with. She told me that there were so many girls in the room, that she couldn't count them.

Did she share a room with Shafarwu, Manamatu and Waharama?

She told me that she shared with other girls, but the other three in the room with us lived together. As we were talking many different people, mostly men, walked in and out of the office to unplug their phones, and as they left yet more people come in to plug in yet more phones. There were tangled wires everywhere on the floor.

I told them I would like to visit their rooms and we agreed that next time we met we would go there.

I was keen to find out about how they pooled their resources. Did they operate a susu system, as did the Mamprusi girls at Tonga and other kayayo girls I had met? Shafarma told me that she and some other girls operated a susu system. However, their scheme consisted of only 50psws per day. This was done between five girls, so that every five weeks one girl would get Gh12.50 cedis amounting to about £6. In other words every week one girl received the susu money that rotated over a period of five weeks. She then said,

'But mummy this susu is not plenty so I don't spend it, I want to save it more, so when I get my susu every five weeks I give it to someone else to keep because it is not up to much.'

'Who is that?'

'I give it to my older sister to keep for me.'

The older sister was not her real sister but an older girl from her village of Nisanu.

I asked her how much she had managed to save so far in Accra?

'I save Gh80 cedis.'

This was about £35-40 Sterling, which wasn't bad. It appeared that many girls not only saved with the susu alone. There appeared to be other private savings they made. This was often kept with someone else. Yet this practice was not always secure as it was sometimes stolen from the 'treasurer' or the person chosen to look after the money, as was the case with Poppy. Also I had heard that those looking after the money did at times abscond, taking the money with them. All in all I felt it would be better for the girls to save their money, perhaps at a women's savings bank, which would allow them to deposit small amounts and where it would be at least safe.

I wondered if those who joined the susu schemes ever didn't pay their daily dues or refused to join in completely. Did some kayayo refuse to join the susu schemes?

A ring tone went off the same as mine and I rushed to get the phone from my bag only to find out it was one of the charging phones buried amidst a mass of tangled wires on the floor.

Shafarma told me that,

'There is one girl called Maryam. She doesn't want to pay the susu money to the group...she will not show her money to her sister...she will not give the susu.'

She went on to tell me that nobody knew what she did with her money and when they asked Maryam about the money she made, she told them that they should leave her alone as they were not 'carrying her loads', she was.

Osama came back into the office, still munching his biscuits. He checked his charging phone and went out again.

'Do people often call you from the village asking for you to send them money?'

Waharama could hardly answer for giggling and kept covering her beautiful face with her hands. She told me that usually they didn't ask for physical cash, but rather asked them to buy things.

'What things?'

'They ask for Maggie cubes, onions, fish. We pack it in a box and someone, they write the name of our mother on the box. Then we put the box on the bus.'

They then told me that when the parcel eventually arrived at Tamale station or a place near their village their mother would come to collect the box from the bus. The girls told me they usually left the box at the ticket office where we were now sitting and when the bus from Tamale left the ticket office men gave it to the driver.

It had been quite a long morning and the girls had to get to work. We agreed that next time we met we would go to visit the girls' rooms deep in the market. They ran off together in a group and I made my way precariously out of the inner recesses of this market.

Chapter Eighteen

Poverty Pays

Some days later I was waiting at Debele trotro station for Lameen. He wasn't there. I rang him, he rang me. This continued for several minutes. We were both in different places but couldn't figure out our exact locations. After some time I saw him coming towards me with Salima. He told me he had been searching but unfortunately hadn't been able to locate the other girls. I said we should just then go with Salima to visit her room, as she lived in a separate room to the other three 'runaway' girls, Waharama, Shafarma and Menamatu.

We started to make our way through the labyrinth. It had been raining and some of the makeshift shacks seemed to be almost floating in large puddles. Thick mud lined the narrow tracks between the shacks. It stank as this mud was mixed with other waste as there was no drainage. Some of the alleys were so narrow, that my body touched the walls on either side as we made our way through. Yet people were surviving in this nightmare. They would sit on their stools, the putrid water around their ankles, lighting a fire on a coal pot, cooking their evening meal.

As we continued on deeper and deeper, music could be heard booming out of the many small sheds selling CDs and pirate videos, mainly from Nigeria. Just as the notes from one tune began to fade, a new melody would take over a few yards ahead. Sometimes there was an amalgam of two or three different tunes competing for precedence. Small children ran naked in the mud, some stood in metal bowls having their evening baths. The environment was disgusting yet people went about their daily business just as any other the world over. Ladies would finish their work and go back to a hairdressing lean-to to have their hair done with a pedicure, children would sit on the floor in the dirt outside their shack doing their homework in the half light, women would sit outside, now in the flooded pathways, cooking their evening meal.

It was some time before we reached Salima's room. Salima lived in a room with twenty other girls, which measured 3.85 by 3.60 metres. This meant each girl had approximately 19cm of sleeping space each when lying along the longest side. The room was made from bits of plywood hastily nailed together. They had managed to cover the bare cement floor with a large piece of white plastic linoleum, which they had picked up from somewhere. The room was spotlessly clean. Their flip-flops (all twenty pairs of them) were arranged meticulously outside the door in the mud. This was what you had to step into as soon as you got out of the room. The room was a few inches off the ground on sticks. A bare piece of wire led to a single naked light bulb. This dangled precariously from the low ceiling. The girls seemed very proud of their little 'room' with its white lino floor. The shack was not very high and you could hardly stand up. Salima walked over to a switch nailed to the wall halfway up the plywood and switched on the dim low energy bulb with such pride. She glanced back at me coyly with a look as if to say, 'we are actually quite posh here, we have light and a lovely white floor which many of the other houses don't have.'

I felt so humbled I wanted to cry. There was no fan however and I was sweating copiously. The street outside was packed, and as the door was ajar the people outside were able to look in at 'the stranger', and more and more of those loitering around in the street just started to enter the tiny shack, whether they lived there or not. It became more and more crushed and stifling.

Bits of string, held up by nails bashed haphazardly into the walls criss-crossed the ceiling. A jumbled mass of clothes drooped from this intersection of twine traversing at different angles just below the ceiling. Boxes piled high, adorned with Chinese scripts and filled with items they planned to take back to the village, were placed neatly on a high shelf which wound round the perimeter of the room. 'Check Check bags', the formidable African 'suitcases,' were stuffed with clothes and goods piled high in any available corner.

As I observed Salima I noticed she seemed to be limping as if she was in pain. I asked her what was wrong. She told me that yesterday she had been carrying a heavy load of corn. It had been too heavy and she had told the lady who had asked her to carry the load that she wouldn't be able to carry any more. However, the lady insisted she carry the whole load. While walking she had tripped on a pothole and had injured her back. She had wanted to go to the doctor but had not had the money. She told me that when she dropped the corn all the people in the market were shouting at her so she just got up and ran away taking her empty bowl with her. Now she was afraid in case she bumped into the load's owner again, a market lady.

'I'm sure if she see me again she will beat me.'

We all sat staring out at the bright sunlight through the open door that led into the street. Suddenly the sunlight was blocked. It was a human shape, the shape of a woman. We couldn't make it out, it was only an outline as the bright sunlight around it glared in our eyes. As the shape entered we saw it was Shafarma who had come to visit Salima. She was amazed to see Lameen and I amidst the semi-darkness of the room. I asked her where her younger 'sisters' were (Waharama and Menamatu) and she said she had left them at the other room but she was sure they would soon follow her.

There was no running water and no toilet facilities in the room and I asked them how they managed when it came to going to the toilet and bathing. They told me that there was a small public shower about a five-minute walk from their shack. Also there was a 'bucket toilet' across the road. This was different to a flush toilet and consisted of a structure with pieces of scrap wood and corrugated iron, hammered together to make a small kiosk usually less than one metre square. A deep pit was dug inside and then another piece of wood placed on top with a hole, here you could squat and go to the toilet. Once the pit became full up a new one was built in a nearby empty space. The toilet would be different from a urinal, which would normally be at another place. Often in a public toilet one must go to different areas according to whether one wants to 'wee' or 'poo'. You pay accordingly, with one paying substantially more to go for a poo, which must be disposed of in a different way to urine. Often a urinal will not consist of a deep pit but rather a stone or some tiles which will be intermittently washed down with soap and water. The girls went on to tell me that the smell of the toilet sometimes wafted into their room. However in another way they were happy as the toilet was nearby and that they didn't have to walk far to the toilet as in the 'deep night' they got frightened. I asked them what they were frightened of. They said,

'As that time of night it is not only human beings who go to the toilet...you can meet a ghost.'

I remembered reading about the 'sonya' in the Dagomba kingdom, the witchcraft meant to travel at night, which was sometimes seen as a red light and said to eat the souls of its victims. Many of the girls were very superstitious and their ancient beliefs travelled down with them to the city. It was the leitmotif flowing within their lives and shaping the lens through which they observed and made sense of the new world in which they now found themselves.

Yet what must have been my biggest shock about the kayayo was still to come. It was only after I had gained some time to reflect that I realized that the exploitation of these innocent, hardworking little girls with whom I was now sitting surpassed that of almost every other soul in Accra. It was to be a revelation. I discovered that, taking into account other factors such as water supply and toilet facilities, that these poverty stricken girls were paying more per square meter for their accommodation than billionaires were probably paying for their flats and rooms in prime parts of London, New York or Tokyo!

I asked them how much they paid for their 'room'. Sabina had told me insouciantly,

'We pay Gh1.50 (75 pence Sterling) cedi each per week. We pay this because we live in a wooden house, the girls they live a block house, they pay 2 cedis (£1.00 Sterling) each per week.'

At first glance paying Gh1.50 (75 pence Sterling) each a week doesn't seem much. The girls were charged per person so the more they crowded into the room the more the landlord creamed off. Houses and flats in all the parts of Accra I knew of and indeed most of the rest of the world only charged rent per room, not by the number of people in it.

When one multiplied what each girl paid per week with the number of girls in the room which was twenty, this came to Gh30 cedis (£15 Sterling) a week (Gh40 cedis for a block house). When multiplied again by four this totalled around Gh120 cedis a month (£60 Sterling) (Gh150 cedis for a block house). To begin with this is three or four times the average cost of a room in a poor part of Accra. An average room in a poorer area, made of blocks and with some kind of washing and toilet facilities included in the compound, would be between Gh30-50 cedis a month. The girls were paying between Gh120 and Gh150 per month, this was THREE TIMES the average price of comparable property in Accra. In Sterling this would be £60-£75 per month dependent on whether it was a block or wooden shack. This would be an average price for a room in an average but not wealthy area of London. However, the kayayo girls in this and other shacks at Debele had no place to wash or go to the toilet. The girls had to wash twice a day, in the morning and evening. In addition they needed water to wash their clothes daily. A bucket of water normally cost on average between 30-50 pesawas per bucket depending on water availability. With this one bucket most girls had to wash both themselves and an infant in addition to their daily laundry. So all of the kayayo girls with whom I was now sitting were paying more or less 1 cedi a day for water to bathe. This would take into account the days they may take extra water for some laundry, cleaning of the room and so on. If this was multiplied by the number of girls in the room, which was twenty, it totalled Gh20 cedis (£10 Sterling) per day for water or a crippling Gh600 cedis (£300 Sterling) per month. Who in the western world would pay £300 a month for their water bill?

Yet it didn't end there.

On top of this preposterous amount had to be added the money that had to be paid daily for toilet services. This could also most likely reach 1 cedi each per girl per day. To use the flush or bucket toilet one normally had to pay approximately 20-30 pesawas and to use the urinal 10-20 pesawas per visit. If we assumed the girls visited the toilet on average four times a day it would probably reach approximately one cedi per day, taking into account they also had to buy toilet paper from the lavatory attendant. This would be approximately again 1 cedi per day as was the cost of bathing. Another Gh600 (£300 Sterling) per month. If this was added to the rent of £60 per month, and 'water bills' of £300 per month, the girls were paying in total £760 per month. Making allowance for miscalculations and variations over the cost for buckets of water and toilet services, we could say on average they would be paying £600 per month. Also they had to pay the 'light bill' for their one bare bulb. It was amazing how far the tentacles of Ghana's electricity generating board reached.

An average room in London, a room that included toilet and washing facilities, would range from £350-400 per month. A room in a more prestigious area would perhaps be between £500-600 per month. But again the comparison does not end here. It is important to note that this room in London, Tokyo or New York would have windows and curtains. It would have electric sockets and the roof wouldn't leak. There would not be gaping holes between the tin roof and the wooden wall. The walls would be solid without gaps between planks of wood. There would be a pavement on which to step out into when you left your house. There would be hot water and heating. There would be some kind of floor and wall covering. It would be painted. The kayayo girls had none of this. They were paying more for their 'room,' that in most countries would not be deemed fit even for a dog or pig, than were people in some of the most expensive cities in the world.

Many people would never believe there would be profits to be made, comparable to property in New York or London or Tokyo, in one of the most squalid slums in Ghana and indeed Africa and from a group of people, who even by African standards, were the lowest on the rung of an already bottom heavy ladder. Even the most deprived and impoverished in Accra's society could look with relief when contemplating the kayayo, as they knew in their heart of hearts that they, at least, were not as unfortunate and despised as these girls. At least they were one or two rungs up the ladder, and not at the very bottom, which was where these poor girls were precariously balanced.

Yet the painful irony in all this was that the poor girls were full of gratitude. They told me they were 'blessed' because 'their men built rooms' for them. These people were the men from their tribe, the Dagomba. They told me their men were kind to them. They were actually happy to live in this shack. Moreover, because they were paying for their daily needs in such a piecemeal fashion, pesawa by pesawa, day-by-day, hour-by-hour, they were also unaware of the scale of their exploitation and the financial burden it was placing on them. If they had calculated just how much they had been spending they would have realized they would have been much better off to rent a room and pay monthly.

Yet paying monthly is almost unheard of in Accra, with most tenants having to cough up a year or two years rent, in advance. For example, if your rent was £100 per month, you would have to give the landlord £1200, that is the full year's rent in one go, in advance. There was no way the girls could have done this. The situation of rent payment in Accra makes it very easy for individuals to exploit those at the very bottom like the kayayo. Yet even the girls who slept outside, like those at Tonga market, still had to pay exorbitant amounts of money for water and toilet facilities, plus the added extras to men who were supposed to be 'protecting' them or turning a blind eye to their sleeping arrangements.

I was keen to find out about the owner of the room. Salima told me that he was a Dagomba man from their own tribe. She told me that every Sunday he came to collect the Gh1.50 from each of the twenty girls in the room. I noticed there were also a number of babies. I asked them what time he generally came.

'He can come anytime...so every Saturday we gather together and one girl she collect all the money from us so that it will be ready when the man comes on Sunday.'

The heat and stench of the room was becoming unbearable for me. One girl, called Rabi, got some cream out of her paint pot and started rubbing it into her legs. There seemed to be literally hundreds of flip-flopss lined up outside the entrance to the room and I wondered how they remembered whose was whose. The white lino floor, frayed at the edges, was cool and clean and gave the shack a homely feel. The girls seemed very proud of their little room with its white floor and electric light. They were happy and painfully unaware of the extent of their exploitation. Yet it is worth considering that almost all people living in this sprawling slum had to pay similar amounts each day for water and toilet facilities in addition to their rent. It is the paradox of poverty in this city that those at the very bottom often have to pay more for water, sanitation and rent than the more affluent.

Another important point was that the rent itself only constituted a small proportion of what the girls paid. A large part went to the owners of toilets, bathhouses and those that sold water by the bucket. Many people had told me over the years that those owning such places were 'raking in the money' and it would be interesting to find out just how much they actually made. In times of severe water shortage those selling water can increase the price substantially. It had become a racket that affected the poor more than any others.

As we had just been discussing how the Dagomba men built rooms I was keen to find out if it really was true that every Dagomba girl lived in a room, which was the exact opposite of the Mamprusi girls that I had known for so long, who had always slept outside. When I asked the girls in the room they said,

'Dagomba girls don't sleep outside, only Mamprusi and Sisala girls. The Mamprusi girls they sleep outside at Wiase Station.'

I had been hearing that Wiase Station, a large bus station in downtown Accra, was another place where a large number of kayayo lived and so was keen to go there. They did not mention the Mamprusi girls of Tonga, maybe they were unaware of this market, it being so far from their stomping ground.

I asked Shafarma why she thought the Mamprusi girls slept in the street, and she told me it was because they didn't want to pay. The other girls laughed.

'Who don't want to pay?'

'The Mamprusi girls.'

Salima then said that it was difficult to see Dagombas sleeping in the street.

'Why is that?'

Sabina and Shafarma and the other friends agreed, that it was because there were Dagbani men in Accra and Debele who 'help them'. They told me the men 'help them' because they build rooms for them. Shafarma went on to say,

'As for the Mamprusi men, they are not many, so the girls don't have anyone to build rooms for them.'

We went on to talk about the Dagomba and Mamprusi generally. Despite being from a similar geographical area, and possessing similar linguistic and cultural backgrounds, here in this strange and alien city, there seemed to be little connection between the two tribes. There was a slight difference in the language, but Mamprusi was a different dialect from Dagbani, rather than a distinct language. I thought of their great and common ancestors, Tohadzie the 'Red Hunter' who married the Malian princess. How one of his kin, Naa Gbewaah, gave birth to the three sons that founded the Greater Dagbon Kingdom. It was said that the people of Nunun, Mamprugu and Dagbon considered each other as brothers, because of their shared and great common ancestor, Naa Gbewaah. This certainly didn't seem to be the case now.

They told me again that,

'Dagomba and Mamprusi can't be equal because they don't want to pay...it would be shameful for Dagbani people to sleep outside.'

'Why then don't Mamprusi people feel shame when they sleep outside?'

'We don't know why they don't, it is their habit to sleep outside.'

Due to the rain that was now beating down outside, the door had been closed and the inside of the shack had become even darker. Shafts of sunlight peeped in through the cracks and gaps in the wooden walls and the large gap between the wall and corrugated iron roof. Suddenly there was a loud knocking at the door. I thought it might be the landlord coming to get the rent. Sabina went to open it. It was the two younger of the four 'runaway' girls. They had followed Shafarma and had come to visit their 'sister' and other village friends on their day off. On seeing us they looked both shy and surprised. We sat in silence for several minutes. The shafts of sunlight lit up only fragments of the room and its inhabitants. I saw Waharma's large almond shaped eyes and the edge of her shoulder, Shafarma's cheek with its long vertical tribal mark, Sabina's prominent forehead and the extremities of some adjacent check check bags. A shaft of sunlight peeping through another crack lit up Menamatu's hand, which was resting on her cheek, and a faint flickering from the same shaft catching the corner of her eye glittered. As the girls moved the shafts fell on different parts of their bodies. As we continued to sit in the waltzing light beams, rain thundered on the tin roof above, lending the eerie scene an orchestral backdrop befitting the climax to a horror movie or thriller.

After a few minutes of watching this strange light show I started to wonder why they continued to stay in such appalling situations. Looking around me at the squalor and overcrowding and what they were forced to pay for it, I couldn't help asking them again whether they preferred the village to 'this'. Shafarma again spoke, having to raise her voice to drown out the thunder from above.

'Yes, we think more of the village...there you don't have to buy water and food.....we go to farm together and chat with our friends along the way.'

Often in Accra they could not walk together during the day as they did in their villages. Their routes and hours were determined by the customers that they came across each day as they trudged the streets, trotro stations and markets.

I remembered that some days ago Shafarma had told me that she preferred the village because of 'simpa', a kind of Dagbani dance. I wanted to find out more about this and asked the girls in the room.

'Yes we do simpa in the village...but sometimes we do it here...we do it on Saturday nights in the market...this Saturday there was an outdooring (christening)...the people doing the outdooring they invited us to dance for them at the celebration. As we are many they gave us 50psws each (25 pence).'

This was probably just enough for them to go and buy a bucket of water afterward to bath. But then I guessed that the people doing the christening probably also had little money and 50 pesawas per person was all they could afford. Once again I was reminded of the loaves and the fishes, small amounts get divided again and again, everyone living on smaller and smaller fractions and portions.

I wanted to find out if the girls here, who lived in this room, were spared the torture of having to be gnawed by rats while they slept. This was what was happening nightly to the girls at Tonga. Did the room shield them in any way from this? It did not seem to be the case. They told me they too were bitten by rats as they slept. As with the girls at Tonga, this resulted in blood being found on the parts of their bodies the rats had been biting during the night. Waharama wanted to speak, and she smiled, covering her mouth with her hand. As she did this her hand lit up in the narrow stream of light piercing though a nearby crack in the wall, her almond eyes glittered as another ray hit her face through a hole in the tin roof.

'You have to be careful not to leave food on your hands at night, as they come and nibble the food on your hands and bite your hands too...the food attracts the rats, if the rats are pregnant they bite us more.'

I later looked this up and found it to be correct, that rats did tend to bite more when they were pregnant. I asked them about the other pests, the ants, cockroaches, mosquitoes and bed bugs. Waharama continued giggling, the ray of light now dancing on her cheeks.

'We have them all - cockroaches (called pedacheriga in dagbani), mosquitoes, and ants. The ants when they bite it is very painful.'

All of a sudden Lameen stood up. He then took it upon himself, through a very authoritative announcement as if on a loud speaker, to ask all the girls in the room if they had 'run away' or if they had told their parents that they were here. All the girls chorused that 'their parents knew'. Lameen then told them in his own language,

'We will ask your parents and check.'

They all roared with laughter. As we watched them rolling and laughing, the fragments of light tiptoed over them chaotically in the darkness. I decided it was time to leave. We said our goodbyes and the girls got up to see us back onto the muddy track outside their door. They cheered and waved as we disappeared into the distance, the rain beating down on us.

It was the first day of May when I arrived once again early on Sunday morning at Abusia trotro station. Two days earlier, along with another two billion people, I had watched the marriage of the royal couple, William and Kate, live on TV and been enchanted by the fairy tale wedding. Now, as I entered the trotro station in very different surroundings, a bus from Tamale, filled to the brim and almost toppling over from the amount of luggage on it, was just arriving. It parked at the bay and its cargo of people and goods gushed out. Many kayayo were amongst them, making the long journey down from the dusty north.

On arriving at the ticket office I was yet again greeted by about fifty mobile phones being charged all over the floor and on boxes, chairs and trunks. Once again extensions were plugged into extensions. About four old-fashioned TV sets were piled on top of each other in one corner. A very well dressed, distinguished looking man was sitting in the room. Everyone was addressing him as Dr Mehtab. I asked if he was indeed a medical doctor but was told he was a traditional herbal doctor. Not long after Lameen arrived, somewhat worried and flustered, and told me he had been unable to locate any of the girls, Shafarma, Menamatu, Salima and Waharama. He told me they just roamed around 'the whole of Debele' and as the market was so vast he was unable to locate them. He also couldn't remember the way to Salima's house. It had been so deep inside the market with so many twists and turns he or I would never again remember the way. Lameen then went on to tell me he had been looking and asking around for the girls the whole morning without any luck. He then introduced me to another very young girl he had just met. He said she also lived in Nisanu, which was the same village as the other girls, and suggested I talk to her instead. I told him we had already started to build up a relationship with the other girls. It would be best if we stuck with them. Lameen then went out again in a vain attempt to try to locate the four.

I stayed behind in the ticket office with the girl standing silently in the middle of the room, not really knowing why she had been brought there. I was stumped as to what to do. I couldn't talk to her. The others in the room were engaged in some animated conversation that seemed to engross them. Suddenly I remembered I had bought some photos of the 'runaway girls' that I had taken the week before. I showed the tiny girl the photos of Shafarma and the others and she immediately lit up. She started smiling and said that she knew the girls and that they lived in her room!

Today we had wanted to visit the room of Waharam, Shafarma and Menamatu. We waited for Lameen to return and told him the good news. We debated and decided that the best thing would be to go to their room and see if any of them were around. It was Sunday so the possibility was high. I ate my 'breakfast' of biscuits and kalyppo orange drink, as I had got up so early I hadn't yet had time to eat, and we set off in single file, the girl in front followed by Lameen and I at the rear.

As always we walked through unimaginable squalor. Skeletal electrical wires, dangerously criss-crossing the tracks above our heads, were haphazardly attached to numerous 'residences', making their way, often illegally, from poles to houses. The houses for the most part had no foundations and when it rained, almost daily at this time of year, it became almost impossible to stop the water from seeping in. It seemed like a long walk through the mud until we reached the wooden shack. The little girl, whose name was Kadima, insisted on carrying my bags. In the distance I could see lots of girls and Waharama recognized me and ran toward me smiling, taking my bag from Kadima. I entered the room and several girls and a baby were asleep on the bare cement floor. As in all the rooms, there was no furniture. Furniture would only take up valuable floor space that could accommodate another 'body'. Like in Salima's room bits of string were tied to the ceiling criss-crossing the room from one corner to the other. On these clothes were hung.

I sat down and opened my rucksack full of shoes, clothes and belts. I handed them out and they grabbed them with glee. Some light-hearted scuffles started to break out over the clothes, which ended with a lot of them falling on the floor or on top of each other laughing. Waharama got her hands on some nice white high-heeled shoes. She loved them and tried them on. She stepped outside her hut into the narrow track and all the neighbours around roared and cheered with approval and said she looked great. Someone called out,

'They would look nice with three quarter length jeans!'

Even though they were only Primark, for her new

white shoes straight from London were unimaginable luxury. Definitely a change from the flip-flops. We started to talk, but as in Salima's room a few days ago, it became unbearably hot, the tin roof sucking in the sun's heat. Everyone was perspiring profusely, so much so that the girl standing above me was actually dripping her perspiration onto me, like rain. Also everyone was so excited and talking at the same time that it was difficult to conduct an interview.

So we decided that we all, myself, Lameen, Shafarma, Menamatu, and Waharama, should head back to the ticket office. I was worried as Salima would not be able to come, so Shafarma said she would send one the girls round to her room to tell her to come and meet us at the ticket office later. It was difficult to walk back, always having to look out for gutters, food sellers and slippery rotten fruit, and navigate around trucks and carts. The air was awash with aromas.

On arriving at the trotro station, Shafarma, who was uncharacteristically quiet, sat down on the cement floor. She seemed subdued. I asked her what was wrong and she told me she was sick. Yesterday she had carried a heavy load and it had affected her heart. She told me she hadn't seen a doctor about it, but she showed me where the pain was in her chest. She told me that yesterday she had had to carry a very heavy load of cassava. She seemed angry despite her pain and started to explain,

'Even when I tell my customers it is getting too heavy they just keep adding more and more into my bowl.'

She then told me they make her carry loads 'so heavy it pains.'

Over the years I have often observed the kayayo carrying heavy loads. They are weighed down to such an extent they can only bear the weight by constantly bending at the knees intermittently in a kind of rhythmic way, perhaps to transfer the force of the weight for short periods to other parts of their bodies. Whenever I see girls walking in this way, they look in unbearable pain, and I realize the weights they are carrying are indeed beyond their capacity. They are at the tipping point.

It was a few minutes later that Salima arrived. She had received the message and made her way down. She quickly sat down and proceeded to listen to Shafarma who continued to talk.

'But it is not only this that they do wrong...many times they will not pay me.'

'Why do you think they try not to pay you?'

Lameen interjected. He said that most of the time the girls cannot even understand what their customers are saying.

'They don't speak the same language,' he added sadly.

The girls were passive bystanders, not even able to argue their case. They could do nothing if their customers refused to pay them. They were at the mercy of everyone, even those of 'their own people', their own tribe, those who the girls believed were supposed to care for them and who also inhabited this market that sprawled for miles and miles. I kept looking at Shafarma on the cement floor and could see she was very sick.

As with the girls at Tonga I asked them about their diet. What they appeared to eat consisted just of carbohydrates with no nutritional value. They replied,

'We only want our stomachs to be full so we don't care about meat or vegetables.'

In the distance, on the corner of one of the bus lanes I gazed at a group of three young kayayo girls sitting on their upturned bowls and falling onto each other in uncontrollable laughter at their private jokes. Next to them, two more sat braiding each other's hair. They always seemed not just happy but joyous. I have never seen such joy exhibited in people before as I had seen in these young girls.

I asked Waharama about her foot which had been knocked by a 'hit and run' driver, and she told me it was now getting better. She showed it to me and I saw that most of the swelling had now gone down.

I wondered if they ever reported these incidents to the police - the incidents of not being paid and hit and run drivers. From what the girls told me they went to the police only as a very last resort. In Ghana generally I have noticed that people tend to avoid dealing with the police. They told me that when there were any problems they went to a chief, and they informed me that they had their own chief here in Accra.

'If there is any problem we go to him as we are all of one tribe.'

Lameen said that you had to try to settle things at home before going to the police. I remembered an interview I later had with the local police in downtown Accra. They told me they rarely had any dealings with the kayayo and this explained why. They would generally never attempt to go to the police station unless they were taken there by an accuser, or as a last resort. They would hardly ever go on their own volition. Lameen told me that another reason they didn't go to the police was because of language problems, they didn't speak the same language, 'They can't speak Twi'. He also added gravely that they 'feared the police'.

The girls complained to me, as had all the kayayo girls before them, about being unable to rest. They told me that whenever they sat down outside someone's store they would be moved on. Shafarma told me the shopkeepers usually asked them,

'Why are you sitting outside my shop? Are you waiting for a customer?' If we say no or they ask customers in their shop if we are waiting for them and they say no, then they tell us to go away...so it's very difficult even to find somewhere to sit.'

A Twi speaking lady called Gladys who sold 'tealeaf' at the trotro station popped into the ticket office, to greet me. I often bought tea and fried egg from her stall.

They told me that throughout the day they often would not see each other. They were dispersed across the sprawling market or even beyond in downtown Accra, depending on where they are sent with their loads. Often they have to trudge back miles to this trotro station as it was often the only place they could rest without being disturbed.

'If we try to rest anywhere else we will be moved on.'

But then Shafarma interjected and told me ferociously that 'even here', at the trotro station itself, they were harassed. If the bus drivers wanted them to move they drove their buses or cars towards them so they had to get up quickly and run. She told me that the other day, they had driven so fast that the girl did not have time to gather up her tahili and they crushed her head pan under the bus's wheel.

Salima also told me that one of the drivers had said that the kayayo girls 'were so many' that they should use their cars to knock them down one by one. I asked who had said this and Shafarma told me it was a lorry driver.

I asked the girls why they thought it was only usually the girls that came to Accra to work. Shafarma said,

'The men they concentrate more on their school

than ladies, and also the girls they lack 'mother care''.

'What do you mean by this?'

She told me that often the women got sacked from the father's house. This was usually due to the father taking on another wife. The women, their mothers in fact, then have nowhere to go and little income, and as a result were unable to look after their daughters. It appeared the boys tended to stay with their fathers. Shafarma continued, sadly.

'Many times the mothers don't tell their daughters why they have had to leave their father's house...other times the children will stay with the father but the mother is still sacked from the house.'

Shafarma went on to tell me that they can 'sack the mother for any reason' so they can take a new wife. The 'sacked wife' was then unable to look after the children on her own and so sent the girls to Accra.

Lameen went on to say that the men will often bully the older wife, once he gets a second or third wife, as he knows that she is now infertile and therefore 'expired', so that whatever she says he will provoke her. If she retaliates he will use this as a reason to 'sack' her, or 'divorce' her. She was therefore in a no win situation.

The same stories were emerging over and over. The lives of the kayayo, from one market to another, from one region to another, from one tribe to another, appeared to follow a similar pattern of misery. I then asked Salima,

'Do you feel sad that because of these things you can't go to school?'

Salima told me that they would all like to learn to read and write and they felt sad when they saw others reading and writing and they couldn't and I remembered the wonder which they, only some weeks earlier, had shown when they watched me writing in my book. It was a painful, hopeless situation for them.

Just then the bus that had earlier arrived from Tamale drove off, going back once again. The bus as usual was piled high with luggage and full of kayayo girls. They leant out of the window shrieking and waving goodbye to their friends still sitting on their upturned bowls beneath the parked cars and under the shade of nearby buses and trucks. Even myself, standing at the ticket office entrance, gave them a big wave goodbye. They were going to the remote, dry villages, like Bundugu and Wialu. Hundreds of miles away in both distance and culture. I also thought it was time to say goodbye and we agreed to meet again the following Sunday at the ticket office.

It was now late May, the rains were coming strongly. I would soon be returning back to the UK. Today, Sunday, rather than go to the ticket office at the trotro station I was waiting at the main Debele trotro station, as we were going again to the girls' rooms.

After some time I spotted little Menamatu's maroon striped Portugal football jersey in the distance. The four girls walked behind Lameen in a line, from tallest to smallest at the end, like the seven dwarfs. It's impossible to walk next to each other in this market. It was just too crowded.

Soon after entering the market, and after walking down some incredibly narrow alleys criss-crossed with washing lines, we passed what seemed to be scores of tiny, low level dark cupboards in rows. The space between either side of the row was under a metre, barely enough to squeeze through. I guessed they were used for storing grain. However when I bent to peep inside the darkness I saw they were full of kayayo girls and their babies. When the door was closed there would be no natural light inside, no air, they were like cramped dungeons that opened out onto open sewers.

Yet I couldn't help thinking that to live in this hell, they were paying more per square metre than prime London or New York real estate. It was surreal.

I saw a small chemical store selling cheap, locally produced drugs. I asked the owner, a well educated man called Isaac what type of drugs were most in demand from the kayayo.

'The drug they purchase most is painkillers, as the work is so arduous they are often in pain at the end of the day...they carry loads that are too heavy for them and also overwork, the painkillers alleviate the pain brought on by this.'

He also told me they at times bought Valium. This had been cheap and easy to buy over the counter until very recently when the government advised pharmacies and chemical sellers to restrict is dispensation. He then told me,

'Many kayayo come and ask for cytotech. Whenever I tell them I don't have the drug they won't believe me.... but they keep coming here to demand it. They worry me too much. Because of this harassment now whenever they come and ask for the drug I tell them that I've never heard of it before.'

'What happens then?'

'They start to tell me that I do have the drug, that I am lying, and that I have to sell it to them.'

This evidently shows the desperation they find themselves in when they are pregnant. They know little about family planning, are coerced into sexual relationships or raped, and then when they become pregnant often through no fault of their own, they had no safe recourse to medical care, but had to rely on 'back street' methods that could kill them. It was so sad.

We crossed the main road onto the muddy waterlogged tracks, which moved us deeper into the bowels of the market. After walking in single file, marching like a row of soldier ants, we began to hear wild shouting in the distance. As we approached it got louder and I saw crowds gathering. I knew there was some kind of trouble ahead. As we neared the crowd we saw two kayayo girls fighting it out. Crowds teemed around them, cheering them on as if it were a major entertainment spectacle. Gladiators came to mind. Lameen, who was somewhat ahead of me, looked at me full of anxiety and started screaming,

'Quick, quick...get a picture...'

All around me mobile phones were clicking and flashing, capturing the moment on camera.

Seconds later scores of people were proudly displaying the photos they'd captured of the 'fight' on their mobiles. It was as if they had been to a rock concert and had managed to grab a picture of a famous artist. The fight died away and as I continued to walk along the track in the now slowly fading light people were shouting out at me,

'Hey, did you see the fight?'

……as they proudly displayed their mementos on their phones for everyone to see.

Shortly after we arrived at the girls' little shack it started to rain, it was seeping in through a crack in the corner of the room and also dripping down through some cracks in the ceiling. Buckets had been strategically placed to catch it all. Because of the rain many of the girls had sought refuge and the place was packed. I wanted to ask them and find out about the rent they paid. The shock of what I had heard from the girls in Salima's room last week was still reverberating through me.

One of the older girls in the room started to explain.

'Some time back the girls, we all contributed together and we bought this room. It cost us Gh200.

Now we don't pay rent. But now if you wanted to buy this room it would cost more. Probably 600 cedis.'

House price inflation reached even the most humble of places! They told me, and emphasised again that it was some years back. They had all contributed 10 cedis each. I couldn't believe it. This group of young girls, had actually bought their own house. It made economic sense. They now no longer had to pay rent and were free from the clutches of the landlords.

As she sat braiding her friend's hair she added,

'When you contribute you are free, than if you are always paying for a rented room.'

I wondered how many other girls in the market had bought their own rooms. How enterprising they were.

The room, though basic, felt cosy inside. It was made of wooden planks nailed together. It had a corrugated iron roof and a cement floor. It was rudimentary but it protected them from the elements. As in all the slum shacks, what seemed like hundreds of pairs of flip-flops were neatly lined up outside the door, and no one would dare to come in with their shoes and 'dirty the floor'.

Some were braiding hair, others trying on the clothes I had brought. Others were lying on each other just relaxing. It was 'their day' away from the insults and backbreaking labour of their daily routines. As in the other room, a shelf had been attached about two thirds of the way up the wall. On this were placed various 'barrels' in which they stored their belongings and the things they planned to take back to the north, such as their cooking pots and dishes, their cloths for marriage, sewing machines, and their 'new clothes', which were in fact the cast offs of people in the far off lands of Europe and Asia.

They then told me that, some weeks ago the lock on their room had broken and they had not been able to replace it. They were afraid someone would come and steal their goods.

'So how do you lock the door now?' I asked.

'We tie it with a piece of string.'

I measured the room. It was 3.72 by 3.20 metres, which gave each girl 18cm of sleeping space if each one lay the longest side down along the widest side of the shack. They were indeed packed like sardines. Nevertheless, these young girls had done well. They had mainly come alone to this massive city and bought their own little property. Even though for many it would be considered disgusting and horrible, they were proud of their 'house'. The room conveyed neatness and cleanliness, the abode of house-proud young females. Everything was neatly packed away above ground, making more room for sleeping; the dull yellow light cast warm shadows over the place. Their buckets for washing themselves and their clothes and saucepans were neatly packed into two separate corners. They told me the 'light bill' came every month and they paid five cedis a month.

Shafarma, who was drinking tea from a plastic cup, passed some to me and I took a sip, I passed it back and then asked for some more. Big cheers went up. The stranger actually liked their food and drink. I asked 'for more!'

As always the girls told me the usual stories of the hardship of their jobs. 'It is too heavy,' they told me, 'my shoulder and neck pain all the time'. They told me that sometimes they carried things from Abusia station to Wiase station. This was about an hour's walk. If they were lucky they could do this journey several times a day and get Gh3 cedis each time, making almost Gh10 cedis (£5 Sterling) a day, they also told me it was possible to earn even Gh25 cedis (£12.50 Sterling) a day. Yet some days they could walk around all day and not get a single load.

Why did they think that it was difficult to get work?

'We are too many for the work...too many of us come to Accra now.'

The rain had started to subside and the roar of the rain falling on the metal roof became a gentle pit pat. I saw this as my opportunity to make a run for it before it started to gush down again. I said goodbye to the girls. I realized this would probably be my last meeting with them. I also thought of the girls at Tonga I had not seen for a long time now. I told Shafarma, Waharama, Menamatu and Salima I would go and visit their parents in the village, I would travel up to the north of Ghana. They all laughed.

'You cannot find our village, it is too small, you must not go there as you will waste your money.'

Like Rebecca and her group I guess they doubted I would find it, although their village was much more accessible, being quite close to Tamale. The girls stood in a group outside their hut and waved goodbye. Lameen and I made our way back to the trotro station, sometimes wading ankle deep in putrid water.

I was now coming to the end of my time with the kayayo girls, and as always I felt moved and somehow exhilarated by their determination, their refusal to give up, and their indomitable joy. They appeared to experience delight just by the mere fact of being with each other, by sharing and working together to achieve something, to make their mark on the world, however small it was. By working and saving together, saving cents, pennies and pesawas, little by little, they achieved their modest dreams.

Chapter Nineteen

Revisiting the North

I was keen to get an early start for what was to be a journey to the north far different from my previous fiasco of dust clouds, potholes and broken down cars. I had decided to catch a plane to Tamale, a short forty-five minute 'hop' from Accra where I would catch a taxi to my hotel and then on to the village.

About a week previously I had suffered an accident, cutting my foot badly. My foot now had six stitches and was bandaged up. I was told to return to the hospital every two or three days for the dressing to be redone and hoped I would be back from Tamale by that time. I was also on crutches and was in a lot of pain, having basically to hop along on one foot. But my time was running out. I had no time to wait for recovery.

I caught a taxi to the airport, which I shared with a man who was taking his young son, aged two years, to the 37 Military Hospital. The boy had an arm cast and was going to get it removed. After about ten minutes of driving through the usual go slow traffic, our taxi was stopped. Two enormously fat policewomen appeared in front of the windscreen blocking the view. The taxi driver vainly tried to pretend he hadn't seen them, which was a bit difficult seeing the size of them, but he tried nevertheless. We crawled along slowly for about another thirty seconds pretending to look in the other direction. They then jumped on top of the bonnet as if to say, 'if you dare to drive on now, just see what happens to you'. The taxi stopped, and they screamed at him,

'Drive over there, drive!!'

Myself, the man and his son duly got out, fearing a

spat that could go on for epochs. We went to find another taxi, the boy with his arm in a cast and myself with my crutches and my bandaged up foot. We resembled the walking wounded. Not surprisingly we soon found another taxi and not long after I got down at the airport, leaving the man and his son to continue on to the hospital.

Less than an hour later, I arrived in Tamale. Oh how different from my last trip! There were many NGO signs flagging the road from the airport into town. One said,

'CAMFED When you Educate the Girl Child...Everything Changes.'

How true! Driving along I noticed that on every lamp post getting into town was a Vodafone advert. Not long after the taxi drew up at the guesthouse.

On arriving, I asked the young man at the reception desk if he knew of anyone who could interpret for me and accompany me to the village the following morning. He said he knew of a lady and would go and ask her this evening. He later sent a message that the woman would come to meet me at 7am. I was pleased as on this occasion I would be able to have a woman as an interpreter. Here in Tamale, unlike in the markets of Accra, there were people from all walks of life. Later on that evening I watched the man from the reception approach me while sitting at the dinner table. He apologized that 'in the end' he couldn't get the lady but 'not to worry', he has found a man who would be able to come instead. I was disappointed but what could I do? At breakfast the next morning I asked him what time the man would be arriving. He apologised, saying that 'in the end' the man couldn't come but the lady was now coming instead!

An exquisitely beautiful young woman soon arrived, dressed in white from top to toe. Her head was wrapped in a long white headscarf and its tassles swished and dangled down her back. Her name was Hazirah. She was tall and slender with incredibly long legs. He eyes were wide and her face had an incredible symmetry about it as if her features had been designed by computer software. It was almost perfect. Her skin was light copper coloured. She had a shy, humble air.

We walked to the taxi rank in order to catch a shared taxi to Nisanu, as by now I hadn't the money to afford to charter a private car all the way there.

I hobbled on my crutches through dilapidated streets lined with Vodafone emblazoned shacks selling all manner of things. Tamale is like a typical low-rise bush town, like an overgrown village in many areas. At the taxi rank most of the taxis were in various stages of disrepair some almost falling apart. As we drove through the town, donkeys, cows and goats freely wandered some of the streets. Piles of scrap metal consisting of bits of old cars and motorbikes were piled high at the sides of the roads, bicycles and mopeds roared past. The number of cars that could be seen in Tamale was far less than in the large cities of southern Ghana. The northern region is noticeably poorer than the south. Traditional mud adobe houses were mixed with vodafone painted shacks. Everywhere was awash with a distinct smoky smell reminiscent of sandalwood. Flame trees were in full bloom and many of the ubiquitous neem trees lined the streets.

Hazirah and I eventually arrived at the large village of Nisanu. It consisted of many traditional adobe compounds, scattered over a wide area. The taxi drew up at a small shack, which was the town's police station. We had to wait ages for the taxi driver to fix his car. Hazirah, who had hardly said a word since we met, possessed the demeanour of a frightened deer. She was an extremely beautiful girl.

Soon the taxi driver started to rev his engine and we got in. When we arrived at our destination we found ourselves in the middle of a field with numerous rounded compound houses, all looking identical. We passed lots of small kiosks full of girls sewing and making garments with black Chinese made hand-held sewing machines. Empty plastic bags of sachet water and black plastic carrier bags were strewn everywhere, hitching and hooking themselves onto thorn bushes. Men were busy (as this was the dry season) putting on new coats of mud and cement mix to cracked houses. I entered a compound comprising of four round huts around a cement compound floor.

The huts of the compound were usually rectangular for men and circular for women. Married men had separate rooms. Unmarried women slept in the room of a senior woman. Children and girls slept with their mothers or foster mothers. Boys aged six and seven slept in the entrance hall. A characteristic of Dagomba huts linking them with the style of huts found in northern Nigeria from where they claimed to originate, was the band of decoration found around the entrances to the senior wives' huts. Broken china and sometimes whole plates were set into the wall made of plaster, mud and cow dung.

A few people on seeing us came out of their huts and crossed the open compound into the main hut at the front. We greeted each other in the customary way and I told them why we had come to the village. I read out the directions to Shafarwu and Menamatu's houses, and showed their pictures to the people in the compound. I definitely did not want a repeat of the last saga where I was talking to the wrong parents about a girl I had never met! Surprisingly for me nobody here recognised the girls. They told me they had never seen them ever before. I then showed them pictures of some of the other girls. Thankfully they recognized Waharama.

My leg was beginning to swell and an older lady who spoke good English told me I had to change my shoes as they were causing oedema. She gave me a pair of flip-flops and rubbed some ointment into my foot, which she said would stop the swelling. She told me she was a retired nurse, but she said, she was still strong and wanted to continue working, 'they need nurses' she told me.

'Why should I just sit at home when I can help?' she asked me indignantly. She told me she was almost sixty but most people said they couldn't believe it and I assured her she also didn't look her age.

There was another man sitting in the large, round room where we were seated. There was also a baby fast asleep on a multi-coloured coconut fibre mat. After some minutes another girl entered the hut. She also spoke very good English. She was the daughter of the retired nurse. She looked thick set and strong with muscular arms and chubby hands. Her deep-set eyes, buried beneath her prominent brow, were strong and focused. Both mother and daughter were strong willed and articulate. The daughter told me she would take me to Waharama's house, and her mother insisted on taking my number. The mother was Earnestina, the daughter Kubura. Kubara started to chat animatedly on our journey, while poor frightened deer Hazirah receded further into the distance, outdone by her more pushy age mate. Both were eighteen years old. I asked Kubura if she had ever 'gone to do kayayo' she said she had never been 'as she was schooling'. Hazirah also had never gone, both were busy at school. I saw in these two girls the potential of all the kayayo if only they were given the chance. Hazirah wanted to be a nurse and Kubura a doctor.

My foot was throbbing and was getting increasingly

dirty as we trudged through the dust. The bandage was becoming loose and dust was entering inside the dressing. I started to worry that the wound would become infected. After about fifteen minutes we reached Waharama's hut. It was a five-roomed compound house of thatch and mud, almost identical to the one we had just left. On the walls near where I sat mobile phone numbers had been written down. I had noticed this had been done at a lot of compounds I had visited. Warharama's parents were called Munif and Sahar.

A small boy was sleeping on a mat and another boy of about eight years was also there. This was Waharama's brother. The family comprised of four boys, who the father told me were fifteen, twelve, and eight years plus a baby. He said Warhama was twelve, which would have made her the same age as her brother, but they were not twins and I realized the father was just guessing their ages. A few minutes after we sat down, Sahar moved to the centre of the open compound to pound TZ, and I was left with Hazirah, who sat still, upright and silent while Kubura took the reins and asked all the questions I had brought poor Hazirah to ask. I felt quite sorry for Hazirah, she wanted to do the work but was too shy to interrupt Kubura. While sitting there I could see many of the bright enamel pots decorated with coloured flowers, which were such prized and sought after possessions in these villages. These pots were also one of the main reasons why many girls travelled so far to Accra. They wanted the money to buy them to prepare the necessary utensils needed for marriage. I was wondering whether Warhama had bought them here.

I asked Waharama's father what he remembered as the happiest day in his daughter's life. He said it was the Dangban festival. But he said ironically, it was also at that time when he experienced some of the saddest moments in his daughter's life.

'When the festival was happening Waharma was very happy. She was dancing and wearing a new dress and new shoes...but after the festival my daughter got severe malaria...we thought she would die and we took her to the hospital. This was quite recent. It was not long ago. After she recovered she went to Accra for kayayo. This is the first time she has gone and she has been in Accra for three months.'

Munif's wife Sahar suddenly stopped her pounding and looked up, she held up three fingers as if to emphasise that her daughter had been gone for three months.

I asked if they would like Waharama to go to school, they both said yes but they had 'no money'. I asked if Waharama's money would help her siblings to go to school. The parents agreed that their daughter's money would help.

'What will your daughter bring back from Accra?'

Her mother pointed across at the flower patterned enamel bowls, which were strewn across the floor of the compound. She then resumed her pounding.

'What is your most treasured possession?' I asked the father.

He told me that he loved music and his most treasured possession was his battery powered radio which I could see hanging from a nail on the mud wall.

I asked if I could to speak to Sahar and Kubura told her to come over and join to our circle. Kubara then went and continued with the pounding that Sahar had just stopped. The constant thudding of the wooden mortar was unremitting. I then asked Sahar what she treasured most. She told me it was her cloth (dress), which was red.

I looked up at the sky, it seemed to be darkening and

I wondered if it would rain. The wind gained speed and blew up whirlwinds and spirals of dust, the trees started to sway. I didn't want to be caught in a deluge.

I wondered if Waharama's parents ever worried about their young daughter, who could be no more than about twelve years old, living so far away from them in Accra.

'Yes, we worry. We fear she will get pregnant.'

'Does she have an older sister or relative with her?'

'No, Waharama went alone.'

'How did your daughter get the trotro fare to Accra, did you give it to her?'

'No, Waharama went out and told a friend that we needed a bag of rice. The friend gave her the rice and she told them we would pay for it later. Then she sold the rice and used the money to get to Accra...I only found out about the rice later, after she had gone.'

'Did you have to pay back the money?'

'Yes, I had to do it small small (in instalments) but now I have finished.'

Waharama's father told me he had never encouraged or suggested to his daughter that she should go to Accra. He said it had been Waharama's idea.

'Do you miss your daughter?'

'Yes we both miss her.'

When I asked what could be done to improve the situation in his area, something that might stop the girls having to go to Accra, he told me that 'if the girls were working here', that is in the northern region, they wouldn't have to go to Accra. He suggested that vocational training would help the girls, and suggested dressmaking as a possible skill they could learn.

I told Waharama's parents, Munif and Sahar, about the Mamprusi girls in Accra. How they slept in the streets and how their babies were sometimes snatched and I wondered if they knew about this.

Munif told me sadly how he had also heard about this happening and added that people often did this for ritual purposes. He also said he knew about the very young girls who did the 'babysitting' and added that this was not good.

After some time we bid farewell to Waharama's parents and once again attempted to find Shafarwu's and Menematu's houses. We had the house names, the directions and the area but just couldn't seem to find them. The pain in my foot was getting worse and worse and the bandage was starting to fall off and unwind. I just had to hobble on with my crutches; I had no other choice, especially as it appeared I was now in the middle of nowhere, miles from any roads or transport. Hazirah and Kubura helped me to carry my water bottle and bag. We entered into another compound house and proceeded to ask those inside if they knew any of the girls in the photos. After scrutinizing the photos for some time the women in the compound reluctantly told us that they did not recognize any of the girls

Soon, in the distance we spotted a sizeable crowd of girls and women sitting under the swaying branches of a giant neem tree, the rays of the ferocious sun undermined by its thick foliage. I mistakenly thought that with so many girls nearby of the same age as those we were looking for, we were now bound to find someone who knew them. But yet again we were to be disappointed. We passed the photos around, together with the names of the houses but nobody seemed to know them.

I was beginning to want to give up, I was getting tired, my foot was throbbing and the sun was blistering. While walking through this large village I couldn't help noticing the numerous men throwing second glances and admiring Hazirah. She was attracting a lot of attention. As we continued to amble along Hazirah and

Kubura chitchatted in their language. Then they began to talk to me. They began to share their secrets.

'When the men get a younger wife they just ignore the older wife and her children. They will not even look after the older wife again,' Kubura declared despondently.

Hazirah waited, appearing to examine Kubura's face for the appropriate time to interject and then added,

'And the men, they don't want to take care of the children.'

And then Kubura said something very significant.

'That's why there are so many kayayo, the men have so many children and they can't look after them. Then the boys become armed robbers and the girls go to kayayo in Accra.'

Hazirah was now losing her reserve and shyness, but only very slightly. I think the injustice of it all provoked such strong passions they erased her inhibitions. She said softly but indignantly,

'The men, all they want to do is take wives and pay bride price, and then they divorce and marry again then divorce and marry and so on.'

Now it was again Kubura's turn. She declared,

'They beat the wives a lot.'

'Why?'

'The men say they beat their wives because they talk.'

Then both Hazirah and Kubura stated simultaneously as in a chorus,

'And women, we the women are not supposed to talk. We are not supposed to talk when the men are talking.'

Hazirah added cautiously as if unsure how far she should go,

'If you ask for housekeeping money they beat you, if you ask for money for food they beat you.'

It appeared from the tone of gentle indignation in her voice that Hazirah was talking from experience, even though she was not married, and I wondered if her mother had gone through these ordeals.

I looked up and saw two women sitting under a nearby tree feeding their babies. We showed them the pictures but they also did not recognise Shafarma, Menamatu or Salima. By now I must have walked at least a couple of miles. After some time we reached the junction where Salima had told me she lived. Due to my fatigue and the endless disappointments the enthusiasm and drive with which I had begun the day was beginning to wane. I now seemed to be asking the questions out of a vague sense of contractual obligation, almost mechanically, like a reflex action. I asked the women beneath the shifting branches of the shea nut tree, the now seemingly useless question and waited for the familiar response. Yet this time I sensed something new. There was animated talk in dagbani. The lady stood up and pointed in the distance. Kubura said we should follow her. Within minutes we were being led into a large compound house where, we were told, lived Salima's parents.

We reached Salima's compound just as I thought I could no longer walk anymore. The girls kept commending me on how well I was doing, walking so far, despite my injury. A heavily pregnant lady sat beside me, another sat opposite feeding a baby, her large emaciated breast dangling. I asked to see Salima's mum and the women both told me, chuckling, that on seeing me Salima's mother had ran off, declaring she was going to the toilet. We waited for some time and Kubura asked if someone could go and buy us soft drinks and biscuits. We were all famished. Soon after Salima's father arrived. He was a very tall slim man, and he was wearing jeans and a grubby white T-shirt with 'Mobil' written on the front. He had the air of an ancient patriarch surrounded now as he was by his ever-expanding progeny. He was holding a small baby girl whom he told me was his latest child. I could see Salima's features in his countenance, his long narrow face, and prominent forehead. His moustache extended down past either side of his mouth to the extremities of his face, and his teeth protruded, reminding me of a rodent. His name was Mohammed and he told me proudly that he had fathered twelve children from his three wives. At this Kubura and I glanced at each other, sharing between us a surreptitious smile. She threw me an expression which said, 'see I told you...he is one of them!'

We asked him why it was he had so many children when he obviously couldn't take care of them all. He told us that although he didn't have the means he would take care of them 'by God's Grace'.

We showed him a photo of Salima just to make sure we hadn't ended up at the wrong family as had turned out in Poppy's case. He gazed at it for a while as if he wasn't sure. Maybe he had so many he couldn't remember who was who. I was reminded of a story someone once told me of a king in a small African state, who purportedly had over one hundred wives. While waiting at a traffic crossing he saw a beautiful young women saunter past. He informed his driver that he 'wanted that woman as his wife'. The disconcerted driver then had the uncomfortable and embarrassing task of reminding the king that the said women 'was already his wife, he had married her some years earlier!' Whether or not Mohammed was having the same problem, I didn't know, but after a short time he looked up and told me that it was indeed Salima.

I then remarked that Salima had informed me that it had been her father, in fact himself and one of his wives, that had instructed her to go to Accra. Mohammed looked slightly embarrassed.

'Well, it was Salima's mother-in-law, my third wife, she worried me to send Salima to Accra and then I agreed. The money and the things she will buy will help her when it is time for her to marry.'

'But why did you not inform Salima's real mother, surely she would want to know?'

'At the time she was in the deep bush and there was no mobile phone, so we couldn't tell her.'

'Couldn't you wait?'

Mohammed once again insisted it was his third wife who wanted this. I remembered how many kayayo girls I had spoken to had described to me this same type of scenario. That co-wives didn't like catering for and feeding the children of other wives and will often collude with their husband, who most often favoured the newest and youngest wife, to get rid of them. This was what obviously had happened to poor little Salima.

The lives of the kayayo girls were, it seemed, shaped and determined by a multitude of malevolent forces. Firstly, tradition dictated they marry a man of their father's choice. The father's decision was generally not based on the welfare of his daughter, but often some other reason relating to owing or gaining a favour. The mothers sometimes encouraged their daughters to leave their homes and villages due to rivalry, expecting the girls to return with goods which would out-do or surpass those of their neighbours or co-wives; step-mothers pushed them out due to jealously and resentment. These girls were the innocent victims of village stage dramas concocted from an array of incessant personal animosities and rivalries. They were sacrificial lambs used to score points with neighbours, friends and kin. Even those that left of their own free will, were in many ways swayed by the innermost jealousies and conflicts operating within their communities, often feeling they were 'worthless' in the eyes of those around them, if they didn't go and come back with goods and wealth.

Once removed from their villages the animosities towards them continued. This time from their customers who exploited them, their neighbours who abused them and stole their meagre earnings and menfolk who sexually harassed and raped them. Yet these poor little girls rose to the tide. They were full of joy, worked hard, shared everything, and even prospered. They were miraculous!

I looked up again at Mohammed. Kubara was seated next to him opposite me, her mouth now pursed in anger. Frightened deer Hazirah sat still and silent beside her. I continued,

'Are you not afraid that something bad could happen to your daughter, she is so young and she doesn't even have an older sister with her?'

'Yes, I am afraid but we are praying nothing will happen to her, we are worried about pregnancy, but we pray that God will give her what she wants and she will come back.'

Salima's mother, who had now returned, stood timidly amongst the crowd of her large extended family that had been gradually gathering in the central compound. She was a small woman with a petite face as round as an apple. She smiled in a way which made you think she in fact did not know what to do, or say. As if she was unsure what was exactly going on, why she was there and why we were there. I tried to speak to her, but she bowed her head, laughing while covering her mouth.

I asked her how the money that Salima earned would help them. Did it help to pay for their other children to go to school?

Salima's mother just stood there, smiling at what Kubara was translating, she continued to smile, cover her mouth and look down at the ground.

Then Mohammed, sitting on his plastic chair, surrounded by his large family, said in a resentful tone that what his daughter would bring home would not help the family generally, it was only for her marriage. He then added,

'She will not even bring back a shirt for me.'

Dark clouds began to gather above and I thought it would rain. A sudden wind raised the dust from the earth taking with it pieces of litter that swirled and floated around. The smell of yams being fried rose with the wind. There was a momentary silence. Only the distant sounds of children playing outside the compound could be heard. Mohammed waited for his next question. Aysha, his wife, continued to stand, smiling awkwardly.

I asked him how many of his children went to school? He told me that eight of them in total went to school, five boys and three girls. We heard the roar of a motorbike outside. The boy had at last returned with our biscuits and drink. He drove into the compound slowly on his bike, which looked brand new and shiny. He had bought us Fanta and cream crackers. Kubura, Hazirah and I whoofed them down hungrily. We were all starving. Many other people in the compound were also now eating TZ and okra stew from the ubiquitous flowery patterned enamel bowls that the kayayo girls brought back with them from Accra. Mohammed continued, his teeth now seeming to protrude more than ever.

'The girls go to primary which is completely free, we don't have to pay, but we must buy books and uniforms and this costs (is expensive).'

Mohammed then said he wanted to marry me. I

replied no, I wasn't interested. His wife roared with laughter, much more than anyone else.

I asked Mohammed if he wanted to have any more children. He replied that he did, and that he 'wanted to reach twenty children before he would stop'. He continued, not noticing the sly, repressed smirks circulating between Kubura, Hazirah and myself.

'Salima's mother is no longer giving birth but my other two wives are still producing so I will have more.'

I then asked if he had ever 'sacked' (divorced or chucked out) any of his wives. He replied that no, he had never sacked any of them.

I asked the parents jointly what had been the happiest memory of their young daughter so far. They said it had been at one of the Ramadan festivals. Salima had a new dress and she was very happy. But at one other Ramadan festival she had also wanted a beautiful dress to wear that day but they didn't have money to buy it and she was very sad. They told me that the things that made them happy more than anything was the local dance. I guessed this must be the simpa, and I remembered how the girls at Debele market had also told me how they loved dancing the simpa.

Then Kubura out of the blue said,

'Oh when the boys do go to Accra they come back with funny ways of dressing. The boys they pull down their trousers half way down their buttocks, and their underpants will be showing and coming up.'

Everybody laughed and I thought of the boys in London, where this style was now so fashionable. Poor Hazirah sat now feeling even more excluded and ineffective. She had come to help with the translation but had hardly been able to say a word the whole day. Now Kubura had become the life and soul of the conversation and everyone was roaring with laughter at her jokes.

I asked again if they could think of any other reasons why it was always girls that were sent mostly to the south to work. I saw that Hazirah's chest was heaving up and down with the slow rhythm of her deep breaths, her eyes suddenly closed. She took another long, deep breath as if preparing for some insurmountable assignment. Her eyes opened wide, she looked at me, then Kubura. Just like a frightened deer. Then she said,

'Peer pressure.'

She gave a sigh of relief as if to say, 'I've done it now, I've said it, it's all over'. I quickly gave her the credit and acknowledgement she desperately needed.

'Yes, Hazirah, you're right, it's a very important reason and one that has been mentioned to me many times.'

She looked relieved and proud, in her inhibited understated way.

It was time to leave, rain had started to fall, but still only gently. So with Hazirah now displaying her newfound confidence, Kubura newly aware of her latent talents as a comedian and myself hobbling along with my crutches, we walked slowly to the bus stop at the nearby junction.

There was a small covered eating spot made from bamboo and thatch adjacent to the stop so we waited inside, shielding ourselves from the now heavy rain. Inside were about half a dozen people, both men and women, eating boiled yam with groundnut powder out of flowery patterned enamel bowls.

The taxi arrived and Hazirah and I said goodbye to Kubura. I gave her back the flip-flopss her mother had kindly lent me and put my own shoes back on. The taxi drove at top speed back into Tamale, and I could see the white skin forming over my knuckles, as I took in deep breaths, trying to avoid looking ahead. In Tamale I said goodbye again, this time to Hazirah, and I told her that I hoped I would see both her and Kubura again if I ever came back to Tamale.

After arriving back at the guesthouse, I rushed out again quickly to the nearest pharmacy to buy a new dressing for my foot. The old one was now almost hanging off and barely covered the wound. The Frafra lady at the 'Kwik Pharmacy' insisted on bathing and dressing the wound herself, and even refused to take payment when she had finished. People in Ghana are often so kind and unselfish.

The next morning I flew back to Accra, this time in reverse order I watched the parched ochre landscape dotted with massive green shea, neem and mango trees transform into the thick, lush green of the south.

Chapter Twenty

The Triumph of Hope

It was now June. I would be leaving Ghana in a few days, having lived there for fifteen years. This last year I had spent with the kayayo, the people who had fascinated me since my very first days in the country. For me it had been an honour and an astounding voyage of discovery to learn about these brave, hard-working and fiercely independent young women. Yet my time with them had come to an end. I didn't want it to end. I wanted to find any excuse to be with them longer. I loved their world, the special world they had created between themselves within this gigantic city. A world which allowed them to survive and fulfil their needs and dreams.

It was early Sunday morning and I was walking through the market with George, listening as usual to his plans for European travel and visa applications. Today the market had an unusual atmosphere of stillness, as if everything had been frozen in time. I felt that I would be able to come back years later and everything would still be the same, just as it was now, at this moment. Even the usual colours seemed to have lost their vibrancy. All looked washed out, sun bleached.

I couldn't see anyone I knew. Emptiness engulfed me. It was as if I had been dropped into an unknown area where everything felt familiar but all that had been familiar had disappeared. Where were all those characters, those hearts and souls, I had come to know so well? Those personalities that possessed such determination that nothing could crush them? There was only hollowness all around me, a thin hollowness like cheap tin that crushes and breaks into cruel shards when broken. How could I leave this market without being able to feel once again the warmth of these girls? These girls I had come to know and love. I looked around again and could see no one, hear nothing.

We turned the corner of the Blue House, and came to the mango tree. If I walked a few steps further this enchanting world that I had come to cherish would be behind me. I would have said goodbye without one last time being able to see anything that was part of it. I wanted to linger. I refused to put it behind me. Not yet.

I watched three kayayo girls, heavily loaded, walk past silently, in the frozen landscape. It was as if I was being allowed to peep into another world. They seemed distant, separated from the reality in which we now stood.

Suddenly Rebecca appeared from behind the corner of the Blue House, as if from nowhere, baby Madihah on her back. She untied her, putting her down on the ground. She could now walk, and the toddler stood smiling at me confidently in her tiny plastic shoes. The patterns of the newly grown leaves above us etched themselves over our faces as they swayed with the breeze. It was as if everything had come full circle. A year ago I had met Rebecca and the then baby Madihah exactly at this spot, under this tree and it was today, my last day, that I was again with them.

I told her I would be leaving that day. She smiled but I didn't think she realized I would be going for good. We continued to linger. In the distance I could see a small girl, in fact a child, walking along the road. As she approached I realized it was the little girl, Martha, who always loved to crochet. She stood in front of me silently as if expecting a reaction.

Rebecca spoke first.

'Mummy, look, she is wearing the skirt. Doesn't it

look beautiful?'

I was amazed.

'Martha,' I said, 'the skirt is lovely, you are so clever and have worked so hard.'

She continued to stand in the empty street. The sounds and colours around started to disappear, as if they were being sucked out of landscape. Only the shape and colour of her skirt seemed to matter now.

'Look,' said Rebecca, pointing to the first stripe of her skirt, near to her tiny waist, 'you remember when we first met Martha, she was knitting with this colour, the yellow...you remember how we went to the shop to buy her some more?'

Yes I remembered.

George's finger pointed to the next stripe.

'Look at this...the red, I remember when we bought her this colour, it was the night Rebecca was beaten by Shagba. Do you remember?'

Yes, I remembered.

Then Rebecca spoke.

'Look at the blue, I remember we bought this when we took Madihah to hospital, the day she hurt her head, do you remember?'

Yes, I remembered.

George pointed to the green stripe. Martha stood still, stiff. The landscape around her was distorting, its shapes becoming amorphous, running into each other, all colour had been bleached away by the sun, the sound had been stifled, muffled. Large black birds flew around but they, like everything else, were silent. A pungent odour filled the air like burning plastic. Only Martha breathed life. Martha and her skirt, whose colours were increasing in intensity as if they were taking on a life of their own.

'Look at this colour, look, look, the green, we bought that the day that all of Poppy's savings were stolen. Do you remember?'

Yes. I remembered.

George continued.

'This colour, the purple.'

This time I spoke.

'George, that was the day we discovered Poppy had got her tealeaf job, she was so happy, do you remember?'

George looked at me smiling. 'Yes I remember.'

Rebecca moved towards Martha. The surrounding landscape no longer existed. It had become a monochrome blur. Martha's skirt became luminous and it started to glow amidst the cold greyness that surrounded it. Rebecca touched the next stripe. She bowed her head for some time, then looked up at me. Tears were running down her cheeks.

'Mummy, this colour the pink, do you remember the day we bought this for Martha, remember we drove to the shop in the car, that was the day Madam Gifty at the Spot got her new job, do you remember?'

'Yes, Rebecca, I remember that day.'

George now sat down onto the ground under the stunted branches of the tree above, his legs splayed out on the uneven, cracked pavement. Now we all were surrounded by greyness, even the shapes and outlines of adjacent houses and trees had disappeared. Martha continued to stand still. Erect. Stiff.

Rebecca was now bending on one knee with her forehead, now clasped within her hands, leaning against her upright knee. I could not see her face. Little Madihah walked silently over to George, sitting between his outstretched legs. She stared blankly at Martha.

There was now deafening silence. The black birds had gone. There was nothing or nobody except us. Rebecca stood and walked over to George. She sat down next to him. She was weeping. George too hid his face in his hands. I walked over to him. I lifted his face. I stared intently into his large, dark eyes. Tears then began to roll down his cheeks. Then I too I started to cry.

We held on to each other. It was difficult for us to look at Martha. The colours blinded us. They were the colours of life, of our pains and agonies, of our regrets and humiliations, our losses and defeats. But, they were also the colours of our determination and willpower, of our joys and loves, of our victories and accomplishments in the face of often unimaginable adversity, they were the colours of all that we must suffer and endure in our lives.

We continued to hold each other, squeezing harder and harder, and with this strength we faced the blinding colours, these colours that represented our existence. Then slowly their vibrancy began to fade. We relaxed our grip. The shapes, sounds, hues and familiar aromas of the surrounding landscape returned. Martha came over to us. She stood looking into our eyes, all of which were still full of tears. As we sat there clinging to each other, we contemplated the skirt, its patterns, and colours. We touched and felt its texture. Martha smiled. She then turned and walked silently away into the distance. We watched her until she disappeared.

Rebecca stood up first and tied Madihah to her back. She gazed at me and then walked around the corner of the Blue House.

She was gone.

George and I walked for a while and separated, each going our own separate ways.

Next day as the plane rose above Accra and for the last time, I looked down upon the giant hands held together in prayer outside the Action Chapel in Spintex Road. I realized that it was only by being and acting together, just as the young kayayo girls; together as families and friends, as villages and towns, cities and nations and ultimately as a planet that we can achieve anything in our dreams.

We had a lot to learn from them.

References

1. Government of Ghana. Office of the Vice-President. *The Savannah Accelerated Development Initiative. (SADA) Synopsis of Development Strategy* 2010-2030. October 2010.

2. GhanaToGhana.com *'Hunchback killed for rituals'* March 30th 2012

3. *'Ghana's Sakawa Superstition – Magic in a Digital Age'* Grahanghana@worldpress.com 6th April 2011

4. The Good Funeral's Guide. *'Abusua do funu – The family loves the corpse'* 3rd February 2012.

5. Harden, Blaine. *'Dispatches from a Fragile Continent'* Harper Collins 1990.

6. Howell and Barwell. *'Bearing the Weight. The Kayayo Working Girl Child.'* 1987

7. Joyonline. *'Sakawa murder in Nima'* September 24th 2011

8. Koranteng, Adu, *'Saving the rice Industry from total collapse.'* The Statesman 14th April 2008

9. Mahama, Ibrahim, *'History and Traditions of the Dagbon'* 2004

10. Modern Ghana, *'Police arrest third suspect in Sakawa murder case.'* 11th May 2011

11. Moore, Charlotte. *'Oxfam says livelihoods of Farm Workers being destroyed'* The Guardian. Monday 11th

April 2005

12. Myers, William (Eds). *'Protecting Working Children.' 'Children's work in Urban Nigeria; A case study of young Lagos street Traders.* Zed Books in association with UNICEF 1991.

13. A study commissioned by Response NGO in association with UNICEF. *'Listening to the girls on the street tell their own story.'* 1997.

14. A report conducted by the Organisation of African Unity (OAU) and UN Children's Fund o Africa's children. *'Africa's Future'.* OAU

15. UNICEF Ghana, *'Examining the sexual Exploitation of children on the streets of Accra.'* 2007